THE BED I MADE

Lucie Whitehouse

BLOOMSBURY

LONDON · BERLIN · NEW YORK

First published in Great Britain 2010

This edition published 2010

Copyright © 2010 by Lucie Whitehouse

The moral right of the author has been asserted

Bloomsbury Publishing, London, Berlin and New York

36 Soho Square, London W1D 3QY

A CIP catalogue record for this book is available from the British Library

ISBN 978 1 4088 0913 6

10 9 8 7 6 5 4 3 2 1

Typeset by Hewer Text UK Ltd, Edinburgh

Printed in Great Britain by Clays Ltd, St Ives plc

Mixed Sources
Product group from well-managed
forests and other controlled sources
www.fsc.org Cert no. SGS-COC-2061
© 1996 Forest Stewardship Council
FSC

www.bloomsbury.com/luciewhitehouse

For Polly and Sophie

Chapter One

I was standing on the shingle bank when they towed her boat back in. The last of the sun was slipping below the horizon, pulling the dying day after it, turning the water of the Solent black. On the far shore, two miles away across it, the lights of the mainland blinked on. The lifeboat was coming up from the Needles, its orange decks a bright mark in the gloaming, but the throttled-down rumble of its engine reached over the surface of the sea like a growl. At a distance the hull of the sailing dinghy was barely visible; it bobbed childlike on the wake of the bigger boat.

The stones crunched under my feet as I started to move. Behind me, the wood that reached down to the rough beach had become amorphous, the branches and tangled undergrowth suddenly a dark mass which met the sea's approach with silence. I broke into a run but I had come further than I thought; it seemed a long time before I reached the tarmac path again. I ran through clouds of my own breath, sucking in lungfuls of air heavy with salt and tar and the stink of rotting seaweed.

I had been on the harbour front in the morning when the flare had gone up. At first I hadn't remembered what it was, the rocket's long whistle, the moment's pause before the cracking sound and the streamers of smoke descending through the white sky. A minute or so later, though, a battered blue car raced past and was abandoned on the quayside, the driver's door left open, and a bicycle flew round the corner and was flung down, its back wheel still spinning. Two more men came running from the road by the roundabout. The lifeboat's engine was already roaring and

1

in a matter of seconds it was gone from the harbour, a skirt of churning water behind it, out into the Solent where it powered up and fled. The people on the quayside had watched until it disappeared from sight. I asked a man outside the lifeboat office which I'd seen on the corner. 'Local woman's missing,' he'd told me. 'Out in her boat.'

I didn't know why it felt so important to be there now when the boat came back in. I left the tarmac path, met gravel as I climbed the slope away from the sea wall, and then, at last, I came out on to the road again, heart pounding in my ears, calves burning with acid. Another couple of hundred yards and I reached the river bridge. There in front of me was the town, scarcely more than a village: the stout stone buildings hunkered down beyond the quay, ready for whatever came at them, the brick chimneys of the George hotel standing four-square and resolute in the twilight. I could see the lifeboat again and heard it slow as it came inside the harbour. Less than a minute later, the engine was cut and silence fell.

It was as if the town had taken an inward breath. Nothing moved. The pavements were deserted, the roads empty of cars. Those parked on the quay waited for the next ferry with their engines turned off. The breeze that had played melancholy music through the rigging of the yachts during the afternoon had died away, and the boats sat motionless on their moorings. Even the seagulls, keening since dawn, were mute now.

As the bridge brought me to the harbour, I made myself slow down. I had no right to be conspicuous here. Instead of following the pavement on to the quay, I kept back by the wooden barrier that divided the ferry lanes from the road. Two of the lifeboat crew were on the pontoon already, the high tide lifting the platform so that their heads and shoulders were visible above the edge of the quay either side of the little boat's mast. Their voices were low, and too far away for me to make out. On the deck of the lifeboat a man in a heavy waterproof jacket paused at the stern for a moment to look down at them, the rope he was coiling hanging in slack loops between his hands. Behind him, the lights in the cabin went out.

2

There was another man standing on the quay wall directly in front of me. Despite the cold, he was wearing only jeans and a thin shirt. He faced away over the harbour, silhouetted against the sky so that his body was hardly more than a black shape, an absence of light or an intensification of the darkness. He was tall, remarkably tall, and the breadth of his shoulders suggested power but he was gripping the top of the metal railing as if he were trying to keep himself from being blown away by a wind which no one else could feel.

Suddenly he turned. He was crossing the tarmac with long strides, coming towards me. I drew back but the barrier was only knee-high and offered no cover. I was directly in his path. His head was down, his eyes fixed on the ground. I willed him not to see me but, just as he passed, he looked up.

He wasn't much older than I was: perhaps thirty-five or -six. His hair was dark and there was several days' stubble on his cheeks but in the glow of the streetlamps, his skin had a lunar pallor. His eyes were wide open but moved over me without seeing. The rest of his face was blank, as if there were no expression that could reflect what he was feeling, and as he went by, the air around him seemed to tremble with the force of it.

I stood still for a minute or two after he'd gone, listening to the quick sound of his footsteps as they faded, feeling the sweat cooling on my skin.

They had found her boat, I realised, but they hadn't found her.

Chapter Two

When I woke the next morning, my T-shirt was twisted around my torso as if I'd been wrung out while I slept. Since coming to the Island I was finding it hard to fall asleep at night and harder still to wake up: I watched as the clock chewed its way through the small hours and then surfaced from a dreamless oblivion to find the watery light of late morning seeping through the curtains, the sun already nearing the top of its shallow November parabola. The disorientation of waking in an unfamiliar bedroom usually meant I started the day with a few easy seconds but today the sequence of events which had brought me here replayed itself in my mind immediately, as if the key images had been sketched into a flick-book and I only had to thumb the corner to see them all dance before me again.

To stop them, I got out of bed at once and walked the two steps to the window. Outside, the static silence of the night before had lifted: there was a car coming round the roundabout, its engine audible through the old glass, and two others waited at the temporary lights on the bridge. Seagulls wheeled over the estuary, their wings flashing white against the sky, their cries rising like unkind laughter.

I put on the jeans and jumper I'd thrown over the back of the chair when I'd undressed and pulled my hair off my face with my hands, retying the ponytail that had worked itself loose against the pillow. The stairs dropped steeply down off the narrow landing into the kitchen where I had put my boots by the radiator to dry. Their leather was still clammy when I slid my feet in.

4

Stepping out on to the path, I locked the door behind me and pocketed the key. The house was in the middle of a row of cottages originally inhabited by Victorian coastguards. I hadn't recognised it when I'd first seen the picture on the internet; with Dad, we'd always stayed at the further end of town, where the backs of the houses looked out over the marshes. A brick corridor and a wrought-iron gate separated the terrace from the street and, to reach it, I had to pass the fronts of several of my new neighbours' houses. Each one was narrow, with only a kitchen window and a door above a single step. On the other side of the path were areas of yard perhaps ten feet square, some with flower pots and hardy roses still just in bloom, others occupied by tiny outhouses or spinning washing lines. I strode along with my head down, not wanting to have to engage with anyone, but there was nobody to see me anyway.

The gate clanged shut and I was on the pavement. I crossed the small road and passed the Wheatsheaf pub on the other side. It was open already and the yeasty aroma of beer seeped out on to the street. I remembered this shortcut to the newsagent's from years ago, when Matt and I had spent our pocket money there on pink rock that said 'Yarmouth' all the way through and which we'd sucked into points so sharp that they'd cut our tongues. I didn't remember it like this, though; everything seemed slightly too small, as if the whole town was a scale model built at eighty per cent of the proper size. The fish bar wasn't open yet but the smell of cooking fat was heavy in the air outside the café next door whose board offered all-day breakfasts, and egg and chips. In Quay Street the magnifying mirrors in the chemist's window display – more than thirty, I guessed – glinted in the light like big round eyes.

The smell inside the newsagent's two doors along hadn't changed in twenty years: carpet made damp by wellingtons and deck-shoes, seasoned with wet dog and newsprint. I breathed it in, olfactory time-travel. The atmosphere, however, was different: it hummed with the barely suppressed excitement of those who have been close to a disaster. I was one of only three or four customers but the air was alive; everything seemed to vibrate with it.

5

The woman at the till flicked a glance at me. Her eyes stopped for a moment on the side of my face, registering it, but then moved away: I wasn't the person she was watching for. She leant her hip against the counter, folding her arms high across her chest, and went back to talking to her friend, face confidential. I walked over to the magazines and pretended to browse, hoping they would forget I was there and take up again where they had left off. They kept their voices quiet, however, and though they were only a few feet away, I strained to hear what they were saying about the thick fog apparently due to roll in over the Channel. Had they been talking about something else when I'd come in?

In the end I gave up the attempt to eavesdrop and bought a copy of the *County Press*. As the woman handed me my change, I hesitated. I wanted to ask her if there were any developments on the news that would be in the paper but I couldn't. In a town this size, it was possible – likely – that she knew the missing woman personally.

I hurried back the way I'd come, feeling the cold against my cheeks like a damp cloth after the muggy warmth of the shop. The sky was the same white as it had been the previous day, unmarked by any texture or line in the cloud, and infused with a dirty light. I felt claustrophobic under it all of a sudden, as if it were a stifling blanket being lowered down over my face.

At the house again, I spread the huge paper over the kitchen table and searched for the story. I found it at the bottom of the third page. It was short, just three paragraphs.

Fears for Yarmouth Woman
There are serious fears for the safety of a Yarmouth resident after her sailing dinghy was found floating off the back of the Island near Freshwater Bay.

Lifeboats from Freshwater, Yarmouth and Lymington joined the coastguard helicopter in the search for Alice Frewin, 34, after she was reported missing by her husband. Mrs Frewin's boat, a scow named Vespertine, *was recovered by the Yarmouth crew on Thursday evening and towed to Yarmouth harbour.*

6

Peter Frewin, the missing woman's husband, had believed her to be visiting family on the mainland but raised the alarm when his wife's sister claimed that there had been no arrangement between them to meet and he discovered her boat had been taken from its mooring in the Western Yar. The search continues but, with sea temperatures now low, hopes for Mrs Frewin's safe recovery are fading.

Next to the story was a photograph. I leaned over the table to look at it more closely. The newsprint blurred the picture and she hadn't been looking directly at the camera, but with a shock of recognition I realised I'd seen Alice Frewin before.

Three days earlier, my first full day on the Island, I'd gone walking in the afternoon, partly to distract myself, partly to start getting my bearings again. At the end of the passageway I'd turned right and walked the fifteen or so yards to where the street met the town square. There, too, little had changed. The grocery was still on the corner, its green-striped awning rippling in the breeze, and opposite it was the yacht chandlery whose stone step, I remembered, had a deep groove worn into it by centuries of feet. Then there was the Bugle pub, the white walls of the little branch of Lloyd's bank, the café in the wooden hut at the start of the pier. The garden of the George hotel was screened by a thick hedge. Two people had been in evidence: a grey-haired woman pulling a canvas shopping trolley and a man on the bench by St James's church on the other side of the Square, bending slowly to pet the Yorkshire terrier which snuffled round his feet. Apart from the look of the few cars parked at the kerb, there was nothing much to suggest that I hadn't been teleported back to the 1950s.

I had taken the road that led off the Square by the grocery: the High Street. There were more tiny local shops: a jeweller, a florist, a place selling old-fashioned women's clothing. Signs on the doors of a gift shop and a restaurant said they would be closed until spring. A faded poster outside the police sub-station proclaimed the importance of the Neighbourhood Watch.

The shops ran out as the street went on and then I was walking between two facing rows of houses, some cottages, some substantial properties, in a range of architectural styles. There was a huge Gothic mansion, its leaded windows obscured by the lush magnolias that dominated its garden, and a little further along, the four-storey North House, so fresh-painted and pristine it wouldn't have looked out of place in Kensington. Smaller but equally beautiful houses came after it and I looked surreptitiously through their windows, seeing the ornaments on their sills – the vases and plates and photographs – and the ordered rooms beyond. Occasionally in the houses on my left, I could see all the way through to the Solent, past the easy chairs and kitchen tables positioned for the view. Only in one of the rooms was there a light on, the yellow glow of a lamp pushing back the creeping grey of the afternoon.

The High Street came out at a common that sloped steeply to a tarmac path along the water's edge. I'd made my way down across the long autumn grass and followed it, letting my feet fall into a rhythm with the grey-green waves that slapped at the concrete sea wall. Their briny smell mingled with the scent of mud and wet grass. Across the Solent, the mainland was little more than a thick green stripe; above it, another bank of cloud was massing.

Along the length of the path there were benches and on the last one, furthest from the houses, a woman had been sitting. Her posture had caught my attention immediately. She was perched on the edge of the seat, the tension in her body palpable even at a distance, as if she was primed to spring up in an instant, fight or flight. She wore a khaki parka jacket, its hood rimmed with fake fur, and one of her hands pinched the material of it close to the base of her throat. The other held a cigarette that she brought to her mouth with darting movements. Her hair was long and blonde, and the wind blew it about her face.

Her anxiety mirrored mine so closely it was as if I was looking at myself, and I had been filled with a sudden desire to talk to her. 'Excuse me,' I said, approaching. My voice was thick; it had been almost a day since I'd spoken. 'I'm sorry to ask but do you have a spare cigarette?'

She'd looked up sharply and I realised that she hadn't been

aware of me in the minutes that it had taken to walk along the front towards her. Her eyes were glistening, as if she had recently been crying and was on the verge of tears again, but a flicker of interest that died almost as soon as it sparked told me that she'd noticed the side of my face. I turned away a little to hide it. A moment passed and then she reached into the pocket of her coat. Marlboro Reds: too strong. I took one anyway and wordlessly she extended her lighter.

'Thanks. Do you mind if I . . .?'

She waved her hand quickly over the bench, granting permission.

It had rained around lunchtime and the seat was covered with fat drops of water that the wind hadn't yet dried. I cleared the worst of it with the arm of my jacket and sat down, careful not to trespass into her space. The wind buffeted me, too, and I tucked my hair behind my ears to stop it whipping round my face. There were only a handful of boats out but coming up the Solent, midway between us and the mainland, was a large yacht, its huge white sail fat with wind. Out of the corner of my eye, I could see her watching it, too. Her legs were crossed now and her top foot bounced to a hectic secret rhythm.

'That's a beautiful boat,' I said, tentative.

She'd glanced at me, surprised that I had spoken again, and brought her cigarette to her lips. She looked exhausted. Her eyes, though bright, were underscored with dark rings. Her hair had been recently highlighted – expensively, I thought – but it was dirty, the roots dark. 'Yes,' she said. Her foot kept bouncing. 'Do you know about boats?'

'Not really. I mean, no, not at all.'

She turned to watch it. It was moving quickly enough for its progress to be visible against the line of the mainland. Already the mouth of the Lymington River where I'd caught the ferry the previous day was far behind it.

'Do you?' I said.

'I sail.'

'I should learn.'

'Learn,' she had said, turning to face me again as she stood up to go. The look in her eyes had been suddenly fierce. 'Learn to sail.

9

Sometimes I think it was the only thing that kept me sane in this place.'

I looked at the photograph for a while and then I folded the paper away and went upstairs. There was a second, even smaller bedroom next to the one I had been sleeping in and it had the same view. I'd decided I would use it for work and I'd pushed the single bed back against the wall and moved the table in front of the window. Now I sat on the chair I'd brought up from the kitchen and looked out. Visibility was closing down. The first of the fog the women in the newsagent's had been talking about was already swirling round the tops of the masts in the harbour, and on the other side of the estuary the line that separated the wood from the sky was furred. I thought of her out there, gone for at least thirty-six hours. I hadn't understood the significance of fog earlier but now I did: if there was any chance at all she was still alive, fog would make it almost impossible to find her.

I brought my focus back inside the room. My notebooks were stacked on the corner of the table and next to them was the manuscript. I pulled it towards me and turned the pages until I found the place about halfway through at which I'd left off a week ago, in what felt like a different life. I needed to start working again now, to bury myself in the analgesic detail of it, force time to pass. I planted my elbows on the desk, hands either side of my head as if to hold my eyes in place over the text, but though I tried to engage with the words, they swarmed on the page like bacteria. I tried again. The book was a crime novel which had won a number of awards, and I'd wanted to make a good job of it: I'd spoken to the author and been touched by how pleased he was about the French edition for which I was translating it. I read the paragraph again, trying to get a sense of how it would work, but now my eyes kept wandering towards my laptop. In the end I lifted the lid and booted it up. My mobile was switched off so that I couldn't hear the calls and texts but it meant that I was out of touch for anyone else who might be trying to contact me: Dad, Helen. I should check my email at least, I told myself.

I felt my heart accelerate as I opened Outlook. Twenty-three new

10

messages, about half from him. I deleted them without opening any. On most, the subject line had been left blank, as usual, but the final one, timed only half an hour earlier, had a title. *At least let me talk to you.* I clicked on it and pressed delete again.

By three o'clock, the air in the house was stale, as if I had sucked every particle of goodness from it. I needed to go outside and breathe the air off the sea, regardless of the cold or the mist. I knew, too, where I wanted to go.

I drove without the radio on, listening to the sound of the engine. The inside of the car with the rattle of cassettes in the door compartment, the nest of newspapers and road maps and old paper coffee cups in the footwell of the passenger seat was comforting, a capsule of the familiar. 'I've still got you, car, haven't I?' I said and then felt foolish. As I crossed the bridge, the mainland was shut off from view by the shifting mist. The sea was a milky green now and the sky pale grey, the point where they met indeterminable. The light was fading; there was perhaps an hour of it left.

I had to look for signs to Freshwater Bay; I'd never driven on the Island. I had been too young, and my memory of how the various towns and villages connected was hazy, a collage of images of tracks and lanes and summer hedgerows with no practical particulars. I came down a hill at the top of Norton and found myself on a long street of semi-detached houses behind unkempt patches of garden, some of their curtains already drawn against the evening that was fast encroaching.

When at last I found the bay I pulled into the public car park and left the car next to the only two others there. It was pay-and-display but I didn't bother with a ticket: I didn't have time. No one would check anyway: the bay was deserted, not a soul on the pavement. There was no one on the stony beach either, and the café was closed for the winter, stacks of chairs visible through its lace curtains. I wrapped my coat around me, feeling the cold reaching into my bones.

The track I was looking for was behind the Albion hotel. Earlier walkers had turned the ground under the stile to heavy mud but they were long gone now; I was alone on the down apart from a few grazing cows. I watched my feet as I began the climb. In my

11

memories, this place danced with sunlight and its blue reflection off the sea; now it was done up in flat shades of brown and green and grey, the grass punctuated with scraggy thistles. My heart began to beat faster, the slope steeper than it seemed. The morning's breeze had dropped and the silence was so deep that I could hear the sea murmuring against the bottom of the cliff away on my left.

When I reached the fence at the top of the first incline, I stopped a minute to catch my breath. The Albion was below me now, shrunken already. In spring the bay would be inundated with people baring flesh on the first days of weak sunshine, buying ice cream and buckets and spades, but for now it had settled into timelessness, the view of dun fields back towards the north face of the Island the same as it might have been fifty years earlier or two hundred.

My thighs ached as I started up the next slope but I didn't stop again: I had to get to the top before the light went. Now the grass had become the soft, mossy sort that never seems to grow and its surface was flecked with the shale of the white chalk underneath, as if the cliff's scalp was showing through. To my left the land sloped away and I corrected my direction again and again to stop myself veering nearer the edge, which hid itself behind banks and folds in the cliff-top.

After perhaps fifteen minutes, I reached the top and the stone cross set up in memory of Tennyson, who had lived at Freshwater. Even here, where wind stole the heat out of the warmest summer days, the air was still. I circuited the monument and then, without knowing I was going to do it, I turned and walked to the edge.

Even from a few feet away, it looked as if the grass was disappearing from sight to incline gently to the sea but four or five steps further uncovered the truth: a sheer drop of three hundred feet. The grass simply stopped, became air. I leaned out, made myself look. There was no beach below, just a few feet of rocky rubble and then the sea, lapping insistently away at the back of the Island. The nearness of it, the dizzying possibility, took my breath away. Here it was, available to anyone who walked up here, unmarked and unfenced, raw as a knife. It would be so easy. In my knees there was a sudden urge forward.

No.

I took a couple of quick steps back and sat down. The wet grass was cold through my jeans at once. My legs were shaking and a wave of nausea swept over me, bringing a rush of saliva into my mouth. The ground seemed to tilt under me. I looked at the view to try to steady myself. People said you could see France from here on a clear day. Could they see us, too? *Do you see this, Maman?* a voice cried out in my head. *Can you see me now?*

It was only a hundred yards before the surface of the water mingled with the dusk and the thickening fog. It lay still and glassy, the only movement in it the direction of the tide, invisible from this distance. From directly below, though, where it touched the shore, there came a gentle heaving like breath, a drawing back and forth as if it moved with the lungs of someone underneath.

Alice Frewin. This is where her boat had been found, floating in the Channel off the back of west Wight, the blank loneliest face of the Island. Had she still been with it by the time it floated past the cliff here? Or had she slipped over the side near the Needles and let the water take her? How long would it take to drown or die of exposure, for the temperature of the water to alter the balance of one's mind, numbing everything out while one's body shut down? Was it brave, what she'd done, to make the decision and carry it through? Or was it braver not to jump, to carry on?

A band of fog swirled up off the sea towards me, shrouding the view forward completely, so thick I thought I could taste it. A moment of sheer terror: the light was suddenly almost gone. I could see the edge and the monument behind me, but beyond that little more than the grass around my feet. I stood up and started back down the hill, running now, conscious all the time of the edge. The thought of falling – jumping – so compelling only seconds ago, was now horrific. I imagined it, the breathless rush of freezing air, frames of white and green and grey flashing past my eyes as I plunged, faster and faster and faster. Then my body lying smashed at the bottom of the cliff, the water coming to feel it, to lap at me and touch me.

The damp and mist made the grass slippery. I fell over twice, soaking the knees of my jeans and cutting my hands. The fog was growing thicker all the time. It moved in spectral swathes, like floating gauze. I stumbled on and came, I thought, to the place from which I would see the hotel. It was invisible now, swallowed up. In front of me there was only a shifting white wall. I spun around, hoping for a landmark, the monument, by which to navigate but the way behind was closed, too. I took some deep breaths, trying to suppress the panic. To my right, a long way below, there was the gentle hush, hush of the water, and for a moment it was as if I heard Alice Frewin's voice in it, lulling and hypnotic, calling me over: *Kate, Kate*. I started humming aloud, making senseless noises to block it out.

At last I reached the bottom of the path, then the road and the car park. I got into the car and slammed the door. Reversing, I swung round too fast and almost hit the old silver Metro parked alongside. As soon as I was moving, I switched on the radio. I needed to hear music or a human voice, the babble of a DJ. I wanted to be reminded that somewhere a normal world was carrying on. Coming to this isolated spot in the dusk and the fog had been stupid beyond belief. That urge to jump, however momentary, had been real.

I didn't go back to the cottage straight away. I had no idea where I was going; I drove for the sake of it, for the illusion of purpose and momentum. Where the road ran close to the sea, the fog rubbed everything out. It moved in patches so dense that at times all I could see in front of the headlights was an impenetrable yellow cloud. In the worst of it, I put the car down into second and crept forward, afraid of hitting something, an animal or a person looming up suddenly to be thrown on to the bonnet, seen too late.

Four or five miles further on, however, the road seemed to climb and the fog grew thinner and then dissipated altogether. In the very last of the light, the landscape here was a charcoal sketch. Everything was in shades of grey and black: strong upward strokes for trees, thick hatching for the hedges that bordered furrowed fields. The clouds hung overhead, unmarked by stars or the moon. This was an old darkness, out of time: it was never dark like this in London, where light poured out into the night from a million windows.

Chapter Three

Helen's response to my decision hadn't been a surprise. 'The Isle of Wight?' She'd put her hand out to stop me picking at the crocheted blanket and made me look at her.

'I want to go away.'

'This is really sudden.'

I'd broken the eye contact and focused instead on the orderly who was bringing round another trolley of tea. He moved slowly through the ward, handing out polystyrene cups to those who could take them. He brought us two and put them down on the table that Helen had pushed aside so that she could sit on the bed. Behind her a nurse was drawing the curtains. It was a week since the hour had gone back and it had been dark for some time already. The huge windows reflected the room back at itself, the rows of beds and lockers and vinyl chairs. Visiting hours were nearly over; I'd given up hope by the time I heard her voice asking for me and then her decisive steps down the corridor. She'd come straight from the office, as soon as she'd been able to get away, and it seemed she would be working at home later, too: I could see papers sticking out of her bag. She looked as stylish as ever – her outfit today a black woollen dress that traced her shape without clinging, and snakeskin pumps – but her eyes were tired.

She'd smiled a thank you for the tea and waited until the orderly had moved on. 'Listen,' she said. 'Don't make any decisions now. Wait till you're out of here.'

'I'm not ill.'

'I know. And I'm sure you do need a break – you've been working too hard again, haven't you? You look shattered, even apart from the rest of it. But why not just have a holiday?'

'I need to go for longer than that. Six months, maybe a year . . .' I couldn't explain what I wanted without getting into the reasons. 'I've made up my mind.'

She had frowned. 'But why the Isle of Wight? You could go anywhere.'

'Dad used to take us there on holiday.'

'That was years ago. And it was summer, wasn't it? It'll be dead in winter.'

I'd refrained from telling her that that was one of the reasons I had chosen it. I wanted somewhere dead. Somewhere cut off and removed from my life.

'God, your poor face.'

I'd felt the cut on my eyebrow strain against its stitches as I grimaced, and said a silent prayer that it wouldn't start bleeding again.

'And what about Richard? Won't he mind if you suddenly disappear off the face of the earth?' she asked.

'He'll understand.'

'Will he?'

'Yes.'

'You've told him you're here?'

'He's going to America today. He'll be on the plane.'

'I'll ring him for you. Leave a message for when he arrives.'

'No.' My voice was louder than I'd intended and the vehemence of it caught the attention of the women in the two beds opposite, who looked and then quickly glanced away again, as if they'd witnessed something embarrassing. Helen drew back a little, too, and I felt guilty. I would have understood if she hadn't come, given how things had been between us recently, and my heart had filled with gratitude when I'd seen her but now I wanted to be alone, to close the curtains round my bed and pull myself into a ball under the crisp hospital sheets.

'At least tell me how it happened,' she said, with a new stiffness.

'I was on the Lillie Road on my bike and a van came up just before the bridge and knocked me off. I was thinking about something else, it was too close and it clipped me with the wing mirror. I didn't have time to put my hands out.'

'How did you get here?'

'Taxi.'

'Where's your bike now?'

'At that corner shop by the bridge; they said they'd look after it for me.'

'Do you want me to go and pick it up?'

'No,' I said, slightly too loudly again.

She looked at me and I saw that she was debating whether or not to say anything. 'You don't have to do this, you know,' she said at last.

'What?'

'You're doing it again – this is another of your over-the-top reactions. I don't know what's happened and you're clearly not going to tell me but I can't believe it's worth dropping everything to go running off to some place where you don't know anyone. I mean, do you know even one person there?' Her voice was low but full of frustration. 'Why does everything you do have to be so extreme?'

Exhaustion broke over me and I let my eyes close for a moment. When I opened them, she was picking up her bag. 'I'm going to leave you to get some sleep,' she said. 'This isn't the right place for this conversation.' She waited, giving me one more chance to apologise, explain myself, but the moment passed. I lay back against the pillows and listened to the sound of her feet on the lino as she walked away.

The nurse came and drew the curtains round my bed. They didn't meet in the middle but left a vertical sliver about four inches wide. Through it I could see the last few visitors saying their goodbyes. It was odd to be lying in pyjamas in this place filled with strangers, on public display at just the time I felt most vulnerable. I turned so that the undamaged side of my face touched the pillow. Ten minutes later, the night sister turned off the main lights. My Anglepoise lamp was bent all the way down so that it cast a circle scarcely larger than its own circumference on the pillowcase behind my head. I could feel its heat on my hair.

Eventually the muffled sounds around me had stopped. I listened and beyond the rumble of the air-conditioning, I heard life going on outside on the Fulham Palace Road, the low whirr of a bus going past and the business-like trundle of a black cab. It was all so familiar but this evidence of the normal world had seemed then to be coming from a million miles away, like old starlight.

In the morning, satisfied I wasn't concussed, they had let me go. I'd still felt too shaky to walk so although it was only two stops to Earls Court, I had taken the Tube. I had forgotten about the tide of morning commuters. It was five years since I'd been part of it, travelling to work every day in carriages packed so tightly that every journey required physical intimacy with strangers. The translating meant I was no longer subject to the same forces, the great flood into the offices of the City and West End, the staggered ebb home. I charted my own trajectory through the days. But Richard did this: suits, offices, meetings. Mostly he took taxis to work but very occasionally he went by Tube. I'd felt a surge of panic until I remembered that he was away. It was the wrong line for him anyway. I leaned my head against the glass partition, and the rhythm of the wheels over the track resolved into a chant in my head – *Whatever it takes; whatever it takes* – until I stopped it, imposed another over the top: *You lied to me; you lied to me.*

Back at the flat I took off my coat and sat down at my computer. I brought up Google and typed it in: 'Isle of Wight rental property'.

That evening, when I'd finished packing, there had been two boxes at the door of my flat: one with the dictionaries and papers for work, one with my coffee pot and printer. My suitcase, filled with the most basic of my clothes, waited only for my wash-bag in the morning. Everything else that was personal – ornaments, the rest of my clothes, those of my books with any sentimental significance – had been tidied away into the cupboard in the tiny hall and the highest shelf of the wardrobe. I'd phoned Helen to apologise for my behaviour at the hospital, skirting away again when she tried to ask about Richard. She was still against my going to the Island but she'd accepted that I wouldn't be persuaded and put me in touch with her assistant, Esther, and her boyfriend, who had been looking for a new place and were going to take over my lease for six months. Esther had been around to see the flat after work and though I had always been fond of it, seeing it through a stranger's eyes, I was aware all of a sudden of the phone-box dimensions of the kitchen, the ill-fitting carpet, the stain on the bedroom ceiling from the time the guttering had clogged with dead leaves and overflowed. I had felt defensive about my life here, as if its inadequacies had been exposed. Esther was ten years younger than me and the flat was much more suitable for someone her age, just starting her career and with a first-job salary, than for someone of mine.

I had known I wouldn't sleep. Earlier the landline had rung. I'd hesitated to pick it up but thought it might be the woman from the cottage again.

'Kate?' Richard's voice had been full of surprise at getting through.

'No,' I'd said and dropped the receiver as if it had burnt me. The phone rang again immediately so I unplugged it from the wall. My heart was thumping against my ribs and I went straight to the kitchen and opened a bottle of wine, hands fumbling at the foil around the top.

A little after midnight I poured the last of it and sat down in the wicker chair by the window. The room was full of shades: everywhere I looked there were versions of Richard and I still playing out what we'd done here as if we'd been leaving a slipstream of our own molecules all the time. It was familiar, this sense that we had layered up a history here. Before, when he'd been away, I used to look around at the sofa we'd had sex on, the table where we'd eaten dinner, the bed we'd slept in, and felt that I was among my accomplices, not alone. Now, though, overriding all those others, came the memory I was determined not to have. I shoved it away.

I turned my back on the room and looked out of the window instead. The blinds were left open, as they always were, for the view of the flats opposite. I felt as if I knew the people who moved around in them. I knew their routines and the hours they kept; I knew I'd worked too late if all their lights had gone out. Though I'd never spoken to any of them, I would miss them. In a strange way, they were my community here; they had given me the sense that there was life going on. At the same time, though, they had served to highlight my isolation. Sometimes, late at night, I had felt as if I was standing on a bank by a railway line, watching those lighted windows and the people in them as if they were racing past on a fast train that somehow I had missed.

Driving out of London the next day, everything had seemed invested with significance all of a sudden: the grocery shop and café at the bottom of the Earls Court Road, the petrol station where I stopped to fill up, the Fuller's brewery just before the turn-off at Chiswick. Shockingly, I had started to crave Richard. Everything was connected to him; every shop I passed, every stretch of road. There was a pain behind my breastbone as if I had swallowed something that had lodged in my windpipe, and the pressure was making it hard to breathe. Suddenly I hadn't been leaving the current Richard but an earlier version, the one in whom I had invested so many dreams, the one with whom I'd spent days in bed, hardly thinking of anything at all. The new Richard was gone and the one I was driving away from was the one I loved.

Two hours later, I'd arrived at the ferry terminal in Lymington. At the ticket office my will almost failed me. More than I could ever remember wanting anything in my adult life, I wanted to go back to London. The ferry ride across the Solent had turned into something else in my mind, the strip of water now Atlantic in significance.

The girl at the counter waited patiently for me to speak. There was the chatter of approaching voices: the first foot passengers disembarking from the boat which had just docked. It would be returning again in a few minutes, either with me or without.

'Come on,' the man behind me had muttered under his breath.

I had thought of my flat. Helen was going to give the spare keys to Esther later on. It wasn't mine any more, not until April anyway. I couldn't go back there. I opened my purse and handed over my card.

As I returned it to my bag, I'd seen that the screen of my mobile was lit up. Sure enough, the call was international. He'd rung four times during the night, leaving messages that I'd deleted unheard. It would be six in the morning in New York now, though, and clearly he was already awake. I flushed with anger. Did he really think I would answer him? The phone had been on silent before but now I turned it off completely.

On the ferry, I took a seat in the lounge on the top deck and watched from the window as we began to wend our way down the Lymington River, past the mudflats on one side, the yacht club and marina on the other. Out towards the mouth of the river where the wind had a freer run, the boat juddered and the bottles behind the bar began to rattle. I put my coat back on and went out on deck. The air smelled like salt and ozone and diesel but also somehow clean. The sea was flecked with white, and spume flew up around the bow. Two hours from London, I thought, but it was a different world.

Ahead lay the Island, a line of wooded green rising out of the water. My hands became raw with the cold but I stayed out for the rest of the journey anyway, holding on to the railing, watching the land come into sharper and sharper definition, like a photograph developing. The buildings along the shore at Yarmouth grew larger. There was the George hotel, tucked in next to the castle, and the yacht club and the row of large houses out towards the Common. On the other side, near where the ferry came in, was the harbour with its white spinney of masts. It was all just as I remembered it and I felt my spirits lift. Helen was wrong to think my coming here was a mistake.

The house was three minutes' walk, if that, from the harbour. The owner was a woman in early middle age, with the premature lines and ruddy cheeks of someone who had lived a good portion of her life outside. She was wearing a pair of navy trousers in heavy cotton and a chunky sweater. Her jacket, a waterproof, hung on the back of one of the chairs at the foldaway kitchen table. My own outfit, a pair of skintight jeans, a polo neck and black leather jacket, although simple, felt suddenly attention-seeking and wrong.

'Ouch,' she said when she saw the cut on my brow and the deep purple-grey ring beneath my eye.

'I fell off my bike,' I said. 'Hit the kerb. I should look where I'm going.'

'I don't know why you people do it – cycle in London. Seems like madness to me.' She went back to making the coffee. When it was ready, we went through to the sitting room. It was large, spanning the whole width of the building and opening through sliding glass doors on to a paved area with a small wooden picnic table and a cluster of empty terracotta planters. At the end, beyond the patio, were wooden double gates. The room itself was plain, the armchair and sofa upholstered in oatmeal, a porridge-coloured carpet. There was a pine coffee table and an amateurish watercolour of yachts over the fireplace. It had the functional feel of most rental places, nothing of value or quality left to damage or steal.

'You know it gets very quiet here in the winter?' She looked at me over the rim of her cup.

I told her about my work, emphasising the advantages of peace.

'You're not married? No partner?'

'No.'

'There's internet here, if that helps,' she said. 'For your work, I mean. The last tenant asked for it.' She finished her coffee and stood up. 'I'll show you the rest.'

I followed her up a narrow staircase to a landing barely large enough to turn around on and saw the two bedrooms and a bathroom whose uncompromisingly avocado fittings suggested the 1970s weren't over yet. Back downstairs in the kitchen, the cooker's digital clock said it was twelve. Odd that it was still so early; I felt a whole day should have passed already. It was the journey; not only had it removed me from the mainland, it had dislocated my sense of time, too. Distance, though, was what I wanted. I wrote her a cheque for the deposit.

When she'd gone I went back to the harbour front for the car. It took me twenty seconds to reach the wooden gates and drive it into the yard, and perhaps three minutes more to open the sliding doors and carry the suitcase and the boxes into the house.

Then, the doors locked again behind me, I sat down at the kitchen table, my legs going from under me all of a sudden as if in shock at how quickly I had achieved it, bringing myself here to this place. There was no noise at all from the town; no cars passing or voices on the street. Little by little, the sounds of the house itself pressed themselves on my attention: the low vibration of the fridge whose phases resolved every minute or two with a mechanical shudder, the irregular drips of water from the tap into the steel sink, the surge of the central heating when the temperature dipped below whatever the thermostat had been set at. I leant forward and put my head in my hands. What the hell have I done? I thought.

Chapter Four

I hadn't been afraid the night I met him. On the way back to his house I had looked blithely out of the taxi window at unfamiliar streets and thought to myself that I had only been to that part of London once before, crossing it on a bus for a reason I'd forgotten. He had had his hand on my thigh, his fingers curling in to press on the soft flesh on the inside, and it seemed to weigh heavier than a hand should. I had smiled as I turned my face down to my shoulder, baring more of my neck for him to put his lips against, knowing that the driver was flicking his eyes to watch us in the mirror.

Helen and I had been out for supper in Soho. She had been tired by the time we finished eating but I was suddenly full of energy, excited that it was Saturday and we were out, the streets busy, full of possibility. 'It's too early to go home,' I said, draining my glass. 'Come on. How often do we celebrate your getting promoted?'

'It's nearly midnight,' she said. 'I've got stuff to do tomorrow.'

'More work.'

'Well, yes but . . .'

'Is this the Helen who only used to leave a club when they started sweeping? Come on – one more.'

We found a place round the corner. Neither of us had been there before. It was crowded with people dressed more smartly than us and when at last we were served, there was nowhere to sit. We were shunted away from the bar and found ourselves standing by an arrangement of dramatic red flowers, birds of paradise and amaryllises, by an alcove near the door. The room was hot and airless. I saw Helen stifling a yawn and felt bad: I shouldn't have dragged her on; we should have gone home.

Afterwards I couldn't have said how it happened but suddenly they were talking to us, him and another man. His friend, who focused on Helen almost immediately, was tall and peered down at her with pale strained eyes. His light brown hair was cut very short, as if he was adamant no one should think he didn't know he was receding.

The first thing I noticed about the man who turned to me was his eyebrows. They were thick and black, and arched up so that he seemed permanently to be asking a question, one to which he already knew the answer. There was something griffin-like about his expression; there was dry humour in it but also a challenge, as if he was saying: surprise me. He was watching me intently but didn't speak. It was strange: it should have unnerved me but instead I found myself responding to the intensity. It was like suddenly finding myself in a spotlight.

'You're in suits,' I said eventually, to break the silence. 'You and your friend.'

'We've been at work.'

'On a Saturday evening?'

'Until about an hour ago, yes. It's been a big week.' His voice was accentless and somehow confidential, as if we'd known each other a long time and he was telling me a piece of information whose importance only I would understand.

A new group of people came in from the street and, to make room for them, he took a step towards me. I took a corresponding step back into the alcove and, in doing so, lost Helen from direct sight. There were a few seconds in which neither of us spoke. We looked at each other, and one of his eyebrows lifted, as if he was daring me to look away first. His eyes were a colour I hadn't seen before – light brown, like toffee – and there was something Persian about their shape. In their corners were lines which the remnants of a tan made more pronounced. I put him in his late thirties. One side of his mouth was rising. I smiled back, feeling the start of a bubbling hilarity in my stomach, but in the end it was me who broke the eye contact. I took a sip of my drink to find that, apart from the ice cubes, the glass was empty.

25

'I'll get us some more,' he said. 'Gin and tonic, yes?'

Before I could say anything, he was on his way to the bar. I came forward a couple of steps. The man with Helen was leaning against the wall next to her now, his rucksack between his feet. He was talking – something about Spain – and I waited for him to break off but a minute later the new drinks were back from the bar. 'That was quick,' I said. 'It took us ages to get served.'

He made a face that suggested he hadn't noticed one way or the other and took a mouthful from his glass. Then he stepped closer to me and we were back in the alcove again. He smiled and I looked at his mouth. His lips were full but in no way feminine. His hair was cropped close to his head and so thick that it looked not silky but velvety. I suppressed an urge to put out my hand and stroke it.

A trio of women in cocktail dresses had moved to our side of the room for the waves of cooler air that came in when the door opened, and they pushed us closer together, so close now we were almost touching. The three or four inches of space between us came alive with tension. Suddenly and without taking his eyes off me, he took my hand and threaded his fingers through mine. He brought our hands up next to my face and pushed me lightly back against the wall. His mouth moved closer to mine but ten or twelve seconds passed and he didn't kiss me. Go on; surprise me, his eyes said. This time I held his stare, making no movement either towards or away from him, wanting him to know I could play this game, too. I saw him register it and then, at last, he leaned the small extra distance and his lips touched mine for perhaps a second. The frisson spread over the whole surface of my body.

He moved away and took a sip of his drink.

Disorientated, I struggled to think of something to say. In the end, I asked what he did. It sounded like ridiculous drinks-party small talk after what had just happened.

'I'm a property developer.'

'What sort of property?'

'Residential – sometimes in the UK but mostly overseas. We're working on a project in Andalusia at the moment.'

'Enjoy it?'

'Of course. I wouldn't do it otherwise.'

He was watching me as if he was trying to work out what I was thinking. I was suddenly determined not to give him any idea. I would surprise him, I thought, if that was what he wanted.

He kissed me again but this time his lips stayed on mine, and for seconds before and afterwards our mouths were so close that we were breathing each other's breath. His arm was on the wall next to my head, simultaneously creating a barrier between me and the girl who was pushing against us, and fencing me in. The pit of my stomach felt tight, the hilarity becoming a different sort of excitement.

When he pulled away again, Helen was standing behind him, wearing a questioning expression. 'I'm exhausted,' she said. 'I'm going home. Are you coming?'

In front of her, visible only to me, his eyebrows twitched up. I looked at Helen and then back again at him, at his mouth. I shook my head. 'I'll be all right,' I said. 'I'll stay and finish my drink.' I raised the glass towards her, as if it were proof of my need to stay, but found that it was empty again.

'Can I have a word with you?' she said. 'Outside.'

'I'll be back in a moment,' I said to him. He took my glass.

I followed her as she pushed a way towards the door. We reached the pavement and I took a deep breath of the fresh air. It was much cooler than inside but still warm. Some of the heat seemed to be rising from the pavement, the concrete radiating the sun which it had been storing all afternoon.

'Tell me you're not going home with him,' she said.

Until that moment, I hadn't really thought beyond what it had felt like when he kissed me. 'No,' I said. 'Of course I'm not.'

'You've just met him. You haven't got a clue who he is.'

'I know that.'

'I don't want to leave you in the middle of Soho when you've been drinking.'

'Relax. I'll have one more, then I'll get a taxi.'

She looked at me appraisingly. 'Will you?'

I felt a surge of rebellion against her. Who was she, I wanted to ask, to pass judgement on me like this? 'What if I do?' I said. 'What if I do go home with him?'

'You met him two minutes ago – in a bar. He could be an axe murderer.'

'He's not an axe murderer.' I laughed. 'He's a property developer.'

Helen closed her eyes briefly, as if she were trying hard not to lose her temper. 'Come home with me. You can sleep in my spare room.'

'No. I don't want to. When did you get so old and . . . censorious, Helen? Why are you like this? And why shouldn't I have some fun?'

'Are you having fun? Are you – really? I don't think you know what you're doing these days. You work all day and all night, or not at all. You drink far too much – I know you don't tell me the truth about it. And this isn't the first time you've done this recently, either, is it?' She waved her hand backwards.

'Oh come on, it's not like I do it often.'

'There was that guy two weeks ago.'

'That was different, that was . . .'

'How was it different?'

There was a few seconds' silence and for the first time in our fifteen years of friendship, I saw how I could dislike her. 'Just forget it,' I said, and my voice sounded cold even to me. 'I'll speak to you later.' I turned away from her and walked back in. Just inside the door, I glanced back to see if she was still standing there but she had already gone.

His friend seemed to have disappeared, too, but my man was standing just where we'd been before. He'd been to the bar again and I took a mouthful of gin from the glass he handed me.

'Not going home then?' he asked.

Later, the cab dropped us outside a red-brick mansion block. Soho had been busy still but once the sound of the taxi's engine had faded into the distance, his road was quiet. The streetlights shone bleakly down a long avenue lined with BMWs, Mercedes, Jaguars. Nothing moved, not a car, or another person, or even the leaves on the trees. He closed the front door behind us and put his hand in the small of my back as we climbed the wide staircase to the first floor and went along the corridor. The door of his flat opened into a hallway almost as large as my bedroom. On the wall there was a single picture, a stark black-and-white line-drawing which looked Japanese. Through a door to the right, I could see a dining room: a glass table with an iron structure, eight matching chairs. The carpet was cream.

He snapped another switch and we went through to the sitting room. Most of the rooms I knew were full of stuff: soft chairs, candlesticks, piles of books and magazines, lamps, prints on the walls; this one had two low black leather sofas and a glass coffee table. There was a flat-screen television and an expensive stereo on the shelf by the fireplace but otherwise the room was empty. For a reason I couldn't identify, the difference was exciting. He came up behind me and turned me around, putting his hands around my face, pressing his thumbs behind my jaw, moving his tongue into my mouth.

Later, pinned under him, I pushed his shoulder, making him stop.

'I don't know your name,' I said.

'Richard.'

'Kate.'

'Nice to meet you.' He raised one of his eyebrows and the challenge was there again. I narrowed my eyes a little and looked straight back at him.

In the morning I woke up alone. I ran my palm over the bed where he had lain and took a handful of the sheet and pulled it to my nose. It smelt of his body, a light soap scent mixed with a deeper musk note and sweat. I lay in bed for a minute, remembering. We hadn't slept until the alarm clock on the night table had read half past five and the gap in the curtains began to let in the first grey dawn light. I thought about the muscles in his shoulders and how his back had tapered to his waist and the cleft in his buttocks. It was clear he went to the gym. Black hair covered his chest and ran in a line from his navel into his groin. I thought about how he had held my hip, his thumb pressing the bone, his fingers reaching round to dent the flesh of my backside.

Suddenly afraid that he would come back and be annoyed to find me lazing presumptuously in his bed, I swung my legs over the side. The varnished floorboards were cold on my feet and the insides of my thighs ached. I bent slowly down to pick up my skirt and heard footsteps outside the bedroom door.

'You're not going yet,' he said.

I turned, unsure whether or not it was a question. He was leaning against the jamb, a large towel tucked in around his waist, his hair wet and slicked back. His eyes moved over me, making me acutely conscious of my nakedness. The satin skirt with its peacock-feather pattern hung limply between my fingers, its rich blues and greens contrasting with my pale flesh.

'Stay for breakfast – I've been out to get it. The bathroom's down the hall.'

I hesitated, then laid the skirt gently on the edge of the bed. By the doorway he stood aside to let me pass and I tried to look as though I were confident, walking naked past a man whom I'd known fewer than twelve hours and yet who had spread me across his bed like a merchant laying out a piece of cloth.

The bathroom was humid with the rosemary scent of expensive masculine unguents. I rubbed the steam off the mirror and looked at my face. I had a glow to which I had no right after so little sleep. In my eyes there was a strange light and it took me a few seconds to identify it: a mix of pride at my daring with a small measure of exhilarating fear. I opened the glass door of the shower cubicle and stepped on to its slatted wooden floor. A storm of water fell from the ceiling and I turned my face up into it. I searched my mind for the name of the feeling that coursed through me and found that it was a vivid awareness of being alive.

As I was using the comb that he had left by the sink, there were footsteps in the corridor. 'There's a dressing-gown on the back of the door,' he said.

It was the sort found in expensive hotels: a waffle fabric in heavy white cotton. Helen had one just like it, and I had always coveted it. I tied the belt tightly round my waist and went through to the kitchen where he was making an espresso with a Gaggia machine not much smaller than the one in my local Italian coffee shop; engine-like, it covered four feet or more of the lovely marble work top. I stood awkwardly for a moment taking in the expensive sparsity of the room, the butcher's block, the Sabatier knives on the metal strip above the counter, until he turned from the melon he was slicing and ushered me on to a chair at the table. A minute or so later he slid the chopping board on to the table and sat down next to me. It struck me that there was something practised about his ease.

'Do you do this often – go home with strange girls from bars?'

He laughed. 'Of course not – do you?'

I pulled a mock-offended face. 'Are you surprised I came back with you?'

'What you really want to know is whether I think less of you for it.'

'What makes you think your opinion carries any weight with me at all?' I said, raising my eyebrows at him.

He looked momentarily taken aback, then laughed and leaned across to kiss me, putting his hands on either side of my head. The odd excitement that I'd felt in the pit of my stomach the previous evening renewed itself. After a moment, he pulled away and looked at my face. Again, the intensity of his stare was like a beam of light, so strong it was disorientating. Then he stood and scooped me up, lifting me from the chair and carrying me across the room to the counter. He set me down on the edge of it and kissed me again before pushing me backwards and parting the dressing-gown. His mouth hovered over me. For a second, I thought he was going to bite me. Then, glancing up and smiling, he lowered his head.

Later I left his flat and stepped out into the bright light of a Sunday afternoon. My low-cut top and the peacock skirt were obviously evening clothes; everyone who saw me would know I hadn't been home. My high shoes and the ache in my thighs limited my steps. A couple were unloading boxes from the back of a Mercedes estate and I stopped to let the woman cross the pavement in front of me. In the back of the car there was a small boy strapped into a seat and he watched me impassively through the glass. I caught his gaze and smiled but his expression remained solemn, dappled by the patterning of the leaves of the cherry tree overhead.

I was in no hurry to find the Tube station. He had offered to call me a cab but I wanted to walk. The world felt distant, removed from me by lack of sleep and by my unfamiliarity with the area. The distance gave me a feeling of power, a sense that the world was a backdrop against which I could act, rather than an unchangeable fact of which I was an insignificant feature. Just around the corner there was a café and at one of the tables on the pavement a couple was reading the papers, both comfortable in jeans and T-shirts, she holding a mug between her hands, he leaning on his elbow, absently pressing up the crumbs of a slice of cake. They looked at ease, contented, but I didn't envy them. I felt wanton and electrified.

Chapter Five

The fog that had swallowed the Island had cleared entirely by the morning, even over the estuary. In its place was a sullen dank that darkened everything: the walls of the buildings where I cut through to the newsagent's seemed damper than before and the tarmac in the Square shone a wet charcoal grey. It was colder, too; coming into the café on the corner, the contrast between the mordant wind and the muggy warmth inside had momentarily taken my breath away.

I watched as condensation ran in lines down the plate-glass windows. From my table at the back, the whole interior of the little café was visible, all the heavy pine tables with their cruets and the miniature model lighthouses holding the menus in place. In the small glass cabinet by the till was the selection of Danish pastries and cakes; behind it a doorway led away to the kitchen.

It was late again: quarter to twelve. My body clock was completely out of kilter. Last night, the insomnia had been its worst yet; when I'd turned off the light and lain in the dark waiting for sleep, the moment on the down when I'd been drawn to the edge kept replaying itself in my mind. I was shocked by how close I had come: the memory of it had started my heart racing and then I had thought about Richard again. I remembered hearing the muffled sound of St James's striking four o'clock.

The smell of bacon filled the air and my stomach growled. When I'd finally come in from driving I hadn't been able to make myself eat at all. Now a bacon sandwich seemed a good compromise between the breakfast which I'd slept through and the lunch for which it was still too early. The customers who had been in for coffee were slowly paying and leaving and the waitress circulated, clearing away their dirty cups and wiping the tables with slow arcs of her cloth.

The local television news last night hadn't mentioned Alice Frewin and there was no radio in the house. I'd been to buy a paper before coming in but discovered that the *County Press* only appeared weekly. I bought a copy of *The Times* instead and now had it spread out on the table in front of me like a prop. In London I thought nothing of sitting in cafés on my own but here I felt oddly self-conscious. I was twenty years younger than anyone else in the room and the only person alone; the other customers were in pairs or threes and greeted the waitress by name. Several times I looked up, aware of eyes on me.

I'd finished my sandwich and was attempting the crossword by the time they came in. The room was busier again with the start of lunchtime and the table in front of mine was now the only one free and clean. They were a pair of women in their late sixties, I guessed; through the window I had seen them greet each other in the Square. The one who sat on the side of the table nearest me had been lagged like a boiler in multiple jumpers and a green quilted jerkin but quickly began shedding layers once inside. They broke off from their conversation about the cold to order omelettes and tea and I went back to grappling with the crossword. I was months out of practice.

A few minutes later I heard it, a voice lowered and confidential: 'Well, something must have been wrong.' Without moving my head, I flicked a glance in their direction. It was the one with all the jumpers who'd been talking, leaning forward so that her bust rested on the edge of the table.

'I don't like to think about it,' her friend said quietly. She had a neat grey page-boy cut and her fringe swung as she shook her head.

'I can hardly think about anything else. I saw her in that boat a thousand times, in all weathers. Rain, wind – it hardly seemed to matter to her, did it? Maybe I even saw her that morning, going out – I wouldn't have thought anything of it. And to think that that might have been the last time . . .'

34

'Margaret! Don't be ghoulish.'

'Well! How am I ghoulish?' came the response in a quick whisper. 'It's no good pretending to me that you're not thinking about it. And thinking's not going to influence anything, is it?'

The waitress appeared at the end of my table and reached across for my plate. 'Can I get you anything else?' she said. The woman with her back to me turned a little to look at me, as if she'd only now become aware of my presence.

'Another coffee. Thanks.' I wasn't ready to go yet. I lowered my head and wrote out the letters of an anagram on a paper napkin, hoping to disappear into the background again or at least to look preoccupied and oblivious. A minute or two passed and I thought they'd stopped. I worked out the anagram and was writing it in when the voices were lowered again.

'That poor man, though,' said the woman with the page-boy.

'Poor? Do you think so?'

'Don't you?'

'Why would a woman up and do that all of a sudden – do away with herself? What made her?' Margaret's voice was full of wondering conspiracy.

'You can't think he had anything to do with it, surely.'

'Well, something happened.'

'He treated her like a queen. That was plain. That house, the boat, all those foreign holidays – money no object.'

'How long have they been married?' Margaret said. 'No children.'

'It's that generation, isn't it? They all leave it late; jobs, careers – that's what's important to them. My daughter-in-law's the same – career, career, career. She's thirty-seven now, been married for eight years. I've stopped asking.'

'She didn't work, though, did she? She wasn't one of those.' Margaret lowered her voice still further.

The waitress brought my new cup of coffee and in doing so drew the attention of the neat-headed woman. I caught her eye as I looked up from the paper and I saw her realise I'd been listening. Pointedly she turned back to her friend and changed the subject. 'The bins were kicked over again last night – did you see? Rubbish all up the street. It's time someone gave that boy a proper hiding.'

I left the café and went back down Quay Street. At the bottom, a few people were waiting by the gate to meet foot passengers from the ferry just arriving. I stood and watched as the handful of cars loaded for the return sailing and then crossed the road on to the quay wall. The water in the harbour was steely green today, taking its grey from the sky, and the wind rocked the boats on the moorings, making an eerie staccato music through their rigging. The lifeboat was in, tied up in its bay. Just ahead of me, a seagull landed on the path, its object an abandoned sandwich. It anchored the bread with its foot and tore at the crust, gulping down the pieces with a singular lack of elegance, regarding me all the while with suspicion, as if I might try and challenge it for the meal.

As I came back through the door of the cottage, my mobile rang once to tell me I had a text message. I took it out of my bag and looked at the envelope on the screen, hesitating. It was getting harder to ignore him. Now I wanted to dial his number and scream at him: 'How could you do this to me? This is me.' Shamefully, though, the ebbing of the fear had also left room for the insidious part of me that wanted just to erase the past week and go back to how we had been before. I wanted *my* Richard. The thought sent a stab of pain through my chest.

I locked the door behind me, sat down at the table and opened the message.

I'm at the airport now, coming back today, and I need to see you. What I did was wrong but let me apologise, Katie. I love you – you know I do.

Wrong? What he did was *wrong*? I threw the phone on to the table. *Katie*. He was the only person in the world who called me that apart from Dad and Matt. It was so calculated: in that one word he knew I would hear his voice, the low tone suggesting we shared things that no one else did, the echo of all the times he had murmured my name into my ear. I imagined him in the departure lounge only a few seconds earlier, thumbs moving over the keys of his phone with customary speed, the second of his early-morning double espressos in front of him. I sat back heavily, winded.

After supper, I sat in front of the television and tried to concentrate on the news. I'd been here for five days now but I still didn't feel even slightly comfortable. During the afternoon I'd been at my desk again but it had been impossible to focus on work; instead I had surfed the internet, read halves of articles on the *Atlantic Monthly* site and looked at the programme of films I was missing at the BFI, all the time trying to work out where he would be, whether his plane would have taken off, whether he was halfway yet. He would certainly have landed by now, past nine o'clock, so where was the barrage of calls? I had pictured him going through his usual aeroplane routine: turning his phone on as soon as the wheels touched the tarmac, standing up before the seatbelt signs were off and then agitating around the baggage carousel, incensed at being held to anyone else's timetable even for a few minutes, dialling my number over and over.

Why hadn't he rung? My mobile was on the pine dresser by the sliding doors, moved deliberately out of my direct line of sight: while it had been on the arm of the sofa, my eyes were flicking on to it every few seconds. Now, suddenly, in the semi-darkness of the corner of the room, the screen started to flash blue. I stood up immediately, feeling sick. The number wasn't his, however. It was Esther's.

'Kate?'

'Is everything all right?'

'There was a guy here.'

'What? There – in the flat?'

'He rang a few days ago – he thought you were still here. I wouldn't have let him in just now but he surprised me – he buzzed, said he was passing and thought he'd try and pick up the book he'd left, to save you asking me to post it on.'

'Which book?'

'I didn't see. Look, I probably wouldn't even have rung you but – well, it was weird. He didn't go straight away. He went downstairs but then he just stood on the pavement opposite, looking up at the window. He was fine when he was up here – quite charming, actually – just came in, took the book off the shelf, said thank you at the door and went. But then . . .'

The blood was pounding in my temples. 'Does he know you saw him?'

'Yes. I went over to draw the blinds – he was looking straight at me.'

'How long was he there?'

'I don't know – five minutes, maybe. It was kind of creepy – he was just standing there, in the middle of the pavement, looking. And Steve's out tonight.'

'Did he ask you where I was?'

'No,' she said. 'Doesn't he know?'

I took a silent breath and tried to make my voice sound calm. 'I'm really sorry about this. I didn't think he'd come round when he knew I wasn't there. He's OK; he's just a bit . . . intense sometimes.'

'No, I'm sorry, I shouldn't have called. I just thought you should know.'

When we hung up, I put my coat on and went out, leaving my mobile behind. I wanted to be away from it now. I'd known he would carry on ringing the flat until he found out I'd moved but I hadn't guessed he'd go there once he did. He'd done it so that she would tell me, pass the message on.

I walked through the town for as long as I could but the lighted areas were small and I was going faster even than usual to ward off the cold that worked its way inside my coat. I did the circuit twice, along the harbour front, the Square, up to the common, back down again by the terraces that lined Tennyson Road, but I began to feel unnerved: it was a Friday night but there was no one to be seen. There were lights on behind the curtains of the pubs and in the cottages up towards the common but not one person on the pavement. Everyone was locked away. I felt like the only person alive, the sole survivor in a plague town. Or perhaps I was the ghost, wandering the streets alone, unable to break through and reach the living again.

When I got back to the cottage I checked my phone straight away, wanting to pre-empt the beep that would tell me he'd left a message. He hadn't called but there was a text: *Where are you? I wonder.*

The first time he'd come to the flat, I'd waited for him at the sitting-room window, standing to one side so that I wouldn't be visible if he looked up from the street. A little after eight, a taxi had pulled in and I watched him get out. My stomach turned over when I saw him: it had been real, then, that night. He came up the steps and I'd jumped at the sound of the buzzer even though I was expecting it.

I hadn't known whether he would call me. Purposely I had said nothing to suggest I cared one way or the other. When I'd left his house that afternoon, I told myself that whether or not we saw each other again wasn't the point. The night could be seen as an isolated incident, a brief step out of bounds, an adventure. It would be something to remember when I got old and needed to remind myself that I had taken risks and been daring. Nevertheless, it was true he'd intrigued me. He was different. It was there in the way he looked at me, eyebrows arching as if he were calling me out, and in his deep self-assurance. There was also the physical connection between us.

He hadn't mentioned meeting again until I had been standing inside his front door. We'd spent the past four or five hours back in his bed, his body enclosed in the circle of my legs, his nails tracing lightly up the outside of my thigh while we talked. It was a strange bantering conversation, like a game of tennis between two people trying to assess the other's level of skill, each registering their opponent's best shots, producing their own. At the door I had turned awkwardly towards him and smiled, pretending to look for something in my bag. He took a step forward, tipped my chin upwards and kissed me lightly. I resisted an urge to lean into him. 'Give me your number,' he said.

He called two days later. I was at the table in the sitting room working at the computer, the blinds left up for the view of the flats opposite, as usual. The sound of the phone startled me but his voice carried me straight back inside the bubble which had seemed to surround us as soon as we met. He hadn't called for one of the brief exchanges of information – a date, a time – that I'd sometimes had with other men and that left me with a transactional feeling; he asked how my week was going and listened to my answer.

He'd suggested dinner on Friday and I'd pretended to check my diary. When I hung up, the display told me that we'd been on the phone for half an hour. Too excited to start work again immediately, I stood at the open window and looked out. The couple in the top flat had gone to bed while we'd been talking. Though it was June and warm, there was a breeze and the wind caught the litter in the gutter and blew it in scudding gusts along the street, rushing, then settling, moving on again.

The restaurant he'd taken me to was in Kensington, a tiny place with eight tables, tucked away near a gallery and a boutique on what was otherwise a residential street. The chef and the one waitress chatted to one another through the serving hatch and it felt like another sign: they were French. Richard discussed the wine for two or three minutes before he ordered and when the bottle arrived, he examined the label before taking a sip and rolling it thoughtfully around his mouth. Whenever I tried the wine in a restaurant, I hurried through what I thought was expected of me, spinning it out just long enough that there was a chance people would think I knew what I was doing, embarrassed to keep anyone waiting. Richard, by contrast, was perfectly at ease with the idea that the waitress should stand by until he was satisfied.

While we waited for the starters to arrive, he reached over and took my hand. He looked at it as if it were something whose details were worth remembering. His own fingers were long and straight, with short dark hairs on the back of the sections before the second knuckle. He ran a single finger across my palm, his nail touching my skin, and the touch sent a shiver through me.

'You told me you're a translator. What language? Or languages? Not Spanish by any chance?'

'French. Mostly English into French. I do some technical manuals, sales brochures, that sort of thing, but mostly it's books – novels.'

40

'Bright girl.' He dipped his head slightly.

'Did you doubt it?' I raised my eyebrows in the way he did.

'Do you think I'd be interested if you weren't?'

'I don't know. Maybe you like daft women – some men do.' I glanced away, smiling. When I was a teenager, I'd comforted myself for not being one of the better-looking girls with the knowledge that I did well at school and could meet the clever boys on their own terms, often beat them.

'I like clever women. I need someone who can keep me interested.'

I took a sip of the wine, which was really good. I would never have said that: it sounded so arrogant. I thought it, though: I liked clever men and wouldn't go out with anyone who couldn't at least hold his own, if not beat me in arguments. There was an honesty in Richard's saying it out loud that impressed me.

'So why French?'

'My mother was French.'

I saw him register the past tense. 'You grew up speaking it then?' he said.

'Yes, until I was ten. I kept it up; I had a French friend and I did it at university, spent a year at the Sorbonne and then worked in Paris for a couple of years after that. Anyway,' I said, feeling uncomfortable, 'we're only talking about me. Tell me something about your life.'

'What do you want to know?'

Everything, I thought. 'Where did you grow up?'

'Here – London. I did my degree here – economics – then I did post-grad in the States, at Harvard. I worked in banking for a bit, then I set up my property business. I'm not cut out to work for other people.'

Over coffee, he leaned in as if to whisper something. I leaned in, too, but realised that he was reaching for my leg under the table. His fingers slid up my thigh, pushing the hem of my skirt higher. Hidden by the tablecloth, his thumb caressed my flesh through the fine gauge of my tights. Memories of Sunday morning came back to me and I flushed. 'Why are you single?' he said quietly.

'Why are you single?'

'These things happen.' He smiled, went on stroking. 'Am I coming home with you tonight?'

I looked up.

'You seem shocked. Surely you can't be?' There was a suggestion of laughter in his voice. 'After all, technically, you've already *given yourself to me*, if I remember correctly. And I'm certain I remember that quite clearly, if not at all correctly.' The smile was moving round his mouth and his eyes were full of it, too.

'You were granted temporary access to my body,' I said, giving him the same look. 'As was I to yours. But giving myself to you – I'm afraid that's much more complicated.'

His eyes, suddenly, were unreadable but then he grinned and slid his hand an inch higher. *Engaged*, I thought ridiculously, heady with wine and the sensation of daring myself and getting away with it, *one partner in a high-stakes game*.

In the taxi he traced his fingers lightly over the nape of my neck. I stopped talking and gave myself over to the feelings it sent running through me. As we climbed the stairs to my door, I was conscious of the weight of his stare on my legs and bottom. As soon as we were inside, he moved towards me and kissed me. We were standing directly under the main light in the sitting room and the blinds were still up. I wondered whether any of my neighbours across the street were watching and what they would make of this scene, so different from the usual one of the outline of my head bending into the yellow halo of the desk lamp.

Chapter Six

As he had known he would, Richard had frightened me by going to the flat. For much of that night I thought about him standing motionless on the pavement, looking up at the windows, and the image grew in resonance and power until it seemed to become symbolic, a statement of intent. Over and over again I had to remind myself that he didn't know where I was and no one would tell him. Only three people knew, anyway, and of those Helen was the only one he would be able to find. I'd made her promise not to tell him and, however strained things were between us, I knew I could trust her. Richard's going to the flat was a gesture of intimidation, born of frustration at not being able to reach me. I mustn't let it work; I had to hold my nerve if I was going to get free of him.

The shadow of the image was still on me in the morning, though, and I knew that if I stayed in the cottage, it would leach the whole day. It would be hard to concentrate enough to work. On the drive to Freshwater, I'd seen a signpost to Totland Bay and I decided to walk there. Matt and I had loved Totland when we were children. There was a café down on the beach with tables outside where we'd sometimes had tea and we used to buy ice creams there, too, disgusting Dad by choosing the plastic cones with a red bubble-gum ball at the bottom. The little town above the beach had had a newspaper shop which sold penny sweets, buckets and spades, and nets for shrimping. The memory of being there with them gave me a feeling like homesickness.

The tide was in, covering the mud on the banks of the estuary, and as I crossed the bridge out of Yarmouth, the water dimpled with the breeze and refracted the light from the pale sun struggling through the cloud. The land lay low around the river but beyond it to the south there were gentle hills covered with fields which rose in stripes of late-autumn green and brown. In Norton someone had a bonfire, and the smell of burning leaves mingled with the cider scent of apples left to rot on the ground.

When I reached it, my Totland had gone. This was a different place. An air of neglect had settled over the town, which seemed to have aged away from the time of my memories just as I had. Autumn cast an unflattering light over the huge Victorian villas on the road to the beach; they looked empty and down at heel. The pub on the corner was closed, as was the fish and chip shop next door. Only the combined grocer's and post office on the other side of the road seemed to be open. Everywhere I looked there was further evidence of dereliction: paint peeled; curtains sagged on their rails; weeds grew unchecked. It dawned on me that what I was seeing was not just a holiday resort out of season but poverty. And again, there was no one on the street.

What sort of lives did people live here? What sort of life could you have if you were young here? It wasn't just money; in the poor areas of London that I knew there were people on the streets going about their business, talking, shopping for food, walking dogs; music filtered out from the windows of flats and passing cars. Here it was silent. I thought of Alice Frewin telling me how she thought that sailing had been the only thing that kept her sane. It had sounded like melodrama but I was starting to see how, if one's mental balance was off, it could be oppressive here.

Surfing the internet the previous day, I had found myself typing her name into Google. I had been thinking about her a lot; if my mind wasn't flooded with pictures of Richard, it returned to the cliff-top and how I'd imagined I'd heard her voice calling me, offering me her way. I'd shaken my head to get rid of the thought. Most of the entries that came up were part of genealogical surveys detailing Frewins of the nineteenth century in Australia and Canada. There had only been two for her, the *County Press* story I'd seen, and then another on the website of a magazine called *Wight Living*. The page had shown a collection of photographs taken at a charity fundraising dinner in Cowes and there was one of them, Mr and Mrs Peter Frewin. I'd clicked to enlarge it and they filled the screen. She was wearing a black dress in what looked like silk, the cowl neckline revealing the pale skin at the base of her throat and over her collarbone. Her hair had been blow-dried and hung from a side parting in a shining golden sheet which broke over her white shoulders. Her husband stood behind her in a charcoal suit and tie, his hand on her elbow. I compared his face to how it had been the night they had brought her boat in. On the quay he had been expressionless, only the wideness of his eyes hinting at the catastrophe that engulfed him. In the picture he was smiling a little for the sake of the photograph but the angle of his body, his hand, showed that his real attention was focused on Alice. She was looking more directly at the camera but it had seemed to me that there was something blank about the look in her eyes, absent, as if she was elsewhere and it was only really her body that had been there, going through the motions. Neither of them looked comfortable, I'd thought, but perhaps I was letting my knowledge of what had happened to them since then colour my interpretation.

All the other photographs showed what I took to be pillars of the local community in various attitudes of wine-sipping, laughing, sitting at tables adorned with extravagant flower arrangements. Most were in their fifties and sixties, seventies even, but there were three or four others in their thirties. Somehow, though, they seemed to belong to a different type. Alice was current, the length of her dress and the opaque tights right up to date; they wore outfits which had evolved over their journey from the catwalk to the high street, become domesticated, and their shoes were smart but not sharp like Alice's, whose slim ankles were bound around with heavy studded straps. The older people, too, looked jolly, pleased to be having a night out with a nice dinner, the men in sports jackets, the women in matching floral two-pieces. If the backgrounds hadn't been the same, I might have thought that the photograph of Alice and her husband was one of a different set entirely, included by mistake.

I walked on and a little further up the street I came across something that surprised me. One of the bay windows was filled with a set of shelves on which books were propped open to show their covers to the street. On the top level there were recipe books, a guide to dog grooming and two Jilly Cooper novels. In the middle there were thrillers by Len Deighton, Frederick Forsyth and Ken Follett, and on the shelf below that, there was a copy of *Bleak House*, two Thomas Hardys and a volume of Tennyson poems. A handwritten sign on the shop door said it was open.

Inside I found myself in an L-shaped space, the foot of the shape the front room in which I was standing, the longer part running all the way through to the back of the building. The walls were covered by shelves which reached almost to the ceiling and there were Turkish rugs in reds and ochres over the varnished floorboards. In front of the sash window at the far end was a pine table with a lamp and a laptop computer at which a man was sitting. He glanced up as the bell above the door announced my arrival and looked at me over a pair of steel-rimmed glasses balanced halfway down a straight nose. He had short silver hair which had retreated a little at the temples and was sixty, maybe slightly older, I thought. There was something rather patrician about him: he would have looked as at home in a toga as he did in his plaid shirt. I gave him a quick smile and moved into the part of the shop which was out of his line of vision, not wanting to be watched.

The window display had given a false impression of the stock, which was not in the jumble that I'd expected. The books were arranged alphabetically and though all were second-hand, they were in good condition. Theirs was not the unlovely used-bookshop aroma suggestive of house clearances but the library flavour of those that still had something to offer. Interspersed among the bestsellers there were classics – a complete set of Jane Austen and a fair representation of Dickens and Eliot – and also quite a few new titles. I looked up. The man behind the desk was typing, squinting at the screen over the top of his glasses, and I moved along the shelf. There was A.S. Byatt, *The Great Gatsby*, Alan Hollinghurst, *Portnoy's Complaint*. It was like meeting old friends, small pockets of my former life, before the Isle of Wight, before Richard even. I couldn't think now why I had left my own books in London. I had to buy some of these; I wanted them around me again.

It took a while to choose and when I glanced over, I realised that the man was watching me. His glasses had slipped still further and his sharp blue eyes were now completely visible over the top of them. His expression was serious and as I went towards the desk, my movement made him start. There was no till and he added up the prices pencilled inside the front covers mentally before putting the books in a pink-and-white-striped paper bag from a pile on the floor.

'You're not from the Island, are you?' he said suddenly, as I turned to go.

'No. I'm just staying in Yarmouth for the winter.'

He nodded. 'Good. Well, enjoy the reading.'

Out on the street again my happiness at finding the books, the moment's connection, quickly dissipated. Of course he knew I wasn't from round here, though: my jacket, my shoes, even my bag made me conspicuous. And then there was the black eye.

By the time I got back to the cottage, it was dark. The cold had reddened my cheeks and my fingers were stiff where they had held the parcel of books across my chest. I made a cup of tea and went upstairs to my makeshift study to check my email. It was Saturday so I didn't expect much, if any, but there was a message. It was from Richard and the whole of it was written in the subject line: *If you want to be alone, then be alone.*

At the beginning, I had always slept better on the nights he was with me. Sometimes if I was on my own and I'd stayed up working so late that the street below the flat had finally gone quiet, I put off going to bed. I knew that as soon as the lamp went out, my ears would become hypersensitive and the near-silence inside the building would grow into a sound like the fizzing when a record ends. Then every small noise within it, in the flat and on the floors below, would become significant, evidence of the intruder who had broken in through the old back door on the ground floor and was now slowly working his way upstairs. My bedroom shared a wall with the top landing and though I told myself that the creaking I sometimes heard out there was just the sound of the wooden staircase settling as the temperature through the building dropped, there were nights when I had to turn the light back on, get out of bed and nerve myself up to look through the glass spy-hole in my front door to check that no one was there. Often on those evenings I would go to the kitchen afterwards and pour a glass of wine or brandy to take back to bed.

With Richard I didn't even notice the quiet. Sometimes I tried to stay awake longer than him so that I could enjoy the feeling of security and listen to the sound of him breathing but by the time we turned off the light, it was always very late, often near morning, and I fell asleep immediately.

It was unusual for him to sleep longer than me. In fact, I was surprised by how little rest he seemed to need. Given the hours he worked, I thought that he would spend a significant amount of the spare time he did have catching up on missed sleep, but in fact it seemed as though his lack of opportunity for rest had lessened his body's need for it.

Near the beginning, though, when we'd been seeing each other for a couple of months, he'd been in Spain for a week. His flight had arrived into Heathrow late on Friday evening and he'd come straight to my flat. He'd looked exhausted when I opened the door and though normally he was up before me, the next morning I'd been first awake. I'd lain quietly for a minute or two looking at the rise and fall of his chest and the muscle in the arm which he'd flung across the bed towards me and then, filled with a sudden enthusiasm, I got up, made some coffee and went to my desk in the sitting room. I liked the idea of working while he was asleep, knowing that he was there, and I also liked the thought of him seeing me working when he woke. His work ethic was inspiring; I was pushing myself harder than I had for some time. The energy I felt now reminded me of the state of strange exultation that I'd had at university and in my early twenties when, strung out on coffee and nicotine and lack of sleep, I'd felt that the world was so full of excitement and possibility that I could go free-running over the rooftops of London without thinking of falling, vaulting from building to building with fearless ease. This, I suspected, was how he was all the time.

The sun, which rose behind my building and moved slowly round during the day to set behind the block across the street, spilled its light further and further down the red-brick façade of the flats opposite. Their blinds were still drawn. As sometimes happened when I knew I would be interrupted, I immediately found a deep concentration and worked well for the hour or so that passed before I heard Richard's feet padding softly over the carpet. I carried on working, my head bent over the manuscript, and he came up behind me. My hair was loose, hanging down my back over my new silk nightie, and he took hold of it near the end, gathered it into a ponytail and wrapped it carefully around his fist until his hand was tight on the nape of my neck. Then he'd pulled my head back against his lower stomach. On my shoulders I felt the heat of his skin, still warm from the bed, and in the semi-mirror of the window, I could see us, his bare torso, my face against it. His musky scent was in my nostrils and I wanted to turn around and run my tongue over his skin, kiss his stomach, but my head was held firmly in place. He'd caught the delicate new hair at the base of my scalp and it was pulling, a little painful but not unpleasurable.

'Why do you work so hard?' he said.

I tugged my head so that I could turn and answer him but he either didn't notice or chose to ignore me. 'I don't work nearly as hard as you do,' I said.

He laughed, tipped my chair on to its back legs and turned it round so that I was facing him. I kissed him, the tip of my nose fitting into the indent of his navel. Then he'd lifted me up and carried me through to the bedroom again. A block of sunlight was falling through the narrow window on to the bed now and I watched it play on his skin as he moved over me. 'You didn't tell me,' he said afterwards.

'What?'

'Why you work so hard.'

Because I don't have anything else. The words came into my head straight away and though I'd never thought it before,

I recognised the truth of it at once. Richard was watching my face and raised his eyebrows in the manner which was already so familiar to me. 'Well,' I said. 'If you're going to do something . . .'

'And that's one of the things I like about you, Katie,' he dipped his head to kiss my breast again. 'Why we're so similar. No half measures.'

Chapter Seven

Two days after I walked to Totland, I woke to find that I'd been taken over by a dreadful, wrenching anxiety. The night before, lying in bed in the dark, I'd felt an emptiness just beyond the horizon, exponentially gathering momentum like a breaker waiting to crest. It pressed at the edge of my thoughts and I'd closed my eyes and pulled the pillow tight around my head, praying that sleep would ward it off and deliver me safely into the next morning.

But now the feeling was in my stomach, a spasming, nauseating anxiety that left no room for any positive thought or even volition. Panic was all there was. I turned on my side and curled into a foetal position but it only spilled further into my body, a viscous liquid slowly finding its level again. Getting out of bed was impossible. It wasn't just that I couldn't see any reason to: a paralysis had taken hold of me, as if my brain had lost the ability to send instructions to my limbs. A familiar sense of agoraphobic limitlessness stretched and stretched until I became the centre of a world that I could fall through for ever without coming to anything solid.

One afternoon when I was twelve, Dad and Matt had gone to look at a neighbour's new telescope and I had been left alone in the house for the first time. As soon as the front door closed behind them, a strange quiet had settled. I wandered from room to room, enjoying the peace and the subtle air of difference that seemed to have come over the familiar things. I had a vision of myself as an adult, the house and the furniture and objects in it mine to do with as I wanted. I was the owner, independent, and my roles as daughter and sister fell away.

51

Then the feeling had changed. The silence became oppressive, a great weight that threatened to crush me. There was nothing in it, no distractions, nothing but more of the same: silent time rolling on into an empty future. It had been a mild day, still only April, but sweat broke out on my forehead. There was no structure to anything, I suddenly understood, nothing apart from what you could make. I'd recently learned about agoraphobia and I hadn't been able to imagine it. Then, though, I could: it was panic at the sheer limitlessness of everything. There was nothing to keep you rooted down.

That was the first time I'd had the feeling but I had come to recognise it since then, to sense it rolling towards me, gathering pace and momentum like an avalanche. The only way to deal with it, experience had taught me, was to throw things in its way, create barriers of distractions – work, going out with Helen, talking to my brother, the flings with the men whom I saw for a week or two and then pushed away before they got close, trips to galleries and concerts and films: anything that could ward it off, even for an hour. Now, though, here on the Island, I was cut off from my old life and the little structure it had offered me. I was on my own.

If you want to be alone, then be alone. Richard's last message ran through my mind, finding its mark over and over again. He knew exactly how to get to me, of course; he had learned me inside out, storing information about me with an avidity I had loved. He had asked me question after question about my life, as if he had been swotting for a cool metropolitan version of *Mr and Mrs* in which prizes depended on him providing the correct answers. He was so different to my previous boyfriend, David, a teacher and a sweet man whose avuncular warmth had reminded me a little of my father. I'd tried with David, I'd really tried, but I'd begun to feel first stultified, then smothered by his mildness and his references to 'settling down', an expression and idea which I'd loathed. It had been three years since we'd split up and in the months before I'd met Richard I'd started to wonder whether I'd been stupid to throw it away. The excitement I felt with Richard, however, the intensity of his focus, was confirmation that I'd been right: stability wasn't enough.

One evening at our table in the corner of the French restaurant in Kensington – it had become our regular haunt – the candle enveloping us in a private cloud of light, we had been talking about friends and I'd told him my theory that being with other people is the only insulation against the sharp edges of the world. Part of it, I told him, as he rubbed his foot up my shin under the table, was the feeling that there were people to help you and look after you, of course, but the other part was simple distraction, that being with others and being involved in the business of their lives was padding against the hardness of things.

'That's what you're really afraid of, isn't it?' he'd said, his foot stopping all of a sudden. 'It frightens you more than anything else. Being alone.'

I looked at his face. His eyes were watching me carefully. 'Yes,' I said.

That first day I didn't get out of bed except to stagger to the bathroom where I was very sick. I ate nothing and my stomach was emptier and emptier, the throwing up only exacerbating the aching until I was no longer sure what was hunger and what was the voracious anxiety. I didn't open the curtains but was aware periodically of the light changing behind them, the dim daylight becoming dusk and then dark again.

The following day, I had no choice but to get up. I was too hungry; the pain of it was clawing at my stomach. I stood on wobbling legs. The bed was rancid, the sheets soft with sweat. The stairs seemed steeper even than usual and I put my hand flat against the wall to steady myself. In the kitchen there were a few slices of bread left and I ate them straight from the bag, feeling them melt against my teeth. A cold draught blew in over the linoleum tiles, mottling the flesh of my thighs white-blue and making the bones in my feet numb. I went upstairs and got out the spare blanket I'd seen in the wardrobe. It was old and the grey wool was rough against my bare arms; it smelled of dust and the bare pine shelf. The stitching round the edge was done in contrasting red wool and sharp tears came into my eyes. I remembered a blanket that my brother had had in his cot, his in palest blue, the stitching also in red. I remembered my mother's hands tucking it in around him.

Irregular hours were one of the things that Richard and I had had in common. When he was abroad, he sometimes phoned me very late. The first time, I had been asleep and answered the phone anxiously, wondering why anyone would be ringing at nearly three o'clock in the morning. 'It's me,' he said and I sat down in the wicker chair in front of the window, suddenly wide awake. 'I know it's late there but I wanted to talk to you.' A thrill went through me. This was what I wanted, someone who didn't follow the rules but called when he needed to, regardless of the time. There was a drama about it, implicit excitement. Why wait until the morning, office hours? We talked until the sky above the roofs opposite began to lighten through shades of blue so stunning I didn't want to look away. I described them to him. He told me how he thought the estimate he'd been given by one of his contractors was too high. 'They're trying to rip me off,' he said. 'I'm not having it. They'll regret it.'

I laughed. 'That sounds very serious.'

'I am serious. There's hundreds of thousands of pounds at stake here, sweetheart; I'm not fucking around. People have to learn that they can't outsmart me.'

I reached for the throw that I kept on the arm of the sofa; though it was summer, it was chilly in the flat in the early hours. Richard's business attitude, the macho posturing of it, made me laugh sometimes, though of course he'd be furious if he knew. On the other hand, there was a part of me that found the sheer self-confidence of it attractive. In him, I saw for real the strength that sometimes I only pretended.

I came to love the phone calls; there was something so intimate about them. In bed, we were the same as every man and woman, the same bodies, the same positions, even if they did feel better with him than anyone else. Our telephone calls, though, were unique; no one else could have had the exact same conversations. When he called me late at night, I had the sense that our voices were cocooned in the darkness, our two spots on the earth's crust illuminated by the connection between us. But the calls did nothing to stave off my physical longing for him – the opposite, in fact. I craved him. Sometimes when he was away, I imagined him so vividly that I thought I could smell him, the traces of rosemary soap on his skin, the human warmth underneath. I ached to kiss him, unbutton his shirt, put my hands on him.

About three months after we met, he rang from Spain. It was two o'clock in the morning and though I was in bed, I was awake, reading. I'd hoped that he might call and had the phone on the bedside table. I said hello, hearing myself smile.

'Hello, Katie.'

'Is everything all right? You sound . . .'

'I'm a bit drunk. OK – I'm missing you, I admit it. I hold up my hands. Tell me, that game you were talking about – do I stand a chance of winning?'

I felt my heart lift. 'Well, I don't know. It sounds to me like I'm winning,' I said, with the bravado that was getting harder to fake the stronger my feelings for him became. 'You'd better watch out in case it's you that ends up giving yourself to me.'

I heard him take a sip of a drink, the ice cubes chinking against his glass, and then a laugh full of pleasure. 'Oh, I miss you,' he groaned. 'Why aren't you here? I want to fuck you so badly.'

In the bath the following day I lay motionless and let the water settle so the only movement was a trembling across its surface as I breathed. I thought about what would happen if I died. How long would my body be here before anyone came looking for me? It could be weeks. The ends of my hair floated on the surface. Had Alice Frewin thought like this? Had she imagined the boats out looking for her, finding her body? Had she hesitated at the last minute, trod water trying to keep her face above the freezing waves, spitting out mouthfuls of salt water, or had she dived in, dug her way deeper and deeper down into the darkness until the weight above her started to crush the air from her lungs?

I stayed in the bath until the water was cold. The phone hadn't rung since Richard's email, I realised, three days before. I had cut myself off from him, run from him in horror, but somehow he had reversed the situation so that now I felt as though it were him who had severed contact. True to his word, he'd gone. He'd left me alone.

The day after that, I had to go out. There was nothing left to eat. I wasn't sure how many days it had been since I'd left the house – three? four? – but it seemed an incredible idea: inside, there was structure; outside, anything might happen. I had no choice, though. Talking myself through the actions, I put my long coat on over my T-shirt and found my ankle boots. My purse and the key were still on the counter from the last time. I took a deep breath and opened the door.

A strong wind was blowing, funnelling down the passage and biting at my bare legs. I put my hands on my thighs to stop my coat flying up. In the Square, against the cloudless petrol blue of the evening sky, everything seemed supernaturally bright, as if I had been wearing a blindfold which had now been removed. It all seemed so definite and beautiful but distant, too: alien.

At the checkout at the corner shop I waited with mounting impatience while the assistant, a woman with salt-and-pepper hair and round eyes that almost closed when she smiled, slowly scanned and packed the food. My hands were shaking with hunger as I took the notes out of my purse and when at last she gave me the change I dropped it and the coins rolled off in different directions, fleeing under the racks and spinning merrily away from me. I got down and scrabbled for them. The floor was cold on my bare legs but the coins now meant much more to me than their monetary value: they seemed to symbolise everything. Suddenly I was blinking fiercely against hot tears. The assistant came out from behind the counter and helped me, retrieving three coins and putting them gently into my hand. As she curled my fingers over to make sure I had them this time, she smiled at me again and in her face I saw the unmistakable softening of pity.

The following afternoon I got properly dressed for the first time since it had started. I needed more books. They had some at the newsagent's, I had seen them tucked away in a corner at the back, but it was the Totland shop I wanted. There was something more than the books there; though the owner had identified me as an outsider, it had felt familiar to me, a like-minded place.

Passing the mirror on the landing, I caught a glimpse of my face and, despite my hurry, I had to stop. I looked hollowed-out. My skin was colourless apart from the rim of bruised purple in my eye socket, now subsiding into shades of rotten yellow and green, and the livid line under the spidery stitches that itched constantly. My eyes stared dully back at me, the pupils huge with lack of light. I touched my cheek and the skin felt dry and older than I ever remembered.

I was nervous about driving but I didn't want to be out of the house for any longer than necessary. I went slowly, praying that I wouldn't meet a situation which required a swift response. It occurred to me on the way that the shop might be closed – I wasn't sure what day it was – but when I arrived, the lights were on. I took a minute to try to calm down before going in; I didn't want a repeat of yesterday.

Inside, the atmosphere of unfussy order and peace was the same. The man behind the desk looked up as the bell announced my arrival. He recognised me and mouthed hello, and I turned to see another woman already browsing, her attention focused on the chunky paperback in her hand, shopping basket tucked into the crook of her arm. I nodded to him and moved out of view. Despite my determination to be calm, I felt the same overwhelming desire for the books that I had had for the food. I wanted to snatch them up and take them all back to the cottage. Five, I told myself; any more would look excessive.

I started scanning the rows, finding things I hadn't noticed before. What would be more distracting, I wondered, old favourites or new stories? Behind me, the telephone rang and was answered. The man kept his voice low, as if we were in a library. Looking up, I realised his quietness was in deference only to me: the other woman had gone. A sudden urgency in his tone caught my attention.

'Where?' he said. A few seconds passed. 'The coastguard? They didn't bring her in themselves?'

Now I was straining to hear and I could just make out the sound of the voice at the other end of the line. I was too far away, however, to distinguish what it was saying.

'And they think it is?' Another pause. 'Right. OK. You've tried his office, obviously? I may do – I think so, yes. If he is there, I'll tell him – no, it's all right. I'll ring you. Half an hour?'

He hung up and I realised I'd been holding myself rigid, hardly breathing. The call was about Alice, I was sure. They'd found her body. For a moment I thought I might be sick, and I quickly put my hand over my mouth. The intensity of the feeling took me by surprise.

'I'm sorry.' The voice came from just behind my shoulder and I spun round as if he'd caught me stealing. 'I have to close up now; I have to go.'

It took a second or two for the words to register. 'No, of course. That's . . .' I remembered the books under my arm.

'Have them.' He was searching for his keys, patting his pockets, shaking his jacket to hear them.

'What?'

'The books – have them.'

'I couldn't; I wouldn't feel . . .'

'Please. It doesn't matter at all. I'm sorry – I hate hurrying you like this but I really do have to go.'

He followed me out of the shop, turning the light off and locking the door behind him. I got back into the car and watched in the rear-view mirror as he went down the hill towards the war memorial, his slightly bow-legged stride quick for a man of his age. He was going to find Peter Frewin, I knew it.

Chapter Eight

I'd spoken to my brother less since he'd moved to America. The cost of transatlantic calls, especially from a mobile, meant that when we talked now there was a third party involved in our conversations, the clock ticking through the minutes, racking up the pounds or dollars. Most of the time, we kept in touch by email but today I wanted to hear the sound of his voice with the Bristol accent that it had retained despite all the years since he'd left home and the move to another continent.

I called him at midnight: seven o'clock in Baltimore. With the exception of the man in the shop in the afternoon, it would be the first time I'd spoken to anyone in days. I hesitated before dialling the number, nervous all of a sudden at the prospect of speaking to my own brother. The phone rang and rang but when at last he answered, there was delight in his voice.

'How are you?' he was asking. 'How's the Island?'

I swallowed quickly, not wanting him to hear the lump that had come into my throat. 'It's cold,' I said. 'And it was foggy and now it's windy.'

'But you're enjoying it?'

The question was so far from the mark that I couldn't think how to answer. *I've got no one to talk to and the day after I came here, I met a woman who drowned.* I could say it, of course I could, but I couldn't really tell him how I felt; as soon as he'd picked up the phone, I'd known that. In Matt's eyes, I was the one who knew how to handle things, the one who helped and solved problems. I'd been the person he rang when he was seventeen, at university a year early and out of his depth in London. A second-year by then, I knew my way around and enjoyed showing off my new sophistication as much as I'd enjoyed helping him out. If I told him how I really was now, it would reveal a side of me he had never known and it wasn't just for his sake that I didn't want that. His perception of me was important for me, too: I needed him to think of me as capable and strong. While I had that, I still had the façade of my old self at least. If I kept it, I could perhaps rebuild myself behind it; if I lost it, then there would be nothing left. There was another element to the feeling, too: pride. I couldn't bear him to know that I'd made such a mess of things, especially when now, having always been the less worldly of us, he'd got everything right.

'Well,' I said. 'It's fine, yes. It's good.'

'I was really surprised when Dad told me. I've been meaning to drop you a line but we've been doing trials at work and Charlie's had a chest infection.'

'He's all right though?'

'Getting better now but Mel was really worried – we both were. His temperature was so high. But why did you move? I didn't even know you were thinking about it.'

'You know, I felt like I needed a change.'

He laughed. 'And you couldn't just go on holiday like normal people?'

'As if you'd know what normal people do.'

'All right,' he said, a little defensive but also a little pleased. I felt a flood of affection for him. I wished that he was here so that I could put my arms around him and press my face against the chest which had been parallel with my forehead since he was thirteen. He'd inherited Dad's height, as well as his love of physics. It had been like growing up with a couple of tall aliens who communicated in a code beyond my ken. But the geek in Matt was accompanied by a kindly diffidence that, over the past four or five years and much to his bafflement, had made him popular with women despite his elongated frame and its tendency to stringiness. And here he was now, his life all in order: the research job at Johns Hopkins that he might have been born to do – something to do with magnetic imaging, as far as I could make out – marriage to Melissa and then, a year ago, the arrival of Charlie. I wondered how he had made it all happen.

'Oh, and I split up with Richard.' I tried to sound casual.

'Shit. You OK? What went wrong?'

The lump was back in my throat, hard as baked clay. What had I told him? I tried to remember. The truth was so far buried under layers of lies and half lies that I couldn't be sure what he knew. But anyway, of everyone in the world, he was the last person I could tell. The thought alone made me wither.

'I'm fine. It wasn't meant to be, that's all.'

'Come on, you really liked him. You loved him. You've never talked about anyone like that before.'

'I'll get over it.'

'If it would help to talk . . .'

'I said it's not a big deal. Just leave it.'

He was silent for a few seconds, and I could tell that I'd hurt him. 'Well,' he said eventually, 'if you change your mind, you know where to find me.'

'Right. Thanks.'

There was an awkward pause in which I felt bad.

'Look, what are you doing for Christmas?' he said. 'We spoke to Dad and Jane last night and we suddenly thought, why don't you all come out here? I'd love to see you – Mel would, too. We could have a big family Christmas.'

One side of me felt an immediate yearning. I'd only seen emailed pictures of his house, a two-storey white clapboard place with a screen door and a long lawn out front, but I imagined going there, spending the holiday with them all in a fug of family warmth, feeling part of something. But the other side recoiled from the idea: how could I go there, tainting their happiness with the hash I'd made of my own life, making light of everything to keep up the pretence but seething with it all behind the façade, simultaneously pleased that I could hide it and angry that they, the people to whom I was supposed to be closest of all, were fooled? And how could I go from this isolation to that? It would be like coming up out of a mine into bright sunshine. No, impossible.

'Let me think about it,' I said.

'Dinner's ready, Matthew.' Melissa's voice reached me at second hand.

'Well, I'd better go,' he said.

'Yes, you better had.'

'You should come, though. Do think about it.'

When he hung up the silence began to settle in the house again like snow and I felt a yawning disappointment. What I'd really wanted was to talk about Alice. I wanted at least to try to articulate to someone the intensity of what I'd felt earlier in the afternoon, the sense that there was some sort of connection between she and I, that we were two sides of a coin, heads and tails, and it was only that one moment on the down that separated us. I had pulled back, I had made that decision, but the moment had been so fractional, such a tiny blink of time, that it seemed only chance that I was still here while she was gone. I felt pity for her, pity that made my stomach ache, but it was tinged, too, with something else: guilt. Survivor's guilt.

Of course I couldn't have told Matt any of it – even the thought was ridiculous. Horrified, he would have rung Dad, who would have insisted on coming up from Cornwall and making everything worse. The only person it might have been possible to talk to about it was Helen but I couldn't do that, either.

Because of Richard's travelling, things between us never became routine. He could decide at such short notice that he needed to go abroad that I wouldn't know until the day before or even, when there were emergencies, the same day. As well as the Spanish development, there was a plot of land on the Côte d'Azur which was coming up for sale and because he was also considering investing in a project in New Jersey there were occasional trips to the States. As a result and because it could never be taken for granted, the time we spent together felt more valuable. Sometimes, when he rang me from the taxi that was bringing him to me straight from Heathrow, I was sorry for the couple in the flat across the street with the baby and the settled routine. I wouldn't have traded my excitement for anything in the world.

There were times, though, when he had to shelve supper with me in favour of dinner with investors or when meetings overran and he missed his flights. The disappointment then was like feeling the carpet drop away from under my feet and, the evening suddenly empty, I would open a bottle of wine and drink it. I almost always woke up the next morning to a string of late-night texts and I would be cross that I had let the alcohol depress me and make me forget that because what we had was not ordinary, there was a higher price for it.

More and more often when I was with Richard or on the phone to him, I had to stop myself from blurting out that I loved him. I could feel the words inside, causing pressure in my chest and stomach, threatening to rise up my throat and out of my mouth like shaken Coca-Cola. However much I wanted to say them, though, I didn't. The semi-combative game between us, the bantering exchanges about who had supremacy, appealed to him. He liked the challenge, the competition: it fired sparks between us and, for that reason, I liked it, too. It also appealed to my vanity that I could meet this clever, ambitious man and match him. I loved the thrill of daring to respond to his bait with indifference and firing back a challenge of my own. It hadn't taken me long to understand that for Richard, things acquired value in direct proportion to their difficulty. I wanted him and so I gave him the impression that he would have to work for me.

I couldn't resist trying to put claims on him in covert ways, however. The unpredictability of our relationship gave it an air of unreality; afterwards, the bubbles of time I spent with him could seem dreamlike. I wanted to plant them more firmly and make them feel like part of my real life and so it became increasingly important to me that he meet Helen again and get to know her, at least a little. Despite the tension between us, Helen was still the anchor of my life in London. I wanted her to acknowledge my relationship with him and put her seal on it but I also wanted her to understand. I wanted her to like him. Though I'd hoped she'd relent once we started seeing one another properly, she'd remained sceptical about Richard, which infuriated me. 'It sounds all right,' she said, when I talked about him, 'just don't rush it, OK?'

'Can't you be happy for me?' I would ask. 'I've met someone I really like.'

'I just – oh, I don't know. The guy who was with him that night said he worked him pretty hard. He made him sound a bit . . . ruthless.'

'Of course he's ruthless when he's working – that's why he's successful.'

'You know him better than I do,' she said, and I heard resignation, as if she had decided it was pointless trying to argue with me.

It was important to me, too, that Richard liked Helen, and her opposition to him that first night hadn't endeared her to him. I was sure, though, that if they met properly, things between them would come right. For a reason I couldn't fathom, though, I'd been nervous about asking Richard, and his initial response hadn't been positive. 'What?' he'd said, as he pulled me in under his arm, moving his head slightly so that there was room for mine on the pillow. 'You'd rather we go out to dinner with her than on our own? Or we could stay in and . . .'

'I want you to meet her. She's my best friend.'

'I thought I was your best friend,' he huffed, smiling, and I felt his breath on my face.

'Funny.' I pressed my knee hard against his thigh. 'But if you really don't want to go out, I can cook for us all here.'

So in the end I made dinner at the flat. I was anxious beforehand and abandoned work for the afternoon to slow-cook the Moroccan lamb which I knew they both liked. I cleared the table I used as a desk and laid it up with three places, and vacuumed and dusted as though I was preparing the place for inspectors.

Actually, immediately afterwards, I'd thought the evening had gone well. Richard was great; I'd been worried that the bantering way we talked to each other would strike Helen as odd but he was softer and it came across as a fond sort of teasing. He didn't talk about himself but focused his full-beam charm on her, asking informed questions about brand-management and how media buying was evolving with changes in technology, paying her subtle compliments. I watched her keenly for signs that she was thawing towards him and threw in encouraging remarks and

64

leading questions from time to time, like a parent trying to arrange an advantageous marriage. The next day, after Richard had gone home, I rang for her verdict, excited. 'He's great, isn't he? And gorgeous.'

'Yes, he's very good-looking,' she'd said and, encouraged, I'd pressed her, wanting further confirmation. No matter how much I angled, though, she wouldn't say that she'd liked him and eventually I gave in and hung up, in case my frustration boiled over and caused me to say something I might regret.

The morning after I went to Totland again, I put on the television for the sound of voices and heard that the body recovered from the sea near Brighton hadn't been Alice Frewin but a mother of two from Basingstoke who'd gone missing a month previously. I felt a soaring feeling behind my ribs and made a sharp sound somewhere between a gasp and a laugh. It felt like she'd been given a reprieve, a second chance. I went into the kitchen to turn on the hob and then turned it off again, too agitated now to make breakfast at the cottage. I wanted to go out and hear what the locals were saying. They must have known about the body being recovered; behind the town's closed doors, news like that would have jumped from house to house like fire.

There were people in the Square today: a middle-aged man in paint-covered trousers on his way into the chandlery, and a couple of women by the delicatessen. I went along the pavement next to them and pretended to look at the display of preserves and chutneys while I eavesdropped but they were talking in tones of outrage about some obscene graffiti which seemed to have appeared at the bus stop. The wind of the past few days had moderated and the cloud which had been harried across the sky now lowered itself comfortably down to sit overhead. The flat light contributed to the strange sense of anticlimax which I felt, the crisis which had threatened but not materialised. I bought a newspaper and went to Mariners café where I drank a cup of coffee and listened but the handful of customers were waiting for the ferry and weren't local. Eventually, running out of reasons to linger, I paid the bill and left.

Before making my way back to the cottage, however, I crossed the Square to look for a moment at the display of binoculars and compasses in the window of Harwoods. I'd been standing there only a few seconds when, in the shadow on the glass, my eye was caught by something moving quickly along the ground. I turned round just as it stopped and saw a cat standing about six feet away, quite confidently watching me. He was the image of Magpie, the cat we'd had growing up: spotless black with a white bib, a tendency to corpulence and, it seemed, the same inquisitorial manner – a feline Hercule Poirot. He wasn't at all fazed by me; instead he turned his head analytically to one side and carried on staring. I felt a sudden urge to pick him up and press my face into his fur but, despite the paunch, he was too fast and presented me with only the final inches of a lustrous black tail as he disappeared under the car parked at the kerbside. I crouched down and peered but before my eyes could become accustomed to the dark underneath, I sensed rather than saw someone next to me. I got up quickly and found myself standing slightly too close to Peter Frewin.

I took a swift step backwards. I'd caught only a momentary glimpse of his face before looking away in shocked embarrassment but what I'd seen in that fraction of a second was an expression of utter exhaustion. The deep grey hollows under his eyes and the whiteness of his skin suggested that he hadn't slept in all the days that she'd been missing. He looked frangible, as if the merest touch would shatter him. I'd remembered him as tall and I was struck by his height again; the top of my head was parallel with his shoulder and the neck of the grey jumper he wore under a navy Musto jacket.

'You're looking for my cat,' he said.

'I'm sorry – I didn't know he was yours.'

'Why would you?' He ran a hand over his eyes and blinked widely, as if coming awake. His eyes were a startling aqueous green against the wanness of the rest of his face. 'Is he still under there?'

'I couldn't see – the light's wrong.'

He went down on his haunches and craned his head around sideways, just as I had done. I stayed standing, unsure whether or not I should help, but a couple of seconds later he put his fingertips on the tarmac and pushed himself back up. 'He's not there – must have run out the other side. He's avoiding me; he hasn't been home for days.'

My face must have asked the question.

'He's not mine, really. He's my wife's.' He blinked again, and his mouth seemed to fold in on itself. It felt like an invasion of his privacy to look at him, as if, in his vulnerability, he couldn't help giving away more than was right for me to see. 'Anyway,' he said, 'thanks.'

I opened my mouth to say something as yet unclear to me but he was gone, already yards away, striding down towards the harbour.

Without thinking, I crossed the road and went into the shop on the corner. I walked up the narrow aisle towards the back and stood in front of the open-fronted fridge. I looked blankly at the cheeses and cold meats, my mind full instead of the image of Peter Frewin's face, the pain etched into it like scrimshaw.

'Excuse me?'

I turned around. In front of me was a woman in jeans and a jumper, a huge black woollen coat hanging heavily from her shoulders. She was about my age, maybe a couple of years older, lines just beginning to fan out from the corners of her eyes, which were pale grey and watering slightly. Her brown hair, made wavy by the damp, was parted to the side and tucked behind her ears. She put her hand up and smoothed it, as if she wanted to make sure she was presentable before talking to me. 'I'm sorry,' she said. 'I didn't mean to shock you.'

'No – you didn't.'

'I hope you won't think this is weird but I've seen you around a bit and I've been meaning to say hello. It's always good to have new people here, especially younger ones.' She lowered her voice conspiratorially, as if we were surrounded by pensioners who might take umbrage. 'I'm Sally Vaughn.' She put out a small hand for me to shake, which struck me as a strange formality.

'Kate Gibson.'

'Have you got time for a coffee?'

In my surprise at being asked, I hesitated and she seemed to withdraw a little. 'I'm sorry – you must have lots to do,' she said.

'No,' I said, almost too quickly now. 'Coffee would be good.' Perhaps, I'd realised, being about the same age, she might have known Alice.

'I'll let you finish your shopping and then . . .'

'I'm finished. I mean, I just came in for some cheese.' I took a wedge of Brie from the fridge, wondering why I felt I had to offer a pretext. Looking to see what she was buying, preparing to be embarrassed by the evidence of effort-making home cooking, I realised she wasn't holding anything.

There were two other people at the till, a veritable rush, and she waited out of the way by the door while I paid. The woman behind the counter was the one who had been kind to me before and she patted my hand now as she gave me my change. 'You're looking a bit better, love,' she said. 'That's good.'

Outside we stopped to let a bowed old lady pass, her Jack Russell briefly investigating our trouser-legs before his leash tugged him onwards. I wondered whether, as a local, Sally would choose Mariners café or Gossips by the pier but when she started in the opposite direction I understood that we were going to her house; there were no cafés this way.

I felt awkward and a bit cumbersome walking by her side; she was three or four inches shorter than me and moved lightly, as if she were tripping along on tiptoes. We went down St James's Street, two of my steps to three of hers, past the church and the terrace of white-painted houses whose faces, with their small windows, always looked so closed. Being with someone else changed the feel of the streets; in company they seemed more real somehow, no longer just theatre sets constructed out of cheap wood and cardboard. A ferry was in and we waited for the end of the brief flow of traffic before crossing Tennyson Road.

'How long have you been here now?' she asked.

I had to think about it. 'Almost a fortnight – though it seems much longer.'

'Where were you before?'

'London.'

'God, you must be finding it quiet.'

'That's an understatement.'

She didn't reply and I wondered whether I'd been rude or whether she was waiting for me to ask. 'Me?' she said, when I did. 'Oh, I feel like I've been here for ever. I'm from Portsmouth originally but we moved here when I was seven. I never got round to leaving.' She laughed but the sound of it struck me as hollow.

Her house was beyond the school on Mill Road, one of a red-brick terrace that I had passed before. I waited as she found her keys in her handbag and opened the door, giving the bottom of it a sharp kick with a small booted foot. 'The damp,' she said. 'It swells up and then it sticks. Drives me mad.'

As in my cottage, the door opened straight into a small kitchen. The units and the painted wooden table were white and very clean, and there was a blue gingham blind in the window. She took my coat and ushered me into one of the pine wheel-back chairs at the table. On top of a pile of raffia placemats was a bowl of small, imperfect apples and a GCSE chemistry textbook, which she saw me notice. 'Tom's – my son.' She turned to the sink and filled the kettle. 'You don't have any children?'

The question surprised me, as it always did. It was ridiculous but there was a part of me that still thought I was too young. The textbook made clear exactly how ridiculous: I'd guessed that she was only a couple of years older than me, thirty-four or -five, maybe, and her son had to be fifteen or sixteen if he was doing GCSEs.

I watched her as she took down mugs and decanted milk into a jug. Out of the coat she was as slight as I'd thought she must be, and her hands moved quickly, flitting back and forth between objects as if she checked things by touch rather than sight. She took a tin of biscuits from a cupboard and arranged some on a plate with a doily, and I tried to remember the last time I'd seen a doily in a private house.

'It's only instant, I'm afraid.'

'Instant's fine – great. Please, don't go to any trouble.'

She brought the mugs over to the table and sat down. 'Have a biscuit.' She proffered the plate and I took one, largely from a sense that it would be rude to refuse. She took one herself and began to gnaw at the end of it. 'Did you come to the Island for work then?' she asked.

I explained about the translating, how I could do it anywhere. I wondered as I talked how many days it had been since I'd done any actual work. It was stretching to weeks now. I would have to be careful; before any of this had happened, I'd been ahead of schedule, as I always was, but coming here, the days when I'd been incapable of doing anything: I was losing ground, and I couldn't afford to get the reputation of not being able to work to deadline.

'That sounds interesting – much more interesting than my job. I'm a PA, for a company of solicitors in Newport.'

'Translating has its downsides. It's pretty lonely, for one thing,' I said, feeling I had to offer some consolation. 'This probably isn't the right place for it, not in my situation.'

'You don't think you'll stay then?'

'Not permanently. I don't know anyone here.'

'You know Pete, though. Pete Frewin.' She looked up from where her fingers were following the doily's scalloped edge. 'I saw you talking.' There was a moment's silence and then she laughed lightly. 'That sounded terrible – as if I'm stalking you or something. What I meant was: I noticed you talking to him in the Square before I went into Wavells.'

'That was the first time we've ever spoken. I was trying to stroke his cat – I used to have one who looked exactly the same.'

'You know about his wife?'

'Did you know her?' The coffee was still very hot but I took a big mouthful, wanting to mask my face in case it gave away the extent of my interest.

'Yes. She was my friend.' She was looking down again now and I thought I detected a tremor in her lower lip. 'Since sixth form. All three of us – us and Pete. She went to university on the mainland, in London, but when she came back, we just picked up where we left off. She was . . .' She swallowed audibly.

'I'm sorry. It must be very hard.'

A few seconds passed, then she sniffed as if fortifying herself and looked up again, resolute. Her eyes were watery, as they had been when I first saw her, but she blinked the tears quickly away. 'If we knew for certain,' she said, 'that would help. Poor Pete – he's being so strong but what must he be going through?'

I nodded. There were so many questions I wanted to ask but now it was near impossible. I couldn't probe into her grief. I tried to imagine how it would feel if Helen disappeared and felt a wash of anxiety go over me. 'Was there any warning?' I said gently. 'That she might . . .'

'Not really. She'd been through a particularly bad patch recently and we'd been worried for her then but, if anything, she seemed calmer in the last few days, even excited – as if she'd sorted herself out, found some sort of answer to it all. Of course, it makes sense now,' she glanced away and bit her lip. 'She had found the answer. A terrible answer.' She looked back at me. 'I'm sorry, you don't want to hear all this – and we've only just met and here's me crying all over you.'

'If it would help you to talk . . .'

'You know what I don't understand? She knew that we were here for her, whenever she needed us, Pete and me.' She shook her head. 'Pete was the best thing that ever happened to Alice. The way he loved her.' She looked at me fiercely, as though I were trying to contradict her. 'They were perfect. If he couldn't make her happy, loving her like he did, then nothing would have done.'

To my horror, I felt my own eyes fill with tears. She noticed them and reached across the table to put her small hand on mine. Her nails were neat and painted with clear polish. 'I'm sorry,' she said. 'I'm upsetting you now. We won't talk about it any more. Tell me about you instead. Do you have a partner?'

'No,' I said. 'There was someone but it went wrong.' She looked genuinely troubled, as if it mattered to her. 'How about you?'

'I had Tom when I was eighteen,' she said. 'My father was furious, said I'd wasted myself. I didn't care – Tom was worth every bit of the shouting then. The only thing that bothered me was that I split up from his dad quite soon after. I would have liked him to have a dad. Still, we've done OK, I think. We've managed.'

That night, for the first time in a week, I had trouble sleeping again. For the past few days, I'd been falling into a dreamless oblivion so complete it was as if I'd been anaesthetised but now

71

lying in bed, the faint glow of the streetlights along River Road coming through the thin curtains, I realised something disturbing: I was jealous of Alice. Not for what she'd done, of course not, but for the obvious love she'd had, both from her husband and from Sally. I envied her that. More disturbingly still, however, I realised that I was also jealous of my brother. When I'd put the phone down after talking to him that evening, the house had settled into near-silence around me again and I'd thought of him sitting down to supper in his kitchen with Mel, opening a bottle of wine, Charlie already in his cot for the night. I'd felt it then: the first pang of unmistakable envy. They'd been together four years now and before Melissa, Matt had had another girlfriend for years, too, a shy girl called Rebecca whom he'd met in the labs at university. He could have no idea of what it was like, I thought, to have to breathe life into a cold house every time you walked in, to come home to cook your own supper every night and to eat it alone, never even to have to look for something and find it other than where you'd put it.

This time last year Richard had been in France and had got into London late on a Friday evening. We'd spent most of the night awake, lying in bed talking and drinking the wine he'd brought back with him. The following morning I went to the newsagent's on Earls Court Road to buy milk and a newspaper. Though I'd had almost no sleep at all, I'd felt euphoric. 'What are you doing for Christmas?' he had asked an hour earlier. He was lying behind me, his body tucked in behind mine, his fingers gently tracing over my hip bone.

'I don't know yet,' I'd said. 'Normally we spend it with Dad in Bristol but he's moved now and Matt and Mel have just had their baby.'

'Spend it with me then. Let's have Christmas here.'

'Here? What, in this flat?'

'Why not?'

'Yours is much nicer – and much bigger. Do you really want to spend Christmas picking your way around the edge of the bed to get to the window?'

'Maybe I don't intend to spend much time out of bed at all.'

72

He moved his hand, sliding it off my hip and along the top of my thigh instead.

I wriggled out of his arms and turned to face him. 'You mean it, then? You want to spend the holiday here? With me?'

'Yes. Is that so very extraordinary?' His eyebrows twitched and I laughed and kissed him.

I'd been so excited that I'd had to stop myself hopscotching along the pavement to the newsagent's. I knew that going home with him that first night had been reckless but I didn't care. If I hadn't taken the risk, maybe I wouldn't have had this. Often in the past when I'd felt myself beginning to care about men, I'd experienced something like panic. It was difficult: I wanted to connect with people, I went looking for connections, but I struggled with the reality of getting close to men because I was afraid of losing my emotional independence, being made vulnerable. Even I could recognise the pattern: as soon as I began to see potential in a new relationship, it was as if a switch was thrown in my brain and I deliberately began the sabotage, picking fights, looking for faults.

It hadn't seemed to be happening with Richard, though. Perhaps it was the mock-confrontational banter between us which made me feel as if I was playing a role in a film and kept things light. But perhaps, I'd increasingly thought, it was because we had so much in common. He understood me and my need to be independent. Certainly he understood my need to work and why it was important for me to prove myself; it was one of his defining characteristics, too. 'Thank you for understanding,' he would say sometimes, when he left for his office on a Saturday afternoon. 'You're different. You get me.' I liked the idea of being the person who understood him. And perhaps, I'd started to think, perhaps this was the understanding, the easiness, people meant when they talked about how they knew they'd met the right person.

As I'd walked back up the stairs that morning, I'd heard noises coming from my flat and as I approached the front door, I realised it was music. Richard had put the radio on. The unexpectedness of it, something in the flat that I hadn't done, was strangely thrilling. I put down the papers and milk and followed the music through to its source in the bathroom. In the time that I'd been gone, he'd run a bath and was now in it, hidden up to his chest by bubbles. The sight of him in there, the adult, masculine shape of his body emerging from the childish foam, made me so happy that I burst out laughing. Then I took off my clothes, left them where they dropped and got in with him, lowering myself gently in so as not to send water spilling over the side.

'I think you've got a talent for pleasure,' he'd said, as I leant back against his chest.

'And I thought I was only any good at languages.'

Chapter Nine

I knew that the way to pull myself together now was to work. Telling Sally about the translating had reminded me that it was there, not only an increasingly pressing obligation but also an escape route, a way I could make myself disappear.

Starting the day after I met her, I set out to establish a routine, getting up as soon as the alarm went off, putting on my old cord trousers and making a percolator of coffee. The first day, I only read through the notes I'd written when I'd begun work on the book – they might have been made by someone else for all the memory I had of them – but after that, gratefully, I found a rhythm again and within days I was working at such a pitch that I stood up from my desk at lunchtime feeling sick from the intensity of the concentration. While I was focusing on the text, on finding the neatest, most succinct and idiomatic way of turning the English words into French, I could lose my problems, shake them off.

In the afternoons I went out. Unless it was raining heavily, I walked, just setting out from the cottage and following my feet. On wet days I took the car, gradually expanding my knowledge of the Island, attaching images to the names in my new road map. I went to places we'd never visited with Dad or that I didn't remember anyway. I took the straight road that ran down the south-west facet of the Island, and at St Catherine's on the southernmost tip I parked the car in a lane and walked down to a cluster of low buildings and the single white tower of the lighthouse which presided over the Channel. I was there as darkness began to fall and the lamp came on, strobing across the water like a giant eye, not warning but watching. On another day I went further along the road and came into Ventnor, easing the car down its wet, narrow streets to the shabby centre just above a promenade of closed-up cafés and boarding houses. The palm trees in the beds above the beach were evidence of the town's other, summer life, so remote I couldn't imagine it.

I felt the history of the Island all the time, as if the past was so close to the surface that occasionally it broke through to the present. Nestled among the spongy woods on the slopes of St Boniface Down, white Victorian villas held themselves aloof from the cheap shops of lower Ventnor as if their time of reserve and rectitude had never passed. In Bonchurch I came across an eleventh-century stone church little larger than a garden shed. Rain had made its tiny graveyard verdant and darkened the headstones, many of which bore the names and Victorian dates of those who had come to Ventnor, I guessed, to take the cure I'd read about. A plaque told me that the church was mentioned in the Domesday Book and standing among the graves, listening to the rain dripping through the branches of the trees which pressed at the edge of the cemetery and threatened to overgrow it, I felt even that time wasn't so very far away.

The days began to gather momentum, and November tipped into December. Christmas was inescapable suddenly. Everywhere I went there were signs of it: artificial trees covered with lurid flashing lights in windows and gardens, illuminated Santas leading teams of reindeer across the roofs of pebbledashed semis on the road out of Newport. In Yarmouth there was tinsel woven among the toys and teddies and plastic models that made up the newsagent's window display, and the chemist's blinking mirrors were joined by gift sets of soaps and talcum powder. Listening to the radio in the car or watching television meant subjection to heavy shelling by advertisement.

Ten days after we spoke, I wrote Matt an email to say that I'd decided not to come to Baltimore. I had a deadline approaching, I told him, and Helen had reminded me of a promise I'd made to spend Christmas with her. He would never find out it wasn't true.

Since coming to the Island I had spoken to Helen once and even then only briefly. For the most part our contact, too, was via email; it was an easier medium for both of us. There was something forced about speaking on the phone now, as if we were trying too hard to go back and recapture the time when there was no awkwardness between us and we'd spoken every day as a matter of course. Email allowed us to tread water, to stop our friendship from fading out completely but to preserve the distance that seemed to be stretching between us. I kept my mobile with me all the time and checked my email several times an hour when I was working but the phone didn't ring and her messages were so occasional that I jumped on them as soon as they arrived.

I heard nothing from Richard. I'd thought that later, after the first flush of his anger had faded, there would be texts, emails, phone calls late at night when he'd had a few glasses of wine but nothing came. It was as if he'd forgotten I'd ever existed.

Sometimes, during those weeks, I was quite proud of myself. Every day I went to bed exhausted, having stuck more or less to the pattern of what might be considered a normal day: focusing on the translation, walking until I was tired out, making sure I ate at mealtimes. The nights, though, I couldn't control. In my sleep I ran towards what I dragged myself away from while I was awake: as soon as I lost consciousness, the gates which I kept locked in the daytime swung wide open. I fell with delirious relief into dreams in which Richard – the old Richard, from the beginning – was so real that he might have been lying in the bed next to me. I felt his skin, pressed my face against his shoulder, buried my nose in his hair, his armpit, vacuumed up the smell of him like a homesick child with one of her mother's jumpers. Sometimes I was suffused with happiness, a sense of envelopment and homecoming. On other mornings, though, I would wake with puffy eyes and a sense of desolation, the feeling that just as I'd woken, Richard had pulled free of my arms and slipped out of the room.

Sometimes, though, when I cried in my sleep, it was because the other memories, the later ones, had worked themselves into my dreams. In those it was always dark and I couldn't work out who was talking or where I was or how I would ever get home. Lights shone and were abruptly extinguished. There were slammed doors and footsteps that came and went and sudden, sharp cries. I was chasing someone but I didn't know whom. There were always paths for me to follow, shadowy, twilit tracks that led through woods and cobbled lanes in old cities, but at the same time that I was pursuing, I was being pursued. A beam swept over me and back again like a searchlight and I couldn't stop for more than a few seconds before there were running footsteps which came louder and louder until they were joined by laughter. There was triumph in the laughter, knowledge of certain victory. I ran and ran and ran and when I woke up my heart was pounding and the T-shirt I slept in was as soaked with sweat as if I'd been running for years.

I'd started lighting the fire in the evenings. After supper I would work for another hour or so and then come down to sit in the armchair and read, closing the door between the sitting room and the kitchen and letting the heat build up until the room was really snug. By the second week in December I had finished the last of the five books and needed another batch. I was embarrassed to go back to the Totland shop though really I had nothing to be embarrassed about: he hadn't known I'd been listening. And if I went back, I could pay him for the books he'd given me in his rush to go.

I took the car. It had been threatening rain all day, the sky thickening periodically with pigeon-grey clouds which loomed overhead but then moved off further up the coast just when it seemed they couldn't get any heavier. The wind had a stinging edge, as if it came full of salt from the sea to seek out any cuts and blemishes on the skin. I felt it on my face even after I stepped out of it into the shop.

Christmas had arrived here, too, but in the most modest of ways. There was an arrangement of holly in a tall vase, the branches clearly chosen for their profusion of scarlet berries, and along the windowsills behind the desk there were lengths of trailing ivy. The owner was on the telephone again but he looked up and raised his spare hand in a sort of salute. I worked my way methodically along the shelves, glad that he was talking and that I could browse without any pressure. The conversation this time seemed to be about the safe packing of a book that he was sending to Berlin. After a while the carriage clock on his desk chimed four and, glancing up, I saw that the light outside was gone. Against the glass came the patter of incipient rain.

I chose another five books and went to pay. He'd finished on the telephone now and was writing in a ledger. He looked up quickly when he saw me, held up a single finger while he filled in the sum at the bottom of a column and then gave me his full attention.

'Hello again,' he said. 'I'd hoped you'd come back. I wanted to apologise for the other day – hustling you out. I'd had what I thought was some rather bad news.'

'Actually I've been feeling bad – I'd like to pay you for the other books.'

'Absolutely not. You can put that thought from your mind once and for all.' He took the new books from me, tipping them sideways to look at the spines, nodding slowly as if he had either predicted my choice – heavy on Graham Greene this time – or approved of it. Behind him, there was a sudden angry sound, as if someone had thrown a handful of fine gravel against the window. A couple of seconds later, it came again. 'God, listen to it,' he said. 'That's sleet. You're not walking, I hope?'

'No, I've got the car but it's down by the chemist.'

'Umbrella?'

I shook my head. He frowned, making a deep grid of the fine mesh of lines which crossed his forehead. It seemed odd to me that he should be here in Totland running a second-hand bookshop; he didn't quite fit. In fact, with his academic look, I could imagine him in the languages department of my old university. I filled in the rest of that life for him, too: a bachelor pad filled with shelves and shelves of books, a small circle of faculty friends whom he met for Saturday afternoon pints in pubs in Hampstead. Or perhaps a life with a family, two or three teenage children whom he loved but also liked to escape from into the relative calm of a study in a house somewhere in an unfashionable but more affordable area of suburbia.

'Sorry?' I said, realising that he had been talking.

'I said, I'd lend you one but I gave it to someone else last week, alas, and she hasn't returned it yet. Look, rather than get soaked, and get these wet' – he rapped his knuckles on the top of the pile as if knocking on a door – 'why don't you stay and have a cup of tea with me? I shouldn't think it'll last more than a few minutes but it does sound vicious. Freezing cold, too.'

'That's kind but . . .'

'It's no trouble at all – I was about to put the kettle on anyway. I'm Christopher, by the way – Chris.'

Awkwardly I sat down on the chair that he pulled out for me. He disappeared through a side door and I heard a kettle being filled and cups and saucers being taken from a cupboard. My eyes moved over his desk. The pages of the ledger, now closed, had pink marbled edges, and it reminded me of a notebook of Dad's which I had always coveted. The laptop was still on but it faced away from me; periodically, it whirred, then settled again. I shifted uncomfortably. Why the hell hadn't I made an excuse and left? The sleet threw itself at the window again, malicious, and I willed it to pass over so that I could go home.

'Here we are.' He returned with two teacups, one of which he gave me before retreating to his side of the table. I took a sip straight away, burning my tongue. The cup clattered as it returned to the saucer. He was looking at me and I realised I should say something.

'Thank you – this is very kind of you.'

'No problem at all. As I said, I was about to have a cup anyway.'

'I like your shop, it's . . .' I stopped, uncertain how to describe what I felt.

He nodded an acknowledgement. 'Thank you. It's not the main part of my business but I enjoy it and it gets a bit busier in the summer, when the holidaymakers come in. I deal in antiquarian books, really, mostly on the phone and over the internet. The shop's slightly more sociable, though I still find the winters lonely, I must admit. What do you do? Are you working locally?'

'At home. I'm a translator, English to French.'

'You have family on the Island?'

80

'No. I'm here on my own.'

He nodded again and I was interested to find that I didn't feel as if I had to justify myself. 'I've been back for ten years now,' he said. 'I grew up here but went to the mainland for university and ended up staying until I was fifty.' He laughed. 'I came back when my own children went to college. I can easily do my dealing from here, especially now with the internet.'

'I came here years ago and I associated it with being happy.'

I hesitated. I was filled with a sudden urge to tell him the whole reason I was on the Island. Weeks of words were welling up into my mouth. Perhaps it was his kindness or the calm he emanated. Maybe it was because he was older I felt he would understand. But I didn't like the idea of spilling my secrets to someone I'd just met, the emotional incontinence of it. And for all his kindness, there was nothing to suggest that he was taking a special interest in me. He was just a decent man behaving as decent people did, no more than that. I pushed the words down again and kept quiet. He asked me more about my work and we talked about places we both knew in France, moving from the subject of Gascony to Alexandre Dumas and then on to other writers. We had a surprising number of favourites in common.

All the time we were talking I thought about the telephone conversation I'd overheard. Obviously he must know Peter Frewin very well to be the person people called when they were trying to find him. And if he knew Peter he would also certainly have known Alice, maybe equally as well. There was no way I could raise the subject, though, without revealing that I'd been eavesdropping last time and even if I angled at it another way, approached it in seeming innocence, I was sure he would guess. What, I couldn't help wondering anyway, would he be able to tell me about Alice? Though I'd been moved when Sally had said how much Peter had loved her, afterwards I'd found myself remembering the women I'd overheard in the Mariners, the implication of the one that he might have been at the root of her unhappiness. I could hear the woman's reedy voice quite clearly: 'Well, something happened.'

'There you are, it sounds as if it's stopped,' he – Chris – said eventually. He stood slowly and picked up our cups. 'You'll have to come and have tea again after Christmas – if you'd like to, that is.' Returning from the kitchen, he handed me my parcel from the desk. 'Don't forget these.'

He followed me to the door and took the books back while I buttoned up my coat. He handed them over again and then rested his hand lightly on my forearm. 'It's been a pleasure,' he said.

Embarrassed, I thanked him again and said goodbye, still feeling the imprint of his touch even through the thick wool of my coat. The bell above the door rang merrily but then I found myself out on the street and my fleeting moment of connection was over. Though the sleet had stopped, the wind was still rushing the trees, gusting, then whispering, shivering the branches as if in admonition. There was no one else on the pavement and the orange of the streetlights gleamed uninterrupted on the wet road. I walked briskly back to the car, trying to put from my mind the idea that behind the curtains in the melancholy houses unseen eyes were watching me.

Chapter Ten

I hadn't realised until a few days before Christmas last year that Richard's mother had Alzheimer's. I knew his father had died some time earlier and I'd had the impression that his mother had, too, though as soon as he told me about her illness, I wondered whether I had jumped to that conclusion because I had heard him talk about her in the past tense, as people sometimes did about elderly relatives with serious mental-health problems. She still lived in their family house in Highgate, he said, the one in which he had grown up, having made him swear that he would never put her in a home, and the money his father had left was used to pay for round-the-clock carers. 'She's very ill now,' he said. 'I want to spend some time with her over the holiday. In case . . .' he looked away.

'Of course,' I said.

'I'm taking four days off. I'd like to spend two with her and the other two here, with you.'

I hoped my selfish disappointment at having so little time after all hadn't registered on my face. 'I understand,' I said. 'Would you like me to come with you, though? Can I help?'

'Sweetheart, it's kind of you to offer.' He kissed me lightly on the forehead, something he hadn't done before. 'But she gets confused by new people. Also, it upsets me when people meet her now. She was beautiful, my mother – elegant.' He looked away again and I saw that he wanted to leave the subject alone.

As our holiday couldn't be long, I decided that it would be perfect. I bought a Christmas tree from the market on North End

Road, wildly miscalculating the size. It protruded from the boot of the car as I drove carefully home, its tip bent against the inside of the windscreen, and it dropped needles over the upholstery and all the way up the stairs as, red-faced and scratched, I half-carried, half-dragged it to the top floor. I'd also bought ivy which I put across the top of the pictures and on the mantelpiece, and a big sprig of mistletoe to hang by the door.

On Christmas Eve I went to the delicatessen and bought cheese, cold meats and two loaves of bread, one sourdough, one with apricots. I got olives, pickles, pâté and several other things which hadn't been on the list: amaretti biscuits, cheese straws and a bottle of Muscat. In the evening I baked a ham, which even I recognised as overkill, and made mince pies, listening to the carols from King's while I sprayed pastry crumbs round the kitchen and got a bit drunk. Later on, as I turned out the lights before going to bed, I stood at the window and raised my glass to the flats across the street, wishing them a Christmas as happy as the one I was going to have.

By the time Richard arrived at three o'clock the following afternoon, I was ready. I'd opened my presents and rung Dad and Matt to say thank you. The vegetables were prepared and the turkey – ostrich-sized – had just gone into the oven. We were eating late because he'd already had lunch with his mother and her carer. I'd washed my hair again and put on my favourite black dress. As he crested the top of the stairs, I saw that as well as his usual overnight bag, he was carrying a large paper one with cord handles. He held it away from me, then put it down and pulled me with him under the mistletoe. 'Look at this place,' he said. 'It's a Christmas explosion.'

In the sitting room, he opened the bag and handed me two bottles of Burgundy. I fetched glasses and joined him on the sofa. He was wearing dark jeans and a navy cashmere jumper. 'What?' he said.

'I'm just thinking I don't see you in casual clothes very often.'

'That's because I've been working so hard since I met you.'

'Are you saying you ever work less hard?' I teased.

'No. Would you like your presents?'

'Let me give you yours first.' I stood up to fetch them from under the tree. I had been excited at the idea of buying them, both because I wanted to give him presents and also because it was the first time in three years that I'd had someone, a man – the word 'boyfriend' didn't seem right to describe Richard, somehow – to buy for, but it had turned out to be hard. Everything I looked at seemed charged with significance and though I wanted to give him gifts that reflected how I felt, at the same time I didn't want to reveal myself. The three presents that I put on the coffee table were the result of many hours' deliberation.

I had taken care with the wrapping and the parcels were neat as hospital beds, tied with ribbon. The first was a Ray Charles recording he'd been looking for, and his smile when he saw it made me smile, too. Next he opened the biography of Stalin which he'd mentioned and then the wallet in oxblood calfskin which I had wrapped only at the last minute because I had loved looking at it so much.

'I'll think of you whenever I use it,' he said, putting his fingers against my cheek. He reached around the side of the sofa and pulled the bag forward. 'These are yours.'

Inside there were ten or twelve parcels of various sizes. 'Are they all for me?'

'Some of them are Christmas things but yes, they're all for you. Leave this one till last.' He reached in and took out a square parcel about four inches by five, then sat back while I unpacked the bag. There was a pot of Stilton and a bottle of brandy, Belgian chocolates and a box of biscuits. There was a large bottle of the scent I wore – he'd made a note of it, I thought – a Mont Blanc fountain pen, and a set of La Perla underwear in pale pink silk. 'That's to share,' he said.

When I'd opened them all, the table was covered. 'It's too much,' I said.

'I wanted to buy them for you.' Then he handed me the small parcel which he'd kept aside. When I took the paper off, I saw that it was an old jewellery box, the tooled ruby leather beginning to wear at the corners. He watched my face while I struggled with the tiny catch, then took it back, opened it easily with a flick of his thumbnail and held it out to me.

On the ivory satin bed inside there was a gold bangle. The band was plain, just a slim ring, but the clasp was ornate. I eased it out of the box. Each end of the oval finished in a lion's head so that when, like now, it was fastened, they were muzzle to muzzle. I looked more closely at their faces – there was something human about them, the way the locks of engraved fur streamed back from their foreheads like hair and the expression in their eyes, not a brute rage but a savage, intelligent hunger.

'Fierce creatures for my fierce creature.'

'It's extraordinary,' I said, without thinking.

'I'm glad you like it. Here.' He took it from me and I held out my arm while he put it on. I turned my wrist slowly, watching how the reflection of the lights from the tree gleamed on the gold. The lions faced each other off.

'It suits you.' He caught my hand again and stroked the inside of my arm gently with his finger. I wondered how his lightest touch could evoke such a rush of desire. He read it in my face and smiled knowingly. Then he pulled me round on to his knee and kissed me, fingers already reaching for the black pearl buttons down the front of my dress. The wrapping paper on the floor crunched as I stood up, one foot on either side of his knees, and he ran his hands up my thighs, lifting my skirt, then catching the sides of my knickers and pulling them down in one quick movement. I sidestepped them and lowered myself down over him, watching his face as he leant back and closed his eyes, his mouth falling slightly open. His hand skimmed up from my waist and slipped between the open buttons. I couldn't have cared less that the blinds were up. I watched the different expressions of pleasure pass over his face like the reflections of clouds across water and my hair fell into his eyes.

'Happy Christmas, sweetheart,' he said afterwards, laughing against the side of my neck.

'La petite mort,' I said.

'What?'

'That's what the French call it – orgasm. The little death. Because it's the death of loss and desire – just for a second all human cares drop away.'

86

'You never bore me, you know that?' he said.

I straightened myself out, did up my buttons and went through to the kitchen. As I lifted the roasting tin from the oven, the bangle moved down towards the back of my hand. I looked again at the two strange faces. Fierce creatures for a fierce creature, I thought. Of course he thought I was fierce, though. That was exactly how I had presented myself to him. I should be pleased – I wanted him to think that I was unpredictable and exciting, untamed.

I owned almost no real jewellery, certainly nothing like this. For my twenty-first birthday, Dad had given me a single diamond on a fine white-gold chain that had belonged to my granny but, other than that, everything I owned was costume. That must be why this seemed strange. Also, though I was ashamed even to think it, it was a token of ownership, obviously a lover's present, and I liked the thought of him making a claim on me, annexing me.

He put on the Ray Charles and opened the second bottle of wine. He was trying to give up smoking but when I went through to the sitting room again, he had pushed up the sash and was leaning out of the window. Above the roofs of the houses opposite, the sky was navy. The street below was quiet and the streetlamps pooled their light down for no one other than the tabby cat from the ground-floor flat who stalked his territory undisturbed. Richard put his arm around my waist and squeezed.

We got drunk that night, drunker than we'd ever been before together. By about three in the morning, all the lights in the flats were out and we were alone in the world, marooned on the sofa, he stretched to full length, I tucked in between him and the back, my head resting on his shoulder. The candles along the mantelpiece had burned down and now all the light in the room came from the tree, which sparkled now and again as the draught from the ill-fitting window-frame turned the baubles. I'd been hilariously drunk earlier on but was mellow now, two steps from falling into a happy sleep. I was wondering, though, about something he'd said.

'Richard?'

'Hmm?' He was winding a strand of my hair around his finger.

'Do you think you'll ever work less hard?'

'Why do you ask?'

'I don't know – if you had a family, for example. I don't mean taking on fewer projects, just delegating more, letting Neil do more of the travelling.'

I felt him shift under me but kept my eyes closed.

'You know why I have to work so hard, don't you?' he said. 'You get it?'

'I know why I do – because I need to prove myself, be as good as I can.' I pressed closer to him again, the tops of my arms suddenly registering the falling temperature in the room. The heating had been off for hours.

'Exactly.'

A minute or so passed. He'd stopped playing with my hair. In the silence of the flat I listened to the sound of his breathing. If we hadn't had so much to drink, perhaps I wouldn't have asked. 'Who are you trying to prove it to?'

His answer was immediate. 'My father.'

I felt his chest rise under me. 'Even now?' I asked gently.

'Oh, it'll never stop.' He seemed to spit the words out. 'I go on thinking that if I hammer the point in enough perhaps the old bastard might be forced to acknowledge that he was wrong.' He snorted. 'Or maybe not – nothing I ever did when he was alive did it: results, Harvard, the first development.' He sat up suddenly, dislodging me.

I sat up, too, and put my hand on his shoulder. He was turned away from me now, sitting on the edge of the seat as if he might spring up at any moment. Instead he picked up his whisky glass and downed the last half-inch in one.

'OK,' he said, 'imagine this. You're twelve years old. One day you have an argument with your mother – she's lost something, you get the blame again. Every little thing that happens, you get the blame. Anyway, you storm off up the garden to simmer down a bit and you fall asleep in the long grass. It's late by the time you wake up, almost eight, and you know you'll be in trouble again for staying out. You sneak back into the house through the back door but just as you get to the bottom of the stairs, you hear voices in the sitting room. And what's your dear old dad saying? He's telling your mother that he's worried because he thinks there's something *not quite right* about you. Can you imagine that? You're twelve years old, for fuck's sake. I felt like I'd been fucking branded.'

The next day, Boxing Day, we had driven out of London into the countryside, looking for a pub for lunch. I'd never been in Richard's car before; in fact, I realised, I hadn't even seen it. He had a navy blue Mercedes SLK whose inside was still redolent of fresh new leather, a different species of animal altogether from my battered Ford Fiesta. I watched him surreptitiously as he negotiated us out through West London. His leather jacket was laid on the back seat and he had the sleeves of his jumper pushed up to just below the elbow, the hair on his arms thick and dark. He drove with the focus I now thought of as particularly his, not letting his attention wander for a moment, cruising through spaces so narrow I feared for the wing mirrors, never ceding to anyone. Out on the M4, it occurred to me that he was playing the road like a computer game, changing lanes, overtaking, eating up other drivers like Pacman. He'd been quiet since we'd woken and I wondered if it wasn't only the hangover, if he was regretting telling me about his father, revealing too much. I didn't try to make him talk and there was silence between us for much of the way. I wondered what I could say to make him feel better. I didn't mention our speed, which at times was frankly terrifying.

The place we stopped at was a few miles off the motorway, not far from Marlborough. It was in a pair of old black-and-white cottages knocked through to make one, and while from the outside it had looked dark and old-fashioned, I realised as soon as we went in that we had stumbled on the local gastro-pub. The floorboards were exposed and the chalkboards made much of the menu's organic sourcing. Richard's Mercedes had been one of several in the car park. I thought about suggesting that we find somewhere less obvious but he had already pounced on a table that was coming free.

After we'd ordered, I went to the loo and when I came back, I was surprised to find that he was gone. When he returned, it was not from the direction of the lavatories, as I'd thought, but from the front door. He was putting his phone into his pocket as he looked up and saw me. 'My mother's carer,' he said, sitting down.

'Is everything all right?'

'I'll see her tomorrow.'

I hesitated. 'It must be terrible.'

'It's very hard for her, obviously, but from my point of view, at least I had the years with her while she was well. That's more than a lot of people.'

I looked away. I was used to his questions about my life, his hunger for information, but though he'd alluded to my relationship with my mother several times since I'd skirted the issue at our first dinner, I'd never told him any more. Helen was the only person I'd ever really told. I knew there was nothing for me to be ashamed about but somehow I did feel ashamed. And I didn't want people to feel sorry for me, either; I hated that. I pretended that I hadn't noticed the hint, if that was what it was, and looked round instead. The place was packed, a number of the tables pushed together to accommodate large groups. Two little girls in matching woollen dresses and red ribbed tights were lavishing attention on the pub dog, an old liver-coloured spaniel who lay in his basket by the fire with a look of weary tolerance. The air was full of the smell of roast beef and the spices in the vat of mulled wine on the corner of the bar.

We both had the beef, which was delicious, and Richard insisted I have a slice of lemon tart. He watched me while I ate it, amused by my enjoyment. In my early twenties I'd had a boyfriend who had always made me feel that liking puddings was symptomatic of unattractive gluttony and there was something liberating about not having to pretend about it. I felt a rush of appreciation for Richard and suddenly I knew I should tell him about my mother. If we were going to have a future, I would have to and telling him now was a way of letting him know, without saying it, that I trusted him. It might also mitigate his regret at telling me about his father.

I took a large mouthful of wine and looked at him. 'My mother left us,' I said.

'What?' He was caught off-guard.

'When I was ten and Matt was eight, she went back to France, shacked up with a man who owns a restaurant in Lyon. That's why we stopped speaking French at home.'

Now he was watching me intently, eyes moving over my face.

'We hardly saw her at all. She used to come over once a year for a few days at Easter, bring us chewing gum that Dad didn't like us to have, but that was about it. Dad looked after us.' My face was red with the same embarrassment that had pierced me when, two days after it had happened, Josephine Wright had asked me about it at school straight out. 'Is it true?' she'd said. 'My mum says your mum's buggered off.'

'It was dreadful for Dad. He used to be a research scientist but there wasn't any money in it so he gave it up and retrained as a physics teacher so he earned a bit more and had the holidays. He's shy, my dad – I think he found it really hard to start with, standing up in front of a room of teenagers day after day. He did it, though.' Now I'd started, the story was coming more easily; it was spilling out. 'He's incredible – I didn't realise till I got older how much he'd given up. It's only in the past couple of years that he's even had anyone else serious – he was single until Matt and I went to college, and even then he found it hard. I think it took him years to get over her and then he didn't want to risk getting close to anyone again in case it didn't work out. He wouldn't have risked it, for our sake.'

'Why did she leave?'

'Oh, I don't know. She met him – restaurant man. Maybe she thought she was too young to be tied down. Maybe we weren't the exciting English life she'd had in mind when she came here.'

'Was she happy? She must have regretted leaving you, surely.'

I shrugged. 'I don't care. She made the decision – the rest of us just had to live with it.' The feeling I got when I thought about her was rising up through me and I didn't want to talk about it any more. I took another sip of my wine and looked away, over to the fireplace where the dog, now abandoned in favour of ice-cream sundaes, was snoozing gratefully.

'I'm glad you told me,' said Richard. He half-stood, and leaned across the table to catch my face in his hands and kiss me. 'It means a lot that you trust me.'

91

'Urgh,' said one of the little girls. 'That's disgusting.'

Richard grinned and sat back down again. 'Sorry,' he said, nodding an apology to her. 'But it was very important. I won't do it again.'

'OK, then,' she looked away, suddenly shy.

We had the heater on in the car on the way back and I leaned my head against the window and drifted in and out of a wine-induced doze while Richard gamed our way into London. He was humming quietly and I felt the strengthening of bonds between us, a drawing closer.

When we turned the lights off that night, I lay awake. There was a breeze outside and the streetlamps around the garden square behind the building were casting shadows of the topmost branches of the trees on to the strip of ceiling in front of the arrow-slit window. I watched as they moved gently back and forth like stroking fingers. Richard was on his side facing me, his hand resting in its familiar place on my thigh. His eyes were closed but he wasn't quite asleep. He'd been tender with me all evening and just now when we'd had sex, too, as if what I'd told him earlier had cracked the tough shell I'd presented him with before and made him aware that I, too, had fragilities. There was a dull ache in my torso that I couldn't locate precisely to either my heart or my stomach and I realised that I was mourning these days already. 'Wouldn't it be good if we could be together like this always?' I said quietly into the darkness.

'Hmm.' He was almost asleep now but his fingers moved across my skin and brushed lightly over my pubic hair, before resting there.

'Why don't we do it?'

'Hmm?'

'Why don't we? Move in together?'

His eyes came open immediately. I turned to look at him. The thin gap between the window and the blind let in enough light for me to see that he was suddenly wide awake. 'Sorry – that was a bit of a surprise,' I said.

'It certainly was,' he said, and there was a touch of relief in his voice, as if he'd taken me for serious at first and now realised I was joking. The ache changed, became a pang of alarm. What I heard was distance, and a little of our new closeness seemed to evaporate. I knew I should leave it, have the conversation another time, but I couldn't stop myself.

'Is it a ridiculous idea?' I said.

He hesitated. I watched his shadowed face and it occurred to me that he was deciding how to compose it, how he was going to handle this situation that I had suddenly thrust on him when he was happy and comfortable, tired and slightly dazed with food and wine and sex. He was working out how to handle me.

'Sweetheart,' he said, moving his hand back on to my thigh. 'You know I'm not ready. I've just got out of a long-term relationship. I need a bit of time before I can commit to anything else. Come on, you know that.' His voice was coaxing now, as if he was talking to a recalcitrant child.

I felt a rush of anger and shifted, dislodging his hand. 'Actually, I don't know. I know you were in a long relationship but that's all you've told me about it – in six months.' I realised as I said it that it was true and also that I'd never asked. At the beginning I hadn't wanted to press him until he was ready to tell me or to give him the upper hand in our semi-joking battle of wills by letting him know that I thought about it, and then, after time passed, I hadn't wanted to think about him with another woman. 'You can't really expect me to understand when I don't know what I'm supposed to be understanding,' I said. 'I mean, obviously it was important but I thought perhaps this might be important, too.'

He groaned. 'Don't be like this.'

'I'm not being like anything.' I turned away from him, embarrassed to have abandoned the lightness I'd calibrated so carefully and revealed that I had hopes for our future. I knew with a swift certainty that I had misjudged things. If he felt about me as I did about him, there was no way he would be reacting like this.

'Please don't cry,' he said, his voice sounding as if it came from a distance.

'I'm not crying,' I said, furious. I didn't turn back to him and he made no move towards me. We lay like that for some minutes. I waited for him to go to sleep so that I could get up and go into the sitting room to order my thoughts without causing a scene. His breathing, though, stayed the same.

'I don't know what you want me to say,' he said eventually.

'You make it sound as if I'm putting you in an unbearable position,' I said. 'I'm not, OK? It was just a stupid, off-the-cuff, spur-of-the moment idea. Just forget about it – it's not important.'

He sighed. 'Of course it's important.'

I turned round. 'Look, I got it wrong. I'm sorry. That's all we need to say. Subject closed.'

He grabbed my wrist, pinching my skin against the edge of the bangle which I was still wearing.

'Ow, that hurts, Richard.'

He gripped harder. 'I'm just trying to understand what you want from me.'

'I don't want anything. I just want you to let go.'

He did then and my arm dropped as if it were a dead weight. To my shame, I felt tears in my eyes now and I turned away from him quickly before he could see. This time, though, he moved across the bed and put his arm around my waist. 'Sssh,' he whispered. 'It's all right. It's all right.'

My body was rigid with tension and I couldn't make myself relax back against him. 'I just don't understand why it's such a big deal,' I said.

'For fuck's sake.' He was out of bed in a second. The half light cast shadows over his body and it looked different to me now, hostile. I couldn't imagine how only minutes ago I had pressed myself against it so willingly.

'Why are you so angry?' I wept, sitting up and pulling my knees to my chest.

'You just have to keep pushing, don't you? Why can't you just leave it alone? You're ruining everything – you're making me do this.'

'What?' I heard the note of alarm in my voice.

'You're doing this. You're making me tell you. I can't move in with you, Kate,' he lunged towards me and brought his face right

94

up to mine, making sure I couldn't look away, grabbing my wrist again and holding it hard. I could smell the alcohol on his breath and, partially masked, the cigarette that he'd had after supper. His eyes were completely cold. 'Because I'm married to someone else.'

Chapter Eleven

Last year it had drizzled on Christmas morning but today the sky was as blue as if it were June. Looking over the harbour from my bedroom window, I felt a pressing need to be outside and I got dressed and left the house straight away. As soon as the door closed behind me, though, I realised that the sun was deceptive. There was no heat in the day at all; instead it was so cold that the air tasted metallic.

Coming up Bridge Road towards the Square it was hard to miss the word that had been spray-painted on to the wall of the churchyard. BOLLOCKS was spelled out in red letters three feet high, clearly legible to the nearest-sighted of the congregation at the morning service. Even for me, it was shocking – the sheer unlikeliness of it. In London, graffiti was everywhere; I scarcely even noticed it. Here, however, it was extraordinary, almost anachronistic. I remembered the women I'd heard talking outside the delicatessen the morning I'd met Sally, though, and the graffiti at the bus stop; evidently it wasn't an unknown phenomenon. But who was doing it? I'd hardly even seen anyone young here, let alone a gang.

In the Square every shop was shut, even the corner shop which I'd only ever seen closed at night. The café at the far end was shut, too, and beyond it, the pier extended over the water like the beginning of a bridge which had run out of steam. Walking out on to it, I could feel the sea slapping against the thick wooden struts which anchored it into the seabed. The water changed colour wherever I looked at it. To my left, down the channel towards the Needles, it was a dappling aquamarine, its surface denting and pixilating where the wind blew at it, but beneath me, in the shadow of the boardwalk, it was a deeper, darker green. Away from the shelter of the buildings, the bitterness of the wind made my eyes stream. When I reached the end I leaned against the railing and looked over to the mainland, which the sterile light had brought into high definition. The towers of the oil refinery at Fawley were sharp as needles. There were only two yachts out, one down near Hurst, the other near the entrance to the Lymington River, tacking now to get out of the path of one of the few ferries that would be running today.

I turned around to look at the town. There were lights on at almost every one of the windows at the George, the rooms full of people who'd come for a smart hotel Christmas. It would be packed for lunch later. I scanned along to the yacht club and the large houses that bordered on to the water. There was a flagpole in the garden of the huge Victorian house with the crenellated roofline; the flag, a Union Jack, had been savaged by the elements and now flapped in faded tatters. Below me, a handful of scows like Alice's faced the end of the pier like a congregation in front of a pulpit, headed neatly into the wind. I wondered how Peter Frewin would be spending the day, without her.

I turned the other way and saw that the ferry had made good progress, moving towards the Island while I wasn't looking as if it were playing a game of Grandmother's Footsteps. My hands were beginning to hurt with the cold but I didn't want to go back to the cottage; at least while I was out, I could pretend to be part of the world. Inside, it would only be me and the reality of my decision to stay here alone over the holiday. Dad and Matt would ring from America later but I knew the call would make me lonelier, with its background of happy voices and then the silence when the receiver went down. Well, it didn't matter anyway, I thought: I would get drunk.

Back at the house I lit the fire, switched the oven on and poured a glass of sherry. There hadn't seemed any point in cooking a turkey just for myself so I'd bought a chicken instead with the idea of roasting it today and eating the rest cold. I peeled the vegetables,

97

washed the knives and put the chicken in the oven. After that I went through to the sitting room and stood at the sliding doors looking at the yard. There was no view over the wooden fences on either side and, from the ground floor, it was impossible to see over the gates at the end. When I'd been at the sink scoring the sprouts, a couple I hadn't seen before had passed in front of the window on their way to a house further down but it was quiet now, no voices or music coming from either of my neighbours. The silence started to flood in and I quickly switched on the television to block it.

I poured another glass of sherry and took it upstairs. The bed was already made but I tweaked the blanket so that it lay straight and hung up the shirt that I'd left over the back of the chair. My book was lying face down on the carpet, pages splayed, and I picked it up, marked my place with the envelope I used and put it on the bedside table. Out on the landing again I stopped in front of the mirror and looked at myself. My hair was knotted from the wind but there was some colour in my cheeks from being outside and the ring under my eye and the stitches were now long gone.

I turned and paused at the door to the second bedroom. The manuscript was on the desk, along with the handwritten translation of the latest chapter. I went in for a second to look at it, then picked up the pen and made a small correction to an awkward sentence. I'd told myself that I wouldn't work today but now it seemed preferable to hanging listlessly round the house. As a compromise, I decided that I would just type up the pages that I'd already done but when I finished them, I found myself going on to the next section and by the time I looked up, an hour and a half had passed. My glass was empty, the house was filled with the smell of roasting chicken and I could make out the sound of carols on the television. Before going downstairs, I opened up my email account just in case there was anything. Perhaps Dad had emailed to wish me a happy Christmas before we spoke later on. When it came up, the home screen told me that there was indeed a message and when I clicked on the inbox there it was.

Richard Brookwood.

My hand stopped on the mouse. I glanced away, then looked again, in case I'd imagined it. I highlighted it, ready to press delete, but I hesitated. I took my glass downstairs and refilled it, feeling my heartbeat in my ears. Back at the desk, I didn't think any more; I clicked and opened it.

It was three words: *Happy Christmas, sweetheart.*

The floor seemed to shift under my chair, as though a small seismic shock had rippled beneath the house, and there was a sudden, sharp pain in my chest. I pressed my hands over it and breathed hard. After a minute or so, it moved and lodged itself under my sternum as a severe muscular ache. Christmas Day. It was so typical of him, so calculated. And those three words: did he remember saying them to me on the sofa a year ago, afterwards, when my hair was in his face and we were laughing? I banged my forehead down hard on the edge of the desk in anger at myself for opening it and the pain felt deserved and good.

I deleted the message, snapped the lid of the computer down and went out on to the landing. Instead of going downstairs, though, I went back to my bedroom. I opened the wardrobe door and slid my hand between the T-shirts piled on the shelf until my fingers touched what I was looking for. I held the box for a moment, hesitant, and then flicked up the little catch. I hadn't worn it since October but the lions on the bangle gleamed up at me as if newly polished, their eyes as fierce and hungry as ever. I thrust the box to the back of the wardrobe again. I shouldn't have looked at them – I should never have brought it here in the first place. The ache under my breastbone intensified.

From downstairs came a smell of burning. I ran down and opened the oven, unleashing a cloud of acrid smoke. The bacon which I had laid over the chicken was black; I picked it off and flung it into the sink. Underneath, the skin of the chicken itself was shiny and parched, but when I stuck a skewer into the join between the breast and thigh, the juice ran a cloudy pink. I covered it with foil and put it back in the oven. Then I sat down at the table and put my head in my hands. The reality of where I was, my utter isolation, struck me like a hand across my cheek. What was I doing here? Why had I let him win by terrifying me into cutting myself off from everyone? And why hadn't I gone to the States with Dad and Jane? What was I proving by staying here on my own?

I was summoned from my self-pity by a knock on the door. I jerked up. The table was out of view from the door and I sat as if paralysed. Was the email just an opening move? Had he found me?

The knock came again but this time on the large window over the sink. I spun round but the face looking at me through the glass wasn't Richard's. It was Helen's.

For a moment I looked at her in shock. Then I came to my senses and went to the door. She came in, closed it behind her and then, before we had spoken a word, she put her arms around me.

We salvaged what we could of the chicken and I peeled some more vegetables. 'I can't believe you're actually here – in this kitchen,' I said, turning from the chopping board to look at her again.

'Well, believe it. It's me.' She was at the table, sitting sideways and watching me as I moved around. She'd had a Louise Brooks cut since I'd last seen her, and the cropped fringe and two shiny black wings of the bob framed her face dramatically, making her look pale and sophisticated. I wondered if she'd seen anyone on her way from the harbour – she must have done; how else would she have found the cottage hidden away here? – and if they'd done a double-take at this bit of 1920s Hollywood glamour beamed in from another world. Her scrutiny was making me self-conscious: I knew she was noting my grubby cords and the hole in the elbow of my jumper, the contrast between them and her tight black jeans, cream broderie anglaise jacket and huge red ceramic beads.

'I feel bad,' I said. 'Aren't you supposed to be at your parents'?'

'They've got my sister and her husband. That's enough for anyone. I could hardly leave you here on your own on Christmas Day, could I? The only reason I didn't tell you I was coming was I knew you'd try and stop me.' She picked up her large shoulder bag and rummaged in it for her cigarettes.

'I can't tell you how much . . .'

She held her hand up. 'No, don't say it again.'

By the time the vegetables were ready, the shadows were lengthening and the strip of sky visible from the kitchen window had changed from its earlier blue to a dull white, the sun smothered

100

by cloud. Despite the fire in the sitting room, the house was cold and I put the boiler on so that the radiator would be warm while we ate. The draught from under the kitchen door was ghosting around my ankles.

Afterwards, Helen put her mince pies in the oven to heat up. 'So,' she said, sitting back down. 'Are you going to tell me what this is all about now? Why the hell are you here?'

I looked at the table top and ran my thumb over the edge where the Formica veneer had chipped away. I'd known this was coming. I wanted to tell her, I really did, and surely now when, despite everything I had done, she had sacrificed her Christmas plans to come here and find me, I owed her the truth. But I couldn't do it. It wasn't because I didn't want to admit that she had been right about him, though; I was far beyond that.

She was looking at me, waiting.

'Because I'm an idiot,' I said. 'Richard was lying to me.'

She frowned. 'About what? You knew for ages that he was married.' Our eyes met and I looked quickly away again, remembering telling her and how that had played out between us.

'The day I had the accident,' I said, snapping off another chip of the veneer. 'You know he was going to the States? He stayed with me the night before. In the morning I went out to get breakfast and he didn't hear me when I got back – the door hadn't closed properly behind me. He was on the phone.'

'To who? His wife?'

'His son.' Blood flooded into my cheeks. 'It was my one condition, after I found out he was married. He promised me he didn't have children.'

'He knew about your mother?'

'Yes. I told him.'

'He's such a *shit*.'

'It's my own fault. Only an idiot would have believed him – an idiot who wanted to.'

'Esther says he's been to the flat.'

'The night he got back from America. He's left me alone since. He's trying to punish me. He thinks that if he leaves me alone for long enough, I'll get weak and go back to him. I got an email today, though – the first in weeks.'

'Christmas Day,' she nodded, rolling the biggest bead on her necklace between her fingers. 'Predictable, if he was going to. You didn't write back?'

I shook my head. 'I won't. I can't.'

She stopped playing with the bead and looked at me. 'You're frightened of him, aren't you?'

Again I broke the eye contact. 'I don't know. Maybe.'

'Has he ever hurt you – physically?'

'No.'

'You'd tell me?'

'Of course.' I stood up and went to take the mince pies out of the oven, glad of the opportunity to turn my face away. The pies had got properly hot and they burned my fingers as I lifted them from the baking tray. I breathed deeply and silently and then sat back down, sliding the plate on to the table between us. Helen was watching my face, trying to read it. 'The thing is,' I said, 'until today, I was beginning to believe he really had decided just to let it go. Now I don't think so.'

'So what do you think he's going to do?'

'I don't know. God, I used to be so dismissive of people who got into things like this. But I get it now – sometimes you know you're being manipulated and you know you'll probably end up heartbroken but you still think it's worth it. I should have left it once I knew he was married, of course I should, but I let myself believe him because I wanted to. I didn't want to go back to being on my own, working all the time, pretending I had a life, when I could have that, even for a few more months.'

'You were in love with him.'

'I thought he was in love with me. You know what really got to me the day I heard him? One of the first things he said was *I can explain*. It made me realise that we were the same as every other sordid affair the world over. It was just as clichéd and pathetic as that.' The memories of that morning came rushing back. No: I would not think about them. 'So,' I said, 'you see why I wasn't concentrating on my bike.'

102

'Why didn't you tell me this at the hospital?'

'You never liked him. I didn't want to admit you'd been right all along – I was ashamed. And I was angry with you for being right.'

'You know I'm not into point-scoring.'

'It wasn't just that. While I thought you were wrong, I didn't feel so bad about how things were between us – you and me . . .'

'I hated fighting with you.'

'It was my fault.'

'It was his fault.'

'No, I let him. I saw his jealousy of you as a sign that he loved me. I was flattered by it.' I breathed out, embarrassed. 'Have you got a cigarette?'

'You don't smoke.' She looked aghast and I had to smile that she was horrified at that but completely calm about the fact that I'd been sleeping with someone else's husband for a year and a half. She passed me the packet and I leant across the table for a light, holding my jumper back so that it didn't catch on the tea-lights she'd found in one of the drawers. Their wax was all liquid now.

'Just promise me you won't write back,' she said. 'However bad you feel. Make a clean break. I want you to meet someone better, someone really good.'

'I don't deserve it.'

'You shouldn't say that.'

'But it's true, isn't it? I know how selfish I am now – you can think you know yourself but you never really do till you're tested. I knew about his wife, but I carried on anyway.' I stood up and went over to the sink. I turned the taps on and scalding water rushed into the bowl, sending up thick billows of steam. In the time that we'd been talking, it had gone dark and the window reflected back only the image of the kitchen and Helen's anxious face watching me. I avoided her eyes and started collecting the saucepans and plates, scraping them noisily into the bin. The first plates sent banks of water over the side of the bowl and they steamed gently on the draining rack as though exhaling delicate

103

last breaths. Helen still hadn't said anything but she stood up and took the tea towel that was tucked over the bar on the oven door. In the glass, our reflections mirrored us as we worked, side by side for the first time in months.

Chapter Twelve

Out on the beach at Compton the next day the wind made it hard to talk. We leant into it as we walked, letting the cold blast away our hangovers. Helen's hair flew behind her like blackbird feathers, and her cheeks and ears were pink. I kept my lips pressed together to protect my teeth from the pain of contact with the air.

The tide was falling and we walked just below the high-water mark where the sea had left the sand firm. The beach here was russet, taking its colour from the cliffs on our right, and the retreating water had left the sand gently rippled, like its own echo. There was surprisingly little man-made debris along the tideline, hardly any of the usual beer cans, bottles and bits of plastic. Instead the wind had brought in a great harvest of seaweed, the waves tearing up the seabed and depositing quantities of black bubbled bladderwrack and the finer red weed whose name I didn't know, as well as the thin stuff that looked like rubber bootlaces.

Helen said something but the wind whipped her voice away.

'What?' I shouted.

'I said, it's so fresh you can taste it.' She picked up speed and ran ten or fifteen yards ahead before turning and flinging her arms wide. I smiled and followed, matching her footprints, inspired by her enthusiasm.

We walked to the end of the beach and then climbed the uneven steps back up the cliff to the car. I closed the door and the sound of the wind receded. In the passenger seat beside me Helen looked startlingly vivid, her eyes shiny. I pulled out of the car park and turned right, back on to the long straight piece I now knew was called the military road. I'd wanted to show her this part of the Island, the drive down to the lighthouse at St Catherine's. It was the bleakest, loneliest part of the coast but even on the days when I'd felt empty on the inside, I'd recognised its powerful beauty. There were only a few isolated buildings out here, and just after Freshwater Bay the road ran so close to the edge that I feared a strong gust of wind would blow us over. The erosion at the back of the Island was dramatic. In hard winters or violent storms, the line of the cliffs could radically redraw itself, whole sections of chalk and clay tumbling into the sea. I could tell that Helen was surprised at the wildness, the occasional farms, the few sheep eking out a living on the wind-harassed grass, the patchwork of fields whose new crops didn't yet cover the heavy winter earth. On our right the sea glittered, picking up the light like fish-scales. Seagulls rose suddenly from the cliffs, then wheeled away again on invisible currents. The sky was pallid now, the blue fading out in the early afternoon just as it had done the day before.

I'd woken before her and had lain in bed thinking about Richard. The night he'd told me he was married, the shock of it had been like a punch in the stomach. I'd felt sick, could barely take a breath. As soon as I'd been able to, I'd told him to go. He'd thrown his things into his overnight bag, every movement full of fury, and I'd watched as he'd picked up the oxblood wallet which I'd handled so carefully and shoved it into the back pocket of his jeans. The door of the flat had slammed behind him and I'd fallen back on to the bed and pulled myself into a ball. A minute or so later the front door of the building had slammed shut so hard that I could feel the reverberations of it through the floor. It would have woken everyone downstairs. My stomach was cramping over and over again and several times I'd thought that I would throw up. I'd been awake for the rest of the night in sheer disbelief, wondering how we could have gone so quickly from being close enough for me to tell him about my mother, to this. I even wondered whether I'd got it wrong, misheard somehow, but of course I hadn't. I'd known how I felt about him – I hadn't lied to myself about it – but the scale of my reaction still shocked me. I hadn't realised it was possible to feel desolation like it.

I'd expected him to ring and try to talk to me the next day but he didn't and there was nothing the day after or the day after that. With every one that passed I became more and more convinced that I had been an entertaining diversion, something to enjoy as long as it wasn't any trouble, and I told myself bitterly that I'd been a fool to believe it could have been real. The knowledge that he'd been married all along scored through my memories, making a lie of them. I barely left the flat and instead stayed on the sofa watching rubbish on television for hours at a time, drinking endless cups of tea, eating nothing. And yet part of me was waiting for the phone to ring or for an email, anything to tell me that he was thinking about me, that it had meant at least something. I wouldn't call him – I didn't want him back, I couldn't have him – but I just couldn't comprehend that it had all been a lie. Even if he had been married, I couldn't make myself believe that it had meant nothing to him. It just didn't make sense to me.

A couple of days into the New Year, more than a week later, I'd run out of milk for tea in the early evening and gone up the road to buy some. When I'd returned, he was sitting on the low step at the front door of the building. I'd stopped dead as soon as I saw him. His head was in his hands but he raised it when he heard my footsteps. In the dull glow of the automatic light, he looked wiped-out. His eyes were small and strained-looking, their usual challenge completely absent.

'I can't do this,' he said.

'What?' My heart had started pounding.

'Pretend I don't love you.' He looked away, as if he couldn't say the words to my face. 'I've been trying to leave you alone to get on with your life but I don't think I can do it.'

I gripped the metal railing round the stairs to the basement flat, feeling suddenly light-headed. I'd wanted to hear the words so much but not like this.

'I'm so lonely. I work and work – what for? None of it means anything – it's all pointless.'

'What about your wife? Doesn't she keep you company?'

He put his head back in his hands and addressed the mosaic tiles that covered the floor under the portico. 'Things haven't been right between us for a long time. It's not a real marriage any more. And she's ill.'

'Really? What's wrong with her?'

'She's depressed – seriously depressed. She can't work, she doesn't go out. All she does is sit at home and cry or stare at the television. She doesn't eat. She says she thinks about dying. I'm terrified that if I leave her . . .' He scuffed the ground with his foot. 'I couldn't live with myself. But I'm so tired of trying to make things better. She's been ill for five years and I just don't know whether she's ever going to get better, whether this is it – for the rest of our lives.' He reached into his pocket and took out his cigarettes. I stood and watched while he lit one and took a drag that suggested proper need. I was surprised; I couldn't have imagined the Richard I'd known for the past six months admitting to a weakness like needing cigarettes. I'd always thought of him as a social smoker, someone who saw it as an amusing minor vice in a life of otherwise effortless self-control.

'Then I met you,' he said. 'And suddenly, there was hope. I began to think maybe life didn't have to be this great cycle of sadness and trying and hopelessness. When I was with you, I felt different – as if there was someone who understood me.' To my horror there was a catch in his voice. His hands were held out now, fingers stiff, as if imploring me to accept the truth or trying to coax the difficult words out of his mouth. 'Don't worry,' he said. 'After what I've done, you should hate me. I just wanted you to know why.' He coughed. 'Ever since Sarah got ill, I've felt totally alone. And you seemed to understand what that feels like.'

The light timed out and plunged us into darkness; I swung my arm to trigger it again. 'The night we met,' I said. 'When I came back with you, why wasn't she there?' I thought of how bare his flat had been, the thrill of the strange emptiness which I had interpreted as evidence of his pared-down, masculine way of life.

'We had a trial separation but it made her even worse. She moved back in a couple of months ago.'

'Which is why you never minded coming here instead.'

'When I met you, we were on the way to sorting things out. We'd talked about divorce and agreed that it was the right thing

108

to do. But then she got worse again. At least if she was with me I could keep an eye on her, stop her doing anything stupid . . . And then she begged me to let us give it another go, told me that she worried about herself, her state of mind . . . I nearly broke it off with you then, I came all prepared with what I was going to say, but when it came to it, I just couldn't do it. I relied on you – the support you gave me without even knowing.'

He stood up suddenly, pulling himself wearily to his feet. 'Look, I'm going to go. I just wanted to tell you this so that perhaps you'd be able to understand a bit. Not hate me, anyway.'

The wind blew along the street and I pulled my cardigan round me. Thinking I was only going up the road for a pint of milk, I hadn't put a coat on and I was suddenly cold. Above us the stars were masked by banks of speeding cloud coloured sepia by the light pollution. 'I don't hate you,' I heard myself say.

He came down the steps until he was next to me. I could feel tension radiating off him. He seemed to be struggling, as if there was something else he wanted to say. I looked at his face and his eyes met mine only with difficulty. My chest ached.

He reached out his hand and very gently stroked the side of my face. The sensation spread out across my skin. I tried to imagine what it must be like, living with someone who was a danger to herself, afraid to end the relationship, that threat hanging over everything.

He took a step away. 'Bye, Katie,' he said.

'Richard –'

With the hand that wasn't holding the milk, I reached up and touched his cheek. He hadn't shaved and the stubble was rough under my fingertips. His eyes widened, as if in amazement that someone might possibly understand. They were shining, the tears I thought I'd heard close to the surface again.

Tentatively he reached up and covered my hand with his. Then he moved mine round so that my fingertips were against his lips. I could feel his breath. His eyes didn't leave mine for a second. All of a sudden, his arms were around me and he was holding me so tightly I thought he would crush me. 'I love you,' he said. 'I love you.'

'I love you, too.' My voice seemed to come from outside me.

And then he was kissing me. The desire that flooded me every time he touched me flowed through me again and the light-headedness returned. The pavement seemed to move under my feet and he sensed it and held me even tighter.

He took the keys that had been looped round my fingers and opened the front door. 'Are you coming?' he said, standing on the threshold. Within seconds, it seemed, we were upstairs in the tiny hallway inside my front door under the mistletoe that I hadn't yet taken down. 'I'll make everything right,' he whispered into my ear. I took lungful after lungful of his scent, breathing deeply as if I could internalise Richard himself, make sure that I was never without him again. 'I'll sort things out with Sarah. We'll be together properly, you and me. I promise.' He pulled back and looked into my eyes. I couldn't look away; it was too much to take in, the swoop from the abject misery of the past week to this new state, the promise of a future that I had only let myself think about in the most glancing of ways even when things had been their best between us.

He undid the top button of my cardigan and traced his fingers over the notch at the bottom of my throat. His expression was serious, the light in his eyes gone strangely flat, and I heard him swallow. My pulse leaped in response to his touch.

'Wait,' I said, putting my hand on his chest. 'Wait.'

'What?'

'Have you got children?'

He shook his head. 'No.'

'You promise me? Because I couldn't . . . My mother . . .'

'I promise. I want them, though.' He held my face between his palms. 'One day, I'd like to have children.'

When we reached St Catherine's I pulled up in the car park with the view out to sea. We'd brought chicken sandwiches and Helen poured coffee from the thermos she'd found in the back of the corner cupboard. When we'd finished eating she rolled the window down a couple of inches and lit a cigarette. 'I understand it now,' she said. 'Why you wanted to come here. I can feel my head clearing already.'

My eyes were on the horizon, the line where the sea met the sky blurring as I looked at it. 'Do you think you'll always live in London?' I asked.

'Depends. I've got no reason to move at the moment and there's work, obviously. But I don't think I want to get old there – there's something a bit beleaguered about old people – really old people – in the city. But if I don't want that, I'll have to move somewhere before then and start from scratch. I wouldn't know anyone.'

'You'd make friends, easy.'

'Would I, though? You meet people through work but how do you do it otherwise, unless you join weird clubs and societies that you wouldn't be seen dead at in your real life? I mean, are you meeting people?'

I hesitated. 'No. But I'm not really trying. It's my own fault.'

'I don't believe this crap about cities being faceless and hostile. It's small communities that huddle together and are all defensive.'

She turned her head to blow her smoke through the sliver of open window. It bloomed outside the car, the heat in the freezing air. 'I'll have to find someone to move with, that's the answer. From now on, I won't go out with anyone who isn't from a picturesque part of the world.'

'Have you met any candidates recently?' I was embarrassed to realise that I hadn't asked in the whole day we'd spent together, and excused myself only by thinking that she would have mentioned it.

'No one nearly good enough.' She laughed. 'Oh, I don't know – it's a vicious circle, isn't it? I don't meet people because I'm always at work but then at least if I work hard, I can afford my flat and have a decent life if I do end up on my own. I could work less hard and still not meet anyone. What are you supposed to do?'

Although she'd only been with me for a day and a half, that evening felt like the last night of a much longer visit. I dreaded her leaving and silence falling in the house again. There was still so much I wanted to talk to her about, to tell her about Richard, but I hadn't found the words.

It was nearly nine o'clock when we finished supper and left the house again, and the sky presented a deep blue background for the

111

cloud that was scudding across it like milk curd, lit by the moon. As we came up Bridge Road, I could see that some Christian soul had been out to scrub at the ragged red letters on the wall of the churchyard; only their ghosts remained visible in the muted street-lighting.

The Bugle Inn was the beautiful half-timbered Tudor building on the Square; its interior, we discovered, demonstrated a more eclectic approach to history. The original flagstones were visible in some places, there were framed prints of characters in eighteenth-century outfits and the ceiling had its original dark-stained beams but the bar was modern, a pine island which extended out into the room. The streets had been empty, of course, so it was a surprise to find the place relatively busy; more evidence, I thought, that the life of the town went on behind closed doors. Three men in their sixties sat on stools at the bar and there was a table of four just behind them. Other voices and shrill female laughter were audible from around the corner. Helen sat down in the bay window and I went to the bar.

'So this is where it all happens,' she said, as I put the glasses down.

'Seems like it.' I took a mouthful of the wine, which was a little sweet but not bad, and looked around. There were enough people in the bar to create a burr of noise that was more than the sum of its parts, and we were flanked by spare tables. No one would overhear. 'Helen,' I said. 'You know you asked me whether I was afraid of Richard?'

She took a sip from her glass and looked at me, suddenly alert.

'I'm not afraid, exactly. I mean, he doesn't know where I am, so even if . . .'

'You think he might come after you, if he did know?'

'I don't know.'

'But you said he never hurt you.'

I wondered how I could explain.

'If he had, you would have walked away, wouldn't you? That's the rule: no matter how much you like someone – or love them – the moment you get the slightest hint they might harm you, you walk away.'

We'd talked about it for years; it was one of our core beliefs, an inviolable principle. Part of our friendship, at least in the early days, had been built on our idea of ourselves as strong, brave women who brooked no bullshit. I couldn't let her see how much of a lie I had allowed that to become. Suddenly my desire to tell her was gone. There was no point anyway, I told myself; it wouldn't achieve anything.

'Yes,' I said. 'Of course. I don't know. It's nothing specific. Just, I know it will have made him angry, that's all, when I refused to talk to him.'

'Let him be angry,' she said. 'He lied and cheated – he deserves it.'

We finished our wine and Helen bought some more. As she handed me my glass and sat down again, my attention was caught by a man coming in. He was tall, easily a foot taller than the woman who came in with him, and I realised with a jolt that it was Peter Frewin and Sally. He hung his jacket on the back of a chair at a table not far from the door and they went to the bar together. Sally spent at least a couple of minutes scrutinising the wine list and in the end asked his opinion. I didn't hear his answer but he sensed the weight of my stare and glanced up to identify who was watching him. I saw a hint of recognition on his face but also puzzlement, as if he couldn't place me. Seeing him looking, Sally also looked over. I smiled but her face stayed oddly blank. I raised a hand; still nothing.

'Someone you know?' Helen asked.

I shook my head, confused. 'Not really. Just someone I've seen around.'

They got their drinks and went back to their table. He was facing away from me and though I was afraid to let my gaze wander over in case I made eye contact with Sally again, I couldn't help it. He was speaking in a low voice, his dark head inclined towards his hands as they filleted a beer mat, and she was leaning over the table to hear him, occasionally putting her hand on his forearm where it rested on the table, keeping her voice low, too. They had their one drink, then left.

'That was the man whose wife was lost from her boat just after I came here,' I said to Helen quietly when they'd gone. I'd told her

113

the story but only in outline; I hadn't mentioned how much Alice had preoccupied me.

'Doesn't look like he wasted much time filling the vacancy, does it?' she said.

'I don't think it's like that.'

By late morning the terminal building was busy with people returning to the mainland. The ferry's propellers were churning the water to a white green. The cars arriving had already rolled off and dispersed, and those going back were loading. I waited while Helen bought a ticket at the desk. Nearby a woman who looked only a year or two years older than us was trying to persuade the middle of her three daughters to pack up the trail of Lego she'd laid along the windowsill.

The steward moved the rope barrier at the end of the room and called for foot passengers to start boarding. Helen returned, adjusting the weight of her overnight bag on her shoulder. She was holding her ticket. 'I feel bad about leaving you here.'

'Don't be silly,' I said, putting on a smile. 'I'll be fine. I chose to come here.'

'You're so lonely.'

'It's fine. I'll get out more – promise. Come on, you'll miss it.' Apart from two or three people down by the door, like the last grains of sand in an egg timer, the room was now empty.

She put her bag down and pulled me into a tight hug. 'You look after yourself. Ring me. And come to London – soon.'

'I will.'

'And promise me you won't answer Richard if he gets in touch again?'

'I won't. Go on – they're closing the gate.'

She gave me a final look and then ran down towards the barrier, her bag banging on her back. I watched her go through and walk up the concrete slip to the gangplank, feeling as though I was watching my old life walking away again.

Outside, I waited on the quay for her to come out on deck and wave but there was no reason why she would think to do so. The ramp clanked as it curled up like a scorpion's tail after the last of

114

the cars. There was a hoot on the horn and a fine stripe of black smoke came from the funnel as the boat began to pull away. I watched until the people out on deck waving to their families were almost invisible and then I turned and went back to the house.

Chapter Thirteen

Later that afternoon, the gale blew up. I'd come to my desk as soon as Helen had gone, hoping to distract myself from the ache in my chest and the familiar emptiness which had reclaimed the house while I'd been out on the harbour front. Eventually I'd found a vein of concentration and I worked for a couple of hours before the first gust rattled the wooden sash and made me look up in surprise. Even as I watched, dark clouds were massing over the wood at Norton and advancing towards the town, casting shadows over the long winter grass on the other side of the road. The first drops of rain hit the window, heavy with intent, and another gust came almost at once to smear them over the glass.

Within half an hour, the wind had gained such momentum that when it buffeted the house, the whole front wall shuddered. The rain came in violent waves, dense enough to obscure the view. The usual half-hour of twilight was bypassed and the blackest night I could remember swallowed everything. There were no stars, no moon; even the streetlamps on the other side of River Road struggled to force out their light. The house felt so completely cut off that it might have been spinning through space, untethered. All night the wind howled around as if it were trying to find a way in. At times, lying in bed listening to it, I was afraid it would break the old glass in the windows and come swirling in like a flood tide, blowing the pages of the manuscript off the desk in the room next door and scattering them around the top floor, filling the curtains like sails. The lamp on the bedside table flickered and flickered again, the power barely hanging on.

Eventually I fell asleep, thinking that by morning the storm would have blown itself out, but when I woke up there was no change. I switched on the television for the local news and saw pictures of yachts toppled sideways in boatyards on the mainland and trees blown like straws across major roads. In Gosport, a man had been killed in his bed when his chimney collapsed and came through the roof into the room where he was sleeping. There were no ferries; all services to and from the mainland had been suspended. I stood at the bedroom window watching new banks of turbid cloud coming up from over the wood. The shallow water of the estuary jumped angrily in response to the wind's taunting; the Solent rolled with waves that fought one another and crashed against the harbour wall, the spray rising twenty and thirty feet into the air.

The storm felt like a protest, a challenge to my decision to stay. 'Why don't you come back now?' Helen had asked. 'I know Esther's got the flat until the spring but you can stay with me till then, have my spare room. You don't have to put yourself through this.'

'No,' I'd said. 'I'm going to stick it out.' And as I'd said it, I'd felt my resolve strengthen. It wasn't just Richard, the renewed need to stay away from the places he would know to look for me. On the beach at Compton on Boxing Day and watching the sea from the car at St Catherine's, I'd felt the start of something, a reconnection. Perhaps it had only been because she was with me but I'd felt myself briefly in sympathy with the Island again. The storm was a test but I'd made up my mind.

In the afternoon I had no choice but to go out. Helen and I had eaten everything that I had bought for the week and I wanted to buy more candles in case the power did go off. I wouldn't sit alone in the house in the dark, especially now. The wind was changing. Although it was as strong as ever, it was no longer buffeting and jostling the house as if displaying its strength but whining and wheedling instead. It came crying round the windows and down the chimney, pleading to be allowed in, like a wretched child or an animal in pain. The sound was upsetting; I felt it in my chest as much as heard it.

At noon the next day there was a lull in the wind and the sky lightened. There was brightness behind the cloud, as if the sun was trying to find its way through, but then it grew dark again and the wind seemed, if anything, to have gathered new force. Helen rang a little after three to suggest that I go up and stay for New Year. I told her I'd think about it but the idea of going to a party was outlandish. I would go up in a few weeks, I decided, after I had handed in the manuscript and when I had shaken off the uncomfortable feeling that Richard's new contact had given me. Though I was distracted by the storm and also by work, if I allowed my mind to wander, it would slip me memories of him like a croupier dealing out cards.

For a time after he had turned up at the flat last year, I had been happy. I allowed myself to believe him when he told me that his marriage was just a formality now, a framework he maintained not because he was in love with his wife but because he cared for her and had promised himself he would look after her, financially and as a friend, until her health improved and she didn't need him any more. I could understand why he hadn't told me, that he hadn't wanted to change the way things were between us or to destroy my trust in him. And every time I thought about how close I had come to losing him, going back to my old life, I felt a wash of panic.

And now we talked about love. If I had been afraid before that telling him I loved him would scare him off or make him feel he had won me too easily, that fear was gone. The intensity with which he behaved around me was thrilling, even sometimes, I allowed myself to admit, a little frightening. When we were together, it was rare for me to look up and find he wasn't watching me. If he could be close to me, he would be. His hands seemed always to be on me, touching my hair or my face, sliding between the buttons of my shirt or resting under the waistband of my jeans. And if we had spent a lot of time in bed before, now it seemed we were hardly out of it. The sex had changed, too. It was never light-hearted or fun any more; instead it seemed to be the physical expression of this new need for a certainty about our feelings for one another. Sometimes my muscles would ache the day after I'd

118

seen him from the force with which I had gripped him, and he me. New bruises started to appear on my skin in the places where his fingers had dented my flesh.

I remembered one evening in particular. He had been in Spain for two days for a meeting with his chief contractor, though we'd spoken so much during his trip that I felt as though he'd hardly been away at all. As soon as his taxi from the airport had dropped him off and he'd come up the stairs, he'd started taking my clothes off, kissing me all the time so that I hardly had time to say hello. We'd made love on the sitting-room floor, the blinds still up and the lights on, if not immediately visible to the people in the flats opposite, then at least clearly so to anyone who stood at their window and looked across. Afterwards he hadn't moved off me but stayed where he was, pinning me to the carpet, my arms under his where he held them on either side of my face. His weight was beginning to get heavy on my pelvis and I shifted, trying to move the pressure off it.

'Where are you going?' he said, looking down at me.

'Nowhere. You're heavy.' I wriggled, hoping that he would get the hint and take the weight off a bit but he didn't.

He lowered his face and kissed me, a little roughly. 'I keep thinking about that night,' he said.

'Which?'

'At Christmas, when you threw me out. Didn't you love me then?'

'Richard . . .' I laughed a little, not seeing how it could even occur to him.

'If you really loved me, you wouldn't have been able to do that. You didn't even try to ring me,' he said. He tilted his head to one side, as if he were considering the thing from a different angle. I tried moving again, increasingly uncomfortable. His sweat was sticky on my skin and the hair on his chest was beginning to make me itch.

'You're being silly,' I said, pulling my arm out from under his and tipping his chin up so that he was forced to look at me. 'How could I love you more than this?'

He seemed to snap out of it. 'I don't know,' he said. He raised his torso off mine and sat up on his haunches. I was struck by the sheer heft of him, the power in his thighs and the muscles across his chest and shoulders. 'Perhaps I'll have to get you to show me.'

By New Year's Eve, the worst of the storm was over. The wind had died away and the final, lighter bands of rain were falling. On the early-evening forecast the satellite pictures showed a better front coming in across the Atlantic. I'd bought a decent bottle of wine in honour of the new year and, just before midnight, I went downstairs to refill my glass. The absence of the wind had left a strange silence, like the feeling of relief after a toothache, and in it the softest sounds had become distinct. The rain was pattering against the window over the sink and I could hear it bubbling down the drain outside. Listening carefully, I could just make out voices coming through the wall from the house next door.

Into the peace, shockingly loud, my mobile upstairs rang once to tell me that I had a message. Helen, I thought, texting from the party. I went up to answer her.

The message wasn't from Helen, though. *I'm thinking about you tonight*, he'd written. *Happy New Year.*

I dropped the phone on to the table. The skin on the back of my neck was prickling. After a moment or two, I picked the phone up again, read the message once more to be sure I hadn't imagined it, then deleted it. I took a couple of large mouthfuls of wine and went downstairs. On the shelf to the right of the fireplace was the packet of cigarettes Helen had forgotten. There were two left. I took one and found the matches in the kitchen. I thought about going outside to smoke but beyond the glass of the sliding doors the yard was in darkness. I took great gulps at the cigarette, aware of the tremble in my hands and the racing of my heart. *I will not be afraid*, I told myself; *I will not be afraid.*

Chapter Fourteen

At the tiny post office I waited my turn behind a couple who had come in to collect their pensions. I was getting used to the pace at which people moved here, the apparent view that errands were social occasions but also the rarity of the barely concealed rage that characterised queues in London. In my hands was the finished translation; I always sent a hard copy as well as an emailed one. Surreptitiously I lifted it as if checking the postcode and brushed my lips against it for luck, a habit which had started with the first book I'd worked on. Richard had laughed when I told him. 'Sweetheart, you're so quaint.'

Walking out into the street again, I had an end-of-term feeling. I was going to have lunch at the café on the pier and then walk up to Totland and along the beach. On my way back I would go to the bookshop. I hadn't been since the week before Christmas, almost a month, and dropping in to see Chris seemed the easiest way of honouring my promise to Helen to make more effort socially. It was still cold – very cold – but the light had the clarity that I was beginning to think of as peculiar to the sea. Bathed in it, everything seemed incredibly bright, somehow super-real.

I hadn't been to Gossips since I'd been back. It was smarter than it had been when we were children, if slightly twee. The wooden floor was varnished and shelves displayed items of retro kitchenware – striped china jars and scales with weights – and black-and-white photographs of the town. I chose a table with views of the Solent at the front and the beach at the George to my left, sitting down just as a pair of gulls flew by the window, one holding something in its beak, the other giving chase. They landed on the shingle in a battering of wings, both issuing their ugly cry, the one in triumph as it swallowed its morsel, the other in indignant disbelief.

I watched the waitress as she worked. A couple of days earlier on one of my afternoon walks I'd seen a sign in the window of the other little café up the High Street advertising for someone part time and I'd gone in to apply. 'Am I being mad?' I asked Helen when I rang her that evening.

'I don't see why. If you've got a gap between books and you fancy it, why not? Give yourself a break from all that time on your own.'

'I don't think it'd pay much but that's not really the point. It'd be fun – it'd remind me of all the waitressing I did when I was a teenager.' In Bristol I'd worked on Saturdays and in the holidays at a café down on the waterfront, and I'd ended up saving a couple of thousand pounds towards my university fees. I'd also waitressed in a brasserie in the Marais during my student year in Paris. It was something I associated with happy periods of my life.

By the time I'd finished my lunch at Gossips and walked up to Totland, it was three. I tramped along, feeling fitter already, enjoying the heat I'd worked up inside my coat. The breeze on my face had a rinsing quality. There were other people on the beach, including a woman walking a large red setter. The fur on its legs and undercarriage was hanging in wet ropes where it had been in the sea and I hurried to get out of the way as it planted itself four-square and prepared to shake.

I walked to the end of the bay and then turned round to see how far I'd come. Everything was clean and sharp, as if it had been glazed: the buoys marking the lobster pots, the pebbly beach, the skeleton of the derelict pier. I took deep breaths of the chill air, feeling the weeks of close work lifting from me. I could see the way forward now. If I got the job at the café I would have a framework for my time. I could get agency translating work – brochures, catalogues – if I started feeling anxious about eating up my tiny savings account. It was mid-January already and with even a degree of structure, the weeks would pass more quickly.

Then it would be time to go back to London and I would have done it, stuck it out.

Surprisingly, there had been no more contact from Richard since his text on New Year's Eve. I'd been afraid that, along with the message at Christmas, it had been the vanguard of a new campaign but that didn't seem to be the case after all. I was glad I hadn't mentioned the second message to Helen; she would have asked again why I was worried and I would have been back in the same position, wanting both to tell her and to conceal it. Keeping quiet had been the right decision.

'Hello again. Is it too late to wish you a happy new year?' Chris looked at the books I'd handed him with the expression of assessment that I had seen before. 'I was wondering if you'd left us, thought maybe the Island had got a bit much and you'd decamped back to the mainland.'

'No,' I said. 'I'm staying.'

He nodded. 'Your reading rate's dropped off, though. Been busy?'

I explained about the deadline.

'Well then, now you've got a bit more time and I know you're still here, why don't you come for supper on Friday? If you've got nothing more exciting on.'

I was taken aback. 'That's . . .'

'Nothing grand,' he said. 'A bite to eat and a bottle of wine. I'm just up the road from here.' He found a piece of paper and sketched out a few lines, marking his house with an asterisk. I looked at it, unsure what to say. 'Eight, eight thirty,' he was telling me. 'I'll look forward to it. You can tell me more about your translating.'

I walked until I was out of sight of the windows before stopping. The little map was still in my hand and I looked at it. I'd been railroaded and it seemed like I was going to have to go – it would be too rude not to. Probably, I thought, he'd guessed how lonely I was and inviting me was an act of kindness. I felt my heart sink as I imagined myself there, making awkward conversation with him and his wife. Putting the map in my pocket, I started the walk back. I'd gone about a hundred yards when I got cross with myself. You're pathetic, I thought; he's being friendly and it's only one evening. And anyway, think about it: if you go, the next time Helen asks, you'll be able to say you've been out.

The view from Mary's Café couldn't compete with the one at Gossips; instead of the sweep of the Solent and the stripe of the mainland with the nest of masts in the Lymington River and the wooded foreshore up towards Beaulieu, the plate-glass window gave out on to the street. Even now, it amused me that this was the High Street; it was one-way only and not wide enough for two cars to pass.

I surveyed the interior of the café from my place behind the counter, enjoying the feeling of playing a game that came with the first-day newness of it all. I liked the way the room had been fitted out. It was the entire width of the building but still only large enough for eight of the pale oak tables. On the walls there were large framed photographs of the Island, not the typical tourist shots but long-distance views of the fields and the higgledy-piggledy roofline at Ryde and the estuary at Newtown. The counter was at the back of the room, another chunky stretch of oak on which were laid out bowls of salads and the three home-made cakes which Mary told me was the winter quota; in summer, she said, she'd make another two. When I'd been in for my interview the previous day, I'd suspected she was about to offer me the job when she showed me the heated pot in the small kitchen and explained that one of my responsibilities would be to take the soup out of the fridge and make sure it was hot by the time people were likely to start ordering it. The bread was delivered first thing and I would need to be in when the baker's van arrived.

Mary was in her mid-forties, I guessed, with a laugh like a fox-bark and an abrupt manner slightly at odds with her warm eyes. Her curly brown hair was cut short, and her denim skirt and cream jumper clothed a figure padded in a way I found reassuring in a café owner. She'd had the place since the previous spring, she told me, her teenage daughter helping out in the school holidays and on Saturdays, but she wanted someone in the week so she had more time to spend with her elderly mother. She'd struck me immediately as someone leading a life so crammed with commitments that she was on the point of losing her grip on them all; this morning when she'd come to open up and show me the ropes, she'd had to go back round the corner to her house in Baskett's Lane because she'd forgotten the keys in her hurry. I was amazed when she told me that she made everything apart from the bread herself.

I'd been wrong, I saw now, to imagine that working here would be much more sociable than translating at home. There had been customers, of course, but not many: five or six for coffee and cake over the course of the morning, another six or seven over a lunch hour that extended from noon until half past two. A couple of them I recognised as locals, people I'd seen in the Square or on the harbour, but the rest seemed to be passing trade. I wondered why the locals didn't come in when the food was so good. Perhaps it was the prices: not extortionate but certainly more expensive than the cafés on the Square. Perhaps, though, it was the rocket and quinoa and alfalfa in the salad bowls.

No one had offered much in the way of conversation. In fact, beyond ordering, none of them had said anything at all: no pleasantries, not even a desultory comment on the weather. They came up to the counter, told me what they wanted, then sat at the tables, facing away, speaking to each other in low voices, reading newspapers if they were on their own. Oh well, I thought, at least it was a change of scene and Mary was nice enough, and another person that I could now legitimately claim to know in Yarmouth. And maybe people would start to talk to me over time, when my face became familiar.

Chris's house was one of the imposing red-brick Victorians on the road up out of Totland towards the Needles. The short gravel drive was overlooked by a number of established yew trees, their shapes illuminated by the automatic light that had come on as I pulled up. The house itself, though, was in darkness, no lights showing at any of the windows. Perhaps he'd forgotten and I was off the hook; I could go back to the cottage and spend the evening reading instead. I'd been apprehensive about coming; even after

I'd talked myself out of my initial resistance, it seemed an alarming acceleration of intimacy to go from being a customer at the shop to a dinner guest. I couldn't just drive off, however, so I got out and went to ring the doorbell. The coloured glass of the fanlight was unlit, too, and there was no sound of movement from inside. While I waited, I looked around. Beside the iron boot-scraper, there was a box of newspapers for recycling: the *County Press* and *The Times*. I was standing on a tiled mosaic area like the one under the portico of my building in Earls Court and immediately my mind dealt me the memory of the evening that Richard had lain in wait for me there, to talk me into taking him back.

I was just about to go when I heard footsteps behind the door and it opened. 'Kate, lovely to see you.' Chris stepped forward out of the gloom to kiss me on the cheek. 'Come in.'

He stepped aside to let me pass. Behind him the hallway was unlit and smelled of dust. In what light reached in from outside, I could make out the shape of a dresser against the far wall and a rim of light around a door which now swung open a little. His wife, I thought, but instead there was the skittering of claws across the tiles and a thump against my thigh as a large dog made contact. I looked down and made out two huge eyes in a golden Labrador face.

'This is Ted,' said Chris, as the dog spun around me, sniffing vigorously, the thick cable of his tail sweeping from side to side. I reached down to stroke his head and he pointed his nose towards the ground to allow me access to the soft place between his ears. 'He has his limitations as a guard dog, as you can see.' He got hold of him by the collar. 'Come on, you, let Kate take her coat off.'

'Sorry about the light – or lack of it,' he said, going in the direction of the door through which Ted had appeared. 'The bulb blew earlier on and I'd forgotten to get any spares. But we're a bit brighter in here.'

My spirits revived a little when I saw the kitchen. It was a large room, the units which made up the L-shaped working area wooden-fronted and topped with marble. A long farmhouse table occupied the far end, which had been extended into a sort of conservatory, its wall made up of a series of glass doors which looked as though they folded back in a concertina to leave the room open to the garden. There was no sign of the Belling cooker I'd been imagining seconds earlier and instead of the dry pork chops and furry boiled potatoes I'd begun to picture, the air was full of the scent of a rich garlicky sauce. Two bottles of wine were breathing on an island counter surrounded by stools; the papers which I guessed usually covered it were gathered at one end into a shaggy pile topped by a pair of half-moon reading glasses.

I handed him the bottle I'd brought and he looked quickly at the label. 'Thank you,' he said. 'That's very nice. Now, what can I get you?'

'Wine would be great.' I ventured further into the room, closely marked by Ted. In the light, I could see the distinguished white of the elder statesman around the muzzle which he was pressing into my hand. There was white in the fur above his eyes, too, and a slight stiffness in the movement of his back legs.

Chris handed me a glass. 'New friends,' he said, raising his own.

I took a large mouthful, slightly embarrassed. Especially now, seeing him in context at home, I was aware that though he was probably in his sixties, he was still a man people would describe as handsome. There was an elegance about his face, a fineness around the eyes and the bridge of his long straight nose. 'This is a lovely room,' I said, making a show of looking around.

'Thank you. I spend most of my time in here; I like sitting at the counter – it's good for thinking. And it's very nice in summer with the doors open.' He walked over to flick a switch on the far wall and the garden was flooded with light. I went to the window and cupped my hands around my eyes. A soft-looking lawn sloped away from the house towards a rim of tall pine trees under which the grass petered out.

'It's low maintenance, which appeals to me.'

'You're not a gardener then?'

'My wife was – Miranda. She died seven years ago. Breast cancer.'

'I'm sorry.'

He smiled gently. I came back over to the counter as he picked up a dish of olives which he offered to me. 'Do you smoke?' he asked, as I bit into one.

127

'Officially, no.'

He smiled again, this time more broadly. 'Miranda begged me for years to give up but I started again when she died and I've found it hard to stop completely since then. Shall we?' He slid a packet out from its hiding place beneath the pile of newspapers.

'By the way, I've asked another friend of mine along tonight,' he said, lighting my cigarette and then his own. 'Peter. I hope you don't mind; I thought it might be a good idea. Before he gets here, though, I should tell you that he lost his wife, too. Rather more recently – in the autumn.'

'Peter Frewin.'

'You know him?' He was surprised.

'No, no,' I said. 'I heard about it – in Yarmouth. In the paper.'

'Of course.' He nodded. 'You know the story then. A very great shame.' He took a sip of wine. 'He won't mention it at all but I thought you should know.'

From the hall came the sound of the front door closing and in a trice Ted was up from his spot at our feet and nosing his way back through the swing door. There was a single joyful bark, the sound of jumping up and a quiet male voice, and then footsteps and a figure in the doorway. I turned my head to see him towering there, the kitchen lights illuminating his face, the hall behind him in darkness.

Chris put a hand on his shoulder as he came into the room, then turned to pour him some wine. 'Peter, this is Kate,' he said. 'She's just moved to the Island; she's in Yarmouth with you, in one of the coastguard cottages.'

'We've met,' said Peter, taking a sip and letting his eyes rest on me briefly.

'Have you?' Chris looked at me.

'When I was trying to stroke Peter's cat,' I said, feeling foolish.

'Oh,' he said. 'Right. Well, I hope you're both hungry; I've made a casserole.'

Peter took an olive from the dish and went to sit on the low floral sofa under Chris's corkboard. There was a basket lined with a blanket nearby but a suspiciously dog-sized indent on the sofa itself. No sooner had Peter sat down than Ted clambered on to his lap. 'Oof,' he said, as the air was squashed out of him.

'Gently please, Ted,' said Chris, opening the fridge door and taking out a butter dish. 'Or it's WeightWatchers for you.'

Peter waited while Ted trod all over him in pursuit of a comfortable position and eventually sat sideways across his knee, obscuring his view. He shifted forward a little and slung his arm around the dog's neck, pulling him back against him.

'Kate, top yourself up,' said Chris. 'Don't run dry.'

I did so, grateful for something to do and noticing that I was already beating him, needing only to refill his glass by an inch while mine was almost empty. It was good, though; I could feel the wine taking the edge off my awkwardness, putting down a layer of insulation. I looked over at Peter, who was stroking Ted's ears, letting his fingers slide over the velvet fur. I glanced away again quickly before he became aware of me watching. He looked tired but much better than when I'd seen him in the Square the day after the body that wasn't Alice's had been recovered. What did he feel like now? I wondered. How long did it take to get over something like that?

'Have you got to know your neighbours, Kate?' Chris was dropping French beans into a steaming saucepan.

'I've hardly even seen them,' I said. 'But I haven't introduced myself. Maybe it's a London thing – living side by side with people and letting them stay strangers. Could I have another cigarette?'

'Help yourself. No need to ask.'

I took one and lit it, feeling as self-conscious as an unpractised teenager. Peter wasn't looking at me but there was a watchfulness about him, something in his expression that made me think he was taking in what Chris and I were doing though he was paying far more attention to Ted. I remembered the first cigarette I'd had on the Island, on the bench at the bottom of the common with his wife, her strange excitement. She'd been so vivid then, I thought, and yet so close to dying.

'I'll go down to the yard tomorrow, Chris.'

'Ah, I was going to ask.'

'We'll need to talk about what still needs doing.'

'I've got a list; I'm afraid it's getting rather long. Peter's helping me look after my boat,' he explained. 'I used to be able to do it all myself but I'm a bit past it now.'

'For God's sake,' Peter said, with a hint of vehemence. 'You're sixty-two. He's got a bad back,' he said to me, 'rather than one foot in the grave.'

I felt myself flush, as if he'd known what I was thinking. My cheeks were getting rosier anyway, as they always did when I drank red.

He tipped Ted gently off his lap and came over to the counter for another olive. I watched the movement in his jaw as he chewed it. There were deep lines at the corners of his eyes and quite a lot of grey in the short hair above his ears. On the cuff of his jumper there was a splash of blue paint.

'Do you like Yarmouth?' he said, picking up the stub of pencil that had been lying on a paper folded to the crossword. He started to flick it between his fingers, under and over and back again, a trick I'd tried and failed to learn at school.

'It's quite quiet,' I said, 'but I'm getting used to it. I like the pier and the walk out to Fort Victoria. And the river's lovely – up by the sailing club and the scows.'

Out of the corner of my eye, I saw Chris shoot a quick glance at Peter. *Shit – Alice's scow.* Peter turned abruptly and went over to the glass doors where he faced away, looking out over the garden. I couldn't look at him: he would see my reflection in the glass. You idiot, Kate, I thought; you absolute idiot.

Chris took the casserole out of the oven and rested it momentarily on the hob. 'Right, this is ready,' he said briskly. 'Kate, if you'd like to sit down. Bring that bottle over if you would.'

My face felt scarlet as we ate, with embarrassment, the wine and also heat: the room seemed suddenly to have become very hot. I kept my eyes down, afraid of meeting Peter's and furious with myself. Clearly, the brief grace period when the wine had just lessened my shyness without affecting my ability to think had ended.

'Kate's a translator,' Chris told Peter, who was passing down a surreptitious titbit to Ted.

'Actually,' I said, 'I'm a waitress.'

'Really?'

'Yep. Just started this week – Mary's on the High Street.'

'Just down from you, Peter. I'll pop in next time I'm in Yarmouth.'

'I just got too lonely,' I said, though neither of them had asked. 'That's why I started it. I mean, where is everyone in Yarmouth? It's like a bloody ghost town at night – no one on the streets, everyone locked away safely behind their front doors. Is there a war on – some sort of curfew I haven't heard about?'

Peter glanced up quickly and there was amusement in his eyes, quickly suppressed when he realised I'd seen. Was he laughing at me?

I insisted on clearing the plates, wanting the opportunity to turn out of view for a few moments. I'd had four glasses now, I thought, and I was starting to feel as though I didn't have complete control over my face; my mouth in particular felt slightly alien, not to be trusted not to smile in inappropriate places. I'd reached that stage of drunkenness, too, where I'd lost any will to stop drinking. Chris had realised it, too, evidently; on the last round of top-ups, he'd added only a tiny amount to my glass. I was beginning to feel better, though; even confident.

Over pudding, I relaxed some more. I propped my elbow on the table and started telling them about the holidays I'd spent on the Island when I was younger. I'd lost my nervousness and the words started to flow. I told them how great Dad had been, how much effort he'd put into making sure we'd had a good time – the barbecues on the beach, the crabbing lines, the boat trips. Chris made small comments but Peter listened in silence and for most of the time I had the floor. It felt good, like a return to the socially successful version of myself I hadn't been for a long time. I could do this: be entertaining, make people laugh. Buoyed up, I carried on, finding myself more and more amusing. We finished the bottle and I cajoled Chris into opening another.

It was when I stood up to help clear the pudding dishes that I knocked over his glass. It had been full and the wine splashed everywhere, over the tablecloth, the other plates, into the fruit bowl. Shards of glass glittered on the leftover treacle tart. 'I'm sorry; I'm so, so sorry,' I said, dabbing wildly with my napkin.

'It's no problem,' said Chris, standing slowly and revealing the wine stains on the thighs of his trousers. 'No, no – Kate, leave it. Sit down – I'll do it.'

Peter stood up, too. 'I should go,' he said. 'I'll see you tomorrow, Chris; thanks for supper.'

'Hang on – you're not driving, I hope?'

'No, I want to walk.'

'Walk? At this time of night? You're both going back to Yarmouth; why don't you get a taxi together?'

'No,' he said loudly. 'I mean, I want to walk. I'll see you tomorrow at the yard.' He nodded in my direction without looking at me, grabbed his jacket from the peg just inside the door and was gone.

The front door slammed shut behind him and I sat back down. 'That's my fault,' I said.

'Don't be silly. He's still very raw,' he said. 'I invited him because I thought the company would be good for him but I misjudged it – it's too early. My mistake.'

'I'm really sorry. And I'm sorry about the tablecloth, and your trousers. Let me do the washing up.' I stood up again and reached for his empty pudding dish.

He put his hand on it, stopping me. 'Put that down and I'll ring you a taxi.' He got up and went out to the phone in the hallway. There was the sound of touchtone buttons. Left alone for a moment, I saw my reflection and beyond the glass, nothing but the darkness. I could feel it as if it were a physical presence, pressing against the windows, waiting for me.

The taxi that came was some sort of people carrier. Chris kissed my cheek and helped me in, stopping me from falling back when I tripped over the seatbelt. The driver was talkative on the way but required only minimal audience participation. He chattered on, delighted, it seemed, to have a new set of ears for his well-practised anecdotes, and I leaned my hot temple against the glass and watched the verge flashing past us. There was a strange buzzing in my ears, as if I were wearing ear-plugs, muffling out the world and hearing the working of my own brain instead. Everything felt distant, slightly too bright, liable to start spinning at any moment.

It was some time before we reached Peter; he'd got much further than I'd expected and I soon saw why: he was striding out, each step covering a yard, his shoulders back, his arms stiff at his sides, hands in fists, walking into the night as if he were marching into battle. Perhaps, I thought, it was conscience trouble.

Back at the house, I fell into a drunken, dreamless sleep. Waking parched at four, I went to the bathroom and drank three lots of water from the tooth mug before going back to bed. Later in the morning, long after it was light, I woke to find that quite apart from the remorse about the evening already side-swiping at me, a pall of melancholy had settled over everything like a fine coating of dust.

In the second bout of sleep, I'd dreamed about Richard, a dream with no beginning and no real end. We'd been standing on opposite sides of a huge iron gate, not ornamental wrought-iron but the sort used to keep people in or out, heavy bars extending from floor to ceiling, banded across in several places. Richard had gripped the bars and I held them, too, but for some reason our hands wouldn't touch. The yearning I felt was painful; I would have given anything in the world to have become smoke and passed through to his side. He spoke and though at first I couldn't hear the words, their effect was immediate: the bars in the upper part of the gate softened enough for him to pass his face through to my side. Our hands, too, suddenly touched and we wove our fingers together, holding on so tightly that I was aware of all our bones. He rubbed his cheek against mine and the yearning intensified. The feel of his skin was gentle but erotic, too, sending a charge through me. Then even that barrier seemed to dissolve, so that where our skin touched, he became me, and me him and all I wanted was to lose myself in him like I used to. He was smiling and I felt a smile forming on my lips, too. He spoke again and this time I heard him. 'While you still want me, I can find you,' he said.

Chapter Fifteen

On Monday it was my birthday. Cards from Dad and Matt had arrived on Saturday and I opened them now, deducing from the fact that the one from Matt didn't have a Far Side cartoon on that Melissa had chosen it. Dad had sent me an iTunes voucher and I realised that it had been weeks since I'd listened to any music. I'd fallen out of the habit, having found it too painful after the break-up with Richard. Also I felt strangely vulnerable when I had earphones in and couldn't hear what was going on around me. That bothered me now.

Helen's card was lying on the kitchen floor when I went downstairs to make a cup of coffee, blown away into the room by the draught under the door. 'Present being held in London as bait,' she had written inside.

Upstairs again, I put the coffee on the table, got back into bed and pulled the blankets round me. Last year I had woken up with Richard. It had been a brighter day than today and the block of light from the narrow window had been falling across the bed when I'd opened my eyes to find him propped on his elbow, looking at me.

I'd put my hand over my face. 'Don't scrutinise me. I look terrible.'

'You look beautiful.'

I kept my mouth closed while he kissed me. 'Wait a moment.'

I'd cleaned my teeth while I waited for the kettle to boil and then I'd taken our coffee through to the bedroom. Richard was sitting up, his back resting on the wall. I felt my usual pang of desire at the sight of his chest and shoulders, the five o'clock shadow.

There was something so glamorous about him, even first thing; I often thought that it was as if he had dropped out of someone else's life and into mine by mistake, expensive cargo destined for somewhere more exciting, lost by accident.

I got back into bed next to him to open my birthday cards. Two pieces of thick paper had fluttered out from Helen's on to the quilt. They were tickets for the opera, the new production of *The Magic Flute* that she knew I wanted to see. I hadn't been able to get tickets: it had sold out almost immediately. She must have brought them then and tucked them away for me, waiting for today, not saying anything even when I'd told her how disappointed I was not to see it.

'What is it?' Richard had said. 'Why are you upset?'

'I'm not – it's just Helen. She's so kind.'

He took the tickets from me. 'I didn't know you liked opera.'

'Well, I've only been a couple of times. I loved it, though.'

He dropped them on the quilt and threw back the covers. 'I'm getting up.'

'But it's only seven,' I said, smiling and moving my arms so that the sheet slipped a little. 'And it's my birthday.'

'I haven't got time.' He left the room and moments later I heard the sound of taps running in the bathroom. Surprised, I got out of bed and took his shirt, my favourite pale blue one, from the chair where he'd left it the night before. Knowing he found it sexy when I wore his shirts, I put it on, leaving the top three buttons undone.

The door was shut, which was unusual, but when I tried the handle it wasn't locked. I went in and sat on the side of the bath, crossing my legs in what I hoped was a seductive manner just inside his line of vision. His eyes flicked quickly towards me and then back again. He was shaving and the basin was full of soapy water. I watched as he lifted his chin, stretching the skin taut underneath it and drawing the razor up the length of his throat, his eyes never leaving their image in the mirror. The edge of the blade flashed. I crossed my legs the other way but without response from either man or reflection. He swilled the razor in the water and knocked it against the side of the basin before drawing another line through the soap up the side of his neck.

135

'Why are you angry with me?'

He said nothing and swilled the razor again. A few seconds passed.

'I said, why are you angry?'

'For fuck's sake.' He threw the razor into the sink, splashing scummy water.

I stood up and left the room, closing the door behind me. In the sitting room, I opened my laptop and switched it on. When it was ready, I started typing up some notes. From the bathroom came the sound of the shower and a few minutes later I heard Richard walk behind me back to the bedroom and then the rattle of hangers as he took a fresh shirt from amongst the ones he now kept in my wardrobe.

I raised my head when I felt him coming across the carpet behind me again but I didn't turn around. I remembered the morning when he'd lifted me from this chair and carried me next door and felt another wave of disappointment. I watched him now in the reflection in the window as he reached out his hand to touch my hair.

'I'll give you your present this evening,' he said. 'At dinner. I'll come and pick you up at eight.'

He took me to Pétrus. I'd heard about it, of course, but never thought I'd go there. The morning's argument, if that was what it was, appeared to have been forgotten. The restaurant, decorated the colour of the claret after which it was named, was as intimate as a cocoon and Richard's attention hardly seemed to stray from me for a second. I looked around, taking it all in but – perhaps because he was used to this sort of place – he seemed oblivious. He ate his sea bass without comment, while I had to restrain myself from exclaiming over almost every mouthful of my lamb.

When our plates had been taken away, he reached into the inside pocket of his jacket and took out an envelope which he slid across the table towards me. 'Happy birthday.' His fingers touched mine as I tentatively reached to take it. For a reason I wasn't sure of, my heart had started to beat faster.

'Open it then.'

I glanced up at him as I slid a knife under the flap. His eyes didn't leave my face. Inside were two first-class Eurostar tickets to Paris.

'I thought you could show me your language skills. Though I'm sure they speak English at the Ritz.'

'The Ritz? Richard, you can't – this is much too generous.'

'Extravagant, you mean. You'll live.'

I looked at the tickets again. They were for early February, two weeks' time.

'What?' he said, seeing my expression change.

'Helen's opera tickets are for the same day.'

'She'll have to swap them then.'

'She won't be able to. It's sold out.'

His face darkened. 'So you're choosing an evening with Helen over three nights in Paris with me?'

'No, of course not,' I said, lowering my voice. 'You know it's not like that. Can't we just move it back a day?'

'No.' He reached over, took the tickets from my hand and put them back in his pocket. 'Do you have any idea how hard it is, making the time to see you?' he said in a voice little louder than a whisper. 'Do you think it's easy, inventing excuses for being away so much? Do you think Sarah doesn't comment on how often I'm in Spain? I'm doing my best – for precious little appreciation from you.'

I felt guilty immediately. 'I'm sorry,' I said. 'I didn't think.'

'Clearly.' He motioned to the waiter for the bill. We sat in silence and Richard handed over his credit card without even checking the amount.

I looked out of the window as the taxi carried us the short distance back along the Cromwell Road to my flat. The neo-Gothic façade of the Natural History Museum loomed up massive and spotlit. I remembered Dad taking us there years ago. Matt and I had stood in front of the skeleton of the Tyrannosaurus rex and imagined being eaten. 'Like a snack,' Matt had said, with reverence. That time seemed impossibly remote now, a different life. How could I have been that innocent little girl?

I was dreading the argument that would erupt as soon as we were in private but when the taxi pulled up outside my building, Richard didn't move.

'Aren't you coming up?' I hesitated, my hand on the door.

'I'm going home. I need to think. This isn't right.'

I got out and turned away quickly, before he could see the alarm on my face. The cab rounded the corner as I struggled to get the key into the door with shaking hands. Upstairs in the flat, I sat down on the sofa without turning the light on, letting my eyes adjust to the faint glow that reached into the room from the streetlamps and the flats opposite. The silence came round me, buzzing in my ears. I replayed the conversations in my head and with each repetition it seemed clearer and clearer that Richard didn't think of our relationship as something that had to be continued, regardless of the difficulty. I hugged my coat around me. His intensity over the past few weeks had led me to believe that I was an essential part of his life now but suddenly that seemed a gross miscalculation. The thought made me nauseous.

Two weeks later, I got on the Eurostar with a deep-seated feeling of guilt, as well as the knowledge that I had caused lasting damage to my friendship with Helen. I had hardly been able to bear telling her that I couldn't go to the opera but I'd made myself ring her: it would have been too cowardly to email. She'd said it didn't matter at all and almost masked the hurt in her voice, and that had made me feel worse.

Richard was great company for those three days. He had been distant with me even after I told him I would go and I'd only seen him once in the fortnight since my birthday, but as soon as we were on the train his mood had lightened. My alarm at thinking he was reconsidering things between us had stayed with me and it was only when it lifted that I realised just how panicked I had been. Being with a happy Richard was like coming into the light again. He seemed especially expansive while we were away, laughing more than usual and being very affectionate. I'd chosen to put it down to his being free of the worry he had whenever we were out together in London that someone he knew would see us. Another voice, however, whispered to me that there was an element of triumph in his good mood, that he felt himself the victor in a popularity contest between him and Helen. I suppressed the voice, telling myself I was being ridiculous.

Richard's generosity during our holiday was extreme. It wasn't only the ludicrously luxurious hotel and meals and taxis; I struggled even to buy any of the frequent coffees we stopped for while I showed him my old haunts. He wanted to see them all – where I'd studied, the house under whose roof my tiny *chambre de bonne* had nestled, even the restaurant where I'd worked, now long closed. He also took me shopping and not in the sort of high-street places to which I usually went. Clothes were difficult. Richard always dressed expensively – I had, when we started seeing each other, looked at the labels of his clothes when he'd been in the bathroom to confirm my suspicions – and so I'd had to raise my game. I had bought a couple of tops at the very furthest reaches of my price range and wore them again and again with different accessories but I still felt dowdy next to him. At Pétrus, he had fitted.

In Paris, he took me to the Galeries Lafayette and made me try on clothes. I was torn: as soon as I put on the things he suggested, I looked infinitely cooler, a more suitable partner for him. And yet I resisted. It was one thing to be with him if not as a financial equal, then at least on my financial terms, but this shifted the balance of power between us in a way with which I didn't feel comfortable at all. I loved the way I looked in the dresses and skirts and shoes, and he pressed me to allow him to buy them, but I refused everything except for one Costume National top. I couldn't accept anything else; it made me feel not like a girlfriend any more but his mistress. It made me feel owned.

My plan for my birthday this year was a trip into Newport. I was going to see a matinée at the cinema and then I would buy a new jumper at the big Marks & Spencer there: whether I was imagining it or not, the Island felt colder than London.

It was good to get out of Yarmouth. I dreaded bumping into Peter in the street. All weekend, whenever I hadn't deliberately been concentrating on something else, my thoughts had gone back to the evening at Chris's. My memory now focused on a few key images, any of which made me close my eyes in embarrassment: I saw myself blithely mentioning the scows and Peter turning away; dominating the conversation and pressing Chris to open another bottle when they'd obviously both had enough; the table covered in wine and broken glass. On Saturday afternoon I'd had to go and pick up the car, and I'd put a note through the door thanking him and apologising. Thank God, he hadn't been in.

If I was embarrassed by how I had seemed to Chris, my feeling about Peter was more complicated. I was ashamed of coming across like a drunken fool in front of him and pained to have reminded him about Alice, of course, but the memory of how he had jumped up from the table and marched off as if he couldn't bear it a minute longer still rankled. Would it have hurt to have taken a taxi with me, rather than walk for miles in the dark? For all Sally and Chris's belief in him, I was suspicious. There was something else going on, for sure. And something had made Alice do it.

Dad called in the evening to wish me happy birthday. Helen was in Munich on a business trip so after he'd rung off, I went upstairs to email a thank you for her card; she'd get it on her BlackBerry. Even over Christmas, when we had spoken so much about him, I hadn't told her about a suspicion that I'd developed only after the trip to Paris, on another occasion when Richard had seemed put out by our friendship. It occurred to me then that he had had the opportunity deliberately to book the Eurostar tickets for the same night as Helen's opera ones. He'd seen hers in the morning and presented me with his own in the evening.

I had never understood why he was so irritated by our closeness. Sometimes he appeared to take it as a personal affront. 'Do you think it's normal? You're in your thirties, not junior school,' he'd said.

'We've been best friends since college.'

'You're far too reliant on each other. It's not healthy. How can I ever hope to have a proper relationship with you when you're always hanging round with her?'

140

'How can I ever hope to have a proper relationship with you when you're married?' I'd snapped back at him, and he'd hung up on me.

When I opened my email account now, I saw his name in my inbox straight away; my eyes still seemed to scan for it first. I clicked on it, heart accelerating.

Happy birthday, Katie.

That was all, nothing else – another special-occasion message. And yet it made me deeply uneasy. It was one thing to write at Christmas and on New Year's Eve but remembering my birthday was different. It wasn't even a memorable date.

Perhaps it was because the message itself was so anodyne, however, that I made the decision to write back. It was a spur-of-the-moment thing, a powerful urge to be free of him which met a sudden, unconsidered conviction that I only needed to tell him to leave me alone in a clear, unemotional way.

Richard, I typed, *thank you for your message. I think it would be best, though, if you stopped writing now. We both need to move on. Kate.*

I pressed send before I could start agonising about it. Then I clicked into my outbox and saw it there, gone, irretrievable, and a flash of disbelieving panic ran through me. I'd done it: broken my silence and communicated with him for the first time since it had all happened.

It was almost ten o'clock but he was still at his computer, obviously, because his response came back within the space of a minute. *You've made such a mistake.*

Chapter Sixteen

It was a relief to go to work at the café the next day, though I'd hardly slept. I wanted to be around other people, even if none of them spoke to me; I needed the mundane – warming the soup, making pots of tea, clearing the tables – to convince me that the horrors I'd imagined were just the stuff of waking nightmare. All night Richard's mail had burned in front of my eyes as if the letters had been picked out in flame. The house had seemed suddenly unsafe, porous, as if he might be able to put his hand straight through the walls and reach me, touch the back of my neck. During the slow-moving hours of the night, the sanctuary that I'd come here to find, had tried to create, felt as tenuous as gossamer, blown away on a single breath.

This was the Richard I knew: destabilising the ground beneath my feet. It had started slowly but by the end of our relationship, I had lived so uncertainly that I didn't trust the earth I stood on not to pitch me over at my faintest misstep. It didn't even take a misstep: changes came without warning, sudden tornadoes that twisted up from nowhere. I was never allowed to be comfortable; instead I swung between extremes. The highs with Richard were so high: there were times – like at Christmas or in Paris – when I felt I could jump out of third-floor windows and land unharmed. Everything was electric and vivid; I looked at other people and felt sad that they weren't living at this intensity. But then a switch in him would be thrown and his sudden coldness, his doubts about us, would plunge me into such despair and desperation that I would do anything to claw back even a little of the happiness.

And that was how, at just the time I saw that I meant something to him, when he started to talk with that frightening focus about how much he loved me, I felt my power begin to slip away.

First it was the anger about Helen on my birthday and the refusal to come up to the flat. That was the pattern: a great high followed by a bottomless low: the treat of a birthday dinner at Pétrus, all his attention, followed by complete withdrawal. But even his winning me round after I found out he was married conformed to the system: he'd left me alone for a week, let me taste the bitterness of being on my own again before sweeping in with his exulting, overwhelming protestation of love. He had played weak while being strong all the time: he had set a trap in which he was the bait, an animal pretending to be injured to lure in its prey.

Once last year, we had had a whole weekend to ourselves. On the Friday Richard had suggested one of his extravagant dinners but I had wanted something lower-key, the sort of evening I might have had with a normal boyfriend. Reluctantly he had agreed and we went to Putney for supper by the river and then found a cocktail place that was open until two. He was in one of my favourite of his moods, a light flirtatious one that was a soft echo of our early bantering. He was openly affectionate, too, leaning over from his stool to kiss me, fingers gently tracing the embroidery on my evening bag where it lay on the bar.

It was past two o'clock by the time we wove our way out on to the street. It had been one of those unseasonably warm days in May and, even late at night, it wasn't properly cold. Taxis passed us with their lights on but Richard wanted to walk. I was happy to; I was revelling in him, this glamorous, happy man who I loved and who loved me. Through the caipirinha haze, everything was glossy. From Putney Bridge, the Thames shone not only with the lights which spilled on to it from either bank but with the moon, too, which hung overhead like a big silver coin. Feeling full of love for Richard, life, London, I slipped my hand inside his coat and pressed myself against his side. Waiting for his arm to come around my shoulders, I pressed closer and butted the side of his chest gently with my head. I felt him turn to look at me and I turned my face up for a kiss, alight, I knew, with tipsy happiness.

His expression killed my joy immediately. The affection of only moments before had been extinguished and his eyes were cold – flat, as if there was no one behind them. He turned away, shutting me out of his line of vision, and walked on.

I searched my brain for something to say but couldn't find anything. I had the same swooping sick feeling as when he had made the taxi drive him home on my birthday, the same sense that I had just taken for granted something about which there was no certainty at all.

We walked in silence for a hundred yards and then he muttered something.

'I'm sorry, I didn't hear,' I said, fearing a snapped response.

'Entropy, I said. Everything decays and goes to ruin. Good things turn to shit. What was exciting becomes tedious. Love dies.'

My stomach lurched.

'This'll fade, just like it did with my wife. It always does.'

'It doesn't have to – not with the right person.'

'How would you know?' He looked away to the other side of the road. A bus was pulling up at the stop there, a single passenger getting on. The bridge was almost empty; most of those who had been out late had already vanished into the night. A light gust of wind blew from behind him and made his soft cashmere coat billow. 'You're a fierce creature now,' he said, 'but you won't always be. You'll get old and tired, stop really living. I'll always be like this – this is what I am.'

If I hadn't had so much to drink, I would never have done it. Full of a sudden fire, I threw my bag on to the pavement and approached the wall. It was between waist and chest height on me, made of stone. I thought about my shoes: heels but only small ones. I could do without taking them off; it was the immediacy of the gesture I wanted, the spontaneity. I put my hands flat on the curved top, feeling how cold it was. Deliberately, no doubt, the wall had been built with no easy footholds; I ran my shoe up the bottom foot or two of it looking for purchase but didn't find it.

Hurrying, feeling the impact of the exercise slipping away, I braced my toes against the stone and then with a sudden upward thrust, much easier than expected, my knee was on the top. I brought the other one quickly up to correct myself. I was kneeling forward now, my hands laid flat on the parapet stone as if I was abasing myself before an invisible deity. Twenty yards below but seeming much closer, the Thames slipped blackly past, its surface not shining now but gleaming with intent. My stomach lurched again and I tried not to think about what might be in the water, the flotsam and jetsam of London life: bottles and crisp packets and larger rubbish: old tyres, shopping trolleys, cooking waste. Bodies – rats, mice, birds. Possibly humans.

There was sweat under my arms. I had to stand up. Slowly I pushed myself up on to my fingertips and raised one knee. The view tilted in front of me and the cane spirit and lime in my stomach tipped with it, letting a taste of acid up my throat. I paused for a second or two to let it settle and then brought my other knee up. Now I was crouched in an undignified manner, my bottom facing the pavement. *Come on, Kate, you can do this*, I told myself. *Just stand up. The parapet's two feet wide. You won't fall.* I lifted my body, unfolding myself with all the speed of an old woman, hating myself for not being able to override my instinct for caution. The curve of the top stone was more pronounced than I'd realised; I could feel it under my feet, making balance harder still. When I was fully upright, I took a deep silent breath and opened my eyes. There was London again, the lights bright and distinct. It was when I made the mistake of looking at the water directly beneath me, streaming out, it seemed, from between my feet, that the nausea came. Vertigo: the fear not of falling but jumping. There it was, the forward urge in my knees, the fizzing in the muscles of my thighs. I looked quickly up again, searching for the distant arc of the London Eye to anchor myself by. Deep breath.

Richard still hadn't said anything. I could feel him standing behind me, watching. Carefully I moved my feet sideways and took three or four steps in the direction we were going, as if it was the most natural thing in the world for me to abandon the pavement and walk an unprotected beam above the Thames. If the drop didn't kill me, I thought, the current would carry me swiftly away beyond help, to dash me against the pilings of a bridge further down. I imagined my body among the intricate iron under-structure at Blackfriars and another flush of fear swept over me. *Girl plunges to watery grave*.

Affecting a casual expression, I turned to look at him. His face was serious but the old challenge, less and less in evidence of late, was there in his eyebrows which were raised, faintly suggestive in the way that I had always found so provocative. 'What are you doing up there?' he said, no concern or alarm in his voice. 'You're scared of heights.'

I risked it. 'Proving to you that I'm still your fierce creature. I'm not going to get old and boring. This is me – the finished product. I'm the same as you.'

He came forward, smiling, and took my hands. I thought he was going to help me down, catch me in his arms, but instead he stopped. 'Now lean back,' he said.

'What?'

'Lean back. I'll take your weight.' The eyebrows went up, daring me. 'Go on.'

The wind seemed to rush past my ears and the bones in my legs felt fluid but gently I leaned back. Our eyes were locked on each other.

'You can go further than that. I've got you.'

The intensity which I had never found with anyone else burned between us like a power source. I felt suddenly invincible, as if I could do anything in the world. I leaned further, letting the weight of my body rock back from the balls of my feet to my heels. From the corner of my eye I could see the river, directly beneath me. I was out over the edge. Adrenalin was surging in my blood.

It was then that his hand slipped in mine. I felt an explosion of terror, a flashbulb that went off white in front of my eyes, obliterating everything.

He tugged me sharply towards him and I fell on top of him down on to the pavement, nearly knocking him over. He held me so tightly I couldn't breathe. 'My darling, my darling,' he was whispering into my ear. 'You know I wouldn't let anything happen to you. It was an accident; I would never have let you fall.'

From then until he went to work at six on Monday morning, he hardly left me alone. He treated me with a tenderness which was

146

almost overwhelming; if I was within touching range, it was rare for his hands not to be on me, stroking my hair or my face or just lying still on my arm or my thigh, as if he was making sure I was there and that the alternative sequence of events – the one in which I had fallen off the bridge and been carried away by the water – hadn't been the one which really happened.

After he'd pulled me back down on to the pavement, he had held me tightly against him for what felt like a long time. His arms trapped mine at my side so that I couldn't move them, as if I were a panicked cat wrapped in a blanket to stop it lashing out, scratching. I wanted to slap him, beat my hands against his chest, express physically some of the terror that had seized me in that split-second when I had thought I was going over. 'It was an accident; it was an accident,' he repeated again and again in my ear, like a mantra. 'I'd never have let you go.'

Eventually the first wave of shock had passed. He felt the tension go out of my body and took a step back, moving his hands to the top of my arms, holding me away from him so he could look at my face. 'Let's go home,' he said. There was a taxi coming across the bridge and he hailed it, collected my bag from the pavement and helped me in. I was moving through a dream world: it was as if everything was strobe-lit and I was getting only one frame of the action in every four.

Back at the flat, he poured me a large brandy, then undressed me with a gentleness that was almost motherly, removing my clothes carefully, undoing each of the little buttons, hanging my top and cardigan on the padded hangers. I sat mutely on the edge of the bed and watched. It was an accident, of course it was; no one sane would do that on purpose. And yet, in a corner of my mind that I didn't want to turn a torch on, I knew there was a question: what if he had been testing me, taking that extra step to see how far I would go? And if it was a test, had I passed?

He turned back from the wardrobe, put his arms under my knees and moved me round so that I lay with my head on the pillows, tucking the quilt around me as if I was a baby. Then he took off his own clothes, leaving his boxer shorts on, and slipped into the bed beside me, reaching out to turn off the lamp. I was lying on my back and he put his arm round my shoulders and pulled me to him. 'I love you,' he said. 'You know that, don't you?'

I didn't answer but suddenly the shock, terror and disbelief commuted into desire. I wanted to feel his weight on me, have him press me down so that I couldn't drop away into the blackness. It was a voracious hunger, a statement of survival, but it contained a furious anger, too. I wanted to bite him, scratch him, kick him. I turned and started kissing him fiercely, running my nails over him, through his hair, down his back. In what felt like seconds, I was pinned and I wanted it but I fought it, too. I was as wild as the lions on my bracelet.

As soon as I'd watched Richard's car pull away that Monday, I'd brought up Helen's number on my phone. She was often at her office by seven but I'd hoped to catch her before her day really started. I had desperately needed to talk to her but when it had come to pressing the button and making the call, I'd found I couldn't. I couldn't tell her what had happened on the bridge, any of it. I knew how she'd react to hearing I'd got up on the parapet and she would immediately have condemned Richard for not getting me down at once. There was no way I could tell her about the accident, how his hand had let mine slip. And I hadn't wanted her to condemn him then. What I had wanted was to talk, to lay my thoughts and feelings out on the table top and look at them, try to order them. She had always been my sounding-board but at that time, at least where anything to do with Richard was concerned, that had been impossible.

The situation had reached a nadir when I'd told her he was married. The day after that dreadful Boxing Day night I'd rung her and told her everything, unable to contain my misery. She hadn't said I told you so, hadn't even implied it, but I knew it had to be behind the comforting words. Then I had been beyond caring, had wanted someone to listen with sympathy and join me in condemning him. I had agreed with her that if he ever contacted me again, I had to harden my heart. I had promised.

When I took Richard back after that, I emailed to tell her: I hadn't been able to admit it face to face or even on the phone.

148

And the morning that I had wanted to talk to her about what had happened on the bridge, I'd understood that I couldn't. I had used up her sympathy. And I had made my choice: him over her.

Things were different now. In the afternoon, when the last of the five lunch customers departed and I was alone, I got out my mobile and rang her, keeping one eye on the door for new customers or for Mary, who'd gone out for a while. It was when I heard the unfamiliar tone that I remembered Helen was still in Munich and probably in a meeting. I hung up without leaving a message; I would call her later.

I'd already tidied the kitchen and swept, so to pass the time before anyone came in for tea, I filled an old ice-cream container with soapy water and started cleaning the tall drinks fridge, taking out all the bottles and scrubbing the glass shelves until I began to get hot. I didn't see anyone at the door and it was only when the bell rang that I realised someone had come in. It was Chris.

I dropped the sponge into the water and stood up, pushing the hair off my face with my forearm. My cheeks were already rosy.

'Hard at work? I've just been into Harwoods for some varnish' – he held aloft a tin, the evidence – 'and thought I'd pop in to see where you are.'

'This is it,' I said, looking around the room, not at him.

'It's rather nice. I'll come in for something to eat another time.' He smiled. 'Look, thank you for your note; there was no need to write. And there was certainly no need to apologise: accidents happen.'

'Not to sober people so often.'

'Ah well – we've all done it. And you weren't that bad – you've got a thing or two to learn if you reckon that's drunk. Think no more about it.'

'No wonder Peter ran for the hills,' I tested.

'Don't think badly of him. Sometimes he does that, just disappears when he needs to be on his own; it wouldn't have been because of you. He'd be embarrassed if he knew you thought that. What's that chocolate sponge like? Have you tried it? I should get back – I've closed the shop – but I'll take a piece with me, if that's OK.'

149

I cut him an extra large slice and put it in one of the plastic takeaway boxes.

'Come and see me soon,' he said, tucking his scarf into his jacket again on his way towards the door. 'And don't wait till you've finished your books.'

Chapter Seventeen

I didn't have a shift on Wednesday so I got in the car and took the military road to Ventnor, wanting the perspective of a wide sky and a view of the sea. The email from Richard was still weighing on me. Helen had seen my missed call and rung back in the early evening but she'd been in a cab on her way to a client dinner, her conversation punctuated with directions to the driver. It hadn't seemed fair to burden her with my worry when she was away and I didn't want to get into it all until we could talk properly. Stoppered up inside, though, without the neutralisation of talking about it, Richard's threat – for I was sure that was what it was – seemed to be strengthening, becoming not less potent with time but more so.

It was too wet to get out and walk so I threaded the car down the steep roads through the town centre and parked on the esplanade where I sat and watched the sea foam up on to the beach, its edge airy as beaten egg white. Ventnor was massed on the hillside above me, pressing down, but the only places open in the row of businesses lining the other side of the road were a greasy spoon with a full English for four pounds and the amusement arcade, whose one-armed bandits flashed garish invitations at odds with the morning's muted palette. The rain fell in fat drops, making a tinny music on the roof of the car. I listened to it and watched as the mist cloaked the headlands beyond the Spyglass inn, then revealed them again, shifting like the sea itself. Nothing in the view would have changed in two hundred years, I thought, when pirates must have made a handsome living along this coast.

I was brought out of my reverie by the sound of my mobile. The number was a landline in central London but I didn't recognise it. I hesitated and the phone went on ringing, insistent. Richard wouldn't call me now, though; he'd know I'd hang up on him. It could be someone offering me translating work: an agency. I answered, catching it just before it stopped.

'Is this Kate?' a woman asked slowly. Her voice was thick, smudged-sounding, as if she'd been drinking.

'Yes,' I said, hesitant.

'This is Sarah Brookwood.'

It was a second or two before I put the parts of her name together.

'Are you there?'

I deserved this; it was fair. 'Yes.'

'He was my husband – did you ever think about that?' She was speaking carefully, enunciating but slurring anyway. 'We were married.'

I was trembling all of a sudden. It was shock, shock at getting the call now, not a year ago, when I'd almost expected it. 'I'm sorry,' I said. 'I am so sorry.'

'It's too late for that. And I'd save your pity for yourself.'

Cold went over my skin, down my arms like a pair of freezing hands.

'Do you know what you're dealing with? Do you? Two nights ago he . . . My collarbone's broken and three of my ribs. I've lost my front teeth.' She was crying now but trying not to. 'It was never like this before – this bad. Normally he can stop. I've been in hospital two days. If I'd punctured a lung . . .'

I shuddered, a sudden spasm, and one of Helen's expressions came into my head: 'Someone walk over your grave?'

She swallowed again, as if she were drooling and wanted to empty her mouth. Her breathing was coming in sobs. 'I hate you for what you've done to me,' she said. 'But I pity you, too. I mean it. He won't let you go – not until he wants to.'

I felt a wave of nausea, the contents of my stomach rising up my throat, and quickly opened the car door. I took deep breaths of the air, smelling the salt, the stale cooking oil from the café. Sweat had broken out on my forehead.

'You're not the first – he's always had women. There have been others even while he's been with you.'

'What?'

'Yes,' she said, pleased to have shocked me. Or hurt me – could it be hurt, that note in my voice? 'Last year he got one of them pregnant. He dumped her straight away, like he always does.'

I swallowed down the acid that scorched my throat. *Pregnant? Last year?* I felt myself rock forward in the seat, my head suddenly too heavy. The world seemed to have pulled away from me.

'But you,' she said, her voice reaching me from the other end of a long tunnel. 'You are different. You've lasted longer than any of them. It's not love – don't make that mistake – but it's something.'

'Why did you stay?' I said weakly. 'If you knew.'

She'd given up trying to hide her crying now. 'We're married. He's my husband. He's my son's father. I didn't want a divorce and – it starts to break you, you don't even realise. And I always thought I could make it better; I thought that if I could just be enough for him . . .'

'It would have been hard,' I said, tentative. 'When you were ill.' The nausea ebbed a little and I pulled the door shut again and snapped down the button to lock it, wanting to feel the shell of the car closed around me.

'Ill?'

'He told me.' There was silence on the other end of the phone and I ploughed on. 'I wouldn't have carried on seeing him, unless . . . He told me that you were going to get a divorce but then you got ill. You were waiting until you were better.'

There was the start of bitter laughter and then she choked. 'He's a liar – didn't you know? He lies and lies and lies. I did try to leave once, last year, but he wouldn't let me; he harassed me till I gave in. No one leaves Richard; he leaves them. He decides.'

I closed my eyes, and said nothing.

'You're starting to get it, aren't you? I've seen the emails he writes you – it isn't over. I hate you for what you did but I couldn't just stand by. If anything happened and I hadn't said something, I couldn't live with it.'

'I . . .'

'I don't have any choice now – I have to leave him. He's broken me, everything I wanted, and I can't take another beating: he'd kill me next time. He'll let me go now because he knows that. But you – run, and just pray he doesn't find you.'

When she hung up, I put my head on the steering wheel and let them come, the images which I had fled here across the Solent to escape. They crowded down on me now like gulls in the wake of a trawler, screeching and triumphant: images of the last time I'd seen him, that final morning in the flat when I'd walked through the open door and heard him on the phone, so obviously talking to a child. Had I made a sound, let the breath catch in my throat? I didn't know but suddenly he had been aware of me in the doorway, had told the little voice that he would call back. 'Katie,' he'd said, standing, seeing the look on my face, taking steps towards me which I'd matched with steps backwards. 'I can explain.'

I can explain. It wasn't that the floor moved beneath my feet; it was more that the floor had ceased to exist and I was there, three storeys above the pavement, without anything to keep me from crashing to the ground. I was unanchored, waiting to fall. I heard my voice telling him to get out. It seemed to come from somewhere outside me, from yards away, perhaps even from the other side of the communal garden whose trees I could see dappling with the autumn light that had matched my spirits and warmed me through my coat only minutes before. I had the post in one hand, the bag of breakfast things in the other, and I gripped them. 'Get out,' I said.

He took another step towards me but now I was backed up against the table in the hall. His hands were on my coat collar, pulling me towards him. I dropped the bag, heard it hit the floor. His breath was sour, his teeth not yet brushed. His eyes seemed huge, the pupils black and enormous, ringed with that strange toffee colour. I looked at them, mesmerised. They were expressionless – utterly blank.

'What did you say?' His voice was almost conversational.

'Get out of my flat.' I twisted, trying to jerk free of him. 'Leave me alone.'

154

He changed his grip and suddenly there was pressure on my windpipe. I took a quick breath, tried again to pull back. Then without warning, he yanked me up from the table and thrust me away from him. I fell backwards, my head cracking against the wall beneath the coat rack, my back jarring as I hit the floor. Pain jolted up my spine. I stayed there, momentarily stunned. He reached down and grabbed me up by the shoulder, lifting all my weight, then pushing me backwards into the coats and shoving himself against me, his tongue forcing itself into my mouth. I moved my head to one side but found his arm already there, blocking it. His fingers held my jaw, pressing it open. I clamped my teeth down and bit his tongue.

He pulled back and looked at me a moment, as if he was amused. 'You always think you can beat me, don't you, sweetheart?' He kicked my legs out from under me and then I was on the floor and he was on top of me, pinning me as he had so many times before. One hand tore at my jumper, pulling it up, exposing my breasts, and the other fumbled with my fly, shoving to get inside my knickers. I squirmed and fought. He brought his face down to mine again, his teeth banging against mine so hard that there was a rush of blood into my mouth. He was undoing his own trousers, yanking down the fly, pulling himself free. The fingers of his other hand were inside my knickers now, jabbing at me, hurting me. He was out of his boxer shorts and he brought his spare arm up and pressed it hard over my throat. I gagged, from the pressure, from fear. Richard was gone, replaced by this furious, vicious man who didn't even seem to recognise me.

'I can't breathe,' I croaked, and the arm came down harder. 'Please.'

He pulled back as his jabbing fingers found their mark and I looked at him and saw triumph in his eyes. Hatred coursed through me, and he saw it. 'Fuck you,' I whispered.

His fist connected with my brow. The pain was exquisite, a firework explosion of agony in the bone and the socket of my eye. The shock of rage that followed gave me a burst of strength far beyond myself and I got my leg free from between his and brought my knee up sharp into his groin. He groaned, closing his eyes for just a second, and I took the advantage and shoved him off me. I scrambled up but he grabbed at my ankle and I stumbled. I kicked back at him, meeting flesh, and then I ran, out of the flat and down the stairs, tearing my jumper down to cover myself, not caring until I was almost in the lobby, steps from the street, that my jeans were still undone. I could hear his feet coming down the top stairs now and he was running but I was too far ahead and I burst out of the building and on to the street, still running when I reached the square at the back. An old lady was opening the gate to the private garden and, without thinking, I dived past her and ran until I reached the rhododendrons which were large enough to hide me.

I stayed in the bushes for almost an hour. Twice Richard circled the garden but he didn't have keys and no one else came in so that he could push in after them. Instead he stalked the pavement around the perimeter, walking as casually as if nothing had happened to disrupt the morning. Through the leaves of the rhododendrons and the cast-iron railings I saw him, the slow, comfortable stride, the pale November sun playing over the shoulders of his suit jacket, and I was afraid that my shaking would set the leaves trembling and betray me. My heartbeat was too loud.

None of the sun reached down to me. The dew was still on the leaves and it transferred to my jumper and chilled me even further. My feet grew numb from standing on the cold soil. I was shivering and shivering, couldn't stop. Blood ran from the split on my brow and I pressed the tissue from my pocket gently against it, wincing silently. The minutes stretched. I looked at my watch. Half past nine. I knew he had a meeting at half ten; he wouldn't miss that. And he was going to New York in the afternoon. He must have gone, surely. I scanned what I could see of the pavement and the garden, then stepped out on to the gravel path. My head was pounding, the pain in my forehead intensifying. A blackbird looked up from pecking at the lawn and cocked its head to one side. There was no sign of Richard.

More than anything now, I wanted my flat. I wanted to lock the door and put the chain across it. I let myself out of the garden and went to the corner of the square. Richard had driven last night, told Sarah he had a meeting in Henley and was staying over. His car was still there, parked two doors down from mine, and I could see him in the driver's seat, the outline of his head and shoulder. My pulse accelerated again. If I stepped into my street now, he'd see me for sure.

I doubled back and used the access on the other side of the square to get on to Earls Court Road. I still had to pass the end of my street but I had distance on my side and I walked behind a pair of women to disguise myself in case he happened to look in his rear-view mirror. Lowering my head to hide my face, I ducked into the library on the Old Brompton Road and found a chair in a far corner, out of sight. I sat there until noon, trying in vain to process what had happened. The man I loved had attacked me, tried to have sex with me against my will – to rape me. It seemed so outlandish; could I have imagined it, or read it in a book and absorbed it into an especially vivid dream? Without the pain, I might have believed it. And yet, I had to acknowledge, I couldn't claim that I had never seen hints of this side of him before.

The library began to get busier and several people came into my corner, where I let my hair fall across my face and looked down, pretending to be preoccupied with the illustrated guide to India that was open on my lap. The tissue against the cut on my eyebrow was soaked.

When at last I left the library and walked back round the corner into my road, Richard's car was gone. My keys were still in my pocket from the trip to buy breakfast and, heart in my mouth, I opened the door to my building. I walked slowly upstairs, light-headed. On the landing I hesitated, listening at my own front door, but there were no sounds from inside. I let myself in, pulse pounding, sending pain shooting through my eye. The orange juice and crumpets I'd bought for our breakfast were still lying on the carpet. I checked the rooms quickly, looking behind the doors, even throwing open the wardrobe, but he wasn't there. It was only when I sat heavily down on the sofa that I saw the note on the coffee table. *Whatever it takes, Katie.*

In all the time that I saw Richard, I had never let myself think about Sarah – not properly, as a person who might be much like me, who had friends and a family, favourite books and films, who might have loved Richard like I did. I hadn't denied she existed; I couldn't: she had been a fact. But I had learnt to turn my thoughts away from her, to convince myself that the force of my feelings for him justified what I was doing. When I did think about her, it was in the abstract. If I needed to mention her to Richard, I did so as 'your wife'. On one hand, I'd felt it would have been patronising to use her name, the sort of instant familiarity assumed towards someone weaker or pitiable, nurse to patient. On the other, it was self-protection. If I kept her as an idea, a circumstance which held us apart, like a missed aeroplane or a sudden unscheduled meeting, then I could cope. If I called her by name, I was forced to face the truth of what I was doing. 'Your wife' was a shade; Sarah was a person.

Now I asked myself how I could have done it, put up the mental smokescreen that allowed me to behave like that. What sort of monster was I? However much I'd thought I loved him, I should never have been able to do it. I was disgusted with myself – sick to my stomach with guilt.

I imagined her terror when he lunged at her, shoving her, dragging her, hitting her. I imagined her smashed mouth, the missing teeth, the broken bones. She'd had every reason to despise me and yet she had thought to warn me, as soon as she'd got out of hospital. The contrast in our behaviour towards each other shamed me.

Just as when it had been me Richard had hurt, my instinct was to go home and lock the door, shut out the world. This time, though, there was something I needed to do first. Instead of heading straight back to Yarmouth, I drove to Newport again. On my birthday, I had seen a branch of Carphone Warehouse and now I went in and asked to change my number. Sarah had taken it from Richard's mobile; I needed to make sure that he could never call me again.

Chapter Eighteen

I lay awake all that night, my stomach clenching with fear. I tried all my tricks for finding sleep but it wouldn't come. The noises in the house – the judder of the fridge, the clicking of the old radiators – had reclaimed their strangeness and each one had me lying rigid now, straining my ears in the darkness for the crank of the front door handle, the sound of breaking glass. My mind was roiling, the memory of that morning replaying itself over and over again – him lunging for me, tearing at my clothes; the deadness of his eyes. *Normally he can stop*, I heard Sarah's thick voice say again. I'd thought when he attacked me that it had been extraordinary, the result of him being out beyond his limits, but it wasn't; it wasn't even unusual.

Towards dawn, I stopped trying to sleep and made a cup of tea. I sat on the edge of the bed watching the first of the daylight infuse the sky, lifting it from a heavy navy to an intense royal blue. A shape, black and scarcely visible, flickered past the window and was gone: a bat, whirling through the last of the darkness. I thought about what it would be like to be so free. The air in the room seemed to thicken, the ceiling to come lower, and suddenly my fear mutated into a furious anger.

I was dressed in two minutes and out of the door in three. On the path I stood and took in great breaths of air, as if I had just broken the surface after a deep-water dive. The air was cold and felt like medicine as it came in across my tongue; exhaled, it made clouds like empty speech-bubbles.

Without thinking, I found myself heading for the path around the estuary. I crossed Tennyson Road and passed Sally's house, the curtains drawn against the first signs of the morning. The stillness of the air heightened every sound: my breathing, the scratch of the loose chips of tarmac under my feet. In the bushes there was the light music of the dawn chorus, but over the estuary I could hear the sharp cry of a seabird. That cry was not music; it was a single sustained sound, a screech more than a note, which echoed in the sky and left a desolate silence when it died away.

The road became a track of mud and shingle, its edge shored up by a stone wall which kept back the tide. It was high water now and the first colour of the sun, a bloodish rose, caught the surface wherever it was disturbed. On the other side, the saltmarshes lay low and dark, brackish water shining here and there amongst them, made glassy by the cold. My anger was beginning to dissipate already, the rhythm of my feet breaking it down. The track found its way between trees, and the estuary disappeared from sight. It was darker again, gloom lingering among the trunks and in the undergrowth as if rising from the ground.

Twenty minutes later, I turned the last corner and saw where the end of the path met the lane to Freshwater. At the low stone bridge over the top of the river I stopped. The estuary was spread out in front of me now like a spill of mercury and at its mouth, hazy in the early-morning mist, I could make out the roofs of Yarmouth, the spire of St James's and the tall red-brick chimneys of the George.

A long way downriver, something was moving. I watched, and saw that it was a rowing boat, making a silent but steady progress upstream. Minutes passed. Only when it was thirty yards away was there any sound at all and then just the gentlest plashing, the slow beat of oars dipping into water and lifting out again. The boat was a silhouette between sky and water, a black shape amongst tones of silver. As it drew nearer, I could see that the rower was an old man. His back was curved but he rowed neatly, waiting for the boat to travel as far as each stroke would take it before pulling the next. The oars dipped then rose, dipped again, and the water shimmered around them. I watched until he was close enough to talk if he turned and saw me and then I moved away.

I followed the lane up the hill and into the small square in front of the parish church. In the graveyard frost sparkled on the grass between the headstones. A robin perched on one of them looked at me in surprise as I went in but made no attempt to fly away.

At the back of the church, hidden from the road, I sat down on a wooden bench. It had been many years since I had stopped believing, if I ever had, but there had been two or three times when I had found peace in churches, not by praying but just by sitting in their silence, surrounded by things built by people whose lives were guided by belief and commitment, who were sure there was a purpose. I found a similar comfort in the gravestones now: they commemorated those who had done it, got through from birth to death, their lives no longer the uncertain skein of difficulty and confusion and fear but facts, the finite dates, the defined relationships: beloved wife, cherished son. Resting my elbow on the arm of the bench, I put my hand across my face and closed my eyes.

I woke to find that it was no longer early. The delicate light was gone, replaced by the frank tone of mid-morning. The sun was out and for the first time in the year there was heat in it. It was shining directly on me, and the thighs of my jeans were warm to the touch. I made a move to sit up straight and felt the stiffness in my neck. My arm, too, was dead from supporting the weight of my head. My mouth had been open: my tongue and throat were dry. I wondered for a moment whether anyone had been past and seen me, then realised I was really beyond caring if they had.

I went the road way back to Yarmouth, walking quickly, wanting to get home and go to bed. There was traffic now and cars sped past me in both directions. I had the strange disconnected feeling of having been awake and asleep at the wrong times; the day already felt old.

As I came down the last part of the hill at Norton, the Solent was laid out in front of me. Today it was blue, taking its lead from the sky, and patched only here and there with the familiar green-grey that mirrored cloud. Its surface was scintillating with gold like a haul of coins and though I wanted to get home, I stopped for a moment. In my exhaustion, the sparkling resolved into thousands of flashing lights.

At the yard just before the bridge, a man was working on a small wooden yacht. Struts against the hull held it upright and the mast lay along the deck, protruding at the stern from the burgundy tarpaulin which covered it. The man had his back to me and was crouched scrubbing at the keel. As I watched, he lowered himself slowly to his knees to work on a patch further down, putting a hand on the hull to steady himself. Something in the movement struck me as familiar.

'Kate!'

For a moment I considered pretending I hadn't heard but he was pulling himself up again, waving. I raised my hand and went over.

'I won't kiss you,' he said. 'I'm filthy.'

'Hello, Ted.' I put my hand down to stroke the blond head which came pressing enthusiastically against my thigh.

'You've met my assistant,' said Chris. 'I've got Peter roped in all day, too, though God knows he's got enough on without indulging me. Peter – Kate's here.'

There was the sound of tools going into a bucket and from the other side, where he'd been hidden by the hull, Peter appeared. He was wearing a large black-and-white marled jumper and paint-splashed jeans muddy from kneeling on the ground. He wiped his hands on a dirty cloth as he nodded hello. His face was closed, his eyes screwed up against the sun streaming across the yard from behind me.

'We're getting her ready to go back in,' Chris said, laying his hand on the side of the boat. 'The sanding's nearly all done now so we're ready to start varnishing.'

'This is your boat.'

'What do you think? She's a bit old-fashioned but I'm not a fibreglass man.'

'Neither of us is.' Peter balled the rag between his hands and tossed it on to the tarpaulin on which Chris had been kneeling.

'I want a boat.' The words were out of my mouth before I realised I was going to say them but it was true: I did want a boat, suddenly and urgently. 'Not like this, though – a rowing boat.' I looked down, embarrassed. I felt Peter watching me.

'Anything in particular brought this on?' said Chris.

'I don't know. No, I do. I saw one this morning at the top of the river just as it was getting light. It was . . . serene.' I thought about the old man, the steady creak of his oars and their reliable course through the water. I wanted to feel even closer to the water than I had today, to go out on it myself, become the machinery between the natural and man-made, river and boat.

'What were you doing out so early?' Chris took his hand off the boat and put it on my forearm, where my sleeve was pushed back. His palm was surprisingly warm, hot even, against my skin, and the feel of it was a shock. I'd read an article once about single women who relied on personal services – manicurists, hairdressers, masseurs – and how they were paying people to touch them. I'd been sceptical but I felt it now, the power in the skin-to-skin contact, the connection.

'I've got a dinghy you can borrow.'

I turned. Peter was looking at me, his eyes still narrowed.

'A rowing boat,' he said. 'Wooden. I'm not using it at the moment.'

'I couldn't.'

'Why not? As I said, I'm not using it. It's not going to put me out if you have it for a while. It's better that it gets used – they dry out otherwise.'

I was torn: I wanted a boat with a desire that I hadn't felt for anything uncomplicated for a long time and yet this wasn't uncomplicated. I didn't want to take anything from Peter: it felt dishonest, given my suspicion of him.

'Have you rowed before?' he said.

'Yes.'

'How long ago?'

I paused, wanting to lie. 'I don't know,' I confessed. 'Sixteen years – maybe seventeen.'

'You'll need a refresher then and I'll have to bring you the oars anyway. What are you doing tomorrow?'

'Working – translating.' I looked at Ted, now sniffing round Peter's boots.

'All day?'

'Yes – I'm really busy.'

'So am I so we'll keep it brief. It'll take half an hour, at the outside. You know where the slip is, in the harbour? I'll meet you there at three thirty.' He turned away and bent to pick up his bit of cloth.

Chris's hand had stayed on my arm and now it slid down and squeezed my fingers so tightly I could feel the bones in them. 'Good,' he said.

Chapter Nineteen

I walked the long way round to the slip the next day. Coming along the harbour wall, I would have a clear view of where Peter was waiting, if he was there on time. I didn't like the idea of getting into a boat with him, it being just the two of us, but if I endured this half-hour, the dinghy was mine. And it was a distraction; while I was in the boat – in company – I hoped that I could slip out from underneath the pall of dread which had settled over me again the previous day as soon as I'd been alone.

When I reached the harbour, I saw Peter at once. He was about five yards from the slipway, idling with the oars, taking small strokes now and again to keep from drifting too far. The boat was wooden, as he had described, and the planks of its varnished hull overlapped tightly so that they had the look of a ribbed cockleshell. It was small, just the right size for me on my own, but it would be tight with both of us.

By the time I had walked down on to the slip itself, he was alongside. 'I'll row for now,' he said, without any other greeting, 'and we'll go up the river a bit, out of the way. Then I'll show you where you can keep her.'

Water lapped over the edge of the slip, threatening my trainers, the most appropriate shoes I'd had. I put my hand on the side of the boat and swung my leg in but as I made to do the same with my other leg, the water displaced by my weight washed back and soaked the foot which was still on the concrete. It was icy but I said nothing and pretended I hadn't noticed. My trainer dripped conspicuously as it came over the side and the bottom six inches of my jeans were plastered on to my leg. I settled on the bench in the stern where he indicated, facing him.

'OK?'

'Fine,' I said.

He spun the boat round with a few casual strokes on the left oar and then, rowing with both, took us across the top of the harbour, past the enclosure where the lifeboat was moored and the pontoon outside the harbour office. I had a sudden memory of the first time I'd seen him, standing on the wall there silhouetted against the fading sky, Alice's scow tied up below and the lights in the lifeboat going out. I risked a quick look at him but it was hard to tell what he was thinking; his face was inscrutable, his eyes fixed on some point behind us, over my head. He was wearing the same clothes as the previous day and I had a clearer view now of the paint on his trousers and mud patches on his knees. There was paint on his hands, too, white among the dark hair on their backs. The size of the boat meant our feet were close together on the boards, my trainers inside his wellingtons, even with my legs drawn back as far as possible. His feet were enormous, almost twice the size of mine.

'Equal pressure on both oars to go straight, just use one if you want to turn,' he said. 'If you need to go forward for any reason, reverse the stroke.'

I suppressed the urge to tell him that I knew. To make the point, I looked away. The harbour was different seen from this angle. As we rounded the long pontoon where the little boats and dinghies were tied up, we passed close to the yachts on our other side, close enough for me to touch. With both our weight, we were sitting low in the water and they towered above us.

'Is it what you had in mind? The boat?'

I realised with embarrassment that I hadn't said anything at all about it. 'It's lovely. Thank you – it's very kind of you.'

He pulled another stroke, leaning back into it to make the most of his body weight. We were coming under the bridge now. Its dark timbers reared up around us and the light was muted. The smell of the river was particularly strong here, that rich salt smell with its fishy top-notes. Oily bladderwrack clung to the supports, exposed by the tide. A few more strokes and we came out from under it again and he turned a little and took us up into the shallower water near the sailing club. Here the scows were moored, bobbing lightly on the water like a group of large coloured gulls. I looked at him quickly but his face was composed. Where was Alice's scow now? It had had an unusual name – *Vespertine*. Maybe he didn't keep it in the water any more. Maybe the police had kept it for evidence.

He held the oars in the water to stop us. 'Your turn. We'll have to be careful when we swap thwarts or one of us will go over the side.'

'Thwarts?'

'The seats – benches; it's what they're called. You move first.'

I stood up gingerly and turned round. As I did so, he ducked over and took my seat at the back. I settled on the central bench – thwart – and braced my feet against the bar in the bottom of the boat as I had seen him do. I put my hands on the oars, which were still warm from his. Turning them so that the blades entered the water squarely, I took a first stroke, feeling the pull of it through my stomach and thighs. I angled the blades so that they were parallel to the water as they went back to take the next stroke, as he had done and as I remembered from years before. He nodded at me. We went up the river, leaving the sailing club behind, passing the larger boats on their moorings. Peter watched the oars and I watched the water behind him, where it fanned out in our wake.

'So you're a natural,' he said. I tried to hide my pride but I felt myself smile broadly anyway. I looked at him quickly and saw that he was smiling, too. The unexpectedness of it took me aback. His face looked quite different. Though his eyes were narrowed against the sun, they didn't look closed and assessing; the fans at their corners looked like laughter lines. He turned out of the sun and met my eye. I looked quickly away and pulled another stroke. I was slightly out of breath from the effort; the boat itself wasn't light and his weight was a considerable load. I didn't care, though; I was filled suddenly with something close to euphoria, the sheer pleasure of moving us through the water and the sound of it sluicing past, the clunk of the rowlocks, the breeze blowing strands of hair into my face. I watched as the muscles in my thighs tensed and relaxed and my feet pushed against the bar.

I took us further and further upstream, glancing over my shoulder occasionally to check our course, keeping silent for fear that if I talked, he'd suggest we turn back. I wanted to go on all afternoon. The river was quiet, and apart from the creak of the oars and the lapping of the water around us, the deep peace was punctured only by the cries of the birds which darted over the surface and the warm drone of a small outboard motor on an inflatable dinghy coming down the estuary. We left the moorings far behind and got up into the shallower water whose edges disappeared amongst the scrubby mudflats. Peter said nothing. He was watching the marshes as we passed them but I wondered whether he was seeing them at all. His eyes were glazed, as though his focus was turned inward, and his lips had gone back into their usual line.

At the top of the river, feet from the bridge, I stopped rowing and let the oars idle in the water.

'Do you want to take us back or shall I?' he said, coming out of his trance.

'I'm happy to carry on, unless you'd like to?'

'No – not if you're happy.'

The effort had made me hot. I'd taken my jacket off before starting, to free my arms, but now I took off my jumper, too, so that I was down to a long-sleeved T-shirt. I turned the boat around, casually using only the left oar as I had seen him do earlier, feeling as if I had been doing this all my life.

'Go in here,' he said, as we came back under the bridge and round the pontoon of the dinghy park. 'You can keep her here for the time being.'

I brought us alongside and he stepped out on to the jetty. The dinghy rocked as his weight left it. He took the rope from the bow and tied it up to a ring. The cold in the air had made itself felt as soon as I slowed down and I put my jumper back on. I picked up my jacket and gently stood up.

'Pass me the oars and rowlocks,' he said. 'Don't keep them in the boat – they're too easy to steal.'

Preparing to get out, I reached for the edge of the pontoon to steady myself but he put out his hand instead. I hesitated but took it. His palm was rough and I felt his strength as he pulled me up out of the boat. Embarrassed by the contact, though, I let go too early. My back foot – the dry one – was still leaving the boat and it caught the edge. I kept my balance but my foot dragged through the water.

Peter was looking at me. At first I took his expression for consternation but then I realised he was trying not to laugh. 'At least you're symmetrical now,' he said, mouth twitching.

I tried indignation but couldn't manage it: the euphoria of the rowing bubbled up and became laughter I couldn't contain. Peter's laugh was low and warm, surprising, but when after a few seconds I glanced up to see his face, he stopped abruptly and shoved his hands into his pockets, looking if anything slightly guilty.

'Right, well,' he said. 'I'll leave you to it.' He turned and headed up the jetty.

I called after him and he turned round.

'Thanks,' I said. 'For the boat.'

He nodded quickly. 'No problem.'

Walking back along the harbour front with the oars tucked under my arm, I passed the queue for the ferry. There were more cars waiting than usual, weekend visitors making the Sunday-afternoon return to the mainland. The oars slipped a little and I adjusted them, holding them tighter against my body with my elbow. My feet were soaked, my hair was a rat's nest and at the base of my fingers I could feel the start of blisters, but it occurred to me that to the non-Islanders I would look like someone with a connection to the water, a local, and I quite liked the idea.

I crossed between the cars and made my way up to the house. Leaning the oars against the wall, I got the key out of my pocket. A piece of paper had been put through the door. It was a note from Sally, written in a round and looping script, asking me for supper on Tuesday.

The breeze which tangled my hair on the river had strengthened during the evening and now blew through the rigging of the boats in the harbour to carry its eerie chiming music across the grass to the house. I lay in bed listening to it, too tired by the rowing and the sleeplessness of the night before to stay awake for long. On the rising tide after breakfast, I would take the dinghy out on my own for the first time, and I tried to focus on that rather than the thoughts of Richard that crept up on me again.

Some hours later, I came suddenly awake. A sharp noise downstairs had woken me. I lay frozen, heart thumping, ears trying so hard to hear that a pressure started to build between my temples. Nothing for a minute or so, maybe longer. Then it came again, a sharp, metallic rap near the bottom of the stairs – the sound of the flap of the letterbox dropping against the door. Though the bed was warm, all the hairs came up on my arms. Without moving even to turn on the bedside light, I waited ten minutes, maybe fifteen, but it didn't happen again. It was the wind, I thought, only the wind.

Chapter Twenty

From the pavement, Sally's house looked warm and alive. The kitchen blind was drawn but yellow light glowed around its edges and through it I could see her in silhouette, moving around in her fluttering, birdlike way. I knocked, there were quick footsteps and in a flurry I was inside and she was standing in front of me slightly nervously. The kitchen was steamy from the pot of pasta simmering on the hob and tendrils of hair were curling around her face. Her cheeks were flushed.

'It's only spag bol, I'm afraid,' she said, taking my jacket.

'It smells lovely,' I said. 'Just what I feel like.'

'I just thought it was a shame – it was really nice to talk to you last time and we've never got round to doing it again.'

'My fault – it was my turn to invite you but I had a deadline and everything else went by the board. But I'm back in the land of the living now.'

She turned away to rattle in the drawer for a corkscrew and I wondered again about the last time I'd seen her, in the Bugle that evening with Helen. She must just not have recognised me. It happened: I thought of all the times in London when I'd failed to identify people approaching me with broad smiles of recognition.

'I've been rowing,' I said. 'I've borrowed a boat and I've been out this morning and yesterday, up the river before going to work at the café.'

'Yes, I heard you were working with Mary. Whose boat have you borrowed?'

'Peter Frewin's. I was talking to Chris Harris about wanting one – do you know him? – and Peter was there and offered me it.'

'Kind of him.'

'Yes, very. He didn't warn me about the blisters, though – look at these; they're huge.' I held my hands out.

'Painful, but give them a week or so and they'll toughen up.'

'I'll get hard pads, like a cat.' I ran my thumb over them gently.

The glass door between the kitchen and the sitting room wore a heavy layer of condensation and from beyond it I could make out the sound of voices. 'I'm sorry,' she said as she handed me a glass, noticing me looking. 'We could sit next door but Tom's watching television. It's best not to interrupt him. This is nearly ready anyway.' She pulled out one of the chairs at the table for me and I sat and watched as she flitted here and there putting plates in to warm, filling a jug with water. The table was only laid for two.

She served the pasta and put her head round the door to the sitting room. 'Dinner's ready,' she said. There was no response that I could hear and she pulled the door gently closed. It was three or four minutes before the television went quiet; the plates sat cooling on the counter. As the door opened again, I turned in my chair to say hello.

He was tall, certainly six foot, and lean; when he passed me his shoulder blades were visible through his black jumper like the start of wings. His hands were in his pockets and his trainers squeaked on the linoleum tiles.

'Tom, this is Kate,' said Sally.

He took the plate that she held out to him and shoved a knife and fork into the back pocket of his jeans before turning round. Eyes the same grey as hers regarded me. He wasn't good-looking – his features were too large for his face, as if they had grown first – but he would be. He knew it, I thought; there was a self-confidence in the way he acknowledged my presence with only the faintest nod. He took a can of Coke from the fridge and went up the stairs behind me. A door slammed, making the wall next to me shudder.

'He spends so much time in his room,' she said apologetically. 'He's got exams in the summer but I don't know if he's working. I know he's smoking.'

'Wouldn't be a teenager if he wasn't.'

'I suppose I should be grateful it's only smoking, shouldn't I, not going round getting girls pregnant? He's only a couple of years younger than I was when I had him. It changes your life, having a baby that early.'

'You've done it, though – had a baby,' I said. 'I wonder if I ever will.' There was a stab of complicated feeling in my stomach as I remembered Richard's baby by the other woman; it could only be a few months old.

'It's not everything,' she said, suddenly fierce. She looked away and we ate in silence for several moments, until the weight of it between us became uncomfortable.

'So what's it like working for Mary? She's always been manic – people round here joke about it. She'd probably have gone pop years ago if it wasn't for yoga.'

I smiled. 'She's only really in for a couple of hours at lunch; the rest of the time I'm there on my own. Not that many people come in.'

'It'll start getting busier in a month or so – once we get into March.'

'I hope so. I did it for the company, really.'

'You said last time you were lonely – working at home.'

'Hermits could translate without feeling over-socialised.'

She wouldn't let me help clear up so I stayed at the table and finished my wine while she scurried about rinsing our plates under the tap, loading them into the dishwasher. When she sat back down, she refilled our glasses again, emptying the bottle. Careful, I thought to myself; remember Chris's.

'When we had coffee,' she said, 'you said you'd broken up with someone. Was that why you came here?'

'One of the reasons – the main one. But I'd been in a rut for a while, without realising it – well, acknowledging it.'

'Were you together for a long time?'

'A year and a half. But it wasn't . . . simple.'

She put her elbow on the table and looked at me. I hesitated but then thought, what the hell: she was open with me. 'He was married.'

173

'That's hard.' She frowned.

'I didn't know for the first six months. It was a total shock. But then, the thought of going back to what things were like before I met him . . .' If I'd known then what he was really like, I thought, I would have run for my life.

She picked at a loose piece of the raffia of her table mat. 'I've done that, too, put up with things I shouldn't. I've made some real mistakes. Particularly in my early twenties, when Tom was so young and I looked round and everyone else from school was off at university or going out all the time. I felt left out – no, actually, I felt cheated. I know that sounds bad. It's better now – Tom's almost grown up – but then? Forget it. I was the girl with the baby.'

'That must have been very difficult.'

'Yeah. But with what my dad was saying about having thrown myself away, I thought I deserved it then. I let people treat me like that. I get really angry with myself when I look back.'

'I'm always telling myself that I'll learn from my mistakes,' I said, smiling. 'But I never do.'

'Glad I'm not the only one.' The bottle was empty and she stood up and took another from the fridge, holding it out to me tentatively. 'Shall we?'

'Oh, why not?' I said. The tenor of the evening was changing. It was the wine, of course, but she seemed to be relaxing, the conversation getting easier. I shifted into a more comfortable position on my chair, tucking one of my legs under the other.

'I've done the gamut of dodgy boyfriends,' she said. 'The ones who never phone, the ones who only want sex,' she lowered her voice a little, glancing at the ceiling, 'the ones who borrow money or just take it from your purse – can you imagine?' She fluttered her hand, indicating the modesty of our surroundings.

'I've never had one of those, thank God, not that I've ever had any money, either. But Richard – the last one – was the worst. He played games. Seeing how far he could push me.' I tapped my nails on my glass, feeling a sudden urge to blurt it all out, try to lessen the pressure. 'And at the end he went for me. He hit me, tried to force me to . . . Anyway.'

'God.'

'It was my own fault –'

'How is it your fault if he hit you?'

'It was my fault I was still there – that I hadn't ended it months before. I didn't know whether I was coming or going – he made everything so confused.' I looked down, realising that I still hadn't told Helen any of this at all. 'Sorry,' I said.

'Talking helps. Stops you feeling like you're the only one.'

'Yes.' I paused. 'Sally, with Alice and Peter – was it something between them that made her depressed? She was depressed, wasn't she?'

She sat back in her chair, surprised at the sudden shift in the conversation. I wished I'd managed a little more subtlety. 'You mean, did he ever hit her?' she said.

'No, no – I mean, were they happy together? You said that he loved her but . . .'

'What you have to understand about Alice,' she said, her voice cooler now, 'is that she was highly strung – unstable. She always was – long before Pete. I could see it the first day that she started at college. Some girls are just like that and there are men who seem to like it – want to look after them.

'Look, I'm not saying Pete's perfect – far from it. He can be difficult. He was wild at college. He used to take boats off their moorings at night and sail them over to the mainland or just drift, lie up on deck smoking. We used to go with him, Alice and me. Oh, there were all sorts of things. When he was sixteen, he worked at the garage in Totland and they let him tinker about with this old motorbike which he eventually got going. Do you know the military road?'

'The one which goes along the edge?'

'He used to drive along there flat out at the dead of night without any lights on. He was too young to take his test, let alone pass it. The police caught him twice. He's always been like it – a risk-taker. He took a massive gamble at the start of his business – sold his soul to the bank, basically. It worked but things could have been really different.'

Again I thought of Richard, the mortgaging and remortgaging he'd told me he'd done at the beginning. I remembered thinking how most people wouldn't have been able to sleep at night, knowing they had debts like that – hundreds of thousands of pounds. He had shrugged. Perhaps Peter was the same, and the cavalier attitude extended to women in his case, too, whatever Sally had said last time.

'But the main thing about Pete was how much he loved Alice.' She was looking at me steadily, almost as if she had heard my thought and wanted to contradict it. 'He loved her when he was sixteen and he loved her when they were married and he loves her now. Everything he did was for her. It still is – he hasn't given up hope.'

From through the ceiling all of a sudden came the thump of bass guitar, heavy as footfall. 'Oh God – I was hoping we'd get an evening off,' she said. 'Excuse me a sec.'

She went upstairs and a moment or two later I heard the sound of gentle knocking. No response. She knocked again, a little louder. There was another thud of bass so profound that I felt it go through the floor under my shoes and then I heard the door crack open. There was a brief exchange of words that I couldn't make out over the music and then the door slammed shut again. The volume stayed the same.

She came back down and we tried to pick the conversation up again but it was hopeless. It wasn't just the music, which reached regular thrashing crescendos; worse was the embarrassment that was coming off her in waves. Every thump of the bass overhead seemed intended to humiliate her and demonstrate her lack of authority. If I'd been her, I would have barged in and unplugged the stereo.

It was a relief to step out of her humid kitchen into the antiseptic cold of the night air. I stood in the lane for a moment or two after the door closed behind me, letting my eyes get accustomed to the darkness. The streetlamps here gave a minimal light which somehow did not spread to illuminate the road but hung in narrow bells beneath the posts. It was only half ten but the quiet had settled over the town again; it was almost as silent as when I had come this way on Saturday morning. I turned to go, suddenly aware of being alone in the dark, and as I did, there was a movement in the upstairs window of Sally's house. I turned my head quickly, just in time to see the corner of the curtain dropping back into place.

Chapter Twenty-one

Sally was right about the blisters. Within days, they hardened into tough pads at the base of my fingers and the pleasure of the rowing was unalloyed even by that mild discomfort. I went out whenever I could: before work or, on the couple of days we'd closed early and there was still enough light, afterwards. I loved the ritual of it: untying and pushing off, the first strokes, the oars growing warm under my hands, the speed with which I could get round the pontoon now and up under the bridge. It was simple, this new proficiency, but I was oddly proud of it.

Today I'd woken to the sound of rain against the bedroom window and it had continued all morning and for most of the afternoon. It was after four by the time it stopped and there wasn't much daylight left but I decided to take the boat out anyway, just for a while; I needed the exercise after being inside all day. I bailed out the rainwater then untied and rowed up to the edge of the river near the mill, where I idled in the shallows, seeing how close I could get to the marshes without running myself aground. I pulled the oars in and leaned gently over the side to watch the wildlife moving in the inches of water: a crab no bigger than a coin, its legs and body still soft and white, scuttling between weed and stone, and a shoal of fish the size of needles moving as one, darting this way and that as though on a desperate search. Strings of bubbles rose from an unseen source: a larger crab, a fish or perhaps a mollusc of some sort, processing the air from beneath the mud.

I stayed in the boat until after dark. The tide carried me up into the farther reaches of the estuary and overhead the first stars began to appear like tiny bulbs in the deep blue. The fading light and the sound of the water lapping against the sides gave me a sense that I was in a world of my own.

Since the supper at her house, I'd been thinking about Sally. She wasn't the sort of person I'd usually have been friends with; until now, perhaps, we hadn't had much in common. She'd had Tom and her life on the Island as a mother; I'd had London, no responsibilities at all except for myself and – after a fashion – trying to make a career. Her nervous energy was so different from the confidence of Helen and the other women I knew. And yet I was warming to her; I was grateful for her efforts to be friendly. And we did have something in common: we were both lonely. I'd thought at first that having her son would insulate her from it but now I thought the opposite. Was there anything lonelier than being disrespected, even despised, in one's own home, by a child for whom one had sacrificed so much? I remembered how he had sabotaged her evening, how embarrassed she had been, and felt sad for her.

Back at the cottage I switched on my computer and emailed Matt; I hadn't told him about the dinghy yet and he would remember rowing up the river years ago with Dad. The view of the harbour from the study window was the night-time one, just the lights along River Road and by the harbour office, and the smaller ones of the boats in the harbour itself; funny how being inside made the outside look so much darker.

I was just about to close the internet connection and turn the computer off when the message arrived, appearing in my inbox with a merry ping.

I haven't given up on you and I'm not going to. It's time to stop playing hard to get now, Katie.

   You never believed I would sort things out with Sarah, did you? Well, I've done it. I've told her that I can't wait any more, that I need a divorce now. She's heartbroken but you forced my hand – you wanted me to leave her, didn't you? So I've done it and I'm free to be with you – I'm all yours.

Come back to me. You've made your point. You're the only woman I've ever felt like this about. We're different – we're two of a kind. Marry me.

I pulled away from the screen as if he had bodily appeared there, inches in front of me. The nausea I'd felt when Sarah rang swept through me again. I'd expected contact after her call but the days had passed and I'd begun to allow myself a small nugget of hope that she was wrong, that he'd given up and moved on, but now here he was, inevitable. *I haven't given up on you and I'm not going to.*

Marry me. I made myself look at the screen again. It was unbelievable – actually beyond my powers to grasp. How could he think – after everything that had happened? Didn't he remember? Had he forgotten why I'd run away? Had he forgotten that he'd almost raped me? *Playing hard to get*: he thought this was a game.

I couldn't look at it any more. I deleted the message, snapped the laptop closed and went downstairs. My heart was still hammering against my chest wall and taking deep breaths did nothing to slow it down. I poured a glass of wine and paced the sitting room while I gulped it.

It was minutes before my breath came more easily and I could impose some order on the riot of dread and fear that had broken out inside me. 'They're words,' I told myself, 'just words. He can't hurt you now; he can't hurt you.'

I poured another glass of wine and stopped pacing. Now I was angry with myself: I shouldn't let him affect me like this; I should be stronger. Come on, I thought; are you going to let him do this to you? Turn you upside down with an email? He's just a vicious bully who's furious because he can't reach you. This is a mind game and he's playing it because it's all he's got. You can beat him.

I repeated the thought over and over, until the repetition began to make it real. Later on, though, lying in bed, the fear returned, not with the panic that made my pulse race but creeping and insidious. The worst thing was that I didn't understand. How could he ever think I would go back? How could he lie so easily about what had happened with Sarah? It was the sheer incomprehensibility of him that was so frightening. Trying to understand him – what he might think or do – was impossible, like grappling with smoke.

When I went to open up the café in the morning, Mary was already there. 'Been here since seven,' she said, tucking her fringe back inside the front of the elasticated mop cap she wore when cooking. 'I want to take Mum away for a bit of sun for a few days – her arthritis is terrible in all this cold and damp, poor thing – and I'm trying to get ahead of myself and get some stuff in the freezer. Make us a coffee?'

We leaned against the counter and drank our cappuccinos. 'You're getting good at these,' she said. 'Look at the foam on that – couldn't do better myself.'

The café was hot from the oven, and the air was freighted with the buttery scent of the muffins that she'd just put in. Despite her cooking mission, she was relatively relaxed; it was good to stand and talk for a few minutes, to be asked my opinion on whether a lower-calorie chocolate cake featuring beetroot might be a bridge too far for the palettes of Yarmouth. In this environment of utter normality, even the idea of Richard was surreal. In company, clearing the tables and taking orders, I felt the power of his shadow diminish.

Mary stayed all day, stopping only for another coffee just before lunchtime. Every half an hour the aroma coming from the tiny kitchen was superseded, the muffins giving way to banana cake, then fruit cake and then on to the soups. The procession of new produce cooling then being clingfilmed, labelled and stowed in the freezer lent a momentum, as if we were making preparations for a siege.

At about half three, she ran out of eggs. 'I'm just going to whizz up to the Co-op in Freshwater,' she said, untying her apron and hanging it on the hook by the back door. 'I've only got a couple more things to do but I want to get it all done today. Won't be long.'

The elderly couple who'd been eking out a pot of tea for the past hour finally paid the bill and shuffled off. I propped the door open for a couple of minutes to let some fresh air in; the vat of soup simmering on the hob was fogging the place up. I got a tray to clear their table, put the things in the dishwasher, then went to the store cupboard to replace the bottles of organic lemonade that had sold over lunch.

As I came back in, my arms full, I saw a figure slip out of the front door. It was a furtive movement; I knew immediately that something was wrong. I glanced at the till – still closed, thank God – then put the bottles down and ran out on to the street. 'Hey!' I called after him.

He was moving down towards the Square with a walk that he could only have got from American cop shows, a ludicrous sort of pimp roll. Despite the bagginess of his jeans, he was visibly thin and his light brown hair was long on the collar. With a sinking feeling I realised I knew him.

'Hey!' I shouted again.

He turned slowly. Sally's son Tom looked back at me, his face a picture of scorn. In his hand was a bottle of the lemonade.

'Give me that. You haven't paid for it.'

'Oh, fuck off, you sad cow. No one gives a shit.' Without taking his eyes off me, he cracked the bottle open, took a long swig, then turned and rolled off.

'Everything all right?' Mary asked when she bustled back in with bags of shopping ten minutes later.

I'd debated whether to tell her and had rung the missing lemonade through the till and paid for it myself in case I decided not to. I didn't mind getting Tom into trouble but I thought Sally had enough on her plate already. It would ruin any chance of our becoming friends, too, if I told her. On the other hand, I thought Mary ought to know, if only so she could be on her guard against it happening again.

'Let me guess who,' she said, when I'd explained what had happened.

'What?'

'Tom Vaughn. Bound to be – it always is, anything that happens round here like that. Stealing, vandalism, any kind of trouble – he's totally out of order. You saw his comment on Christianity

182

at the church over Christmas? We all feel sorry for Sally – she does her best with him but he's beyond her. He wasn't ever a nice child but over the last couple of years he's turned into a right little psycho. The only reason he's been allowed to get away with as much as he has is that people like her.'

'Should I tell her – about the lemonade?'

She shook her head. 'No, I'll have a word. Easier coming from me.' She opened the fridge door and started unpacking the shopping. 'Much more of it and someone will have to get the police involved, though.'

On the phone that evening I told Helen what had happened. I also told her about the email from Richard.

'He's written again? But it's been weeks now.'

'It's probably nothing but, you know, it is slightly worrying,' I said, feeling the gulf between the word and reality. 'He's split up with his wife. I think that's what it's about: she's gone so he's looking for the replacement. I'm the obvious choice.'

'But he knows you won't go back, doesn't he?'

'I don't know.' I took a deep breath. Before ringing her, I'd made up my mind to tell her everything; after all, I'd told Sally some of it and that hadn't been too bad. But now I felt the difference again, the shame of admitting to someone I knew well, someone whose life wasn't a mess, how I'd let it happen, how I'd been controlled by him to the point where I had risked my safety – my life. No, I thought; I had to tell her; I owed her the truth.

'There's something I haven't told you about Richard,' I said.

In the background, very close by, I heard another phone.

'Oh shit, that's my boss,' she said.

'Your boss? Helen, are you at work? It's nearly nine o'clock.'

'I know, I know. We're just flat out at the moment. The TV networks are doing their new scheduling – it's crazy. But it's only for a couple of weeks. Look, I've got to answer this. But I'll call you, OK? Speak soon.'

Later I stood at the sink to clean my teeth. In the small mirror above the basin I looked at my face, the same ordinary face that had looked back at me for years. It seemed incredible that this could be happening to me, that he'd picked me that night out of all the women in that packed bar. But I had been open to it, hadn't I? Lonely and bored, I'd been open to the idea of excitement, a powerful connection. He'd seen that in me and used it.

I spat out the last mouthful of toothpaste and put my brush back into the glass. Before turning off the computer, I had made myself check my email. Sure enough, there had been a message:

I'm putting your lack of response down to the fact that you're temporarily out of email contact.

*   *   *

There was always a single day, I thought, when the outgoing season conceded to the one which would come next. There had been signs before that the winter wouldn't last for ever but the following Saturday, while I waited for my toast to cook, I stood in front of the sliding doors in the sitting room and let the glass magnify the sun's heat on to my face until it made my cheeks rosy. The sky was piebald, patched with clouds, but if I stared, the sun behind them was strong enough that I could see their shapes against the red of my eyelids when I blinked. I slid the door open and stepped out in the yard. It wasn't warm but the cold was tempered, at least. I walked to the end of the yard and back, noticing new leaf buds on the clematis that came over the fence from my neighbour's garden. In the terracotta pots that I'd always assumed were empty there were long slim shoots – daffodils.

After breakfast I spent an hour or so in the boat, poking round the few little creeks and lagoons which I hadn't yet explored, drifting on shallows where the water scarcely seemed to move at all and watching a ragged heron standing storklike on the roots of a long-dead tree while he waited for a snack to swim into view. There was a group out from the sailing club near the bridge, ten or twelve little fibreglass boats that zipped here and there across the river like water spilled on a hotplate. Tucked under their tight sails, fat in padded life jackets, were boys and girls not even in their teens.

As I neared the pontoon on my way back in, I noticed a man standing on the quay wall by the harbour office. He was strikingly tall and there was something familiar about the set of his head and shoulders. Another few strokes closer confirmed that it was Peter, and he'd seen me. As I brought the dinghy alongside, he raised a hand and started down the jetty. I tied up and got ready to get out as his footsteps approached along the boards.

'Pass me those,' he said, as I made to slide the oars on to the pontoon. He took them and held them in the circle of one arm while he extended his other to help me.

'Thanks.' I sprung up next to him, leaving the dinghy rocking, and put my hand up to shade my eyes. His face was in shadow but the sun was streaming from behind him, outlining him and picking out chestnut tones in his dark hair. He was in the blue Musto jacket I'd seen before but a different – cleaner – pair of jeans.

'Dry feet today,' he said, smiling slightly.

'Yes – progress.'

'I was out sailing yesterday,' he said. 'First time this year.'

'In Chris's boat?'

'Mine. I didn't take it out of the water this winter.'

'Is it here?' I turned to look, expecting him to point it out.

'No – in the river at Newtown.'

A few seconds passed. A motorboat – huge, white and ugly, engine growling – had just left its mooring and the dinghies bounced and jostled against each other as its wash peeled across the harbour and passed beneath them.

'I was wondering yesterday,' he said, 'if you'd like to come with me next time? Maybe next weekend?'

Taken by surprise, I didn't say anything.

'Chris will take you out on *Sirene* when she's back in, I'm sure, but in the meantime – if you want to and you don't mind the cold? It's pretty bracing.'

'I can wrap up.'

'OK – good. Saturday, if the weather's decent?'

It was only as I was watching him stride back up the pontoon again that I realised what I'd agreed to. Oh God, I thought; why did I never think before jumping in with both feet? Surely if Richard had taught me anything, it was the need to be wary, and surely if there was anyone of whom to be wary, it was Peter.

Chapter Twenty-two

I asked you to marry me, you stupid bitch, and you think you can ignore me. You know, I always thought you were an intelligent woman. That's one of your little fantasies about yourself, isn't it, that you're clever? Well, you're being pretty fucking stupid now. I gave you the benefit of the doubt – I've given you days now – and still you don't deign to respond to me.

I've sacrificed my marriage and access to my son for you and this is how you repay my trust? Nobody does that to me – I'd have thought you'd know that by now.

You said once that you saw us as two points on the earth's surface, lit up by our connection. I think about that all the time, and do you know what, I think you're right. You might not be talking to me (more playground behaviour – Helen's idea?) but we're still connected. I lie awake wherever I am and I imagine you lying in your bed as well, and I feel our connection.

I can be a very powerful enemy.

It was late afternoon on Tuesday when Sally came into the café, nearly quarter to five, and most of the customers for tea and cake – eight or nine people; a busy day – had paid their bills and gone. I was cleaning behind the counter, clingfilming the salads and idly eavesdropping on the two old ladies nearby when the bell over the door went. Mary must not have said anything to her, I realised; she would have been too embarrassed to come in if she had.

'Hi,' she said, smiling. 'I've just been up the other end of town and I thought I'd come and say hello. It's nice in here, isn't it? Cosy.'

'Would you like anything? A cup of tea? Cake? It's very good.'

'Oh no, thanks. It's just a flying visit, to see how you're doing. Any news?'

'News? No – not really. Mary's away this week so I'm here on my own.'

'Me?' she said. 'No, nothing much. Tom's had half term but that's about all.' She looked around the room and then again at the cakes, her gaze settling on the chocolate sponge.

'Are you sure you won't have a piece?'

'I shouldn't.'

'Go on.'

'No, really . . .'

It dawned on me all of a sudden that the reason she was refusing was nothing to do with her weight or spoiling supper. It was about money: she couldn't afford it. I thought with a pang of the supper she'd cooked for me and the bottle of wine. 'Go on,' I said. 'I'm going to take a slice home. The chocolate one's lovely. I'll get these.'

'It does look nice.' She looked at me with a guilty expression.

'One slice won't hurt; you're slim as a bean,' I said. 'Go on – give the rest of us a fighting chance.'

After she'd gone, the ladies at the window table asked if it was too late for another pot of tea. It was, really; it was five already and I should have been closing up but they were sweet and I preferred to be here than back at the cottage where, however much I tried to distract myself, Richard's emails played on my mind, growing in significance the later it got, and the quieter outside.

It was because of the emails, I'm sure, that it happened. By the time the women had gone and I'd cashed up and given the café a final sweep, it was past six. The last traces of the red and apricot that had streaked the sky as the night came down had been erased, and now there was only the rich velvety black that I never saw in London, the first stars pricking out against its absorbent darkness.

I locked the door, tugged twice on the handle and then slipped the keys into my bag. The walk home was barely five minutes but with no insulating cloud, the air was so cold it felt wet on my hands and face. I felt in my pockets for my gloves.

It was when I looked up from putting them on that I saw him: a man so like Richard that my breath caught in my throat. His height; the way he stood, the shape of his body – identical. I stopped still. He was no more than a hundred yards away, just where the High Street met the Square, looking in Harwoods' window.

I was a few feet from the mouth of one of the alleys that led down between the cottages to the sea. I ducked into it and pressed myself into the ivy that spilled over the wall. My heart was pounding, my armpits suddenly wet. I held myself rigid. Every sound was magnified: the waves lapping at the wall at the bottom of the alley, the low hoot of a ferry over towards Southampton, a car coming into town on the road from Shalfleet. I was terrified that my feet would move, and the loose shingle give me away.

Blood thundering, ears straining, every muscle tense, I waited for the footsteps. I pictured him walking up the road, hands in his pockets, looking in at the end of the alleyway to see me: 'Hello, Katie. Waiting for me?'

I listened so hard that I almost imagined the footsteps but none came. No one passed the end of the alleyway at all. I stood there for five minutes, maybe ten, but then, as I gave a long, silent out-breath, I realised what I would look like to anyone who saw me: crazy. Paranoid.

Think, Kate. Yes, he had been like Richard – the same build, the same dark head – but I'd seen him from a distance and the High Street was poorly lit. His coat, too, had been wrong, full-length. He didn't have one like that and I couldn't imagine him in one; he had a three-quarter-length coat for over his suits or his leather jacket for jeans. But why was I even grasping at these details, when I knew it couldn't be him? He didn't know I was here, there was no way he could, and the emails made it plain.

I knew I still looked for him. In Newport on my birthday, there had been a man with dark hair the same velvet texture as his, and as I'd stood behind him at the checkout, I'd remembered my old urge to reach out and touch. As I'd driven through Shalfleet after the storm at Christmas I'd caught sight of a man with a similar build waiting to cross the road by the church. It hadn't been him – a momentary glance in the rear-view mirror had told me that – but on some subconscious level, I'd realised then, I was looking for him. At first I'd thought it was a vestigial thing, a hangover from the times when he was away and I'd sought traces of him in strangers, just to remind myself. Now, though, pressed into the ivy, I knew it was more than that: I was watching for him.

I waited a couple more minutes before gently standing away from the wall and taking two quiet steps to the end of the alley. I felt foolish doing it but I leant out and scanned the High Street, quickly at first and then again, to make sure.

The obvious route to the cottage was via the bottom of the High Street and the Square, but instead I took a circuitous one along South Street and back around by the church. My heart rate had slowed from its pounding panic but it was still beating much too fast, and now the sweat on my forehead was cold. I walked quickly, conscious all the time of the darkness behind me and the shadows that seemed to stretch and move in the corners which the street lighting didn't reach.

On Saturday I waited for Peter on the pavement in Bridge Road. When we'd made the arrangement, he'd said he would come and pick me up from the cottage. I'd done a double take at that, wondering how he knew where I lived, and then remembered that Chris had mentioned it at dinner. Still, he wouldn't know which house in the row was mine.

We had a decent day for the sailing. Earlier it had been cold enough for my breath to make clouds when I had taken my bottles and newspapers down to the recycling bins but it had warmed up a few degrees, and the sky was the crisp blue which faked summer. I'd felt anxious all week at the thought of today. The idea of it alarmed me in the same way that supper at Chris's had, with its sudden and strange leap in intimacy. I was determined not to make an idiot of myself today, though, and determined, too, not to let my nervousness show. It was kind of him to offer the trip and it would be another chance to try to get the measure of him. I wanted to see if he would mention Alice. Since Richard's emails

190

had started, I'd spent less time thinking about her and I felt almost guilty about that, as though I was letting her down, starting to forget.

It was ten o'clock and several cars passed while I stood on the pavement, people who'd been into Yarmouth for Saturday morning shopping. Another one turned in at the top of the road now, an old silver BMW. The driver was wearing shades against the low sun and it wasn't until he pulled in at the kerb that I realised it was Peter. He reached over and opened the passenger door from the inside.

'Hop in.'

I folded myself down, the seat lower than I'd expected. I turned to look at him, slightly wrong-footed by the sunglasses, unsure whether I should try to make out his eyes behind them.

'Sorry,' he said, pushing them back off his face. 'This low sun really gets me. Ready to go?'

He pulled off and I put my seatbelt on, glad to have a couple of seconds to think of something to say. The radio was on – the news on Radio 4, a male voice that rumbled with a story about missile attacks on the Pakistani border, just loud enough to break the silence.

'Good week?' he asked.

'Yes, not bad. We're a bit busier at the café though I'm feeling a bit funny about that.'

'Why?'

'Not about the café itself, that's fine, but it's time I got another book to translate, I think. Working there feels like playing.'

'Nothing wrong with having a bit of time off. That's the only thing I regret about being self-employed. I would have liked to have gone away after . . .' he stopped.

There was a moment's silence. 'I'm sorry,' I said, 'I don't know what you do.'

'We make a system for containing oil-slicks. Basically, it's a series of long air cushions that lie on the surface of the water round a slick and keep it from spreading.'

'Like a bolster down the middle of the bed?'

'Exactly.' Out of the corner of my eye, I saw the side of his mouth lift.

I turned to look out of the window as we went along the top of the common. The Solent was glittering with the hard light today, the view of the mainland so precise it looked closer than I'd seen it before; I could make out the occasional house up the coast from the Lymington River, even individual trees. I thought of Richard over there; he really wasn't far away. What was a couple of hours in the car and half an hour on a ferry? The distance was all psychological, hardly an obstacle at all. For a moment, staring at the strip of land, it seemed to shimmer with the potential energy of his presence. I blinked hard and looked away.

Peter took his hand off the gear-stick and turned up the radio. 'Do you mind?' he said. 'I'm a bit of a news addict. It's nearly finished.'

'No – of course.'

We were out of Yarmouth now and along the stretch of road bordered on both sides by the old natural wood. He slowed right down all of a sudden to avoid a pair of kamikaze rabbits that flung themselves into the road at our approach. I glanced sideways at him. His forehead was furrowed as he frowned at them, the lines at the corners of his eyes deep where they were visible at the edge of the sunglasses. There was something Slavic about the height of his cheekbones, I thought; they gave his face an elegance that otherwise it lacked. The sleeve of his navy jumper was pushed up, revealing a muscled forearm covered with dark hair. His hands were large with long straight fingers, the nails cut short.

I'd driven through Shalfleet lots of times but I'd never been down to the river. Peter took a left and we went along a narrow lane between the New Inn and a couple of pretty stone cottages. A few hundred yards on, the tarmac road ran out and we came on to a shingle track whose potholes the heavy rains last month must have done nothing to improve. On our right beyond a long grassy bank rimmed with scraggy hawthorns was what looked like the top of the river, not more than forty or fifty feet across. A great number of Canada geese obscured the surface in a moving, honking carpet of black and brown and white. Even where the water was visible, it wore a layer of feathers.

'Bloody things,' he said, noticing me looking. 'They're thugs – huge gangs of them intimidating other birds, eating all the vegetation.'

The track led past a garden bordered by oak trees. In it I could see a green wooden hut with sun-leached curtains at the window and three caravans – one with the rounded shape and windows of the 1950s – that seemed to be shrinking back into the woods behind them. There was another caravan, this one dilapidated to the point of near collapse, at the end of the boatyard in which Peter pulled up and parked the car. Its door was open and he said hello to the men in overalls sitting inside having a tea break. Their 'morning' came back rich in the Island accent that I recognised now, with its elongated rural vowels.

I looked around while Peter took an outboard engine from the boot of the car. The yard was full of boats on struts for the winter, their decks covered by tarpaulins on which pools of rainwater and a scurf of dead leaves had collected. Beyond the yard was a stone-built quay, the top covered in shingle, with a small slipway and ladders to the water. There the river was broader and there were boats on moorings. Gulls rode the breeze-chequered surface. On the other bank, the land lay low and flat, punctuated here and there with trees whose growth was stunted by the salt-poisoned earth. Oddly, it reminded me of pictures I'd seen of Africa, the same palette of mustard yellows, faded greens and browns.

Peter carried the outboard to one of the small wooden dinghies pulled up on to the strip of grass and turned upside down to stop it filling with rain. He righted it and dragged it down to the water, then got in and connected the engine. I passed him the petrol can and the bottles of water he'd brought.

I pushed us off, then sat on the thwart in the middle to balance our weight. The noise of the motor made conversation difficult so instead I watched our wash as it fanned out on the river behind us, a widening white V. We passed a large area of marsh extending down from the quay to the opening of another branch of the river, isolated mud stacks topped with blowing grass and sea heather. In the foot or two of mud which the incoming tide had yet to cover, a tern picked busily, the feathers at its wing-tips ruffled by the breeze. The air was rich with the smell of salt and seaweed and the chemical tang of petrol. We passed more boats, their size gradually increasing as the water got deeper, and a barge-like platform with an industrial clutter of ironwork on deck.

'For laying buoys,' he shouted.

A few minutes later and we were down the river enough to see the Solent. Something moved fast on the periphery of my vision and, turning quickly, I saw a scow cutting behind us, its blood-red sail tight with wind. Immediately I thought of Alice. Had she sailed *Vespertine* in the river here? She must have been here hundreds of times with Peter. Presumably she'd been in this dinghy, had sat just where I was sitting now. I pushed that thought away, unnerved by it. The scow tacked sharply to avoid a muddy promontory and as it zipped in front of us, I saw the boy at the helm was no more than eleven or twelve, his curly ginger hair blowing bright in the wind.

A minute or so later, Peter throttled down the engine and we came alongside a white-hulled wooden yacht. *Beatrice* was written on the stern in black italics. He tied us on and then stood and swung himself up on to the deck. I passed the things and then he pulled me up next to him.

'Have a seat in the cockpit while I get a few things organised.'

It was an old boat, I thought, the fittings on deck all wooden and brass, not steel and chrome like a lot of the modern yachts I'd seen tied up at the quay in Yarmouth. It was a good size but not big; a boat to use rather than a status symbol. For such a tall man, he was surprisingly light on his feet. I noticed the unhurried but efficient way he moved around, taking a long hook out of the locker opposite and retying the dinghy to the mooring buoy at the bow, bringing in the fenders. He slid the hatch back and went down into the cabin.

'Shall we have some coffee before we go?' he called up from below.

I climbed carefully down the wooden steps to join him. He was lighting a ring on a gas stove and filling a tin kettle with water from one of the bottles.

'It's lovely – the boat.'

'Do you like her?' He turned and smiled at me suddenly. 'I've had her five years. I always wanted a wooden boat, an older one. She was built in the fifties.'

I sat on the step while we waited for the kettle to boil. The cabin was much larger than it looked from the outside. To the left there was the galley with the stove and a small square sink and on the right a sloping table for charts. In the middle of the cabin, illuminated by the daylight coming through round portholes, was a fold-down table with bunks on either side. There was a rich smell of damp and diesel.

When the kettle whistled, he made coffee in two enamel mugs and we went back on deck to drink it. The breeze felt newly cold having been out of it for a few minutes but the air itself was mild, especially for the end of February. A pair of swans swam up, their legs powerful beneath the surface. I watched as they arched their long smooth necks to dip their beaks into the water, their feathers white as angels' wings, their black eyes assessing.

The motor started with a wheezy cough and chugged under the floor beneath my feet. Peter let us off the mooring and came back to the cockpit. A cloud of blue diesel smoke hung over the water behind us. A couple sitting out in a boat further down the river raised their hands to greet him as we passed. There were more marshes on our left and then the channel took us out between a pair of beaches that guarded the mouth of the river like cats' paws. The one on our right had signs prohibiting landing.

'It's a nesting area for seabirds,' he said. 'It's to stop people disturbing them or collecting the eggs.'

When we reached clear water beyond the river, he started to put up the sail. The sound of waves moving round us and the breeze in the rigging was loud in the abrupt peace when he cut the engine. I watched while he hoisted the sail and then paid out the rope so that it filled with wind. The boat leaned with it.

'Come and sit over here,' he said. I moved across and braced my feet against the lower seat as he pulled the sail tighter and our angle deepened. The water bubbled and raced past us, suddenly close.

I measured our progress against old posts and trees, and the shore slipped past at a surprising rate. Beyond it, the body of the

Island rose in a gentle swell, richly green. The breeze blew my hair round my face and occasionally we hit a wave that sent up spume I could taste in the air. I shot surreptitious glances at Peter. He was sitting at the back of the cockpit, his hand resting lightly on the wooden tiller, the adjustments he made to our course every now and again almost imperceptible. Even behind the glasses he was squinting into the sun, forehead furrowed again. His right leg was tensed to stop him sliding, the muscle in his thigh curving under the denim.

A seagull floated above us, angling to ride the breeze with an elegance it could never own on land. The mildness of the weather had brought out more boats than I had expected and the Solent was dotted with sails that were white against the water like pointed teeth. I'd dreaded the thought of long silences and awkward conversation but in fact there was something easy about the lack of constant talking. He was undemanding; I was free to look around and watch and let my thoughts wander. To my surprise, I felt myself relaxing.

He took us up until we could see Cowes and then we turned around. I swapped sides and faced the mainland instead. There was a cargo ship between us and the shore, the containers on deck stacked like Lego. 'I thought we could go up the Beaulieu River for lunch,' he said. 'Would you like to steer for a bit?'

'I've never done it before.'

'I'll show you.' He moved over and I sat next to him, careful not to get too close. 'You want to get near to the wind without heading directly into it. You feel where it's coming from? No sudden movements. That's it. If you think you're going too fast, just broaden the angle a bit, spill some of the wind out. It's all about physics.'

'That doesn't augur well for me, I warn you.'

He took his hand off the tiller and let me have it. The sail tightened above us again, the tension lines that he pointed out returning. The shore of the mainland began to move past us more quickly. The sail was no longer blocking the sun; it shone on my face so that I had to screw up my face like he had.

'Do you want my sunglasses?' he said, noticing.

'No, I'm OK. Thanks.' The tiller felt good under my hand. He looked away, watching the progress of a larger yacht ahead of us, and I took it as a positive sign that he didn't feel he had to keep a hawk eye on me. Almost as soon as I'd had that thought, though, I hit a wave with a real thump on the bow, and spray came flying back at us. I heard myself laugh out loud and when I looked at him, I saw that he was smiling, too.

'That's how not to do it,' he said.

The moorings at Beaulieu were all taken so he dropped the anchor instead, the heavy chain rattling out and out until it hit the bottom.

'Thanks for bringing all this,' he said, as I handed him one of the Cornish pasties I'd bought at the delicatessen earlier.

'Thanks for inviting me.'

'Here.' He put out his hand. I passed him the bottles of beer and he took the tops off with his penknife.

'You know, this is the closest I've got to the mainland since November,' I said, looking at the marshes nearby, the grass blowing this way and that.

'You haven't been back at all?'

'No need, really.' I shrugged and looked away but not before I'd seen the question on his face. I was annoyed that I'd brought it up; I didn't want to think about Richard now. For the first time in days, I'd felt the dread receding a little.

'Doesn't the quietness drive you mad, after London?'

'Sometimes, especially when I first got here. But I'm getting used to it now. I still feel like a total outsider, though.'

'Give it two hundred years and the locals will start to warm up a bit.' The sunlight caught his eyes and made them sparkle.

'Are you an old Island family?'

'No, only third generation.' He took a sip of beer. 'My grandparents came over before the war. To some people I'm still an overner.'

'Overner?'

'It's what the Islanders call people from the mainland. Like foreigner – and said with the same sort of inflection.'

'Have you ever lived on the mainland?'

He shook his head. 'I was going to go to London – I had a place at university – but I didn't in the end. I'd give that to the gulls if you're not going to eat it,' he said, indicating the crust of the pasty which I'd put down. 'Go to them before they come to you – best policy.'

I broke it into several pieces and threw them over the side. They'd barely touched the surface of the water before several gulls materialised. 'They were lying in wait,' I said.

'They've probably been tracking you since you left the shop.'

We sat without talking for a minute or two. The water was calmer than out in the channel and we were in the lee of a bank of sedge but the boat still rocked gently. I leant against the cabin side and listened to the waves lapping against the hull. Peter went below and I heard the sound of a pump and then water in the sink as he washed the mugs from earlier. I wished I could just come out and ask him about her. There was so much I wanted to know. One thing, however, was clear to me: I was becoming less suspicious of him. Something had happened with Alice, yes, but I was no longer certain that he was at the root of it, as I'd once been convinced. Nonetheless, a small voice cautioned me that I was no judge of character.

After lunch, he lifted the anchor and we motored out from Beaulieu into the Solent and put the sails up again. We went down to Lymington, then crossed over to come back to Newtown on the Island side. The sky was beginning to cloud over, turning the water a greyer shade of green, and the wind seemed to bite a little harder but I could have stayed out for hours regardless. Like I did when I was rowing, I felt different, somehow more alive. I thought of Alice again and the two women I'd overheard in the Mariners, months ago, before I'd even met Peter. Hadn't they said that she went out in her boat all the time, in all weathers? She'd told me that herself, how she'd thought it was the only thing that kept her sane.

Peter let me take the helm again and I got better at working out where the wind was and steering smoothly. I felt a strange sadness when we came back into the river and he took the sails down, as if the access to something wonderful and otherwise out of my grasp had been shut off again.

On the mooring, I packed up the lunch things while he put the sail covers back on. Then he replaced the hatch-boards and locked them, and we got into the dinghy and motored back up the river to the quay. The light was softening and the tide which had been coming in this morning was now hard away, leaving greater and greater expanses of exposed mud. My nose was beginning to run with the cold.

'That was a good day,' he said, when we were in the car, weaving round the potholes on our way back up to the village.

'I loved it – thank you.'

'You'll have to come again. Come next weekend if you haven't got anything else on. Oh, and it's Pete, by the way. No one calls me Peter except Chris.'

Chapter Twenty-three

The next time I went down to row, I could see even from the harbour wall that there was something in the boat. It was in the middle of the central thwart, just where I sat. I kept looking, trying to work out what it was. I hadn't left anything there, I never did. Whatever it was, it was large, probably a foot across, and a greyish-white colour. It wasn't until I was on the pontoon, pulling in the mooring line to bring the boat closer, that I realised I was looking at a carcass.

I got into the dinghy for a closer look. It was the remains of what had been a substantial bird, a Canada goose or perhaps one of last year's cygnets. There was no head or even much of a neck, just a ribcage to which white, grey and light brown feathers adhered in clumps. The bones of it were as symmetrical as the ribs of a Viking ship. Obviously it had been dead some time: there was hardly any flesh left on the frame or within it, and what little there was had been dried by the sun and wind and rain until it was like biltong, a dark, desiccated substance in which the remaining feathers were anchored. The plumage itself was greasy-looking; there was a smear of something like tar across the largest patch of it and the rest of the feathers were ragged and grimy from post-mortem exposure to the elements. It stank.

How had it got into the boat? Clearly it hadn't flown here and died, just dropped out of the sky; something or someone had brought it here. I supposed it was possible that another animal had done it; a scavenging seagull might just have lifted it, then dropped it again, realising that it had taken on more than it could carry, but it seemed unlikely. It seemed unlikely, too, that if it had been dropped from a height even of five or so feet, it would have landed so neatly; it would have bounced into the bottom of the boat, surely. Might a fox have brought it? Not to a boat on water.

It would have to be moved before I could take the boat out and I didn't want to touch it. In the end I picked up one of the oars and slid its blade underneath the thing like a baker's paddle. Moving carefully in case I dropped it, I manoeuvred until the blade was over the water and then I turned it sharply and tipped the repulsive thing into the sea. For a second or two, its lack of weight kept it on the surface and I watched as it floated, rocking slightly, the feathers darkening as they grew wet. Slowly it sat lower and lower in the water and then, reaching critical mass, it sank. I kept my eyes on it as it went, a few last bubbles rising through the green water to burst on the surface. Finally it was swallowed from view.

Who had done it? Richard was my first, irrational thought but the real answer was easy enough when I thought about it: Tom. It had to be him: the vast majority of Yarmouth had no idea who I was and even less interest, and Mary had said that he was usually responsible for anything untoward that went on. What had she called him? *A right little psycho.* This was a petty act of revenge because I'd challenged him at the café. Pathetic.

It had been threatening rain all morning and while I'd been out in the dinghy it had started, letting down a fine sort of drizzle which grew gradually heavier until I was forced to abandon ship and come in. Now I sat at my desk and watched it falling steadily across the town green and the harbour. There were occasional squalls of wind which carried it sideways and made it hop in the large puddles already accruing in the gutters along River Road.

There had been some good news waiting for me when I'd turned my computer on. Sylvie, the editor for whom I had worked most often over the past three or four years, had emailed to say that she was currently in an auction for the rights to the first two novels in a new literary crime series; it wasn't settled and she might not get them but if she did, she'd been thinking of me to translate; would I be interested? The books – the first had been written, the second outlined – were set in Bristol, she said, which had made her think of me straight away.

I was touched that she'd remembered where I'd grown up. Though we often emailed and spoke on the phone when I was working on something for her, I'd only ever met her once in person, at her office in Paris. As she'd come to the door to meet me, my first impression had been glamour. She was in her late forties, I estimated, and was wearing a knee-length suede skirt the colour of crème caramel and a white shirt with a dramatic gold-and-leather necklace. Her thick dark hair, untouched by silver, was cut in a short bob that swung as she moved.

My second impression had been how much she resembled my mother, both in looks and style. My mother had even had the same haircut when I'd last seen her, the time I'd made a trip to Lyon, wanting to tell her in person that I was starting a career in translating. A part of me, I realised afterwards, had been hoping against all the odds that my news would make her proud of me. Instead she had looked surprised. 'Oh,' she'd said. 'But are you sure your French is good enough?'

While I had been in the dinghy earlier, the lifeboat had gone out. I'd heard the flare go up and only a couple of minutes later the roar of the engine as the boat left the harbour and sped away down the Solent. Now it was on its way in again, its orange decks moving slowly back to its mooring behind the masts of the yachts tied up at the quay. Where had Peter – Pete – been the morning it went out looking for Alice? I wondered. It must have been him who called the emergency services. Had he been there on the harbour when the flare went up?

There was a ping as the computer announced a new message. I clicked into my inbox and saw Richard's name there, seeming almost to pulsate with energy. *Ignore it*, I thought. *Don't read it – just get rid of it.* I clicked to highlight it and moved the curser up to the delete button at the top of the screen but then I hesitated. I stood up and went out of the room for a few moments. *If you don't read it, then he can't get to you*, I told myself; *don't let him in.* And then the other voice. *But what if there's something new? What if he's writing to say that he's found you, that he's coming?*

202

Disgusted with myself even as I was doing it, I went back to the study and opened the mail.

I'm thinking about you today, Katie. I'm thinking about our first night. You know there isn't a room in my flat where I don't have memories of your body against some item of the furniture. The dining table, the sheepskin rug, the coffee table, the counter in the kitchen – do you remember that? You couldn't get enough of me. I remember your body exactly, every detail of it – the scar on your knee where you fell off the climbing-frame at school, the mark of your rubella injection, that mole on your left breast. I remember what your hair looks like against your bare back. I remember how you smell, and how you taste – like rain, I always thought. I'm watching the rain today and thinking about that.

The images he conjured came spilling one after another, just as he planned, no doubt. I was filled with shame and revulsion, remembering how I had been so willing, how I had opened myself to him body and soul, his face that night as it contorted with agonised pleasure, his hands touching my face, my breasts. Quickly I deleted the mail, turned off the computer and unplugged it, as if that would somehow stop the pictures.

I needed to go out now, to be with people for a while and be normal. I would go to one of the cafés. Before I put my coat on, though, I quickly texted Helen: *Is it raining in London?*

Cats & dogs, came the response, and then, in another text about ten seconds later: *Why?*

Water was rushing along the gutters either side of the passageway and bubbling down the Victorian drains. I had an umbrella and my full-length coat but as I ran to Gossips, the rain was so hard that it was bouncing up off the ground and soaking the bottom of my jeans.

I ordered coffee and sat at one of the tables furthest from the counter. The room was busy – busier than I had ever seen Mary's – and there was Motown on the stereo, the chunter of the coffee-maker and a babble of conversation at the tables around me. I waited for the relief to come, for the shadow of Richard to be banished by the normality of it, people sitting together to eat a late lunch on a wet afternoon, but today it wasn't working. Instead his poison seemed to be leaching out to discolour it, to make it seem flimsy and impermanent, no protection at all.

I fought down a fresh wave of panic at losing even that small weapon against him. Yet again he'd known just how to get under my skin, to make me feel that I had traduced myself, let him know things about me that no one should know and which would be used against me. I thought of Tom and his street-tough attitude, his attempt at intimidation with the swan carcass in the boat; in comparison to Richard, he was laughable – almost sweet. Richard wasn't even here and yet he had fifty times the power to frighten me. I nearly laughed aloud now when I thought of Mary's description of Tom with his graffiti and petty theft as a psycho; what would she say if I told her even a fraction of what had happened with Richard? Tom was just a thug, like those bolshy Canada geese on the river at Shalfleet – a teenager at war with the world. Richard was something else altogether.

Psycho – psychopath. I turned the word over in my mind, and heard a click. It wasn't just a word, I knew that, a generic term bandied about by the tabloids when they wanted to whip up a public storm about some 'monster' or other. It was a real thing – a proper mental disorder. I'd read about it once, a big reportage piece in a magazine. A lack of any feeling for other people was what I remembered, and a complete lack of conscience about their behaviour. Psychopaths didn't seem to feel emotion in the same way as most people – fear or love or shame. And lies – there had been a lot about lies, about how psychopaths would say anything, lying without giving it a second thought, almost without seeming to know they were doing it. They were charming, too; in the article, I remembered now, the journalist had written about how she'd felt herself begin to be seduced by one of the psychopaths she'd interviewed, even though she'd been talking to him in prison. He was a handsome man with a soft voice and he'd told her she was beautiful at a time in her life when she'd been vulnerable, she'd confessed, the piece taking an unexpectedly personal turn.

The wheel in my brain was turning and with each revolution there was a new click, a falling into place. The violence against Sarah and me and who knows how many other women – the article had described how psychopaths shrugged off the injuries they'd inflicted on others; in some cases, they'd hardly even seemed to remember them. And womanising, promiscuity – now the floor seemed to tilt under my seat, and the noise in the room receded, like a tide going out. It made sense – it all made sense.

I sat up late on the internet. It was like old times at the flat in Earls Court, except then I had been happy for my neighbours across the street to see me in the light from the desk lamp; now the thought of my face illuminated in the window, lit up to be seen by anyone passing on River Road, made me feel so vulnerable that I pulled the curtains as soon as the light began to fade, twilight coming early because of the rain.

The more sites I read, the more certain I was. On academic and psychiatry pages I read about the psychopath's 'grandiose sense of self' and 'need for stimulation' and thought of his risk-taking and high-handedness in business, the repeated adultery, even the driving, which had been so terrifying. Promiscuity and infidelity came up again and again.

Later on I found myself in chat-rooms where people who'd been involved with psychopaths shared their stories, seeking comfort. There were several cases so similar to mine that it was like seeing my own situation described. Many seemed to start when their victims had been fragile, when they were bereaved or divorced or recovering from illness. A lot featured women who had been lonely for a long time, romantics who wore their hearts on their sleeves even now. In had swept a saviour, a new lover who caught them up in a whirlwind and made them forget all their problems. The attraction was always so strong, the protestations of love so fierce and swift. Then, when the fish was irrevocably hooked, it was payback time. The stories weren't just from women: there were accounts from men who'd met women who entranced them, almost put them under a spell, and then slept with their friends and spent their money before walking out of their lives without leaving so much as a note. Nor was it only the women who confessed to having suffered violence.

In every case I could see the warning signs – the charm, the precipitate declarations, the focus on sex and money, the endless lies. I got angry with myself: how, if I could see it in all of these cases, had I been so blind to it in my own? Then I came across a post from a woman who had been deeply wounded. 'I thought psychopaths were like Hannibal Lecter,' she'd written. 'It didn't occur to me that they walked the streets among us, just like ordinary people.'

Chapter Twenty-four

I'd swapped numbers with Pete so that we could be in touch about going out on the boat again. On the Friday of that week, I'd switched my phone on as I was walking back from my shift at the café and picked up a rather abrupt voicemail telling me that the forecast wasn't good and he had some work which he had to do instead. He might go out the following weekend if I was still interested; he'd call nearer the time.

I knew I'd been looking forward to sailing again but, even so, the extent of my disappointment surprised me. Clearly this was how it started, I thought; they got you hooked with rowing boats and dinghies and then, before you knew it, you were on to the hard stuff. It wasn't only the sailing that I regretted, though; I'd wanted the distraction, someone to do something with for a change.

I felt that need even more strongly now. I was spending hours on the internet, drawn to the chat-rooms even though all they did was make me more afraid. I read stories about men falsely accused by jealous psychopathic women and thrown in jail. I read about men and women who'd had to abandon their whole lives – homes, jobs, families, friends, even their names – to try to get free. There was one case in particular to which I came back again and again. It was the story of a woman who'd met a man in a bar in Toronto. A lawyer in her late thirties, financially successful but a workaholic, she had almost given up on the idea of a relationship and falling in love. For a year she had appeared blissfully happy but then her friends started to worry about her; she lost weight and always seemed exhausted. She cancelled arrangements and when she did show up, it was never on her own; always the boyfriend was there, intense and negative. When the first bruises had appeared she'd lied about them but after she'd turned up bleeding and in a nightie on her best friend's doorstep in the early hours of the morning in a driving blizzard, she'd finally agreed that she needed to leave him, accept help. But he hadn't let her leave. For nine months he pursued her – stalked her – sending abusive letters and emails, breaking into her house, turning up in restaurants where she'd made reservations though she'd gone miles out of her way to avoid the places he might be. In the end she'd changed her name and fled to America, leaving her whole life behind her. And it still hadn't been enough. He'd found her, tracked her down to a small apartment in Portland, Oregon, where he'd broken in and strangled her. The story was posted by her sister.

It had occurred to me that perhaps Pete regretted saying I should come sailing again, and that putting me off was a way of gently rescinding the invitation, but, true to his word, he did call the following Friday. The forecast was better, he said, overcast and not especially warm but with less chance of rain. He was calling from a landline, not the mobile whose number I'd stored; it was the first time I'd seen an Island code come up on my phone.

This time we left the Newtown River and turned to the west. We sailed past the woods that crowded down to the shore along that part of the coast, and then on towards Yarmouth. We passed the shingle bank where I had been standing when I'd watched the lifeboat tow Alice's scow back in, and I turned my thoughts away. I didn't want to think about her here, on *Beatrice*; I didn't like the idea of being in her place.

Pete saw her everywhere, I was sure. He was quieter today, the peace between us somehow different, more melancholy. As we went out by Fort Victoria on the point, I heard a bell tolling, its low funereal sound reaching towards us over the water. It sent a shiver over me.

'OK?' he asked.

'Fine – just a bit chilly. What's that bell?'

208

'It's in the buoy – Sconce, that one's called.' He pointed to a black metal structure rocking slowly on the waves about thirty feet away. 'If it's foggy here, you can't see the channel markers.'

The tolling went on and to me it sounded like a lament for all those who had been lost here – not only Alice but hundreds and hundreds of people, wrecked and drowned, stretching back through centuries. I tried to ignore it but on it went, lugubrious, until it was no longer a lament but warning, premonitory.

With no sun, the water was grey-green. It shifted constantly, the tidal race visible where the channel narrowed between the promontory at Hurst on the mainland and Sconce Point on the Island, the occasional white horse breaking the surface. There was a good breeze for sailing – about a force four, Pete said – and the sails were tight with it. He let me have the helm and moved around on the deck up near the bow putting up a deep maroon sail as well as the main one, pulling the rope hard down to run it up. 'The spinnaker,' he told me, coming back into the cockpit.

He was smoking today, which I hadn't seen him do before. His car didn't smell of cigarettes, either; I would have noticed. He cupped his hand around the flame while he lit one and then held it out to me. 'You do, don't you?'

'Occasionally,' I said. 'Thanks.'

'I thought we'd go down to Purbeck to see Old Harry.'

'Who's Old Harry?'

He smiled. 'It's a chalk stack by the cliffs there, part of the same seam as the back of the Island.' He lapsed back into silence, smoking his cigarette and tossing the butt over the side. I watched him surreptitiously. The Musto jacket had been replaced today by a heavy oiled-wool navy jumper, the collar of a checked shirt just visible underneath. The jeans were the paint-splashed ones but they'd been through the wash: the mud on the knees was gone. He looked more tired than he had last time, older. The circles under his eyes were deep and grey. It was my imagination, of course, but his hair seemed greyer, too, in the short bits above his ears. I offered him the helm but he shook his head.

It wasn't until after we'd eaten that he seemed to warm up a bit. It was a relief; I'd begun to think that he didn't really want to be here, that he'd only come out to honour his promise. I'd filled rolls today with roast beef and horseradish, two each, but he wolfed his down so quickly that I pretended I didn't want my second one and gave it to him. The banana and apple went in similar fashion.

'Here,' I said, keeping my hand on the tiller. 'You take this and I'll make us some coffee. There's biscuits, too.'

'It's OK, I'll do it.'

'No – it must be your turn now.'

It was warmer down in the cabin out of the wind. I filled the tin kettle, then found the matches in the cubby hole above the little stove and lit the ring. There was the sound of the winch up on deck and our angle deepened. I held on to the edge of the sink and steadied the kettle as it rocked on the frame that held it above the gas. Through the portholes on the lower side, I could see only water now.

When the kettle had boiled I climbed carefully back into the cockpit with the mugs. He lit me another cigarette and I sat near him at the back of the boat and listened to the water rushing past, bubbling behind us.

'I'm not good company today,' he said.

'You don't need to talk all the time for that.'

'It's her birthday – my wife's.'

Taken aback, I said nothing.

'I haven't been fair with you. This is why I postponed last week. I thought that you wouldn't want to come three weeks running and I really wanted some company today – you know: to take my mind off it. I didn't want Chris or my mother; I wanted someone who wouldn't fuss. I find your company,' he searched for the word, 'easy. But now I feel dishonest – like I've got you here under false pretences.'

'It's OK.'

'No, it's not.'

We lapsed into silence again but strangely it felt better, open at least. I watched a yacht coming the opposite way and noticed how much more slowly it was going than we were. 'Is that because of the wind direction?' I asked. 'That they're just sitting on the water like that, not really going anywhere?'

He shook his head. 'More the direction of the tide.' He finished his coffee and put the mug down by his feet. 'I've never asked you why you came here,' he said. He looked at me directly for the first time all day. In the setting of their grey rings, his eyes looked particularly green.

'The usual story,' I said. 'Love affair gone bad.'

He nodded but didn't ask anything else. A minute or so passed.

'You know I said at Chris's that Dad used to bring us here on holiday? We came for the first time the year after my mother left us.'

He took his eyes off the sail and looked at me again.

'I associated it with getting your life back together. It was the first place where Dad and my brother and I were at all happy again. It was like a bomb through our family when she went. She'd threatened it – there were arguments and she shouted at him all the time, saying she'd leave – but we didn't think she'd really do it.'

'That's what it feels like,' he said. 'Like a bomb.' He took a small metal clip out of his pocket and looked at it, turning it between his fingers.

There was a sudden gust of wind that seemed to come from a different direction; the sail went slack and flapped wildly; the boat rocked upright.

'Sorry,' he said, when he'd got it under control again. 'I'll concentrate.'

When we came in sight of the chalk cliffs at Purbeck, they were looming up out of the fine mist that rose from the water's surface. Gulls and other, darker birds floated round them, landing on ledges worn into the soft cliff face and on the grass that clung to its top. There was Old Harry, a free-standing pillar of chalk as Pete had described, surrounded by the rubble of a partner column that had broken up and fallen into the sea. In the bay that arced round behind it, there was a long sandy beach lined with huts closed up for the winter, keeping a vigil over the smooth water that stretched back to the Island, now lost in the haze behind us.

'I love it,' he said. 'I think it's one of the most beautiful places on earth. Sometimes when Alice was away I'd come here and spend

211

a couple of days on the boat, just reading and watching the birds and the other boats.'

On the way back, he let me have the helm again, and he tightened ropes and gave me instructions until the boat heeled over so far that I thought the water would start lapping over the lower edge of the deck. We were creaming along, carving a line in the water behind us that I wouldn't have thought possible without a motor. Pete sat on the edge of the cockpit, his feet on the seats, the wind blowing through his hair. He turned to me and grinned, his cheeks and hands red with the cold and wind, some of the light back in his eyes. This was it, I thought, this was what it was like to be really free, to have just the water and the sea and the sky overhead, to be an element among all the others.

Even the darker clouds gathering behind us didn't bother me. I loved the way they changed the light over the water, accentuated the line between sea and sky. As we came back up past the Needles – too soon, too soon, I thought, knowing we were heading home – the white of the chalk cliffs there seemed preternaturally bright against the dark water and the body of the Island behind.

Ten minutes later the first rain began to fall. I hadn't brought either my leather jacket or my ankle-length wool coat; neither had seemed appropriate for the boat. Instead, bearing in mind Pete's forecast, I'd bundled up in lots of layers and a chunky jumper on top. I had nothing waterproof.

The occasional drops grew more frequent and made dark circles on the wooden decks. My hair was damp now and my hands were stiff with cold on the tiller.

'There's an old oilskin of mine in the locker by the chart table,' he said. 'Here; I'll take that while you go and put it on. You can't get wet – you'll freeze.'

He slackened off the ropes a little so the boat was at an easier angle and I went down into the cabin again. I took the cushion off the seat and opened the locker, unleashing a fustier version of the damp, diesel smell of the hull. Underneath a couple of life jackets was a yellow water-skin. I took it out and dropped the lid back down.

It was only when I shook it out that I realised the jacket was too small to be his. He wouldn't have been able to get his arms into it.

As I held it up in the dim light, out of view of the hatch, I knew it must be Alice's.

'Find it all right?' his voice came down.

'Fine – thanks.' I hesitated. Clearly he'd thought it was his – they must have had similar ones. He'd think it odd now if I reappeared without it but, on the other hand, I felt a fierce opposition to putting it on, both for his sake and mine. I didn't want to wear her jacket and how would it make him feel, if I came up wearing it? But was it worse not to put it on, to make a fuss and make him feel uncomfortable that way? Maybe acting normal was the thing to do.

Time was passing. In the end, I took a snap decision and put it on.

I knew I'd made a mistake as soon as I climbed the steps back up. He'd been smiling but when he saw the jacket, the obvious size of it, the smile dropped from his face. I stopped, unsure whether to carry on or go back down and take it off.

'Are you coming up?' he said. 'You can't stand on the ladder.'

I came quickly up and sat down in the corner of the cockpit, at a distance from him. He didn't offer me the helm again and we didn't talk. Instead he ran us up the Solent so tight to the increasing wind that I had to hold on to the edge of the seat. The water hissed past. Every time I moved even slightly, the stiff material of the jacket creaked, making its presence felt, and its damp smell got into my nostrils. I wished I could take it off and throw it over the side, watch the bloody thing disappear in our wake. He didn't look at me.

By the time we got back to the river at Newtown, the rain was falling steadily. I went below and took the jacket off as soon as we reached the mooring, shoving it back under the life jackets and only just resisting the urge to slam the lid down after it.

I'd thought we'd come in early but the tide was some way out and the viable channel had shrunk and was now bordered with banks of stinking mud. The surface of the water flashed with circles as the rain fell heavier and heavier. My jumper and hair were soaked. There wasn't enough water left further up the creek to take the dinghy back to its original place, and the outboard whined as its propeller caught against a rock on the bottom. 'Fucking hell,' he said, loudly enough to be audible over it. He throttled down until we were creeping upstream. Neither of us said anything. Finally he brought us to the only ladder at the quay that was still accessible. Its bottom rungs were slimy with weed and I almost lost my footing and fell backwards.

As we bumped up the lane, avoiding the worst of the potholes, the atmosphere improved slightly. The swarm of Canada geese was quiet, huddled together and subdued by the rain. 'I almost feel sorry for them,' he said. 'Almost.' I looked at him quickly and detected a hint of apology in the lift at the corner of his mouth.

In Yarmouth, he pulled up at the end of the passageway to let me out. 'I'm really sorry,' he said, staring straight ahead. 'It took me by surprise – the jacket.'

'No, I'm sorry,' I said. 'I didn't know what to do.'

'I didn't realise it was hers in there; she hadn't been on the boat for such a long time.' His voice sounded tired. 'Look, I'd completely understand if you didn't want to come out again but – if you'd like to, you've got my number.'

'Thank you. And thank you for today. It was good – really.'

The keys in the ignition jangled as he touched them. I took it as my cue to go and plunged out of the car back into the rain.

Later on, after supper and a bath that almost banished the chill that had worked its way into my bones, I rang Helen. I felt slightly better about the afternoon now but I had the old impulse to lay my feelings out and let her light shine on them. I also wanted to tell her what I suspected – knew – about Richard, I couldn't put it off any longer. Both her home number and her mobile went straight to voicemail. It was Saturday night, though; what did I expect? Other people went out.

Chapter Twenty-five

I take my hat off to you, sweetheart – you're really playing hardball.

Well, if you want to play – if you're sure that's what you really want – let's play. It's always been like that with you, hasn't it? But I'll show you who's strongest. You've got to learn that you're never going to beat me.

You won't come back and you won't tell me where you are so I'll have to find you myself. That's the challenge, isn't it? I could just cheat and ask Helen – it wouldn't be difficult to track her down. But that would spoil the fun so I'll play fair and work it out for myself. I know how your mind works – probably better than you do. How hard can it be?

I put my head in my hands and let myself cry. Fear broke over me in waves, constantly renewing. I was prey – prey that by resistance had made itself a prize. Why had I done it? I remembered the first night he'd taken me to dinner, how thrilled I'd been with myself, how I'd revelled in putting up my mock-resistance. *Engaged: one partner in a high-stakes game.* It was ego, my need to compete, to match him, to be thought clever. I'd laid my own trap.

'The worst thing you can do,' I'd read on one of the advice sites, 'is to challenge a psychopath in a battle of wills. The psychopath's need to prove him or herself the victor brooks no obstacle. By engaging him, you put yourself at considerable risk of violence, either emotional or physical.'

* * *

Sally dropped in at the café the next day. She had taken a day off from work, she told me, to get a bit of personal admin done. It was a grim afternoon; raining yet again. She'd stood on the step to shake her umbrella before coming in but her coat had been so wet that it had left a trail of drips from the doorway anyway. The rain had kept other customers away and Mary was out, so she stood with me at the counter and shared a pot of tea.

She seemed jumpier even than usual, I thought. I'd brought her out a stool from the kitchen but she hadn't been able to stay still long enough to sit on it. Every couple of minutes she would wander away from the counter to look at something – the photographs, the drinks in the fridge, the view on to the High Street – before coming back and having another sip of her tea. I didn't think it was me that made her nervous, I couldn't see why I would, but nonetheless I had the strange sense that there was something she wanted from me: when we were talking, she watched my face closely, and whenever I said something, she waited for a second or two before replying, as if wanting to be sure I'd finished, even when I was telling her the most mundane details of what I'd been up to. I didn't tell her about sailing with Pete, not wanting to seem to be laying claim to her friend. He would tell her anyway, no doubt.

It was only now that I realised how much it must have cost her to approach me that first time in Wavells; she must have really wanted to talk to me to have overcome her shyness like that. Suddenly she stopped pacing. 'Do you ever feel like everything's getting on top of you?' she asked.

'Yes,' I said.

'Tom's in trouble at school – someone's put a brick through the window of the science lab. He swears it wasn't him but his track record's against him. It'll cost three hundred pounds to replace, apparently.' She looked at me and shook her head. 'I'm tired out.'

'Come and have some supper at mine tonight,' I said. 'I've got wine, and I'll cook us something.'

She looked almost wistful. 'Thanks – I wish I could. It's parents' evening, though.' She rolled her eyes and gave a sudden grin.

She was on her way out when Mary came in, water dripping from the brim of a red sou'wester. 'How are you, Sally?' she said, taking it off and running her hands through the front of her hair.

'Oh, fine. Same as ever, you know. I'd better go.'

We watched from behind the counter as she put up her umbrella and vanished down the street towards the Square. 'Funny girl,' said Mary.

It was Thursday before Helen called me back. 'Rushed off my feet at the moment,' she said, 'but it's no excuse: I'm just a rubbish friend. Hey, guess what? Paul just rang. He's getting married to that nutty Swiss girl.'

'No way.'

'Oh yes. Shotgun, too; she's preggers – five months.'

I laughed. 'It would have taken that. Brava!'

'My thoughts exactly.'

I felt a wave of affection for her, my lovely warm friend. 'When's it going to be your turn to get snapped up?' I said. 'I've given up on myself now but I still have hopes for you. Anyone on the horizon?'

She sighed. 'I'm just always at work. And I'm not doing office romance again.'

'How about Saturday?'

'What?'

'You were out, weren't you?'

'Oh. Well, yes, but it was just one of those stupid dinner parties – you know, where you're the only single woman at the table and no one else is drinking because the women are pregnant and the men are all too PC to have a glass of wine if their wife can't. How did it ever come to this? That's what I want to know.'

When we'd hung up, I asked myself why I hadn't broached the subject of Richard. It was because I hadn't felt able to; she'd been in such a light, funny mood that it had seemed inappropriate, and anyway, I loved that we could talk like that again, without any edge to the conversation. I hadn't wanted to ruin it.

*   *   *

I was standing in Chris's shop that Saturday before I acknowledged to myself the real reason I was there. 'Peter,' said Chris. 'He told me what happened on the boat.'

'I'm so embarrassed about it,' I said.

'He thinks he was rude to you.'

I shook my head. 'It was understandable – and he wasn't, anyway. And we both apologised.'

'Least said, soonest mended then.'

'Would you like to come to supper?' I asked. 'I promise there won't be any broken glass in the pudding.'

'Are you going to spill wine on my trousers or fall out of a taxi?'

'I'm afraid not.'

'Well, it all sounds a bit dull, then,' he said, smiling. 'But I'd love to.'

On the walk home, I turned off the main road where it curved to follow the shoreline at Yarmouth and took the track down to the waterfront. I sat on the wooden barricade and watched the water for a few minutes before finding my phone in my bag. I hesitated, then took the coward's way out and sent him a text. I expected the response to take a while, but in fact it was only two or three minutes before it arrived: *That would be good – thanks. See you then.*

Chapter Twenty-six

At eight o'clock the following Saturday I stood at the sitting-room door and surveyed my arrangements. It was cramped, I had to admit – the armchair was pushed right back against the wall to make space for the table which I'd brought in from the kitchen – but otherwise it looked pretty good. I'd bought a tablecloth, new glasses for both wine and water and a vase which I had filled with peonies. There were new plates, too. It had felt extravagant, buying so much, but I hadn't wanted them to have to drink from mismatched glasses and eat their supper from the awful earthenware crockery: nothing eaten from it ever tasted nice because it looked so ugly.

In the kitchen I lifted the lid on the hollandaise sauce and dipped in a teaspoon. The asparagus was already tied in bundles on the chopping board and the goulash was in the oven. Two bottles of claret were breathing on the counter. I'd forgotten how much I loved cooking for other people. I had often abandoned whole days of work in favour of flicking through recipe books and sourcing rare ingredients for the suppers I'd made for Richard. I used to comb the Thai and Chinese grocery shops in the little alleys off Earls Court Road, then spent the afternoon cooking and anticipating the evening ahead. I closed my eyes now against the memory of how those evenings had ended, with us tangled around each other in my bed.

I was wearing my grey woollen dress, the one even slightly smart piece of clothing I'd brought with me. This was the first time I'd worn it since I'd moved to the Island; apart from at the café where I wore a basic black skirt which I'd bought for the purpose at Marks & Spencer, I had been wearing jeans to the exclusion of almost everything else. Even to supper at Chris's, I'd worn trousers. Earlier, getting dressed, I'd reached behind the pile of T-shirts on the shelf for the tangle of tights that I'd shoved there when I'd moved in, looking for some with a pattern to try and liven up the outfit. My hand had touched something hard. I knew immediately what it was: the box with Richard's bangle. I hesitated momentarily, then took it out and opened it. There they were again, those savage faces, their streaming manes. I remembered the afternoon he'd given it to me, making love on the sofa, and snapped the lid shut again, nearly catching my fingers. My instinct had been to take it out on to the harbour and throw it in, let the water swallow it up like the stinking swan carcass. That, though, would be a waste, I decided: it was valuable. I would sell it instead.

I went back into the sitting room now and lit the long candles on the table and the smaller ones along the mantelpiece. When I switched off the main light, the clutter of furniture drew back against the walls and the table became the focus of the room. I was straightening one of the napkins again when there was a gentle knock on the kitchen door.

Through the glass panels I saw Chris. He was wearing a tweed jacket and a pale-blue shirt, newly ironed. The lines of the comb were still visible in his hair. The scent of freshly applied cologne enveloped me for a moment as he kissed me hello and pressed a bottle of red into my hands. I poured him a drink as he eased a box of mint thins out of his jacket pocket.

'Are those potatoes dauphinoise?' he said, inhaling deeply. 'My absolute favourite – Miranda used to make them for me as a birthday treat.'

He leant against the counter by the washing machine and chatted to me while I got the last few things ready. He'd been asked if he would sell the books from a house over in Bonchurch, he told me, the collection of a retired professor from Southampton University who'd recently died. 'There're wonderful things. Mostly natural history, Victorian botany studies, all beautifully illustrated. The son's organising it and I get the impression he'd like to keep them but he's pressed financially. Collectors will go for them, though – a couple in particular – so I hope there'll be good news for him.'

I covered the granary rolls with tinfoil ready to go into the oven to warm and listened to him talking. The house had felt different as soon as he'd walked in; it had taken on new life as it had when Helen had been here over Christmas. It was the ease with which he made himself at home; there was no awkwardness or standing on ceremony, just familiarity and relaxed conversation.

I was filling a pan with water for the asparagus when Pete knocked, and Chris let him in. The room contracted immediately: there wasn't more than six inches between the top of his head and the ceiling. I put the kettle down and moved towards him. He was wearing jeans and a black leather jacket I hadn't seen before, and underneath it a lightweight charcoal jumper with the collar of a pale-grey shirt just visible at the neck. It was ridiculous, I knew it was only the clothes, but he seemed different. He was smiling a little, an odd smile that seemed to concentrate in one corner of his mouth, but I found it strangely difficult to meet his eye. I hesitated, wondering whether he would kiss my cheek as Chris had done, but instead he gave me the two bottles of wine he'd been carrying and moved away.

All the chairs were at the table in the sitting room so he folded himself down on to the third step of the stairs. I handed him a glass of wine, making myself look at him directly. He was freshly shaven, I registered, before I glanced away again to where his big feet overhung the edge of the step. Chris was working his way through the guacamole I'd made, ladling it up with carrots and Kettle chips. Both watched me as I stirred the hollandaise. 'Why don't you go through to the table?' I said. 'There's not much room in there either but it's better than watching me get things ready.'

'Not at all.' The grid of lines on Chris's forehead contracted, as though the idea had offended him. 'We're here to see you. We're not going to sit next door and let you do all the work.'

'I think what he means,' said Pete, 'is that we're going to let you do all the work but we'll talk to you while you do it.'

Having worried that everything in the house looked tatty, when we sat down to eat I had the converse anxiety that they would see how far from casual I'd felt about this supper and inviting them into the cottage. I hadn't been able to iron out the lines on the tablecloth which showed where it had been folded in the shop. *Hey*, I imagined it telegraphing to them both, *look at me. She bought me specially, you know. Life's a bit different here normally.* By the time we were finishing the asparagus, however, I'd started to relax a little, helped no doubt by the fact that we were already at the bottom of the first bottle. I glanced across the table and watched Pete's hands as he buttered the last of his roll. I had rarely seen his hands still, I thought; they were always moving, touching something, holding whatever it was he was subjecting to his scrutiny at any given time. He felt me watching him now and looked over, and I quickly looked away.

They both stood up as soon as I started to clear the plates, and the casserole dish and potatoes were taken from me the second I got them out of the oven, as though I couldn't be allowed to lift anything heavy. It was silly but I quite liked it, the slight cosseting; it made me feel unusually feminine, cared about.

'Did you see in the paper that we lost another chunk of cliff at Brook in the week?' Chris said, after much appreciation of the goulash. 'It was all that rain last week – the clay was sodden. There's been a big landslide.'

'My brother found a dinosaur tooth there once,' I said. 'He was obsessed with fossils – we used to spend hours going along the beach. It was quite damaged, the tooth, but recognisable. He kept it on his windowsill till he went to college.'

'I expect everyone will be out now to see what's been uncovered this time.'

'I'm amazed at the subsidence. I mean, I knew it was a problem but so much has gone. The car park at Compton Bay – it just disappears over the edge. You can see where the parking spaces were marked out but they're only half there.'

'And half the adventure playground's gone at Blackgang – it used to be huge.'

'It's not just the back of the Island,' Pete said, putting down his knife and fork. 'The mouth of the Newtown River, the beaches there – they've completely changed shape even in the past ten years. That bit just beyond the quay' – he looked at me – 'the marsh with all the sea heather – that used to be a meadow, flat enough for cricket. The place is alive – it's shifting under our feet all the time.'

I saw him shoot another glance at the casserole and offered second helpings, which they both accepted. Chris, I knew, had always reminded me of someone and watching the simple happiness on his face as he had another mouthful of potato, it came to me: it was Harry, an old friend of Dad's whom Matt and I had loved, perhaps because he'd talked to us as if we were adults. He'd used to come round on Saturday evening once a month to play chess, and he and Dad would sit at the kitchen table with their chins in their hands, serious as Short and Kasparov, while I made them bangers and mash. I had a moment's insight into how lonely Dad's life must have been then; Harry was the only regular adult company he'd had, really.

Going back to the kitchen to fetch a serving spoon for the pudding, I almost bumped into Pete as he came down the stairs from the bathroom. He put out his hands, as if to keep me at a distance. Earlier I'd cleaned the bathroom and changed the towels. I'd put all my personal things – my toothbrush and deodorant, my make-up – away in the cabinet but now I remembered that, changing my shoes just before they'd arrived, I'd left my bedroom door open. Going up the stairs, he would have seen my bed. We looked at each other, neither of us saying anything. At the table in the other room Chris refilled our glasses and the sound of the wine was suddenly loud in the space between us. I ducked away, cheeks reddening.

The crumble drew more compliments. We finished the second bottle of wine and Pete opened a third. The woollen dress had been a mistake, I thought, conscious of damp under my arms and the flush which hadn't faded out of my face. Though I'd left the windows ajar and there was no fire, the heat from the oven and two other people made the house feel close.

'I had some good news yesterday,' I said. 'I've been commissioned to translate a series of crime novels. The editor's emailed me the first one; I've only had a quick look so far but it's good – really atmospheric.'

'That's great,' said Chris, tracing the inside of his bowl with the edge of his spoon again. 'Well done you.'

'It's a relief because it means I'll have gainful employment after I finish at the café, too, when I go.'

'Go?' said Pete.

'When the lease on this place runs out.' I felt a spasm of fear. No – going back to London was impossible now. I'd have to find somewhere else, somewhere even further away. Maybe I'd have to go abroad.

'And when is that?' asked Chris, reaching over and putting his hand on mine.

'The end of April.'

'Six weeks,' said Pete, turning a cork between his fingers and pressing his thumbnail into it.

'Well, you can always come back,' said Chris. 'You can stay with me whenever you like – plenty of room.'

'Thank you,' I said, touched. 'It's funny: I miss London but I'm not sure I'm ready to leave here yet. I'll have to get a dinghy to row on the Thames.' I flashed Pete a smile; his lips turned up in response but mechanically: the smile didn't reach his eyes.

'Gloomy subject,' said Chris. 'Let's talk no more about it tonight. Is that coffee I smell?'

'It is. Would you like some brandy, too?'

'Ah, a girl after my own heart.'

Pete poured out large measures. I sipped mine, feeling the glow it left in my throat as it went down. I leaned forward, my elbow on the table as Chris lit me a cigarette. The candlelight pulled us into a circle around the table, like conspirators or participants in a séance. I wasn't drunk but I was far from sober. More than anything, I was happy, relieved that it had gone well: the food had been good, things with Pete were back on an even keel more or less, the embarrassment of last time smoothed over, if not quite forgotten. I knew, though, that it couldn't last. It was getting late. The ferries stopped running at eleven and I hadn't heard one for a while. I looked up and found him watching me, his eyebrows drawn into a slight frown.

Chris stood and put his napkin neatly on the table. 'Well, it's been a lovely evening and we must have at least another one before you leave us, Kate, but if you'll excuse me, I'm going to slide off now. I'm getting too old for late nights and I can't handle my booze like I used to.'

'How are you getting home, Chris?' said Pete, as we stood at the door.

'I shall be absolutely fine, don't you worry,' he said, and before I could remonstrate or offer to call him a cab, he had disappeared up the passage towards the gate. The darkness outside seemed to gain potency as the sound of his footsteps died away and I shut the door against it.

Pete was behind me. 'I should go, too,' he said.

'You don't have to. Stay for another drink – if you'd like to.'

He looked at me, his expression unreadable. The strange silence that had bloomed between us in those moments at the bottom of the stairs came again. It was Pete who broke the eye contact this time and looked around the kitchen. Every surface was covered with dirty plates, saucepans, glasses. 'Washing up,' he said, going towards the sink.

'Oh, don't worry; I'll do it tomorrow.'

'It won't take long.' He tipped the inch of cold water out of the bowl and turned the taps on, pulling his sleeves up and rolling back his shirt cuffs. I organised what little was left over, throwing it away or clingfilming it for the fridge. The wine had numbed me and everything felt softer, the edges less definite. Nevertheless, I felt the oddness of his being here so late, standing at my sink and doing the washing up as if we were old friends. The silence was gathering all the time, growing into the pauses in the conversation. At first, to keep it at bay, I talked non-stop. I asked about the boat: the longest trip he'd ever done in it, whether he'd ever go transatlantic. He answered my questions but not at length and eventually I stopped talking and let the silence wind around us. In the window over the sink our reflections found a rhythm, him washing, me taking the heavy dishes as he handed them to me, drying them, putting them away. I began to dread finishing, wanting it to go on. The silence was no longer something to ward off, but familiar, even comforting, as though we were in fact old friends, this evening just one of a hundred where we had stood together

225

and washed up in peace. It wasn't as simple as that, though: there was an odd feeling in the pit of my stomach, intensifying. Alice came into my head all of a sudden, the memory of how her voice had seemed to reach me through the mist up on Tennyson Down that day, calling me over to the cliff edge. I batted the thought away. It wasn't just the unhappiness of the memory; I didn't want her in the room with us now.

It took half an hour to restore the kitchen to normality. I heard the muffled sound of St James's striking one and wondered whether he'd heard it, too. He upended the last bowl of water and it spiralled away. 'I'm going to have that glass of wine,' I said. 'Would you like one?'

Afterwards I wasn't sure exactly how it happened. I could remember hearing the lid of the metal dustbin in the front yard as he took the rubbish out and I remembered getting fresh glasses and walking back into the sitting room to fetch the bottle. We met again in the kitchen, at the same place in front of the cupboard by the stairs. This time he put out his hand not to ward me off but to stop me. He was looking at me, his eyes serious, and I found I couldn't look away. The quality of the air had changed. It felt thinner, difficult to breathe, as if we were at altitude.

I was aware of him coming closer, the remarkable greenness of his eyes, and then suddenly he was kissing me. I took a step back against the cupboard door with surprise and banged my head. He put his hand there, cushioning it. His mouth was urgent. He leaned in, pressing me against the door, letting me feel the weight of his body.

It was thirty seconds, maybe a minute, but in that time I was filled with hunger. I grabbed the pocket of his jeans and pulled him harder against me, wanting to hold on, bring him closer and closer. His hands were in my hair.

And then it stopped. He stepped away from me and the look on his face was sheer horror. 'I'm sorry,' he said. 'I'm really sorry.' He grabbed the leather jacket from the top of the newel post, yanked the door open and was gone.

* * *

The seconds that followed were like the pause after something valuable is broken. For a moment, the air around me seemed simply to hang, as if everything were freeze-framed and there might still be a chance to go back, undo what had been done. I stood motionless until, through the rushing in my ears, I heard the clang of the iron gate at the end of the passage as he flung it shut. The noise jolted the air, and time began to move forward again.

Chapter Twenty-seven

When I woke in the morning my first thought was that I had imagined it. It was so extraordinary, such a step outside the usual bounds of my life now: in London, yes, in the years before Richard, it hadn't been unusual for me to meet someone and kiss them, even take them home, and then there was Richard himself, but that sort of physical contact belonged to a different era, a different me. Perhaps the whole thing had been a sort of drunken hallucination, born of wine and brandy and tiredness after running round all day getting ready. Then, though, I put my hand up and felt the back of my head where I'd banged it, the slight tenderness. Last night, I remembered, my skin had come alive where he'd touched it – my mouth, my cheek, my ears, my neck. I had felt the roots of my hair.

I hadn't been honest with myself, I knew now. That afternoon on the boat with Alice's jacket, hurting Pete had been the major part of my regret but it wasn't all of it. I'd regretted jeopardising his good opinion: it had become important to me. I remembered the strange pride I'd felt that first time out in the dinghy when he'd said I was a natural rower, how pleased I'd been when I'd begun to understand the sailing and when he'd asked me out on the boat the second time. More than that, on Alice's birthday, I'd begun to feel that he was offering a sort of friendship, inviting me into his confidence. And then I had ruined it.

The supper had been an attempt to get things right again between us. I had wanted another chance, an opportunity to make him think better of me. But more than anything else, I acknowledged,

I had just wanted to see him again. I had been physically aware of him from the moment he walked through the kitchen door. I had watched him all evening – sitting on the stairs, big feet hanging over the bottom step; his look of concentration as he tried not to break the cork with the cottage's cheap corkscrew; the way the muscles in his arms had flexed when he handed me the dishes. I had wanted him to kiss me. I had wanted him.

Though the washing up was done, of course – the J-cloth was wrapped around the mixer tap like a scarf, as he had left it – the table was still in the sitting room, the ashtray and the wine glasses I'd never refilled exactly where I'd put them down before it happened. I moved the table back, hoovered, and then went out in the car. I didn't want to sit in the house all day and brood; it wouldn't change anything.

I drove without any clear idea of where I was going but found myself on the road to Newport and then heading for Cowes. I took the turn to Gurnard and went along a road lined with wooden houses of all shapes and sizes, some little more than beach huts, others Swedish-looking, with lots of glass. Coming into Cowes itself, I had the sea on my left, blue today for the most part, its more familiar military green only visible beneath the infrequent patches of cloud. On my right, built on a high bank, were the mansions of Seaview which I knew from the *County Press* were some of the most expensive properties on the Island. They looked out over the Solent with an imperious sense of ownership.

In Cowes, I parked the car on the seafront and sat for a moment watching the small boats coming and going at the mouth of the river. A Red Funnel ferry, much larger than the ones which served Yarmouth, was making its way in, and through the open window I heard the announcement asking passengers to go back to their cars. People were walking on the esplanade, some with dogs, others just ambling. On the back of one of the benches two gulls perched side by side like an old couple.

I got out, put some change in the parking meter and walked for a few minutes, past the hotels and apartment buildings on the front in the direction of the Yacht Squadron, whose flag was beating vigorously in the breeze. I leant on the balustrade and watched the water. On one of the moorings there was a wooden yacht like *Beatrice* and I felt a momentary pang. That was probably it now for sailing, unless Chris put his boat back in before I left and was kind enough to ask me. Another pang, stronger this time. I shoved my hands in the pockets of my jeans and walked on.

I couldn't understand how Pete felt – how could I, or anyone? It wasn't only that Alice was dead, which would be hard enough after so little time: he didn't even have that certainty. How could he think about anyone else? It was wrong of me even to have had the idea. And I couldn't blame him for his reaction. Thinking about the intensity of those moments, the hunger I'd felt on both sides, perhaps it had been best that he had gone, before things had got any further out of hand.

On the way back I bought an ice cream and sat in the car to eat it, watching the seagulls swoop and dive over the water. The ferry had deposited its first lot of passengers, loaded those returning and was already halfway back across the Solent to Southampton. For a moment, I wished I was on it. I only had a few weeks left but now I would have to spend them worrying about running into Pete. Perhaps it would be simpler to go. But no: I'd nearly done it, stuck it out; I wouldn't concede defeat at this late stage. And there was the question of where to go, anyway, now that London was impossible. I had no idea where to run to this time. I remembered the poor Canadian woman again, and quickly slammed the door.

Before I set off home, I got out my phone and sent Helen a text: *Feeling a bit insular. Do you fancy a jaunt out of London next weekend? Cornwall? The Cotswolds?* Having sent it, I had another idea: I would sell Richard's bangle and spend the money on a weekend for us both somewhere nice. We could go to a spa hotel: much more her scene than mine but that would be the point, if it was my treat. I left the phone on the passenger seat, expecting a swift answer, but none came, which surprised me for a Sunday when surely even she wouldn't be in a meeting.

In the end, her response didn't come until after eight o'clock, when I was grilling bacon for supper and the phone's single ring made me jump. *Would have loved to but I've said I'll go and visit my parents – their wedding anniversary. Damn! Another time?*

I'd warded off melancholy for most of the day but at about ten, I gave in to it for a few minutes. I poured the last glass of wine from the bottle that Pete had opened and took it outside into the yard with the cigarettes I'd bought in Cowes. What cloud there was moved swiftly, backlit by the moon so that it looked wraithlike and wan. The air was chill but refreshing, almost sweet. There was no ferry at the slipway and no traffic coming over the bridge on River Road: the night's silence had settled. The first drag of the cigarette gave me a head-rush and I sat down on the step, feeling the cold of the concrete through my jeans. Tonight even the faint music of the breeze through the rigging in the harbour was muted. I took another drag and heard the next layer of tobacco crackle as it caught light.

I had been carrying my phone around all day in the hope that there would be if not a call – I could understand that would be difficult – then a text, saying thank you for dinner or apologising even if he didn't mean it or perhaps making a joke of what had happened, just to take away some of the bite in case we met, but there had been nothing at all. Helen's had been the only message. I'd thought about texting him, making some self-deprecatory comment to assume the blame, but nothing seemed right. I also hated the idea that he might think I was pursuing him.

All of a sudden now, in the darkness at the end of the yard, something moved. I froze, felt my heart tighten in my chest. I listened: nothing except the boom of racing blood. It moved again, whatever it was, this time close to the ground. I let out the breath that had caught in my throat and a second or two later, Pete's cat appeared from under the car. He stood at the edge of the patio, his eyes and white bib bright in the light through the glass behind me.

I stood up, expecting him to dart away, but he stayed still, watching me intently as I approached. When I was close enough and he still hadn't run, I knelt down and put out my hand to stroke him. I'd only touched him three or four times when he moved but instead of disappearing, he came closer and brushed against

231

my knees. I felt the same urge as the first time I'd seen him, that day in the Square when he'd reminded me so strongly of Magpie. Wrapping my arms tentatively around his body, expecting him to wriggle away at any moment, I lifted him up and held him, resting my cheek against the soft fur on the back of his neck. How long we stood like that I wasn't sure but he didn't struggle to get free. He was a solid presence, warm in my arms. I caught sight of us in the glass of the sliding doors and it was like seeing myself twenty years ago outside the patio doors at home in Bristol.

Chapter Twenty-eight

Ignore it, I ordered myself, when I turned on the computer and saw a new message from Richard. *Delete it – straight away*. My finger hovered above the mouse, and kept hovering. In the end I got up and slammed out of the house, storming up the road towards Sally's, then along the path around the estuary. I always walked quickly but now I was almost running, my feet beating out the mantra on the ground: *ignore him, ignore him, ignore him*. Still, however, there was the other voice, the one that came from my gut, not my head: *what if he's found you? What if he's coming? You need to know*. Back at the house, it was that voice that won out and I opened the email, furious with myself for letting him in again.

Do you ever think about that night on Putney Bridge? Do you realise how close you came? You would have dropped like a stone. Remember how quiet it was? There wouldn't have been any witnesses. Who would have known you weren't just a lonely girl with problems who'd decided she couldn't take any more?

You would have done anything then to prove that you were right for me, a fit partner. That's because I got into your head. You let me in, Katie, you gave me the key. Now I own you. The only reason that you're still out there trying to lead your pathetic little life is because I'm letting you.

*   *   *

While it wasn't warm, it was mild enough that week that when I got home from the café, I could drink a cup of tea at the picnic table in the yard in the last half-hour of daylight. The days were lengthening obviously now, each one longer than the one before, the moment of absolute darkness coming later and later. They were strange days, ones whose ends I was glad to reach when I got into bed. I accepted that Pete wasn't going to get in touch and my disappointment began to dull but I was ambushed regularly by memories of the days out on the boat or the supper, memories which gave me a pain under my sternum. I distracted myself with work, that old failsafe.

On Tuesday, I found myself looking at the empty planters outside the sliding doors. The bare soil looked forlorn so after work the next day, when I went shopping in Freshwater, I bought sweet-pea seeds and canes to train the shoots up when they grew. I wouldn't be here long enough to see them flower but they would be there for the cottage's summer residents, people on their holidays. Pete's cat came every day. As if by appointment, he would wait until I was outside having tea and then he would squeeze through the gap by the gate and trot up the yard to wind himself around my feet. The first couple of days, he stayed only until I got cold and went inside but on Thursday, when I stood up to go in, he didn't leave. Instead, moving round my feet so closely that I was afraid I would tread on him, he came with me into the house.

Cupboard love, I thought, as he ran ahead and stood expectantly at the door of the fridge. 'I can't feed you,' I said, kneeling to stroke him. 'I'm sorry. You aren't mine. If I feed you, you'll think you live here, and I'm going soon.'

Undeterred, he stayed. I lit a small fire – surely one of the last of the year – and for two hours he curled up in front of it on the rug. When I put the oven on for my supper, however, he got up immediately and came into the kitchen, where he resumed his vigil by the fridge, looking up at me with imploring eyes. In the end, I caved in and poured him a saucer of milk.

I spent a lot of time that week thinking about where I could go next. It made me so angry that Richard was dictating my plans. On the other hand, however, a small part of me was relieved that

I wasn't going back to that lonely life in the flat in Earls Court. I had started to dread it.

In Yarmouth I had begun to feel part of things in a way I never had in London. Admittedly it was only among a small group of people – I remembered what Pete had said about overners and the real locals taking a couple of hundred years to defrost – but when I went to work at the café now there were people who nodded and said good morning, there were Mary and Chris, Sally. And there had been Pete. I could do it again, move somewhere else and, over time, begin to build another network.

The question was where. I had no ideas.

I was in the back yard on Saturday afternoon when Pete knocked. I'd been watering the pots and came into the house to see him standing on the other side of the glass. My hand fumbled slightly as I turned the key.

'Hello,' he said.

'Hi.' My face was burning.

The breeze riffled through the ivy on the wall behind him, revealing the pale undersides of the leaves. He looked especially tall today, even though I had the advantage of the step. He was in another dark jumper – blue again, this one – and the usual jeans. Looking down to avoid his eye, I saw sand in the stitching of his shoes.

'Are you doing anything?'

'What?' I looked up again in surprise.

'Now, I mean. I'm going to Brook, for a walk on the beach. I wondered if you wanted to come.'

It was a mild day but the cloud which had been thickening gradually since the morning hung low over the cliff-top, creating a humidity, a sense that something was brewing. There was no seismic activity under the Island but there was something volcanic about the atmosphere at Brook. Walking along the beach, I was aware all the time of the red-and-grey cliff that bordered the dark sand. It wasn't a static part of the landscape but alive with constant movement. Water trickled down it as if it was gently weeping, and tiny stones and lumps of clayish rock tumbled on to the beach to join the piles of larger chunks that must have come down in the fall that Chris had mentioned at supper. On my other side, the sea was muted, the dull sunless green disappearing to a steely line at the horizon. At Compton, as we'd driven past, I'd seen kite-surfers but no one was on the water here.

Pete walked a few paces ahead of me, eyes trained on the ground, occasionally stopping to pick up a chunk of stuff that he crumbled between his fingers and then tossed away back up the beach. Among the children and the casual enthusiasts, there were several real fossil hunters out, dotted here and there along the length of the beach, easily identifiable by the leather bags strung sideways across their bodies, the trowels and tiny hammers protruding from the pockets of their trousers and jackets. The hammers were hardly necessary, I thought; the stuff that lay on the beach, uncovered after thousands of years, was scarcely rock; it was little more than compacted mud. No wonder the cliff fell in so easily.

In other circumstances I would have been irritated by Pete's behaviour, the invitation to come with him and then this. Actually, though, I was happy to walk slowly, listening to the water, watching him. It was good to have the opportunity at least to try and order my thoughts. His car had been on the double yellows at the end of the passageway and I was putting my seatbelt on before I'd even realised what I was doing. We'd hardly spoken on the way here either, though it was a good quarter of an hour's journey. Radio 4 had been on and that had taken the place of conversation as it had done before. The only time he'd really broken the silence was when we stopped at the roundabout in Freshwater and he looked at me, puzzled. 'Do you always keep your door locked when you're in?' he'd asked.

It was low tide and though the accessible area of sand was longer than it would be at high water, it wasn't a large beach even now. We'd gone maybe five hundred yards when Pete seemed to give up on the rocks and waited for me. There was a piece of sea-washed glass on the sand by my feet and I picked it up before going over, wanting to make the point. I brushed the sand off it and held it so the light shone through. I'd seen that particular shade of toffee brown before. I skimmed it hard into the sea – four jumps, not bad – and caught him up.

We walked side by side for a while. I had a sick feeling in the pit of my stomach that I recognised from other times that I'd dreaded what was coming. I watched our feet. I was nearer to the sea and the difference was visible in the amount of water that flooded our footsteps when we left them: his softened, the pattern of his soles disappearing, but mine jellified, the shape of my feet lost completely.

'The other night,' he said. 'I shouldn't have done that. I'm sorry.'

'It doesn't matter,' I said, keeping my eyes trained on the ground. 'There had been drink taken, as they say. These things happen – chalk it up as a mistake.'

'No. It wasn't a mistake. But I couldn't . . . I've always been faithful.'

'You don't need to say any more.' I glanced at him and saw his grim expression. 'It's forgotten.'

'I do – I did need to say it. I needed you to understand.' There was frustration in his voice, barely masked, and he kicked up an arc of sand, the clumps of it large enough to be audible as they fell back on to the beach. 'I've spent the last week feeling terrible – guilty and just . . . I don't know.' He took something from his pocket and held it out to me. 'Anyway, I found this for you,' he said. 'Not today – in the week.'

It was badly damaged and darkened from the rock in which it had been hidden for millennia but it was still recognisably a tooth like the one which Matt had found, about two inches long, its point broken. I turned it over in my hand, not sure what to say. 'I can't guarantee it's from the same dinosaur, I'm afraid,' he said.

I smiled, though my throat was suddenly tight. 'Thank you,' I said. 'Don't you want to keep it, though?'

He shook his head. 'It's for you.'

We were quiet again on the way back. The quiet was different, however, as if something had been settled. I fought a bitter disappointment and made myself acknowledge that there had been part of me that had still hoped, even this afternoon, that there might somehow – miraculously – be a chance. Alice. For a second time I found myself hating her with a force of which I was immediately ashamed.

It had been past four already when Pete had knocked on the door and by the time we climbed the uneven steps back to the car park above the beach, the light was fading quickly, casting the fields on the far side of the road into a penumbrous gloom. The land rolled away, ancient and imbued with that strange quality I'd felt here before, the timelessness which I'd rarely felt anywhere else. Today, I found it comforting. *Endure*, I imagined it whispering to me; *endure*. Next to me, Pete was solid in the near-dark. I couldn't look at him directly but I was aware of his hand on the gear-stick, the tightening of his grip on the wheel as he slowed to take the car into the steep corner. The engine was the only sound as we went through the lanes, and the hedgerows passed us in a black blur.

My hand, the one Pete couldn't see, was in my jacket pocket, clenched into a tight fist around the fossil. It was an old habit; as a child, I had often found something small to hold on to and would shove my hand into my pocket or under my pillow at night and grip as though whatever it was – a pebble, a conker, a piece of our Meccano set – had talismanic powers and could keep me safe, ward off the bad.

Chapter Twenty-nine

I watched the mist coming, rising up from the sea, thickening second by second, leaving no room for oxygen in the air it moved through. It would suffocate me, I knew. The first tendrils of it were on my face already, touching me like little fingers, damp and cold. I tried to step back but my feet were too heavy – I couldn't lift them.

Now I was surrounded, the white wall behind me as well as in front, shifting all the time but impenetrable, unbreathable. How long would I last on the air I had? Through the fog there came a light, a single beam which raked from right to left then was extinguished, and then came again. And a bell, low and mournful, tolling somewhere below me on the water. Invisible.

Suddenly she was there, only a few feet away. I saw her dress first, black silk moving like running water, billowing as if the wind was stronger where she was standing. Next I saw her hair, blown sideways like pale flame, longer than I remembered, its ends like flickering tongues.

I blinked and suddenly she was closer, close enough to touch me. The skin of her arms was so pale, deathly pale, and translucent; I could see the bones in the hands she stretched towards me. I didn't want to look at her face, I was desperate not to see it, but she was too close now, I couldn't help it: her face, her lovely face, tracked with tears and scored by the two terrible empty circles that were her sockets.

I woke with my heart pounding, the last image still burning in front of me. I turned on the bedside light and waited for my pulse to slow, hearing my own breathing in the quietness of the house.

It was the fourth night in a row. The first time had been Sunday, the day after we'd been walking at Brook, but then it had only been confusing, a couple of the images – the floating material of her dress, her long hair – superimposed on another dream which I couldn't remember at all. I hadn't known then what I was seeing but, day by day, the scene had revealed itself. I was back on the cliff edge on Tennyson Down, the rocks at the bottom waiting to receive my broken body and Alice's voice calling me – *Kate, Kate* – her hands reaching out to me, begging me to come to her, follow her over. And every day, she was closer and closer and I woke up just a fraction of a second before she touched me.

At the café I found myself watching the street more closely. Even over lunch, when there were usually now several bowls of soup to ladle out and ferry from the kitchen, and several rounds of Welsh rarebit to make, I would look up every time anyone walked past the window. I told myself it was because of Tom. On both Monday and Tuesday he'd passed the window in the afternoon, school uniform bastardised with trainers and a hooded sweatshirt, a leather sports bag – huge but empty-looking – slung over his shoulder. The first time, the window table had been occupied but yesterday there had only been a pair of old ladies taking their time over a teacake towards the back, and the front door was propped open for fresh air. I'd been standing by the counter and tensed, ready to spring out if he tried to come in, but he'd walked past without even looking.

When the women had gone and the café was empty, I got my phone out of my bag under the counter and called Helen at the office. It only rang twice before it was answered but the voice that came on the line was Esther's.

'Kate – hi! How's the Island? I was thinking last night that we should call you about the flat; if you're definitely coming back at the end of next month, we should start looking for somewhere else, right?'

'Actually,' I said, 'I've decided not to come back.'

'Seriously?' I heard the shock in her voice; she was still at the age, I thought, where moving out of London was like taking retirement.

'Yes. I'm sure it'll be fine, though, if you want to take the lease over officially. I'll give you a ring about that in a couple of days, if that's all right, when I've spoken to the landlord. Is Helen about?'

'I'll try her line for you.' She disappeared and there was a painful twenty seconds' worth of musak. 'Kate?' she said, taking me off hold. 'She's just answered another call; can I get her to ring you back?'

I left my phone by the till but reached into my bag again anyway and undid the zip pocket. I found the dinosaur tooth and held it in my hand for a few seconds. Then, feeling foolish, I zipped it back up and went into the kitchen to put the dishwasher on.

There was a single bark from deep inside the house as I rang the doorbell. A few seconds passed and then the coloured glass of the fanlight came alive and there were soft footsteps.

'Kate – what a lovely surprise.' Chris's face lit up. 'Come in.'

'Hello, Ted.' I went down on my haunches and let him mug me, his soft head burrowing into my armpit then coming up to lick my neck and the side of my face. His tail was going nineteen to the dozen, its motion moving the whole of his body.

'Come through. Ted, leave Kate alone for a minute, let the poor girl get her breath back.' We went through to the kitchen, today lit only by lamps dotted here and there: one on the counter, another on the small wicker table by the sofa and a standard lamp in the conservatory area moved closer to the long table on which there was a chessboard with smart wooden pieces, a game in progress.

'Have you got the car?' he asked. 'I'm having a gin and tonic. Can I offer you a weak one?'

I sat on the same stool as the night of the disastrous supper. Today the papers had free rein; the top of the counter was a thatch of newsprint. 'You've beaten me on the crossword,' I said.

'Have I? I've been stuck on the last couple since lunchtime – can't get 'em for the life of me.' He dropped a couple of ice cubes into a glass.

He brought my drink over and came to sit on the opposite stool. I asked him about the books at Bonchurch and when he thought *Sirene* would be ready to go back in the water. Ted sat with his head heavy on my knee, occasionally giving a sigh suggesting the weight of the world was on his shoulders. I stroked his ears, letting the silky fur slip between my fingers, remembering how I'd watched Pete do the same.

'I don't like speaking ill of the dead,' Chris said suddenly. 'But I thought she was a selfish woman – Alice.'

I looked at him, forgetting Ted in my surprise.

'I'm not saying she wasn't charming – she could be, very. And she was good-looking, obviously, and always very stylish.' He rustled beneath the newspapers and slid a ten-pack of Marlboro Lights across to me. 'I never got the impression, though, that much of their relationship was about him. A lot of the time, life with her seemed to be about appeasement, as far as I could tell – trying to keep her happy.'

I thought suddenly of the photograph I'd seen in the magazine months ago, the way it had seemed to belong to a different set from those of the rest of the party, with Alice dressed so fashionably. I remembered the way Pete had been looking at her, attentive, while she looked away, and felt a stab of pain for him, mixed with a streak of unreasonable jealousy.

'Depression can seem like that, can't it?' I said. 'Selfish?'

'I daresay.' He lit my cigarette and then his own. 'I don't think she liked living here. I always had the sense that she was straining to be somewhere else.'

'But I thought she grew up on the Island?'

'Well, she came here as a teenager, when her father retired – lovely man. But I have to say I was surprised when they got married. Not from Peter's side – it was clear how he felt – but from hers. She wasn't a natural Islander, I didn't think; I worried that she would get frustrated here. Peter's business is in Cowes – did he tell you? He needs the water for research, trials. And his workforce is very specialised. So he couldn't move. Otherwise I think he would have done, if it would have made her happy.'

'I met her.'

'Did you?' His eyebrows went up.

'A couple of days before she . . . went. She was on the common, looking at the water. We talked about boats – she said sailing was what kept her sane here.'

He blew out quickly through his nose. 'That's what I mean. Didn't she have everything in the world to be grateful for?' He tapped his ash and looked at me. 'It's him I feel sorry for. And you.'

'Me?'

He smiled, seeing my expression. 'Call me cynical but I suspect an ulterior motive for this visit.'

I felt my face reddening and looked down. Realising he had my attention, Ted bumped his chin on my knee and I started stroking again. There was a single thump of tail against the tiles.

'Look,' said Chris. 'He's going to be here in a few minutes – at half past. We're in the middle of a game.' He tilted his head at the board set up on the table. 'We play quite often. But you're welcome to stay.'

'No,' I said, a little too quickly. 'I won't interrupt. I just came to say hello.'

He nodded. 'Finish your drink, though – no need to dash off.'

I gulped down the rest of it, trying to appear relaxed. The cooker's digital clock read 20.27. I stood up but there was another minute of petting Ted to do before I was allowed to move. We were in the hall, Chris handing me my jacket from the coatstand, when there were tyres on the gravel. Shit.

The automatic light was already on as I went outside: Pete was crossing the drive towards the door. We both stopped, eight or ten feet apart. 'Hello,' he said. I had a moment's impression of him before I looked away: long legs in jeans, his navy jumper, a couple of days' worth of stubble darkening his cheeks.

I glanced behind me but Chris hadn't come out. I looked back at Pete. The brightness of the light made him hyper-real. He was watching me and I had a sudden flashback to my kitchen, the sensation in my stomach as he'd moved towards me. 'I'm just going,' I said. I held up my car keys as if they were proof.

He looked at them, then back at me. 'Will I see you . . .?'

'Around? Probably – maybe. I'd better go – leave you to the chess.'

He frowned, lines deepening between his eyebrows.

I got into the car and reversed out, the gravel protesting under the back wheels. At the roundabout by the war memorial at the bottom of the lane, I put the handbrake on and took out my own cigarettes, glad for once that the roads were so quiet and no one came up behind to force me to move off before I could light one. I was filled with a profound sense of loss.

I parked back at the cottage but didn't immediately go in. It wasn't just that I hadn't left a light on and the house looked dark and forbidding: I needed to walk.

Bolting the gate after me, I went back across the grass, over the road and on to the harbour front. The ferry had just left and was only a couple of hundred yards out, lit up in the darkness like a fairground ride. They were playing the pre-recorded message about what to do in the case of emergency, the tinny voice just audible as the wind carried it back. The water lapped against the harbour wall by my feet, black; further out, it was yellow where the streetlights caught it. I walked up past the lifeboat office and the King's Arms, whose low windows gave out a rosy light on to the street. There were men at the bar, and the tables in the window and by the fire were taken. I carried on past the George and into the Square.

There were only two or three lights along the pier and away from them the boardwalk stretched out into darkness, the wooden shelter at the end with its pointed roof seeming to float above the water, lights shining out from its little windows. I started walking. Apart from the sound of the water slapping against the struts and my feet on the boards, there was silence. The ferry was a long way off now. I felt exposed out over the water, away from the town, suddenly conscious that there was no way back should anyone follow me out here. But who would that be? No one knew I was here. I couldn't be so timorous all the time.

I reached the end and leant against the wooden railing. The air carried the taint of rotting fish; the line-fishers gutted their catch here rather than at home, throwing the heads and entrails back into the water. In front of me, across the Solent, the lights of the mainland lay like a necklace along the shoreline, clustered more densely at the mouth of the Lymington River. Away from the shelter of the town, the breeze was stronger. It blustered round my ears until I turned up the collar of my coat but even then I could hear a whine in it, a gentle echo of the wind that had come crying around the house after Christmas, hurting my heart.

It took me several seconds to understand that it wasn't the wind. It was crying, a woman's crying, and it was coming from inside the shelter. Once I realised, I wondered how I could have mistaken it but even so there was still a moment when I questioned whether my mind was playing tricks on me and the weeping from the dream had crossed over, infiltrated my waking life.

I walked round to the entrance of the shelter, which was built away from the end of the pier to protect it from the wind. On the wooden bench inside, a woman was sitting with her head in her hands, her hair falling forward to conceal her face. I didn't need to see it to know it was Sally: her tiny frame and the huge black coat were instantly recognisable. She seemed not to have heard me so I went to sit next to her. After a second or two she looked up. Her eyes and nose were swollen from crying.

'What are you doing here?' she said, and her voice was almost fierce.

'Walking – I needed some fresh air. Are you all right?'

She ran the ball of her hand under her eyes and sniffed.

'Has something happened?'

She looked at me for several seconds, as if she was weighing up whether to tell me. 'Tom found my emergency fund,' she said. 'Two hundred pounds. I kept it in my wardrobe in the pocket of an old coat. He'd been through everything.'

The little shit, I thought.

'I just don't know what I can do any more. He takes money from my purse but this – how did he even know it was there? I've got nothing now – that was it. Is this my fault?' she asked, turning back to me suddenly, eyes glistening. 'Because I brought him up on my own?'

'No. Don't think that. You do your best for him – it's obvious.'

'Is it?' She got a tissue out of her pocket and started blotting her wet eyelashes, wiping away the mascara that had transferred on to her cheeks. She pushed her hair off her face and tucked it behind her ears. 'I've got to get back. God knows what else he will have done. I had a bottle of wine in the wardrobe – he'll have had that as well.'

'I'll come with you – it's too cold out here.'

We walked back along the pier together. She was preoccupied and hardly said a word but I was glad of her company. The pier seemed even longer now, a great stretch to be covered before we reached the safety of the Square again, the occasional lights along it seeming only to emphasise the loneliness. I could almost see the *Crimewatch* reconstruction.

Outside the Bugle, I stopped. 'Let me buy you a drink,' I said.

'What?'

'Shall we have a drink – or something to eat? Have you eaten?'

She looked at me for a moment as if I had taken leave of my senses.

'Not to worry,' I said. 'It was just an idea. You should get back.'

We could have gone as far as St James's before parting ways but I had the strong sense that she wanted to be on her own. I hung back and let her go.

Back at the cottage, I turned on my computer. The home screen of my email account told me I had one new message. Helen, I hoped, clicking into my inbox, but of course it was from Richard. Before I could stop myself I'd opened it.

I'm enjoying our game, sweetheart; it's an amusing diversion now that all I do with my life is work and talk to my wife's solicitors. I can use up hours thinking about where you might be. You're not in London, I'm pretty confident of that, and you won't be in Bristol now Daddy's gone, will you? I think we can safely say you haven't run into the loving arms of your mother. But don't worry, I've got my ideas and I'm getting warmer all the time. I'm run off my feet at the moment but I'll always make time for you.

One more thing, Katie: if you were ever involved with anyone else – even thought about anyone else – I'd kill you.

Chapter Thirty

The phone on the wall in the café kitchen only ever rang with calls from Mary or the greengrocer's so when I heard Chris's voice I knew immediately that something was wrong.

'I'm sorry to call you at work,' he said. 'I tried your mobile but it's switched off.'

'I forgot to charge it. What's happened?'

He paused for a moment. 'It looks like they've found Alice's body.'

The feeling like cold hands came over my skin. 'Where?'

'A fishing boat . . .'

'No – not in the nets?' For a split second I saw her body among fish spilling out on deck, the shimmer of scales. I felt a rush of nausea and put my hand over my mouth.

'If it is her,' he was saying, 'she didn't move far from where they picked her boat up. They were fishing round the back of the Island, near St Catherine's.'

'Pete – will he have to identify her?'

'The body's been in the water for so long . . . I think it'll be dental records.'

'Oh God.' I put the hand back over my mouth, tried to breathe through my nose. 'Where is he?' I asked after a few seconds.

'At home. The boat radioed in just before seven; he hadn't left for work when the police went round. They're with him now. I've shut the shop and I'm coming down but I thought you should know in case you see him. I don't know how he's going to react.'

There were a number of people in the café so I couldn't stay in the kitchen. I splashed water on my face but it didn't help. I kept thinking of her body, rolling in the cold water off the back of the Island for almost five months. Dental records – what had the trawlermen seen when they brought their net up? I imagined her skeleton dragged back and forth along the seabed all through the winter, the turbulence in the water tearing away her clothes, crabs coming to feed on her flesh. I rushed to the sink and was grateful only to dry-heave.

The policemen, an officer in uniform and another in plain clothes, walked past the window just before eleven. Though the station was at the bottom of the road, I hadn't seen police in Yarmouth more than a couple of times in five months; they had to be on their way from Pete's. I felt so powerless, trapped in the café. I wanted to throw everyone out, lock the door and go rushing up the road, knock on doors until I found his house. But what would I do when I got there? Were we still friends? I didn't even know that.

I thought about calling Helen but realised that almost all of this would be news to her. I'd told her about him at Christmas, the man whose wife had disappeared off her boat, but she knew nothing about our friendship, if that was what it was or had been, or how I felt. I hadn't told her about the dinner that night, let alone the kiss. Why hadn't I spoken to her? She hadn't called back after I'd rung her at the office; why was that? Maybe Esther hadn't passed on the message, or maybe she just hadn't had a chance. *What? In almost a week?* asked a quiet voice.

The news didn't become public currency until three o'clock. I was carrying plates of sandwiches to the window table when I overheard a woman regaling her husband with the details. 'Imagine,' she said. 'In the water since November, nothing left on the body to identify her by. They say the fish go for the face first, don't they?'

'Glenda, please,' came the response but I didn't hear the rest. I managed to get to the back door and yank it open before I was sick into the bucket used for washing the floor. I leant against the wall for a few seconds, dizzy, but there were orders outstanding and I couldn't leave the counter unattended. Inside

I washed my face and hands thoroughly; I'd have to sort out the bucket later.

It wasn't until four that Mary came in with the soup for the next day, elbowing her way through the front door with her hands full. 'You've heard about Alice Frewin?' she said, putting the bowl down on the kitchen counter. 'That poor, poor man. Better that she fill herself full of pills at home, surely, than put him through all these months of not knowing. I feel sorry for her, of course I do – no one in their right mind would ever do it. But to put someone you love through this . . .'

As soon as I got back to the cottage, I went upstairs and ran a bath. In my mind, the woman's voice was still playing on loop – *They say the fish go for the face first, don't they?* Afterwards, in a fresh pair of jeans and with my hair washed, the sweaty, nauseous sensation and the images of Alice were a little less vivid. I took the dinosaur tooth out of my bag and lay down on the sofa holding it, hoping that somehow it would channel my feelings and let him know I was thinking about him.

I woke in darkness, seconds passing before I realised that the banging sound was not in my dream but at the front door. Someone – a man – was calling my name. My first thought, heart thumping: Richard. But no, not him, not his voice. More hammering. I stood up from the sofa too quickly, making my head spin, and reached for the switch. The sudden light hurt my eyes.

I stumbled the few steps into the kitchen and saw Chris through the glass. He was shifting from foot to foot, looking at me, then away down the passageway. When I opened the door, chill night air followed him into the kitchen, clinging around his coat like smoke. He was out of breath, as if he'd been running.

'Is Peter here? Have you seen him?' he said.

'No – should I? I wasn't expecting . . .'

'I'd said I'd cook him supper but when I got back to his, he was gone.'

'You're sure he's not there? Maybe he's just not opening the door.'

'It was open. I've searched the whole house.'

'Have you tried Sally Vaughn's?'

'Yes, first,' he said. 'It was the obvious place.' He looked at me, registered the look on my face. 'He's already seen her today. That's why I'm worried – she told him that Alice was seeing someone else.'

'What?'

'He went to see her this afternoon. You know she and Alice were good friends? Apparently she just came out and said it – *Alice was seeing someone.*'

I thought of how she had described them to me the first time I'd met her. Perfect for each other; weren't those her words? 'I don't understand,' I said.

'Alice had started seeing a new psychologist in Southampton – twice a week. But it seems she only went to a couple of sessions. She kept up the pretence as a cover but really she was meeting someone else over on the mainland instead, a man.'

'How did Sally know?'

'Alice confided in her.'

'But surely that means . . .'

'She knew all this when she went missing?' He nodded. 'And it seems that it might be the reason. Sally said that they'd talked about running off together somewhere, making a go of it, but this man, whoever he was, got cold feet and called it all off. Alice went over one last time to plead with him but he wouldn't budge. Sally thinks that's why she did it – that it was the last straw.'

'Why didn't she tell anyone at the time?'

'She says Alice swore her to secrecy, that while there was still a chance she might come back she couldn't break her promise.'

'What – even after all these months?'

'She only told him today because she thought it would help, she said. She thought that if he knew, it would take the edge off his grief.' He shook his head. 'I've just been round there. She's beside herself that she's hurt him – near hysterical. Could she really have thought she wouldn't?'

I waited a long time for sleep to come. The couple of hours I'd spent on the sofa before Chris had woken me hadn't helped but it was more than that. The inside of my head felt like a maze from which I had to escape before I could rest but though I tried countless different ways through it, each one led to a different set of disturbing ideas and images: Alice's body rolling on to the decks of a trawler with a shimmering, jumping catch; Pete as he heard the truth; Sally crying hysterically. Richard, at the computer. And, less clear, there was a picture of Helen, looking at her mobile as it rang with my number.

Before Chris left I'd had an idea. 'I think he might have gone to the boat,' I said. 'To Shalfleet. Was his car still there?'

'I didn't look.'

'I'll come with you.'

'No, I'll go.' His voice was firm enough to make me look at him in surprise. 'You're tired,' he said, holding the eye contact.

It had been barely half nine by then but after he'd gone I went upstairs, cleaned my teeth and got into bed. I'd stared at *The Mayor of Casterbridge* for a while, rereading the same half-page over and over again until I conceded defeat and turned off the light. My phone was on the bedside table next to the dinosaur tooth and minutes later it had rung, casting its blue glow up on to the ceiling in the dark room. It was Chris, calling from the quay at Shalfleet. 'You were right,' he said. 'His car's here.'

When sleep finally came I had the dream, as I had known I would. I was on the cliff-top again, in the swirling unbreathable mist. Through it came the low mourning bell and the strobe which raked back and forth, watching, searching. I shrank from the light, shielding my face as it approached, putting my hands up to shade my eyes and to block out the shape that was taking on form, definition. The beam passed over and I opened my eyes again, looked behind me for a way down, a path. The figure was moving, coming towards me. My heart was beating, its crazy rhythm at odds with the relentless steadiness of the bell. I had seconds before the beam returned, back the other way. It was moving over the patchy grass, illuminating it stripe by stripe, closer and closer. I scratched at the air in front of my face, needing a breath, just one. My feet were rooted; they wouldn't move. Now the light came

251

on to them, so bright I thought it would burn, but it was cold, ice cold. Through my hands, I could see red, the blood in my eyelids all backlit. The beam stopped; it lingered on me, touched me, but then suddenly it swept off again, as if it had tried me and found me wanting.

I opened my eyes and there she was: Alice. I tried to turn away but couldn't. Her arms were so deathly pale, the skin seeming to melt even as I watched, the bones showing clearly in her thin blue fingers. She was looking at me, forcing me to look at her. My heart beat faster still, so hard I thought it might burst through my chest wall. I raised my eyes slowly. There was her chin, the white cheeks. Higher still, towards those terrible empty grey sockets, the vacancy. I opened my mouth to scream but before I could she reached out her hands and clutched my arm, her grip tight as a knot. 'Kate,' she whispered, and I woke up, the sheets around me damp with sweat.

The body was formally identified as Alice two days later. When Chris rang to tell me, he sounded tired out. 'It was lucky,' he said, 'if anyone can call any of this lucky. They think she must have been caught somewhere for a while – under a ledge or in some sort of sheltered eddy – to mean that the skeleton was almost all in one piece. With the winter we had, that storm after Christmas, the sea was so violent. If she'd been out in exposed waters, it might have broken up entirely, never been found. At least Peter has that – at least he knows now.' He'd paused. 'I can't think of anything more terrible,' he said, 'than what he's had to go through. And those men on the boat – what must they have felt? I just can't imagine. But at least Peter hasn't had to see the body – that's a mercy.'

In the days that followed, I didn't leave Yarmouth. For the most part, in fact, I didn't move far off the circuit that connected the cottage with the café, Wavells and the newsagent, not even taking the dinghy out for fear that Pete might come looking for me and not be able to find me. I couldn't seek him out but I did have to be there if for any reason he needed me.

I wondered whether Sally might come to the café or knock at the cottage but I didn't see her either. I tried to imagine how

252

appalling she must have been feeling about what she'd told Pete, the degree of self-flagellation to which she was subjecting herself. Was it wrong, what she'd done? Perhaps she really had thought there was still a chance Alice might reappear and reveal that she'd spent the winter in some remote corner somewhere. I didn't know. All I knew was that she must be feeling awful, and ashamed, so when she didn't come to me, I went looking for her. I waited until the early evening when she was usually home from work and walked round to Mill Road. I knocked loudly twice but there was no answer. It was the same the next day.

I didn't hear from Helen, either, and I didn't try to contact her. I remembered the small voice that had spoken to me the day Alice's body had been recovered, asking why she hadn't rung back. It was almost two weeks now since I'd left the message with Esther and she hadn't called or emailed or sent even the most cursory of texts. I knew something was wrong – since Christmas we'd spoken so regularly it was as if there had never been a problem between us – but I wasn't ready to address it yet. I wanted to speak to her, to tell her everything that had happened with Pete, but something held me off. The simplest part of it was hurt that she could disappear so completely again. The dominant part, however – I could allow this much without having to go deeper into it – was fear. I was afraid of what could possibly cause her to pull back so suddenly, when the biggest obstacle between us had been overcome. I looked back over our most recent conversations, tried to think of how I might have offended her, but found nothing. And into that space flooded Richard.

Chapter Thirty-one

Alice's remains were cremated at a private ceremony but a memorial service was held for her at St James's in the Square. Just before eleven on Thursday the following week, the church's single bell started to toll, its unmistakable funeral tone darkening the morning and breaking the silence which had settled on the town like a weight.

Chris had told me about the service but not, I thought, with the idea that I should go. Even if he had suggested it, I wouldn't have. It felt inappropriate: I would have been embarrassed for Pete to see me there. The café, though, was almost empty, all the morning-coffee regulars in church, as Mary was. 'It's for his sake I'm going,' she'd said, taking a long black coat out of the cupboard. 'She kept herself to herself but there'll be a lot of people who want to show him their support.'

'I didn't know you knew him,' I said.

'Everyone does. He's popular here – well liked.'

When she'd gone, my thoughts turned back to Alice. My views about her were so confused now. It was as if there were a number of discrete versions of her and I had a different feeling towards each of them. There was the desperate Alice I'd met on the common for whom I felt sorrow and pity but then there was the one who'd been unfaithful, who seemed to have made Pete work so hard to try to make her happy and finally hadn't allowed him even the certainty of knowing whether she was dead or alive. There was also the Alice of my dreams, who reached out those white-blue fingers to grip me. Part of me would have liked to have gone to the church but again, for mixed reasons: to pay my respects to someone with whom I felt I'd had a sort of relationship, yes, but also in the hope that being there, seeing the mourning, might somehow lay her to rest in my mind, end the nightmares.

The service was short. It was scarcely eleven thirty before the bell resumed its monotone lament. A few minutes later there were footsteps and subdued voices in the street; they were walking back to Pete's house this way. I was out from behind the counter and, suddenly afraid of being seen, I drew back against the wall.

My eyes found him immediately. Flanked by Chris and a silver-haired woman with her arm tucked tightly into his, he was at the head of a group of six or seven coming up the High Street. Although I couldn't have imagined that he would be wearing anything else, his black suit still surprised me; in it he looked so different to the Pete I knew, with his scruffy jeans and navy jumper or even the leather jacket and sweater he'd worn to supper. His formality seemed to emphasise his distance from me and the things we'd done together, going out in the dinghy and on the boat, walking on the beach at Brook. Now, in the suit, surrounded by people I hadn't seen before, he seemed impossibly far away.

The woman with her arm through his was in her late sixties. She was tall – five ten even with her slight stoop – and I guessed at once that she was his mother. She wore a black three-quarter-length coat and a hat with a small veil which shaded her eyes but as she turned to say something to Pete, I had a clear view of her face. It was heavily lined, an outdoor face, but I saw the high Slavic cheekbones and a glimpse of pale eyes and knew without a doubt I'd guessed right.

It took them several seconds to pass the long plate-glass window, Pete moderating his usual stride to accommodate her pace, but just as they were about to disappear from sight, he turned his head and looked into the café. I saw him scan the front of the room but I was too far back, out of the small pool of natural daylight that fell through the window on to the floor. Then, a fraction of a second later, his mother spoke again, pulling his attention away. A moment more, and he was gone.

*   *   *

I wasn't usually tired out by a day at the café but as I was walking back to the cottage that evening, a great weariness seized me and it was all I could do to get home, lock the door behind me and climb the stairs to my bedroom, where I lay down and promptly fell asleep. I came round again just after nine, woken, probably, by the hoot of the ferry as it departed. Though it felt too late for dinner, I made an omelette and poured a glass of wine before going back upstairs to my study.

Laid out on the desk were the details for the next couple of days, printouts from the estate-agents' websites of the cottages I had appointments to view. Anglesey – an island off North Wales. A place so remote I hoped Richard hadn't even heard of it. A place to which I had no connection at all, and that was the point: there was no mental trail he could use to follow me there. I'd never even seen pictures of it except the ones on the internet yesterday. At least I'd had links to the Island when I'd come here, I thought. Soon I wouldn't even have that: he'd have driven me away from everything that was familiar. I thought of the poor Canadian woman I'd read about and just hoped it would be enough. *I'd kill you.* I heard the words again as if he'd whispered them in my ear.

I folded the pieces of paper in half and tucked them into my bag next to the ferry ticket. Then I poured another glass of wine and brought Helen's number up on my mobile. I hesitated for a second, then made the call. My heart jumped when I heard the ring tone and I prepared myself for the sound of her answering voice, the breezy 'Kate!' The phone rang six times, seven, and then, as really I had known it would, the answering service clicked in and the automated voice asked me to leave a message. Indecisive, I missed the first couple of seconds' recording time but then I did speak. 'Helen,' I said, 'it's me. Look, maybe nothing's the matter and I'm being paranoid but it seems like a long time since we spoke and I've tried calling and I left a message with Esther but I haven't heard from you. If something was wrong, you'd tell me, wouldn't you? Ring me or text. Just – get in touch.'

I caught the seven-thirty ferry. As I waited in the car for my lane to start loading, I remembered the day after Christmas when I'd stood in the terminal building waiting for Helen to buy her ticket, watching her bag bouncing against her back as she'd jogged down the room, so reluctant to leave me on the Island on my own that she'd almost missed the boat. I'd left my phone on all night and though she would be up by now, maybe already on her way to the office, there had been nothing.

On the ferry I left the car and climbed the stairs to the passenger area. I went out of the heavy wooden door from the top lounge on to the open deck. Below, the ramp curled up after the last of the cars and then came the tug of the engine and white water as the boat began to move away. There was a grey-haired couple at the gate on the harbour and they waved at the young family standing just along from me. The man was holding his small daughter on his shoulders, her little legs in stripy tights hanging on either side of his neck. 'Wave, Emily,' he said. 'Wave.'

In a matter of seconds there was clear water between the boat and the town. Now I could see the pier parallel to us and then, when our perspective broadened, the beach and garden at the George, where the wooden tables had now been set out on the grass for the coming season. A minute more and I could see the whole length of the town where it bordered the shore and stretched out to meet the grassy slope of the common, whose benches already seemed tiny and distant. There were the huge properties with their private jetties and then the row of smaller but still substantial houses further along, one of them Pete's. Over the boat's white wake, gulls wheeled and tumbled, their wings flashing against the bright blue sky, the sun infusing everything with light. Despite the morning chill, I looked back and saw the green layers of the Island's fields and woods as if it was already summer. I would come back, I thought; I would visit Chris, take up the offer of a night or two in his spare room. I couldn't just go and not come back again, not now.

I stayed out on deck all the way across the Solent, letting the breeze blow my hair round my face and watching the cluster of buildings at Yarmouth grow smaller and smaller until they were indistinguishable from one another and the masts in the harbour became a white thicket.

As we reached the mouth of the Lymington River, I smelled the tang of the mudflats. We came inside the breakwater, the marshes on our left, on our right the marina and the yacht club, the small park beyond it. It was all just as it had been the last time I'd seen it, almost six months ago. I felt a wash of apprehension.

Back in the car ready to disembark, I took my phone out of my bag and checked the screen. Nothing. The ramp came down and the car in front rolled away. I started the engine and followed it, down the dip and then up again on to the tarmac of the mainland. Half an hour's ferry crossing but a palpable difference: straight away I felt the expansion, the contrast between the small area on the quay where the cars waited at Yarmouth and the broader lanes here, the train at the platform and the brimming car park. Pulling out of the terminal and on to the main road, I felt as though I'd fast-forwarded twenty years: the traffic moved so quickly.

The road to Cadnam and the junction to the M27 took me through the New Forest, where the sunlight dappled through the trees. A pair of ponies grazed on the verge, indifferent to the thickening traffic of the morning rush. At the level crossing at Brockenhurst I had to wait while the fast train thundered through on its way to Southampton and London.

On the motorway the traffic was moving slowly and it gave me time to make up my mind. For Wales, I should have taken the turn off towards Newbury and the West but instead I took the M3, signposted London. My heart was pounding. I put the radio on and drove, not wanting to think about what I was doing. The car began to eat up the miles: over the great chalk downs near Winchester and then on to the long, featureless stretch north past Basingstoke, Fleet.

An hour and a half later, I was coming into London on the M4, the road rising on to the elevated section above Brentford, passing through the canyon of high-rise office buildings, the electronic hoardings with their advertisements for airlines and Armani and iPods. It was like entering a different world. I was breaking the speed limit but the cars in the outside lane streamed past me.

The rush hour was over and the traffic was suddenly comparatively light. It seemed only a matter of minutes before I was on the road where Helen's office was. I parked the car, turned the radio off and sat in silence for a moment. Then, before I could think about it any more, I got out and went in.

I gave my name at the desk and waited while the receptionist called upstairs. 'Esther?' she said. 'I've got a Kate Gibson here for Helen. Shall I ask her to come up?' She put her hand over the mouthpiece. 'Just a second.' She listened again. 'OK, I'll let her know. She's coming down,' she said to me. 'She'll just be a minute or two.'

I was too anxious to sit. Instead I paced the reception area, looking at the glass sculpture suspended from the ceiling, then standing at the door and watching the street, where a white van was making a delivery to the building next door.

Finally I heard the sound of the lift behind me and the doors opened to reveal Helen. She was wearing a dress in amaryllis red with matching suede heels, her Louise Brooks cut newly trimmed. Over her arm was a pale trench coat. Though I'd put on my black jeans and a jacket for my appointments with the estate agents, I recognised immediately how dowdy and provincial I must appear.

'Kate.' She ran over, I thought to give me a hug, but she stopped before she reached me. 'What are you doing here? You're in London; I didn't think . . .'

'I was worried. I've left messages for you.'

'I got it – last night. I was going to call you.' She couldn't meet my eyes. Hers were travelling round the room, settling for a second at a time on the flowers on the desk, the van outside, the sculpture.

'I've been trying to get you for weeks.'

'I'm really sorry. It's just been so busy.' She shifted her weight from one foot to the other. 'It's mad here.' She looked back at the receptionist as if for corroboration.

'Can we have lunch? I'll come back in a couple of hours.'

'I'm on my way out – I've got a meeting.'

'Or supper? I'll stay in town for the day, wait till you finish.'

'I need to get a cab. I'm running late.'

'I've got the car here; I'll drive you.'

'No.' There was a note of desperation in her voice now and we both heard it.

'Come outside,' I said, conscious of the receptionist's interested attention. She followed me out and we stood on the pavement. I could see she was agitating to get away from me. 'What's going on?' I said.

'Kate, please. Don't . . .' She was biting her lip.

'Richard,' I said, and she gave a small but perceptible start. 'Are you seeing him?'

'No.' Her voice was loud enough to make the delivery man look over. 'No. Look, I'm just in a rush. I'll ring you later – I promise.'

She turned to go and I reached out and grabbed her arm. I had a momentary mental image of Alice, her cold fingers gripping me. 'This isn't about me,' I said. 'It isn't jealousy. He's dangerous.'

She pulled her arm away. There was a taxi coming down the street, its light on. 'I'm not seeing him.' She put up her hand and the cab glided in towards the kerb.

'Helen – please.'

She cranked up the handle and opened the door, climbing in before I could stop her. 'You've got it wrong,' she said.

I stood on the pavement and watched as the cab drove off, the lights at the bottom of the street turning green just as it reached them. Through the window at the back I could see the dark shape of her head, the sharpness of the bob above her white neck almost cartoonish, but she didn't look back.

Panic broke over me. For a moment I thought I might faint. I got back into the car and sat with my forehead on the steering wheel. My legs were trembling. With an adamantine certainty I knew that she had been taken in by him, one way or another. My lovely, kind friend. I thought of how her face had appeared at the cottage's kitchen window on Christmas Day and slammed my hand against the wheel. How dare he do this to her, use her as a pawn. Perhaps, though, an insidious voice said, it isn't a game; perhaps it is Helen he wants now. *No; don't let him get inside your head.*

Richard was so close – so very close. I imagined his breath on the back of my neck, my face, and into my mind came a picture of that last morning at the flat, how he'd thrown me up against the wall and how I'd fallen, jarring my spine, the explosion of pain behind my eye as he'd hit me. Then another set of images, this time of Sarah, her broken ribs. I had to tell Helen now. She had to know the whole story.

I called her mobile but it went straight to voicemail. What could I do? Had she really had a meeting or had she come running out to prevent me from going up, cornering her? Perhaps she'd got the taxi to take her home. I turned the car around and headed for Hammersmith. When I got there, her street was quiet, most of its residents at work, but a couple of mothers with babies in buggies on the opposite pavement looked with exaggerated disapproval and barely disguised curiosity as I banged and banged on her door long after it became clear that she wouldn't answer.

Finally, I got back in the car and took the road back the way I'd come. Out on the motorway again, I put my foot down and pushed the car hard, watching the needle touch ninety, ninety-five. I opened the window and let the buffeting wind replace the London air trapped inside.

I drove until I reached Lymington again but I wasn't ready to go back to the Island: too much was unresolved. Instead I found myself following signs to Keyhaven and then to Hurst Castle. There was the promontory I'd seen so many times from the Island, the huge shingle bank stretching out into the Solent as if trying to bridge it, the white castle hunkered down on the point. I got out of the car and walked, the only person there except for an occasional dog-walker. Almost at the end, I slid down the steep side and pressed myself into the shingle out of the breeze. Then I took out my phone, dialled Helen's home number and left three messages telling her everything that had happened.

'Please,' I said at the end of the third, 'if I'm right and he's in touch with you, please don't think this is about jealousy or wanting him back or not wanting you to be happy. I don't love Richard – that's gone – completely gone. I met someone else, someone so different from him I just can't describe it. Believe me, this is about you – about you being safe.'

Chapter Thirty-two

On the ferry back, I stood outside again. The wind had a sharper edge now and in the darkness the water was black, illuminated only where light fell on it from the windows of the boat and the open decks. I was alone, the few other passengers keeping warm inside. Holding on to the railing, I trained my eyes on the lights of the harbour at Yarmouth as though, if I concentrated hard enough, we would get there more quickly. Down the Solent, the Needles lighthouse blinked its all-seeing eye in the dark.

I was in my car ready to disembark before the announcement came, the engine running while the ramp was still being lowered. There was a rising feeling in my chest as the car came up on to the Island again. I drove the few hundred yards to the cottage and parked but I didn't go inside. Instead, I took my bag and ran, along Bridge Road, across the Square and up the High Street. My heart was racing but it wasn't just exertion. For hours, walking miles and miles along the shore of the mainland, I had thought about two things: Helen and this.

When I reached the row of houses, I hesitated. Which was it? Not the clapboard house on the end but one of the three down from it. In one, no lights showed. In the next, a double-fronted cottage, the pale glow of a table lamp shone through the fabric of a blind in one window; the window on the other side of the front door was dark, light only visible where an internal door was open. I walked along, as if casual, and let my eyes wander towards the window of the third house. Golden light spilled out on to the street and I said a silent prayer but inside there was an elderly couple, the tops of their grey heads visible over the backs of armchairs, the news showing on the television in front of them.

I felt a moment's despair and turned round. What if the dark cottage was his? What if he'd gone away somewhere? He'd said in the car that time, hadn't he, that he hadn't been able to go away when Alice was missing. What if he'd decided to go now? Maybe I wouldn't even see him again.

Just then, however, my eye was caught by a movement in the second house. The light falling into the dark room was interrupted by someone moving in front of the door; for an instant it vanished almost completely.

I walked the few steps to the door, lifted the brass dolphin knocker and, before I could hesitate any more, let it drop back. The sharp rap sounded loud in the quiet street. Long seconds passed. *What if it wasn't him? What if it was, and he didn't understand why I'd come?*

There were footsteps on a wooden floor inside and a carriage lamp came on above my head. The door cracked open and he was standing there. In a second's upward twitch of his eyebrows I registered his surprise. 'Hello,' he said, and stepped aside to let me in.

The door closed behind me and we were standing in the hall, maybe a foot apart. The house was warm; I had brought the cold in on my coat but he was wearing a faded indigo T-shirt that was torn slightly at the neck. We looked at each other and, without saying anything, he reached out and put his hand against the side of my face.

He leaned in and kissed me, his mouth soft. As he pulled away again to gauge my reaction, I swallowed, the sound embarrassingly loud. He smiled, the lines deepening at the corner of his eyes, and kissed me again, this time manoeuvring me a step backwards so that I was against the wall. As he leaned his weight against me, my whole body responded. I put my hands on his back, felt the heat of his skin through the T-shirt, pulled him harder against me. His hands pushed my jacket off my shoulders and then his fingers moved to the neck of my jumper, undoing the little buttons, touching the skin he'd exposed, brushing his lips over it, letting

263

me feel his breath. He moved his hands lightly down over my breasts, the backs of his fingers lingering for a moment on my nipples which I knew he would feel even through my bra and the thick wool. My fingers slipped underneath his T-shirt and found the groove of his spine.

Abruptly he stepped away. I looked up, alarmed, but there was a question in his eyes. He took my hand and led me down the hall and then upstairs. I didn't think about it for a second. I saw a wide landing, sisal mats, a wicker chair, and then we were in another room, dark apart from the light from the hall. My jumper was off in one neat movement. He pulled me against him again and I felt his hardness against my hip. I yanked his T-shirt over his head and saw the shape of his shoulders, the thick dark hair on his chest.

He reached behind me to unhook my bra and seconds later I was on the bed, the feather duvet rising around me like cloud as he pressed me down in to it. My jeans were gone, then both our hands fumbled at his belt buckle. For a few seconds we were naked in front of each other, shy, then he lowered his weight gently on to me and I wrapped my legs around him.

Afterwards we lay on our sides, faces inches apart. His hand rested on my hip. The warm smell of his skin was in my nostrils. Even now, neither of us had really spoken, as if we were worried that we would burst the bubble which for the moment held us safely inside. As he'd come, he had given a sharp cry, pleasure definitely but also pain.

'Are you all right?' he said.

'Yes. Are you?' I moved over and touched my lips against his.

'Yes,' he said but in the light that fell into the room from the landing I saw that his eyes were shining. 'It's been quite a long time.' He put his hand on my arm, feeling the goose-bumps that were starting to come up. 'Let's get in,' he said. 'You're cold.'

We got into the bed and lay facing each other again, our heads on the pillows.

'I like you,' he said. 'I don't know what this is, whether you even want anything at all or . . .'

'I like you, too.'

264

He pulled me towards him, turning on to his back so that I fitted into the crook of his arm, my cheek on his shoulder. 'I've been incredibly lonely,' he said, addressing the ceiling. 'Not alone but lonely. The time I've spent with you – I haven't felt like that.'

I let my hand rest on his stomach, feeling the pulse under his skin. His body was so different to Richard's. There was something solid about him. Richard's muscle came from the gym but Pete's came from rowing and sailing the boat, lugging outboards around. I had always loved Richard's body but now its definition struck me as self-regarding and vain. Pete's physique wasn't honed in the same way but it was naturally fit, honest somehow and strong.

All of a sudden it was as if a window had come open and a cold wind ran over my bare skin. I'd done it – it was irrevocable. *If you were ever involved with anyone else, I'd kill you.*

After a while, he reached over me to turn on the bedside lamp. We were in a small room with cream walls, the ceiling sloping to meet a wooden sash window. The striped blue curtains were open and though lying down I couldn't see anything except the navy darkness beyond the glass, I could hear the sea.

'It'll sound ridiculous,' he said, 'but I can't believe this is really happening.'

'It is – I've pinched myself.'

He laughed and turned over on to his side. He gently stroked my breast, his fingers tracing my nipple. 'Your breasts are lovely,' he said, lowering his mouth. Sensation flooded me, driving Richard out.

The second time was slower but just as intense. My body rose from the mattress to meet his; I wanted to fill myself up with him. I took deep breaths of the scent of his skin, let my hands run over him, learning the shape of his shoulders and the banks of muscle in his back. I forgot not only Richard but myself: my mind emptied.

It was later when I was back in the crook of his arm and he had brought one of the knots in my hair into better light to untangle it that my stomach gave a loud growl.

'Hungry?'

'Yes, a bit,' I said, embarrassed.

'Haven't you had dinner?'

The memory of the day, so thoroughly banished, returned. 'No,' I said. 'I was on the mainland. I went over to look at some cottages but I ended going up to London instead, to see my friend.' I pressed my face against his chest, avoiding his eye.

'It's April, isn't it?' he said. 'You're going.'

After another rumble from my stomach, Pete threw back the covers and got out. I watched as he put his jeans and T-shirt back on, admiring his long lines, the way the dark hair on his body tapered below his navel. 'Come downstairs,' he said, so I hopped out of bed and got dressed again. There was a mirror on the wall and when he'd gone, I went to look in it. My cheeks were flushed and my hair was a nest but I didn't care.

It struck me that the room was quite bare for one used regularly and when I went out on to the landing to go down, I saw I was right. Through the door opposite, left slightly ajar, I saw another bedroom, a pair of Pete's paint-covered jeans hanging over a wrought-iron bedstead. We'd been in a guest room.

Downstairs I followed the noises to the back of the house and found myself in a huge kitchen. In the area near the door were large modern units, wood topped with steel, a range and a huge fridge from which Pete was taking a bottle of wine. Behind him, the grill was on and there were already slices of bread cut from a loaf on the board. 'I haven't got much, I'm afraid,' he said, 'I need to go shopping. But I can do you some cheese on toast.' He unpeeled the foil from the wine and took a corkscrew from the row of utensils on hooks on the wall.

I wanted to stay close to him but with our clothes a degree of formality had returned so I sipped my wine and watched him moving round, grating cheese, arranging the bread on the grill pan, bare feet big on the wooden floor.

Beyond the units there was a wooden table and beyond that again a wicker sofa facing a long window. I went over to look out. There was scarcely a rim of garden round the back; the house, I saw, was perched right on the edge so that the view was all sea, the Solent stretching darkly to the mainland and the irregular lights along the shore there.

I was self-conscious about eating in front of him but at the same time I was so hungry it was an effort not to wolf down everything on the plate in seconds flat. He was sitting sideways to face me, his arm over the back of the sofa, one of his legs folded under.

'What size are your feet?' I said, looking at them.

'Thirteen,' he admitted. 'Huge.'

It was a strange thing; I'd thought that I would find it uncomfortable to be in the house he'd shared with Alice but I didn't feel her presence, even on a practical level. Apart, perhaps, from the wrought-iron bedstead, the style of the house wasn't especially feminine which surprised me, given her apparent liking for fashion. It wasn't sparse but there were no extra cushions on the sofa and no vases or photographs or ornaments on the shelves on the far wall, just books and a small wooden boat that looked from a distance like a scale model of *Beatrice*. Had he put away the things that reminded him of her or had there even ever been any?

There was silence for a moment and into it came the muffled sound of the bell at St James's striking midnight. I remembered how it had sounded only yesterday for Alice's memorial and was suddenly horrified at myself. How could I have thought to come here? I was a monster. My cheeks flamed.

Pete was watching me. 'Did you hear about Alice?' he said.

'Yes.' I looked down, feeling more blood rush to my face. 'Chris told me.'

'All of it?'

'I . . . I don't know.'

'Did he tell you that she'd been seeing someone else?'

'Yes.'

'The man she was seeing,' he said, looking away and out of the window, 'was her old boyfriend. David – he's a banker. They went out for years, from when she was at university till she was twenty-seven. He was the great love of her life apparently.' He snorted. 'So much so that he dumped her when her dad was dying.

'She came back here to look after her dad at the end. She was incredibly sad then but I thought it was just about that. We'd always been friends and so we saw each other a bit and I did my best to be a support – talking, you know. I'd always liked her – more than just as a friend – but other than a bit of a drunken kiss, nothing had happened between us before she'd gone away to university. Then suddenly, after Brian died, she started coming round more and more and we – started seeing each other. We were married within a year and I was so happy about it all that I didn't think to question it. I had this occasional nagging doubt that I loved her more than she loved me but I thought that would come, as she got better, the grief lessened.'

I reached out and put my hand on his foot. 'You don't have to tell me,' I said.

'I want to.' He took a great swig of wine and emptied his glass. 'Alice didn't love me.'

'Pete, that can't . . .'

'I'm not saying that she didn't like me or we didn't get on but she didn't love me – not in the right way. In the end I had to acknowledge it. There were always areas of her life that she kept closed off. At first I tried to get her to open up but she resisted. She had dresses that she kept in suit bags but never wore. A couple of months after we got married, I came home once and she was just sitting there clutching one of them, crying, as if it was dead or something. He'd bought it for her. I tried buying her things, thinking that she just missed that part of her life – living in London, getting dressed up – but I'd missed the point.' He stopped talking. The bottle was on the floor and he picked it up and refilled our glasses.

'Apparently he found her again on the internet, if you can believe it. She was using her maiden name in chat-rooms. She used to go over there to meet him.' He looked at me, oddly defensive suddenly. 'I suspected it; I did. She was happier, much happier – initially I thought that it was this new psychologist she claimed to be seeing but she was too happy for that. But you know, the truth is – and this is why I've felt so guilty – I'd run out of energy. I'd tried so hard but nothing had been enough, and it's hard to carry on loving someone when they don't love you back.'

I'd left my hand on his foot, and now I pressed down slightly, unsure what I could say that would help.

268

'She thought that it was all going to work out, she was making plans to leave me, but he dropped her again. That's why she did it in the end – went out in the boat. It nearly finished her the first time – she just couldn't handle it again.

'The reason I'm telling you this – it all reflects badly on me, I know that; I'm hardly painting myself as the irresistible love-object, am I? – it's because I want you to have the truth. I know I'm sounding heavy and I'm jumping the gun but I want you to know that if you want . . . What I mean is, this – you and me – it's not about Alice.'

I stayed the night. We finished the wine, then went upstairs and got back into bed. We didn't have sex again but he lay behind me, his body following the shape of mine, his arm around my waist. His breath was warm on my shoulder as we murmured to each other and I listened to the sea lapping at the wall of the garden, feet below. We fell asleep with the light on and when I woke briefly and reached over to turn it off, I felt his arm tighten round me. I lay down again, feeling his chest hair tickle my back. Even when things had been at their best with Richard, I had struggled to sleep in his arms but with Pete, it felt different.

I slept dreamlessly until the first light of the morning began to reach in through the curtains. Then I came awake with a start. Richard's words were in my ears again as clearly as if he'd been leaning over the bed to whisper them. *I'd kill you.*

Chapter Thirty-three

I did sleep again but only fitfully, and after I'd heard St James's strike seven, I knew it was pointless to keep trying. I turned over carefully so as not to wake Pete. He was lying on his side, facing me. He'd worked his way over to the other side of the bed during the night but his arm was stretched towards me, its open palm up. His face was open, too, unguarded: his gentle mouth, the large eyelids with their fringe of dark lashes, the cheek with its coat of stubble. I wanted to wake him up so that he would put his arms around me but I wanted him to sleep on, too, so that I didn't have to stop looking at him.

Last night as his breathing had slowed and I felt myself beginning to fall asleep, I'd realised something. In the past his openness about his feelings and how Alice had treated him would have sent me running. However much I'd liked him, that level of honesty – intimacy – would have horrified me and immediately triggered a sabotage campaign, with me finding reasons why I couldn't get involved, imagining faults, starting arguments, eventually conjuring up a feeling not unlike pity for the poor man who'd made the mistake of wanting me. I didn't feel it now: I had no urge to flee.

Should I tell him about Richard, the real reason I'd come here? I wanted to, when he'd been so honest with me. But telling him would mean confessing that I'd taken Richard back when I'd known he was married. Alice had been an adulterer but I had, too. I heard him sigh as he buried his head further into the pillow. I had to try not to think about Richard here, not to let his poison seep in. Maybe it would all collapse, anyway; maybe there was just too much weighing on us. I would take that risk, though. I would take the pain later if it meant I could have this now, even for a while.

I'd kill you. My stomach turned over, and the previous day came back to me in a great swell. Had Helen heard my message? I had to get through to her. She had been seeing him, I was certain about that, but in what way? Her resistance would have made it all the more exciting for him to seduce her. Perhaps, though, that wasn't it; perhaps he was getting closer to her, winning her confidence so that she would tell him where I was. But she wouldn't. She wouldn't betray my trust, not on that. I was certain.

Eventually, Pete opened his eyes. He smiled when he saw me, a slow smile that started with surprise and ended with a grin. He shifted across the bed and put his arms round me. I felt a surge of emotion, happiness but also something painfully like nostalgia, an awareness that we didn't have long. After a few minutes, his hand slipped from my waist to my hip and the feeling changed, becoming a mix of desire and intense longing.

'What are you doing today?' he asked a while later.

'No plans. It's Saturday – no work, or not at the café at least.' Guiltily I remembered the translation, still barely started.

'We could go over to Ventnor and walk along to Steephill Cove, maybe have a pub lunch.'

It was so lovely, so simple – so normal – that I only just stopped my eyes filling with tears. I sat up, turning away a little, and thought quickly. 'That'd be good,' I said. 'But I'll need to go home first – to have a bath and get changed.'

'Sure.' He kissed my shoulder. 'I'm going to get up and make some coffee.' He padded out, lovely in his solid nakedness, and I saw him go across to the other room from which he emerged minutes later in a different pair of jeans and a checked shirt whose sleeves he was rolling up.

I put my clothes back on and followed him down. Cross-legged on the sofa I drank my coffee and watched the Solent beyond the window. The morning was one of those so sharp and clean it was almost too much to take in. Already the sun had set the water sparkling and there were a handful of boats out. Later, I was sure, there would be many more.

'I'll see you at eleven,' I said, when we were standing in the hall.

'Kate,' he said suddenly, as I put my hand on the latch to open it. I turned round. 'I don't want to be secretive about you and me but I think we should keep it low-key. There'll be people in Yarmouth who won't like it – especially not so soon.'

And there's someone you don't even know about who would like it even less. My gut clenched. 'Under my hat,' I said.

He smiled. 'See you in a bit.'

I scanned around as I came out of his front door. There were several people on the High Street but further down, towards the Square; I didn't think anyone had seen me leaving. I'd switched my phone off before going to Pete's but I turned it back on as I walked, hoping for a voicemail or text. However reluctant she was to listen to what I had to say, surely if she'd heard my messages, she would know I was telling the truth. There was nothing, though, not even a missed call. I tried her mobile but it was still switched off.

Back at the cottage, I started running a bath, then turned on my laptop. On a scrap of paper on the table there were telephone numbers; it took me a moment to remember that they were the ones for the estate agents I was supposed to be seeing. I'd never even let them know I wasn't coming. While the computer was warming up, I rang them both and apologised profusely, claiming a family emergency. 'Would you like to remake the appointments for another day?' the second one asked.

'I'm not sure,' I said. 'Can I think? I'll ring again in a few days.'

Heart beating uncomfortably, I opened my Hotmail account: one new message. I said a silent prayer.

I mean it – you do know that?

'You're quiet.' Pete took his eye off the road for a second and looked across.

'No – I'm OK.' I glanced at him quickly and looked away again. The dishonesty of it, being here in the car pretending normality when I knew how thin the membrane between this – us – and the massing force on the other side had stretched.

272

We'd come what I now thought of as the back route towards Ventnor, along the military road rather than to Newport and down. On our right the sea was glittering, more blue again than green. A tanker was tracking across the horizon, its outline sharp in the clear light of the sky. As we rounded the steep bend where the road ran so close to the edge, I remembered something. 'I heard once that you used to come speeding along here on an old motorbike in the dead of night. Apparently you were apprehended by the police.'

He laughed, surprised. 'Guilty as charged. That was my teenage rebellion – the options were limited round here.' He looked at me again. 'I'd forgotten all about that. Who told you? Chris?'

I hesitated. 'Sally.'

'Well, yes. She does like to keep herself up on my business, it seems.' His mouth straightened and I wished I hadn't said anything.

In Ventnor he parked on the esplanade. We were about a hundred yards from where I'd been the day Sarah had called me; I remembered it all. In my bag, my mobile was on silent. I didn't want to turn it off in case it gave Helen the wrong impression but if it rang, Pete would think it odd if I didn't answer and I couldn't speak to her in his earshot.

We got out and started walking. The businesses that lined the esplanade were remaking themselves for the new season. At a café with a small outside area, a woman with a bucket of water and a sponge wiped down plastic chairs; further along, a man was touching up the paintwork at a bed and breakfast. The summer that I hadn't been able to imagine here was coming.

On the path along the cliff-top there were other people, middle-aged couples in walking boots and a man our age struggling to control a boxer that strained at its leash, but after a while, confident we wouldn't meet anyone we knew, Pete took my hand. I galloped along, trying to match his stride, trying to fix the scene in my mind. I wanted to remember it for ever: the soft grass that covered the cliff-top here, the rooks that rose in flurries from the stand of trees beyond the path and the wind-dappled sea that stretched all the way to France like an expanse of shimmering fish-scales vanishing to a steel-blue line. I wondered briefly what my mother would think if she saw me now and decided I didn't give a toss.

After we got back from the other side of the Island, we dropped in at the cottage for my things. Pete sat downstairs and watched athletics on television for a few minutes while I put my toothbrush and a change of clothes in a bag. Feeling dishonest again, I checked my email: no new messages. In the bathroom, I checked my phone.

When I got downstairs again, Pete was not alone.

'Ah,' I said, coming into the room.

'Does he come here often?' He turned to me. The cat known to me as Hercule regarded me with innocent eyes from over the arm of Pete's jumper.

'Yes. I encouraged him, I'm afraid. I think he comes for the squirrel – there's one in the yard and he chases it. He started following me into the house and standing by the fridge. Eventually I gave him milk. Sorry.'

'Cats do their own thing, don't they? He comes home now, too.'

'What's he called?'

'Victor. That's what they'd called him at the shelter.'

'I think he looks like Hercule Poirot.'

Pete laughed. 'The dinner jacket – yes.'

Back at his house we opened a bottle of wine and cooked the steaks we'd bought at the butcher in Ventnor. Afterwards we lay on the sofa. Beyond us the Solent had turned dark and I could hear it lapping on the rocks round the bottom of the sea wall below. I remembered again how I'd heard the water that day on Tennyson Down, how I'd imagined Alice in the sound of it, calling to me, calling me over.

'Upstairs,' he said. 'We're not in the main bedroom.'

'Of course – there's no need to . . .'

'I want this but I feel guilty. I feel guilty about even thinking about it – you.' He moved on to his back and there was silence for a moment. 'I'll always wonder whether I could have done more. I'll always think about her.' He turned his head and looked at me, his eyes very green. 'What I'm trying to say is it might take time.'

'We've got time,' I said, but even as the words left my mouth, I knew it was a lie.

On Sunday we went out on the boat. I'd woken to an empty bed and had got up immediately and gone down to the kitchen. He had been standing by the window, looking out over the Solent. I went to stand next to him, and he put his arm around my shoulder. The window was open and a cool breeze swept in around my bare legs.

'Shall we go sailing today?' he said.

'I can't,' I said.

'I thought you had no plans?'

I hesitated. 'I'm feeling bad about the translation – the weeks are ticking past and it's a tight schedule anyway.'

'You can't work on it all day, surely? Come, and then work this evening. Go on.' He smiled and slipped his hand up inside the jumper I'd put on. His thumb found my nipple and circled it gently.

'This is coercion.'

'Yes,' he said.

'OK, then.' I breathed in the smell of his hair as he bent to kiss my neck, then my jaw. 'I won't forget this, though – how you've lured me off the path of diligence.'

'I should hope not.'

Out on *Beatrice*, I watched him from behind my sunglasses. He sat at the back of the cockpit, one hand resting gently on the tiller, the other shielding his eyes from the sun that shone directly across him. He looked more relaxed again now, though he'd been tense earlier. Just as we'd been leaving the house to get into the car, early enough to think there wouldn't be many other people around, Tom had been coming down the High Street, clearly on his way home from the night before. He hadn't even bothered to try to conceal his cigarette. 'Morning,' he'd said, his voice full of innuendo. 'Pete. Kate.'

'I don't like him,' Pete had said, when the doors were closed. 'I never have. I don't trust him. And this'll get back to Sally now, guaranteed.'

'They don't get on, though, do they? Would he tell her?'

'Information is power, isn't it?'

Now I watched the shore of the mainland as we cut through the water. We were close enough in to be able to see people walking their dogs along the beach. I tried just to enjoy the moment, being out with him on the boat in the sun, but I couldn't shake off the sense that the weekend was unreal, too good. The happiness felt snatched. Already I'd lied to Pete, and not only because I hadn't told him about Richard. I wasn't going to work on the translation this evening. After he dropped me off, I would wait a few minutes until he was back at home and then I would get in my own car and drive across to the ferry. I was going back to London tonight.

'I won't hang around,' Pete said as he pulled in near the end of the passageway. 'We're probably the talk of the town already but we might as well try not to fan it.'

'When will I see you?'

'I've got a meeting over in Southampton tomorrow and dinner with the client afterwards so I'll be late back, probably not until eleven or so. Tuesday? I could cook.'

'Tuesday – OK. But I'll cook.'

He smiled and touched my face. 'See you then.'

I looked at his face for a few seconds, then I picked up my bag and made to get out of the car. Just at the last moment, though, he caught my arm and pulled me back. He kissed my lips gently. 'Sorry,' he said. 'Had to do it – stuff the curtain-twitchers.'

Chapter Thirty-four

I let myself into the house and ran upstairs to get changed. The computer was on standby and I checked my email before closing it down: still nothing from Helen. My wash things were already packed from going to Pete's so I just threw fresh underwear and a clean T-shirt into the bag for the next day; by the time I got there and found her it would be too late to come back tonight: the ferry would have stopped running. I found the car key, locked the front door and opened the sliding door out into the back yard.

I saw him at once. On the wall, about four feet from the ground, Victor was suspended by his collar.

He wasn't moving. The collar was hooked on a nail in the mortar and, not able to touch the ground, he was hanging, the full weight of his body on the strip of leather round his throat. His eyes were almost closed. I put my hands underneath his stomach, took his weight and lifted him gently off.

He was still warm. I crooked him in my arm like a baby and felt through the soft fur on his chest where I thought his heart might be, looking for a pulse. 'Come on, Victor – please.' As I pressed harder, there was a twitch in one of his front legs and he took a terrible strangulated in-breath. His eyes came open, the pupils gone wide in terror. I held him against my body to stop his feeble attempt to scrabble away from me. Whispering to him, I stroked his head, and after a minute or so, he became calmer.

I went back inside and rummaged through my bag for my mobile. Pete picked up almost immediately.

'Kate?' I heard the surprise.

'Someone's hurt Victor.'

'I'm coming now.'

I paced the room, the cat still in my arms, trying to think what to do. He should see a vet but I didn't know where there was one. Did they work on Sundays? Victor looked up at me with eyes full of pain and fear. Milk – would that help? One-handed, I took a saucer from the cupboard, filled it, then put it on the table top and sat down so that he could see it. There was no sign he even knew it was there.

It was another two or three minutes before Pete arrived. 'What happened?' he said, taking Victor from me as soon as I opened the door.

'I'm not sure. I don't know. He was hanging.'

Softly, he moved the fur where the collar had been and saw the weal where it had cut in. We went out into the yard and he crouched down to look at the nail, running his fingertips over the mortar. There was a flurry of fine scratch marks on the brickwork around it. 'This nail – has it always been here?'

'I don't know. I've never noticed it before.'

'He wouldn't have got caught on that himself. Where would he have been climbing to to mean he would fall there? The windowsill's easy for him to get on to and it's not even close. It's not like there's even a trellis or anything.' He ran his fingers over the network of scratches. 'Someone did this,' he said.

The vet was a friend of Pete's and told him to take Victor round. I stayed at the cottage and paced. As soon as I'd seen him hanging I'd known it wasn't an accident. Pete's cat, my house: someone had done it, and whoever it was knew about us.

The vet told Pete that Victor was lucky his neck hadn't broken. His windpipe was badly bruised, however, and he wouldn't have survived much longer. His life, I thought, had been slipping away when I found him. A couple more minutes and that would have been it. I got the blanket out of the wardrobe and folded it into the seat of the armchair. Pete laid him down and stroked his flank until he fell asleep, exhausted by pain and panic.

'Who would do it?' he said, back in the kitchen. 'What kind of sick . . .?'

'Whoever did it knows, don't they? About us, I mean.'

'You think it was Tom?'

He looked at me but I found I couldn't hold the eye contact. 'I don't know. Who else could it be?' Cold washed over me. 'He's always in trouble, isn't he?'

'We'll have to talk to her – now. If it is him, it's gone beyond a joke.'

Mill Road was deserted, not a soul visible, and though it was still only seven, the light just softening, not yet fading, the blind in her kitchen window was drawn. Pete knocked and we waited. A minute or so passed. 'Perhaps she's out,' I said, thinking of the evenings last week when I'd come here myself.

'I don't think so.' He knocked again, harder this time. There was another minute and I thought he'd got it wrong but then there were footsteps inside and the door opened.

It was obvious immediately that she'd been crying: her nose and eyes were very swollen, the lids bruised-looking. The tendrils of hair that curled around her face were damp. She was wearing a white T-shirt and a pair of wide cotton trousers that bagged at the knee and tied with a drawstring around her tiny waist so that the extra material billowed out over her hips. She looked fragile.

She didn't seem surprised to see us. 'Come in then,' she said in a clogged voice, shrinking away into her kitchen. I saw her notice Pete touch my back as he stood aside to let me go first.

I'd been dreading the pulse of bass through the floor but the house was silent. It was as stifling as ever, the heating on full-bore even in April. Sally had backed herself into the far end of the room and was standing with her arms braced against the bar of the cooker as if she was expecting to have to spring out and defend herself.

'It's Tom we wanted to talk about,' said Pete, and I was sure I saw her shoulders drop a fraction.

'What's he done now?' she said.

'This afternoon, Kate found Victor hanging from a nail in her yard.'

'What?'

'It wasn't an accident – he'd been deliberately hung up by the collar.'

'Shit. Oh, the poor thing. Is he all right – alive?'

'He'll survive. Look, Sally, we all know you've got problems with Tom and I know you do your best but this has to be the end – something's got to be done. We don't know for sure it's him yet but he's the only candidate, and that speaks volumes.'

'He knows that we – me and Pete – have started . . . seeing each other,' I said. 'I think that's why it happened.'

She looked at me and her mouth hardened, her teeth catching her bottom lip as if to stop it. It was fleeting but unmistakable: if we had been alone I thought she might have just come out and said it: 'Why you? Why does he want you?' In a moment, it all fell into place. I remembered how she'd introduced herself to me in the corner shop, just after she'd seen me speaking to Pete for the first time. She hadn't been buying anything – she'd followed me in specially. And when I'd asked her about him she'd been so emphatic about their closeness, and how perfect he and Alice had been for one another. She'd been trying to close them away in a bubble, exclude me. At the café, the times she'd been so keen to hear my news, she'd been fishing to see whether I would talk about him. Why hadn't I seen it before? She loved him.

'It wasn't Tom,' she said, turning back to him.

'Sal . . .'

'It can't have been – not if Victor was hurt this afternoon.'

Despite the heat in the room, I felt a touch of icy cold on the back of my neck.

'He got up at lunchtime and we had an argument.' She looked down, hiding her face momentarily, and I wondered whether he'd told her about Pete and me then. 'He went storming off, saying he was going to his dad's in Lymington. It's what he does when he wants to hurt me. He's on the mainland. Gavin rang ten minutes ago to let me know he was going to stay the night.'

The cold was spreading in waves from my shoulders down my arms and I put a hand on the worktop to steady myself. The edges of my vision were pixilating; for a moment I thought I was going to pass out.

'I need to go,' I said, my voice too high. I yanked the door open and rushed out into the street. The cool air outside was a relief but there was no strength in my legs. I half sat, half fell on to the step of the house three doors down and put my head between my knees. When I closed my eyes, there was a picture of that morning. I saw myself lying among the crumpets and milk, the carton of orange juice inches from my face as his fingers stabbed and his sour breath filled my nostrils.

'Kate – can you hear me? What's going on?'

I slowly lifted my head and saw Pete towering in front of me. 'It's nothing,' I said, putting my face back into my hands. 'I just felt dizzy – it was hot.'

His feet scratched on the tarmac as he crouched in front of me. 'Look at me.'

'I'm fine – it's just the shock of earlier.'

'I don't believe you.' He tipped my chin up and made me look at him. 'If something's wrong, I should know. Come on, I've told you everything, all my stuff.'

I hesitated but he was right: he had been honest with me; I owed him the same.

'I think it might be Richard,' I said quietly. 'My ex. It might be him who hurt Victor.'

'What? Are you still involved with him?' He drew back.

'No.' My voice had gone high again. 'I hate him. I'm terrified of him. I came here to get away from him – to hide – but even here, he's in my head. I changed my number but he sends these emails.'

Pete's face was stony. 'What do you mean?'

'They come all the time. He thinks he owns me. He said that if I met anyone else, he'd kill me.'

'Jesus.' He put a hand over his mouth. Several seconds passed. 'Is it real? Do you believe him?'

'He tried to rape me, the day I ended it.' I was just going to say it; I couldn't lie to him any more. 'He was married. I didn't know at first but then I did and I carried on anyway. This is punishment – I deserve it.'

He bent his head and pinched the bridge of his nose. I wanted to yelp with the pain: I'd ruined everything – destroyed it before we'd even had a chance. Time seemed to stretch and with it a force-field between us.

'Do you think he's here?' he said at last. 'Really? Or has he got you running so scared you can't think straight?'

'I don't know. I just don't know.'

'How would he have found you?' he said. 'Who knows you're here?'

'My dad and my brother but he never met them and they would never tell him without asking me. The only other person who knows is Helen.'

'And would she tell him?'

'No. She wouldn't – she promised. But I think he's got to her. That's why I went to London. I'd been ringing her, leaving messages but she never answered. It's never happened before. I went to her office but she wouldn't talk to me. She's involved with him, I know it – I just don't know how.'

'But she must know what he's like?'

'Not everything. Not until Friday.'

There was a man coming down the lane with a dog, looking at us with blatant curiosity. I waited until he was out of hearing. 'I think Richard's a psychopath,' I said. 'I don't just mean that he's crazy – frightening. I mean literally – in the medical sense. It took me so long to see it. Everything's about control. The whole of his life is a power game. That's why he won't let me go – he hasn't broken me yet. It's nothing to do with love; it's possession. Dominance.'

He stood up again and took steps away from me, turning his back. 'I can't believe you didn't tell me any of this before.'

'Why do you think I didn't?' I said, desperate. 'Because I'm ashamed. Because there's so much in the way of you and me anyway. I didn't want you to know. I didn't want you to think I was the sort of person who . . . I wanted it to be – clean.' I stood up, feeling the ground spin. His back was like a wall between us.

'You should have told me,' he said at last. He turned round and came towards me, pulling me against his chest, pressing my face into the wool of his jumper. 'You still should have told me.'

* * *

282

Victor was asleep when we got back to the cottage but he opened his eyes when Pete smoothed his head. He seemed a little better, his eyes less pained, and when I poured him a fresh saucer of milk and put it next to him on the blanket, he drank a small amount. I went round the cottage drawing the curtains and pulling the blinds. Even with Pete with me, I couldn't shake the thought of Richard out there, moving closer, taking shape in the darkness.

We sat at the table in the kitchen and drank large glasses of brandy. 'Even if Helen is seeing him – worst-case scenario,' Pete said, breaking the silence. 'It doesn't mean he knows where you are.'

'I didn't tell you the truth earlier,' I said, making myself look at him. 'About having to work on the translation. I was going to go to London again. I left her messages on Friday, telling her everything – all the stuff that I'd been too ashamed to tell her before. I haven't heard from her, not even a text. Something's wrong.'

'I'll come with you. Not tomorrow; I can't miss these meetings. We've been working on the models for over a year and we need the account – it's a question of people keeping their jobs. But Tuesday. Ask Mary; tell her you'll swap a day. We'll go up and we'll stay there till you've talked to her.'

St James's struck a muffled three o'clock. I tried to resist the urge to turn over again. It had only been a mild day but the air in the bedroom was as soupy as Sally's overheated cottage. I'd already been up once to open the window and Pete had stirred in the bed behind me then but now the glass on the bedside table was empty and I would never get to sleep unless I had some more water. Gingerly I folded back my half of the quilt and eased myself out. Afraid that the light would wake him again, I crossed the tiny landing without switching it on, averting my eyes from the darkness that thickened at the corner of the stairs. I drank at the sink then inched my way back.

I put the glass down as quietly as possible, got into bed and lay down again. I'd thought that I'd managed it but he moved over and put his arms round me, fitting his body behind mine.

'You can't go on being frightened,' he murmured. 'You have to confront it.'

'I know.'

His breath played over the back of my neck, exposed where my hair had fallen sideways on to the pillow. A fluttering sensation spread out over my skin, down my spine and my arms. He touched his lips to the bone at the top of my spine and I felt his nose move through my hair, gently inhaling. 'Don't leave the Island,' he said. 'Stay. Come and live with me.'

Chapter Thirty-five

Pete stood on the doorstep, Victor in his arms. The ivy on the wall behind him moved with the breeze, a shifting carpet of leaves. I suppressed a jump of fear at the thought of him being away for the day, tied up in meetings.

'I'll see you tonight,' he said. 'I'll probably be on the last boat but I'll come round when I get back. If anything happens – anything at all – ring me. If I can't answer, I'll call you straight back as soon as I can.' He leaned in and kissed me. 'Bye. Don't forget to ask Mary about tomorrow.'

After he'd gone, I locked the door behind him and went upstairs. I stood at the bedroom window and looked out. The early sun was playing over the estuary, working with the breeze to create a shifting, sparkling scene. I narrowed my eyes and it reduced to speckling points of dark and light, as though painted by Klimt. I tipped my head towards my shoulders, first one side, then the other, stretching tendons taut with the stress of yesterday. Yarmouth moved sleepily on the other side of the glass. There were a couple of cars coming over the bridge, and on the wall near the harbour, office men were loading fenders on to the back of a truck, taking their time. Now, in daylight, with the immediate shock passed, the fear that Richard had found me began to seem less grounded. It was impossible to imagine him in the scene in front of me – it would need two worlds to collide. There must be another explanation for what had happened to Victor – either it really had been an accident or Sally was wrong about the time Tom had gone over to the mainland. Surely that was it.

There was still more than an hour before I was due at the café so I lay down on the bed again for a few minutes, my head on Pete's pillow. I breathed deeply for the smell of his hair. It was three days, not even that, since I had gone running up to find him and yet everything was different. I was going to move in with him. It seemed incredible but I hadn't needed to give it a second thought. When he'd whispered the words over my shoulder, I'd felt a surge of joy sing through me. It was a real life, here, with him, and I had never wanted anything more.

The café was quiet even for a Monday. Mary had come in to get on with the baking and I served the handful of customers and tried to stay out of the kitchen. Her usual harried air had been replaced by one of complete absorption, but there was an edge to her mood that made me hesitate to bring up the question of swapping my days. Eventually, though, at half three, when the last of the lunchtime stragglers had left and I'd finished the clean-up, I stuck my head round the door and asked.

'Tomorrow? OK. It's short notice but OK; I should be able to manage.'

'I'm sorry to be a nuisance. I need to go to London.'

She filled the last of the muffin cases, sliding the mixture off the spoon with the side of her little finger, and turned to look at me. 'I have to ask,' she said. 'Is it true what I hear on the vine, that you're seeing Pete Frewin?'

I hesitated, then decided just to be straight. 'Yes. It's a new thing, though – really new.'

She reached for the oven gloves and put them on. 'Well, it's quick but life's like that sometimes, isn't it? You have to take it when it comes. I hope it works out for you. You both deserve a bit of happiness.'

'Thank you,' I said, touched.

'Is there anyone left?'

'Oh. No, that was the last of them.'

'Why don't you head off then? I've nearly finished and there's no point both of us being here when we're empty. Buzz off – I'm sure you've got better things to do. Go and buy a dress; that's what people do when they've got a new boyfriend, isn't it?'

Crossing the Square, I'd had the thought that I would spend the unexpected remainder of the afternoon and the evening trying to get to grips with the translation again but as soon as I walked through the door of the cottage, I changed my mind. The house was silent, the hum of the fridge and the clicking of the pipes when I filled the kettle for tea too loud. It would make me jumpy to sit here on my own for hours, waiting for it to get dark. On a whim, I put my jacket back on and went out to the car. I would take Mary's idea and go shopping, find something new to be wearing when Pete came through the door later on. Apart from the evening of the supper when I'd worn that old woollen grey dress, he'd only ever seen me in jeans and jumpers; I would surprise him.

I took the left at the garage in Shalfleet and went via the lanes to Cowes. Out in the woods round Porchfield the trees were infused with the golden light of late afternoon, which spotted through the new leaves on to the windscreen and the road. Everything was lush and fresh and green; the grass on the verges growing long with the warmth, wild daffodils still visible here and there in shaded spots. The sky was cloud-free, marked only by a vapour trail feathering out into the blue.

I hadn't been to Cowes again since the day after the supper, when anything between Pete and me seemed impossible. I knew I'd felt a sort of resistance to it when I'd come to the Island, a desire to stay away from the places which were most like London. The summer regatta drew people from all over the world but even the rest of the year, Cowes felt too cosmopolitan: my Isle of Wight had been the one running twenty years behind the rest of southern England. Today, though, I wanted a degree of urbanity.

I parked the car on the seafront again and took the passageway up from the parade to the top of the old-fashioned High Street. Barely a car's width at the top, it had none of the usual names; instead there were cafés, a couple of art galleries, an ice-cream parlour, a newsagent's, even a wool shop which I was sure had been there when I was a child. There were a lot of places selling

287

yachting wear, of course, and a couple of dusty ladies' dress shops fronted by demure mannequins but nowhere that looked as though it might sell what I had in mind.

It didn't really matter. Just being here was a good thing, away from the cottage and surrounded by other people going about normal business. My phone was in my bag, in the pocket at the side where I would be able to put my hand on it in a second. It didn't ring, though, and there were no text messages, either from Pete, whom I'd hoped might write between meetings, or from Helen. *Don't think about it now*, I told myself; *wait until tomorrow*.

About halfway down the High Street there was a gift shop which also sold things for the house: vases and teapots and glasses. I went in to spend a few minutes browsing and at the back discovered a single rail of clothes on which was hanging an emerald dress in soft jersey fabric. I took it into the changing room and knew at once I had to buy it: it clung in all the right places, skimming my shape in a way that I thought Pete would appreciate. While I waited for the girl behind the counter to wrap it in tissue, I let my eyes wander over the rest of the stock, the cushions and lamps and candlesticks. Here was everything, I thought, that Pete's house lacked: the individual things, personalising touches. I felt an urge to go wild and buy it all but then I stopped.

It was Pete and Alice's house. I couldn't just move in and start changing things. I imagined how I would have reacted if Dad had met someone else straight after my mother had gone, how Matt and I would have felt to watch her shipping her things in. No, anything I changed would have to be minimal, incremental. Even if I couldn't feel Alice in the house, Pete would see her shadow everywhere; his memories of their life there would be fresh and vivid. Were all her personal things – her hairbrushes, her clothes, her scent – still laid out in their bedroom just as she'd left them? Dad had kept everything my mother had left behind, all the half-empty bottles of hand-cream and body lotion that she hadn't thought worth carting back to France. He'd kept them for years, arrayed on her dressing table as if she might be back to use them at any time.

As I slipped my card back into my purse, I was sideswiped by the thought I had been holding at arm's length: was Pete really ready? Or was he just someone who needed a relationship, trying to buy off his grief and loneliness by jumping into something new? I thought of the conversation on Saturday night, how he'd said he'd think about her for ever. I stumbled out of the shop, the bag with the new dress held tightly against my chest.

Further up the High Street there was a café-bar, its double doors open to the street. I went in and ordered a glass of wine which I took to one of the tables by a long window overlooking the Solent. Though it was just before six, I was the only customer. The sun was mellowing and casting a sheen over the water so that the little boats at the mouth of the river seemed to be coming and going in molten gold. I sipped the wine and reasoned with myself, remembering Pete's kindness, his concern about Richard, the way he had held me in the dark, telling me that we would be happy. At once there was an ache in my chest, a resonant emptiness. That wasn't manufactured; it was real. One had to take happiness where one found it; Mary was right. I had to have faith.

An earlier customer had left a copy of the *County Press* at the next table. I retrieved it, hoping to distract myself from further negativity. The local news here was my news now that I was staying; I wasn't going to be a temporary resident any more but a permanent overner. Moving the wine off the table on to the windowsill to accommodate the paper's pterodactyl wingspan, I started scanning the stories of council meetings and yacht races and events at schools. Perhaps there would come a time when schools here became relevant to me, I thought, feeling myself blush.

It was when I turned the second page that I saw it. The piece took up the top half of page five and the photograph a quarter of that. The wine turned to acid; I clapped my hand over my mouth just in time. I forced myself to look again, to make sure, but I'd seen the picture before: it was the one that was used in all his company literature, the photograph of the dynamic entrepreneur, serious but genial, confident. Now I was shaking, not just my hands but all over, shivering as if I was very cold while my face burned. He looked straight up out of the paper as if he could see me.

I couldn't get my eyes to bring the text into focus. Only the headline stayed still on the page long enough for me to make sense of it: LUXURY REVAMP FOR PARADE LANDMARK. I tried again, anchoring myself by key words: Cowes seafront, neglected Art Deco apartment building, luxury flats, Brookwood Developments. Richard Brookwood.

I pushed the chair back and stood up. The room tilted and I steadied myself against the edge of the table. As soon as I thought I could move without falling, I rushed out on to the street. I ran on legs of sponge, the tarmac seeming to undulate under me. Sound ebbed and flowed, rushing in and then withdrawing. My car was parked on the Parade; I couldn't get away without going there.

At the bottom of the passageway down to the seafront I paused, tried to gather myself. He knew where I was, there wasn't a shadow of doubt about it now. There was no other reason he'd come here. Yes, Cowes was lovely, up and coming probably, but he didn't deal in developments this size. His houses in Spain had covered a hillside. I reminded myself how much he travelled, how many projects he ran simultaneously; even if he had this building, it didn't mean he was physically here now, waiting for me to turn up outside. I just needed to keep my head, to get back to the car and get out of Cowes without drawing attention to myself. I could think about the rest when I'd done that.

I left the end of the passage and turned the corner out on to the Parade. I was hardly conscious of anything other than trying to keep calm, regulate my breathing. I could see my car now, only thirty yards away. All I had to do was keep going, hold on. Without moving my head I let my eyes stray across the street to the buildings that faced on to it. I could see it now, the small white Deco block that I'd scarcely registered earlier. I had parked directly across the street from it. There, on the wall of the building, not more than twenty feet away from my car, was the wooden board which proclaimed *Just Acquired by Brookwood Properties* with its logo of three blue lines denoting the brook and three stylised fir trees.

The contents of my stomach – the sandwich I'd had for lunch at the café, the half-glass of white wine – rose up my throat and I swallowed it down, felt burning. I overruled the instinct to run and carried on walking as calmly as I could: if he was here, he'd expect me to run; if he was looking, it would draw his attention. I was only four cars from mine when I saw that parked a little way up the street, facing me now, there was a navy-blue Mercedes SLK. I looked at the number plate.

I stumbled the last few feet to my own car, crouched down by the driver's door, and was sick repeatedly into the drain. It was like food poisoning; every time I thought there was nothing left to come up, another spasm went through me. I was breathing only from the very top of my lungs, unable to fill my chest, and the lack of air only added to my mounting sense of panic.

I unlocked the car and got in, snapping the lock down, imagining him appearing at the window, reaching for the handle. My hands slipped on the steering wheel, sweating. I shouldn't drive but I had no choice. I had to go, get away. I started the engine and reversed out, clipping the wing mirror on the car next door, the sound making me cry out loud with alarm.

I took the hill away from the seafront in too high a gear and felt the car struggle, threatening to stall just on the steepest corner. I had a mental image of it rolling back, crashing into one of the houses which lined the roadside, exploding in a ball of fire, and for a moment, the thought didn't horrify me. I ground the gears, heard the engine protest, and reached the top. I drove out of town as if I were drunk, swinging round the series of roundabouts in fourth gear, cutting people up, overtaking on a blind bend. For that time, ten minutes or more, I didn't care if I had an accident. Fear shimmered like a blade in the air around me, cutting closer and closer.

I was back at Porchfield again, hurtling between the trees whose dappled light had lifted my spirits earlier, when my phone started ringing. I reached over and fumbled in my bag for it, swerving up on to the verge into low branches. A pigeon flew up in front of the windscreen in a shock of wings. I slammed my foot on the brake and stalled the car, flinging myself forward. The name on the display was Helen's.

'Kate?' I heard the crying before the phone even reached my ear. 'I've been such an idiot.'

'What's happened? What's going on? Are you hurt?'

She sobbed. 'You were right. I've been seeing him.'

I closed my eyes.

'I don't know how I let it happen. He rang me in January, begged me to meet him, just to talk about what was going on. It was constant – emails, phone calls at the office. I only said yes to make it stop.'

'Why didn't you tell me?'

'I thought I could shield you from it. I was trying to protect you.'

'Don't cry – please don't cry. Just tell me.'

'I met him after work. I was going to have one drink, tell him you never wanted to see him again and that would be it. But it all went wrong. He cried – in the middle of the Queen's Head. It was packed but he didn't seem to care. He was there with tears running down his face and I thought *I've got you wrong*. I didn't forget he was married or that he'd lied about his son but I just saw someone who'd got himself into something he couldn't handle.'

'But all the other stuff –'

'I thought you must have exaggerated.' She took a breath, trying to compose herself. 'You're my best friend and you've been through some bad stuff but sometimes you judged things wrong, over-reacted. You used to fly off the handle . . .'

I pressed my fingers over my sternum and felt my heart, the force of the beat travelling through the bone. 'So how did it happen? You and him.'

'We stayed there and just talked. He told me about how much he missed you, how he loved you but you'd just . . .'

'Flown off the handle?' I couldn't help it.

'He said you wouldn't give him a chance to explain. I didn't know what to think. He confused me. I went there all hostile, ready to tell him to fuck off . . .'

In the background of the call a car rushed past, right next to her. She was out on the street: my proud Helen crying on the street.

'I felt sorry for him, that's why I agreed to meet him again. At first we just talked about you, then it was other things. I thought he'd try and get me to tell him where you were but he never did – never even hinted. And I started to think that I'd really got him wrong. He was good company – funny, charming, thoughtful.'

'It's a lie – an act. He's playing a game.'

'I know – I know that now. A few weeks ago, I started feeling – different. We went out for dinner one night – just on, after we'd met in the pub. I was sitting there and I looked up and thought, *I really like you.*' She took another audible breath. 'I couldn't tell you.'

'So, what happened?'

'Nothing – not then. I tried not to see him but he kept sending me funny little emails, just snippets that made me laugh. I'd get them in the evening, when everyone else had gone home and it made me feel better, as if I wasn't the only one still working. He made me miss him – I can't explain.'

'He'll do anything – anything. He makes himself what you want.'

'Yes – I know.'

'Did you tell him where I was?'

'No!' The horror in her voice told me it was the truth. 'But I gave in to him. He emailed, said it would be the last time he contacted me and if I wanted him to leave me in peace he would, but I didn't – I said yes. We went out to dinner, and . . . we kissed. I'm sorry; I'm really sorry.' She broke down again and I listened, utterly powerless while she cried.

'Helen,' I said, 'I don't care about any of it. I don't care. But tell me what he's done to you. Has he hurt you?'

'I saw him last night. He'd been out of London for the day but he came to mine on the way back in. I saw him on Friday, too, after you came here. I had to work late so he cooked me dinner – I gave him the keys and he came round and made it so it was ready when I got home from work. It was . . . nice. He didn't pressure me.'

My message, I thought. She'd never got it. He'd deleted it before she heard it. Then I remembered: I'd mentioned Pete – that I'd met someone else.

'But yesterday we ended up . . . it was the first time. The lights were on and he was staring into my eyes. And then he said it, while we were . . . "*You know, Helen, you're really not such a good friend, are you?*" '

293

I waited until she could speak again, listening to her terrible wrenching sobs. I imagined it, the triumph in his voice. He'd beaten her.

'He's coming to see you – he told me. He knows where you are. Kate, I keep seeing his expression,' she said. 'It's like his eyes were empty. It was evil – real evil.'

Chapter Thirty-six

When I got back to the cottage I checked every room, all the spaces and corners large enough for someone to hide; he wouldn't think twice about breaking in. When I was sure the place was empty, I stood for a moment at the study window and looked out. The story of Bluebeard came into my mind, the new bride waiting at the window, the discovered chamber of dead wives in the castle behind her. The bride had been watching at the window for her brothers to ride into sight, though; help had been coming.

Downstairs I heard my mobile ring once to tell me there was a text. I ran down to read it. *Hope everything OK. About to go to dinner but then on first ferry. Missed you today.*

I rang him straight back but his phone was already switched off. At the tone I hesitated, unsure what to say, whether I should tell him at all. 'Pete, it's me – Kate,' I said in the end. 'Richard's on the Island. He's got a building in Cowes, I saw it. He told Helen yesterday he was going to see me. Victor was him – it was definitely him. Can you ring me? Please – when you get this?'

The sun had dropped behind the woods at Norton now and the whole of the yard was in shadow. I went back into the kitchen and looked out of the window there. The breeze had died away and now the ivy on the back wall was motionless. Somewhere in it, audible even through the glass, a single bird was singing, calling out to announce the end of the twilight.

I could feel Richard moving towards me. It was as if he was altering the charge of the air, making it vibrate. I stayed downstairs, afraid to go up now and lose my view of the doors. I hovered between the sitting room and the kitchen, making myself look out into the yard and on to the path for movement, any sign of change.

He knew about me and Pete; that was beyond doubt. Could he know I was here on my own? Pete had walked down to the ferry this morning; what if Richard had been there, somewhere on the harbour? He had been in London last night with Helen; could he have been here by then? Yes – she'd thrown him out. He could easily have driven down and caught one of the first ferries. He could have arrived on the one which had returned with Pete on it. Or perhaps he hadn't seen Pete at all. Perhaps he'd just seen me at the café and followed me. The hairs rose on my arms.

Unable to sit, I paced the two small rooms and smoked the last cigarettes. I thought about turning on the television for voices, the illusion of company, but then I would be less able to hear anything else.

As the last of the light went, I realised how vulnerable I was. So what if the doors were locked; Richard wouldn't hesitate to force them. I wanted to put on every light in the house, drive the darkness back, but by doing that, I would shut off my view of the yard and the path outside, turning the windows into mirrors which would reflect my own image but hide him outside, let him gaze in at me like a specimen in a tank. But I couldn't bear to leave the lights off, either, and sit in the house in the dark.

All of a sudden, I saw what I was: bait, trapped in the house like a rabbit chained down for a bird of prey. Would my neighbours come if they heard shouting or breaking glass? Maybe not: I'd hardly spoken to them. In my first weeks here I had been afraid to, worried that they would have heard the sound of my crying through the walls at night. And after that had passed, they had nodded, said hello, but they had taken my early distance as a sign that I wanted to keep myself to myself, the girl from London with problems.

I had to leave the house. I couldn't stay here on my own; I would go mad. The pubs were open; I could at least go and sit with other people for the next three hours. I would get there in the last of the light if I went now. I grabbed my bag.

Outside, the silence had fallen. The birds were roosting for the night and there was no traffic coming down Bridge Road. I locked the door and ran, my feet blurring beneath me, trying not to look in the dark corners behind the outhouses and washing lines. The gate clanged shut. I scanned the street, making myself look where the light from the streetlamps struggled to reach: nothing. I ran to the top of the road and then across the Square, past the corner shop and the chandlery to the Bugle.

I stood behind the wooden partition that shielded the body of the pub from the doorway until my breathing slowed. The skin on my shoulders was prickling as if all the time I'd been running, there had been a hawk hovering silently overhead, having me in its sights but choosing to wait, biding its time.

When I could breathe normally again, I followed the sound of voices round to the bar at the back. It was bright and there were people, twelve or fifteen, sitting at tables and on stools at the bar. I was safe for now; nothing could happen to me here in plain sight. I ordered a glass of wine and sat down where I was visible, trying not to let my head jerk up every time someone came in from the street. My phone was on the table and the lights from the bar shone on it so that I kept thinking that the screen was illuminated but no one rang. I tried Pete again but got the answering service.

Helen – Richard had beaten her at last. He'd won; he'd proved that her loyalty to me wasn't unbreakable. It was so cruel: he had known that for her, loyalty was the most important thing. People were just puzzles to him, to be analysed and solved – unravelled. Helen's loyalty, my determination not to repeat what my mother had done; he'd found our principles and made us break them. He couldn't bear that anything could withstand him. Anything that resisted him, he crushed.

I looked around me at the other people in the room: the woman behind the bar chatting to one of the regulars, a man with a pint of bitter and the paper folded to the racing, the couple in their early twenties holding hands across the table. We were separated by an unbridgeable ravine: on their side was normality, an evening at the pub, and on mine was horror.

I had been in the Bugle nearly an hour when I had the idea of booking into the hotel. It would be safer than going back to the cottage: there would be other people, and someone on the desk all night. I could text Pete and tell him to come and find me there. Then, though, I had the idea that I would have had hours earlier if I'd been thinking clearly: I should go to the mainland. It was the mainland that was safest now, not the Island. I looked at my watch: quarter to nine. If I ran, there would be enough time to get the car and catch the nine o'clock ferry.

I gulped down the last of the wine and made a dash for it. The barmaid called goodnight but I was at the partition before I realised she was talking to me. All I could think about was making sure I was on the boat. *Run.* I tucked my bag under my arm and plunged out into the darkness.

He was waiting for me on the pavement.

Chapter Thirty-seven

'Hello, Katie.' His voice.

Nothing could have prepared me for the terror. The shops on the Square, the sky, the concrete underneath me – it all pulled away. Only he remained definite, inches away. *Run*, urged a voice inside, but I was frozen. My guts had liquefied.

He was staring into my eyes as if he could read my mind behind them. The weird flatness of his gaze, the force of it like a current, creating a circuit I couldn't break. He was completely calm, certain of his control. Though he was standing in front of me now, he'd been sitting on the pub wall before. He had stood up as I'd come bursting through the door as casually as if he'd been meeting a friend by arrangement. Behind him, the Square was empty. There was not a single person there to call out to.

'It's been too long.' His face had its old expression now, the lift in the eyebrow which dared me to challenge him while the smile said he had all the winning cards. His eyes were shining.

At last I got my voice back. 'I won't let you ruin my life.'

'I'm not going to ruin it. I'm part of it now – that's how it is.'

'What the hell is wrong with you?'

He laughed. 'My fierce creature.'

I couldn't run past him. He was too close, marking me as if we were playing a game, arms slightly away from his sides to catch me if I tried to make a break. Somewhere behind me, just audible over the terrified rushing of blood through my ears, there were distant voices, music. The pub. I whipped round and tried to go backwards but he anticipated me and grabbed my arm. I felt the pressure of his fingers even through my jacket, the sites of the bruises that would come.

I yanked my arm back but he was too strong. I opened my mouth to scream but his hand covered it instantly. Checking quickly that we were still unobserved, he pulled me tight against him as if he were about to kiss me. I felt my eyes widen with horror.

'Don't try running away and don't try screaming,' he murmured. 'I want to talk to you and that's the least you owe me.' There was no challenge in his face now, no humour, however ironic. He dropped his hand from round my mouth and reached into his pocket. The fingers of his other hand gripped my arm harder still and I couldn't help crying out just a little. 'I said, shut up.'

He brought his hand up again and at first I thought he was going to stroke my face like he used to. Then I felt something cold against my cheek. Metal. Grainy – like the grip on a craft knife but heavier. A gun – he had a gun.

'Let's go back to yours,' he said.

He walked side by side with me back across the Square, propelling me along but also managing to conceal from anyone who might look out of a window the fact that he was gripping me. 'No screaming, Katie,' he said, as a car pulled up and parked outside the corner shop. 'It's very easy to make mistakes.' I watched the driver get out. He was moving slowly, had hardly eased himself from his seat in the time it took us to go fifteen yards. An old man; even if I managed to break free, he couldn't help.

In my handbag my phone started ringing. 'Don't even think about it.' He pulled the bag round and reached into it. Then he cut the call off and tossed the phone over the wall into the churchyard. I heard it shatter as it hit stone.

At the door of the cottage he demanded the key. He pushed me in in front of him, making sure his body blocked the way behind me, and closed the door quietly. When he'd locked it, he slid the key into the pocket of his jeans.

'Shall we have a glass of wine?' he said. 'Like old times?'

300

I stared at him. What could I do? I didn't dare make a run for it now. Both the doors were locked: there was no way I could get enough of a head start. He would be on me within seconds.

'You sit at the table where I can see you.' Without turning his back, he picked up one of the bottles Pete had brought to dinner. I'd been saving it, something of his when I thought it was all I would have. Perhaps it would be now. 'This is decent stuff for a change, sweetheart,' he said, holding it up to the light. 'Have you come into money I don't know about?' He pulled open the cutlery drawer and got out the corkscrew, then took glasses from the top cupboard.

'You know where everything's kept.'

He inclined his head gently to one side. 'Your windows are less secure than your doors. Anyway, let's go through. I don't like this poky little kitchen.'

He steered me into the sitting room and on to the sofa. I willed him to take the armchair but he sat down next to me as comfortably as if we were a couple having a night in. He arranged himself sideways, his arm extending along the back of the sofa towards me, and I shrank away.

'Old friends,' he said, leaning across and chiming his glass against mine.

'How long have you known I was here?'

'Long enough.'

'How? Helen said she didn't tell you.'

'Oh, you don't doubt her now, do you? Why would you do that?' He smiled. 'No, she didn't tell me – don't worry. But she works so hard, doesn't she? Always on that laptop when I went round and very trusting about leaving it open.' He took a sip of wine.

I looked away. The blanket I'd arranged for Victor was still folded into the seat of the armchair. In the window opposite, I could see our reflections. I'd forgotten how powerful he was. He wasn't as tall as Pete or as broad but the gym work kept him bulky and strong. His image almost filled the glass, leaving little room for mine.

The window.

301

I made myself look back at him, praying he wouldn't see in my face the idea that had come to me, the sudden flare of hope. Both the doors were locked and the key to the one at the front was in his pocket. I wouldn't be able to break through either: the glass panel in the kitchen was too small and the sliding doors were reinforced glass. I wouldn't have time to undo the catch on the window, push up the sash, but if I broke the pane, the hole would be large enough.

'Why did you do it, then?' I said, playing for time, trying to think. 'Pretending you didn't know, sending me all those emails.'

'Why?' he said, and the anger came back into his voice. 'Did you think it was nasty of me?' His voice was rich with sarcasm. 'After what you did? You cut me off – didn't even have the courtesy to answer my phone calls. You changed your fucking number. I won't be treated like that.'

'You tried to rape me.'

'Rape you? Sweetheart, I don't think there's a jury on earth who would buy that story. How many times had you done it willingly? You can't pretend to me you don't like it rough. Let's have a little honesty, shall we?'

His hand moved over the gun, feeling its shape through the material of his shirt. My stomach turned over.

'I think you've forgotten that I rescued you,' he said.

'What?'

'Remember how lonely you were? All you ever did was work. Admit it – I was the most exciting thing that had ever happened to you.' He laughed.

'I'm never coming back to you.'

His fingers moved under the fabric now and I heard a nail scratch over the handle. 'Do you think that's what this is about? Me wanting you back?'

A flare of terror went through me. I had to move now. He looked at me, his expression a mask of amused contempt, and I threw my wine glass in his face.

I heard a shout but I was moving before I could see his reaction. I flung myself across the room and on to the armchair and I picked up the vase from the side table and hurled it through the window.

I heard the sound of breaking glass, the brittle music of the shards falling on to the concrete outside, and then there was a thump, something hitting the back of my head, a flash of light.

The pain was the first thing. All sensation had centred in my head and agonising waves were radiating from the back of my skull through the tissue of my brain. I stayed still and tried to shut it out, focus. Everything in front of my eyes was red, a red so dark it was almost black. I was on my back and my body was stiff, as if I hadn't moved for some time. I listened, and close by there was breathing, just audible. A current of cold air flowed over my face.

It was some seconds before I even remembered. Richard was here. He had a gun. I'd tried to make a break for it. I pressed my fingertips down, felt carpet under them. I was still in the sitting room. I hadn't got anywhere.

'Open your eyes. I know you're awake.' The voice was very close.

I kept them closed, not wanting to obey his orders, afraid of the pain that would come with the light.

'Open your eyes.'

Until I did, I was powerless anyway. Gradually, I forced them open. I was looking at the ceiling. At the edge of my vision on the right there was the fringe around the bottom of the sofa and when I turned my head fractionally to the left, triggering another wave of pain, I saw the terracotta base of one of the table lamps lying next to me, missing its shade. The weight of the thump on the back of my head – it was what he had used to stop me, the first thing that came to hand. The room was darker, the remaining lamp on the table next to the sofa providing the only light. The cold air was coming through the broken window.

I lifted my head a little and saw him. My legs had been pushed apart and he was kneeling between them, his hands on either side of my body supporting him as he leaned over me. I gave a cry and he laughed. I wasn't aware of my body, I realised; I couldn't even tell whether or not I was wearing any clothes. I moved my left hand to my waist. My jeans were still there, still done up.

'What, you think I'd touch you now? You don't understand me at all, do you?' he said, bringing his face closer. He'd been smoking while I'd been unconscious. How long had it been? 'Everything would have been fine. I would have forgiven you – yes, even after all the shit you've pulled on me – but not now. You've made it impossible. You're worth nothing to me – you're just a whore. A whore like your mother.'

'Fuck you,' I said.

He moved his right hand and picked up a knife that had been lying on the carpet. It was the carving knife. The incredible became real: he really was going to kill me.

I brought my hand up and jabbed him in the eyes. He was almost quick enough but not quite. I missed his left eye but, as he turned his head, my other finger caught his right eye, not the straight stab I'd wanted but enough to cause him to shout out in pain. In the second or two in which he clutched at his face, I rolled back, trying to free my legs from either side of his body. I turned on to my front, tried to scramble away, but he was on me. He caught the neck of my jumper and pulled me up by it. The wool became a line across my throat, constricting my breathing.

He'd dropped the knife in his surprise but now he snatched it up again. I couldn't see behind me but I swung my elbow back as hard as I could and I felt it connect with his ribcage. He grunted and tightened his grip round my throat. My vision was chequering and I felt as though I was rocking back and forth. The carpet seemed to be rising to meet me. I leant back slightly, desperate to take a breath.

He pulled tighter still on the jumper and I gagged. He put his face forward, letting his cheek touch mine. 'You won't win, however much you struggle. Nobody beats me.'

I pulled my head forward the few inches that I could and then I smashed it back, catching him in the face. But the contact came at the point on my head where he'd hit me with the lamp. The pain was disabling. All I could see was colour bursting in front of my eyes, a kaleidoscope of agony.

Behind us, in the kitchen, there was a crash, the sound of the door being kicked in. I couldn't see anything but the pressure went from around my neck as Richard let go of my jumper. I fell forward, my hands meeting the cold tiles in front of the fireplace.

304

He was scrambling to his feet and I put my leg back, knocked one of his out from under him. He grabbed a handful of my hair, pulled the back of my head against his chest again. The knife was in his hand but he hesitated.

It was just a moment but the hesitation cost him because, in that second, Pete seized the poker from the stand by the fireplace and knocked him sideways. He fell, hitting his head on the edge of the tiles. Somehow I got up, scrabbled out of range of the hand that grabbed at me. Pete pulled me across the room but Richard was up on his knees, the light of victory still in his streaming eyes. In his hand was the gun.

'Here's the cuckold,' he said, putting his free hand on the arm of the sofa and pulling himself to his feet. 'Second-hand goods must really be your thing. I've had her seven ways since Sunday, I hope she's told you?'

Pete watched the gun, the poker in his hand useless. 'She's with me now.'

'I wouldn't touch her now. But you have to know something: I was the most important thing in her life – I was, I am and I will be.' He turned the gun towards me. The barrel became a perfect circle. 'Remember our connection?' he asked. 'Two points on the earth's surface.' He stroked his finger against the trigger. 'We'll always be connected, you and me.'

'Richard, please –' I begged.

Pete's voice – not words, just a shout. He lunged, pushing me sideways, and then another noise filled my ears, seeming to push back the walls with its force. A rush of sensation, not pain, not anything but a rush, but pain then, extreme pain, beyond anything I'd thought the body could endure – like fear but tearing, screaming.

I was on the ground again and there was blood – a lot of blood. I'd been shot. He'd shot me. The pain overwhelmed me and it was a moment before I could focus again. I put my hand up towards the source of it and then thought better. Looking down, I saw that the left shoulder of my jumper was a ragged, bloody mess.

'Kate.' Pete's voice, disembodied.

'I'm all right – I'm OK.' The chequering at the edges of my vision again.

'Can you move? Not your arm – can you get up?'

It took an age but I did it. When I opened my eyes again after another spasm of pain I saw them. Pete had Richard on the floor and was holding him there with a knee pressed between his shoulder blades, his hands on Richard's forearms. Richard's face was sideways, crushed into the carpet. He was grunting, ineffectually pushing from his knees to force Pete off him, but Pete was too heavy; he was pinned. The gun was on the carpet six feet away, kicked or thrown out of reach.

'Kate – can you hear me? I need you to call the police. My phone's here – in my pocket.'

Beneath him Richard snorted. 'Why don't you just finish the job?' His voice was muffled by the carpet. 'You've got me where you want me, haven't you?'

'And give you the satisfaction of knowing I was going to prison?' Pete brought his knee down harder.

I found the phone in his pocket but I had to put it down again to dial; my left hand was useless. Blood had darkened my entire sleeve now; it was red to the cuff. I suddenly felt afraid – not of Richard, not now, but of dying, losing everything just when I'd been given so much.

'Sit down,' said Pete, seeing me sway. I took a step away and fell back on to the sofa just in time. And then the answering voice of emergency services.

Epilogue

The scar on my shoulder looked like a second navel, I thought again as I looked at it in the mirror; the unsightly result of an umbilical cord tied up too quickly by a junior midwife at the end of a long shift. Even with the angry redness gone, it was ugly, the stretched and shiny skin with the twist in its middle a permanent reminder. I'd got into the habit, when I was on my own, of letting my fingers slip under the collar of my jumper to touch it and though I was familiar with it now, months later, it still sometimes surprised me, indelibly written on my body.

Over the summer I had worn cotton shirts and T-shirts with sleeves rather than vest tops, wanting to hide it, but Pete had made a point of not ignoring it, of touching it and talking about it, helping me to think of it as just another part of myself. Now it was winter and so there was no question of it being on display anyway: only he saw it, when we were dressing in the morning or when I burrowed up against him in bed at night.

Richard was tried for attempted murder but in the end was found guilty of causing grievous bodily harm. His sentence was the maximum five years, though he wouldn't serve all of it. I'd expected it to be hard to face him in court, to feel his eyes move over me in that amused, assessing manner, and it was. He looked ridiculous in the dock in his tailored suit, like an actor playing the part of someone falsely accused, but the façade dropped for an instant when he heard the verdict and the jury saw for themselves one of the sudden switches I'd described to them in my testimony, the flick-knife speed with which the charming veneer could disappear. He couldn't see all of the public gallery from his position in the courtroom so he hadn't been aware a minute or so later of Sarah standing up from her seat at the back and slipping silently away or of the look she'd given me just before she did, a look that told me that she could relax now, at least for a while.

I'd thought nothing else about Richard could have shocked me but I was wrong. In the weeks before his trial, another side of his life slid out into the light. Brookwood Properties turned out to be an empire built on sand – not even that. For years Richard had been borrowing money against the projected profits from one development to finance the next, repeating the trick over and over again. When the accounts were scrutinised – after they'd been extracted from the labyrinth of companies and holding companies and fronts that he had constructed over the years – it was discovered that there was no value left in them at all. In fact, he was in debt to the tune of nine million pounds. The whole thing had been a confidence trick, a juggling act which he'd sustained with charm and lies – endless lies.

Immediately after I'd got out of hospital, I'd wondered whether I would be able to live in Yarmouth. The local gossip ran at such a pitch I began to feel like an eighth-rate celebrity, one of the train-wreck variety whose lives are played out on the front pages of the magazines which promise it all *Closer, Hotter, Now*. After the court case, however, I felt a change in the water, the turn of a tide, and suddenly I was acknowledged in the street and there were friendly hellos in the shops. The best part of it for me was that I was able to salvage a sort of friendship with Sally, tentative though it still was. It helped that three or four months after it all happened, a new partner joined her firm of solicitors, a divorcé about our age. Over an awkward coffee one morning she told me that he'd asked her out and that she liked him. She'd see, she said, blushing.

Things were also easier for her because Tom was living with his father on the mainland while he went through the motions of doing his A-levels. At the beginning of the summer he and a couple of friends were caught doing eighty along the military road in a stolen car and although he'd only received a caution, the sixth-form college he'd had lined up had got wind of it and declined to take him. Living with Gavin, Sally said, was not as cushy as Tom had hoped; his stepmother had the whip-hand and while she had tolerated his attitude when he was only an occasional visitor to her house, things were different now he was there full time.

I gave my hair a final once-over and put the brush back on the table. With all the physiotherapy, the movement in my arm and hand was almost back to normal. The very tips of my fingers were still numb but apparently even that would go, eventually. The reflection of the room I could see behind me in the mirror was still spare but that was by design now. We hadn't moved across the landing to the main bedroom. It wasn't just that I didn't want to be in the room Pete had shared with Alice but that I liked our room better anyway. Nonetheless, Pete had insisted on redecorating the other bedroom and making it a room for guests, the first of whom was about to arrive.

I went downstairs and found my house key, then gave the kitchen one final scan. Everything was ready: the table was laid, the wine was cooling in the fridge, and the casserole was in the oven. The candles could be lit just before we sat down to eat.

Pete turned from the window where he was watching the ferry make its way across the Solent towards us. I went over and watched with him for a minute or two. It was a cold night and late in the year so there were few other lights moving on the water but it was still a beautiful view, the shifting navy surface with the spill of white moonlight across it. I pressed myself into his side. 'I'd better go,' I said. 'It'll be in by the time I get down there.'

'You're nervous,' he said, smiling slightly.

'No, I'm not.'

'She's your best friend,' he said. 'Everything's going to be fine. Come on, I'll walk down with you.'

Acknowledgements

I'd like to thank the following people for their invaluable help: Katie Bond, Alexandra Pringle and Colin Midson at Bloomsbury; Laura Longrigg; Claire Paterson, Kirsty Gordon and Cullen Stanley at Janklow and Nesbit; Caroline Bland, Katie Espiner and Cordelia Borchardt. I'd also like to thank Paul and Jenny Whitehouse, and Polly and Sophie.

ALSO AVAILABLE BY LUCIE WHITEHOUSE

THE HOUSE AT MIDNIGHT

When Lucas inherits Stoneborough Manor after his uncle's unexpected death, he imagines it as a place where he and his close circle of friends can spend time away from London. But from the beginning, the house changes everything. Lucas becomes haunted by the death of his uncle and obsessed by cine films of him and his friends at Stoneborough thirty years earlier. The group is disturbingly similar to their own, and within the claustrophobic confines of the house over a hot, decadent summer, secrets escape from the past and sexual tensions escalate, shattering friendships and changing lives irrevocably.

*

'A pacy literary thriller ... deeply spooky, compulsively readable'
TIME OUT

'Psychological suspense as elegant as a Swiss watch but as powerful as a locomotive ... subtle, intelligent, accessible, and highly recommended'
LEE CHILD

'Scary, sexy, sultry and shimmering'
DAILY MIRROR

*

ISBN 9780747596257 · PAPERBACK · £7.99

Not
The End

Go to channel4.com/tvbookclub for more great reads,
brought to you by Specsavers.

Enjoy a good read with